Takeoff TOO!

by Randall Garrett

Takeoff TOO!

by Randall Garrett

**Cover and interior illustrations
by Phil Foglio**

**Introduction and commentary
by Vicki Ann Heydron**

Edited by Mary E. Gray

Executive Editor, Kay Reynolds

The Donning Company/Publishers
Norfolk/Virginia Beach
Starblaze Editions

TABLE OF CONTENTS

Introduction

by Vicki Ann Heydron

**When you think of him, please...
remember the joy.**

Those words are *about* Randall Garrett. They were said *to* the audience at the World Science Fiction Convention in Chicago (Chicon) in 1982, and to everyone who has known Randall or his work. I was accepting the Pat Terry Award from a representative of Australian fandom on Randall's behalf—as his most recent collaborator, and as his wife.

I was touched that Australian fans had chosen to honor Randall for the very thing which gave him the most pleasure in writing—humor. He devised subtle (sometimes) puns for his titles. He planted caricatures of his friends in his stories (and was repaid in kind—see Avram Davidson's *Peregrine Primus* for a prime example). He invented plots and applied his gift for style mimicry to poke fun at other authors, literary tricks, overused ideas, and the world in general. Writing was fun for him, and it shows.

The Chicon awards ceremony provided me a unique and deeply appreciated opportunity to speak to the entire science fiction "community," so that I was spared the pain of repeating a sad message individually to each of Randall's multitude of friends. The memory loss Randall suffered in 1979 (caused by a rare viral brain infection) has proved to be permanent. He can no longer make a direct contribution to his writing career.

Sad as that message was, to deliver and to hear, its most important words are quoted at the beginning of this text. I said them with the conviction, still strong, that I was expressing what Randall would have said himself, given the opportunity. Of all things in the world, laughter was most precious to him.

But saying them wasn't easy for me. That speech—indeed, the entire convention—was something of a personal rite of passage. The greatest horror of Randall's illness had been the inability to predict, once his physical survival was assured, the degree of his mental recovery. For over two years I had cared for him personally and continued work we had jointly conceived before his injury, clinging fiercely to the conviction that his "absence" was only temporary. In August of 1981, for the sake of his health and my sanity, I allowed him to be hospitalized.

1

The year between that event and the awards ceremony saw me go through many emotional changes. I emerged slowly from a crippling guilt and sense of failure, and a terror of working "alone."

It finally sank in that failure is impossible without control—and I had held no true control over Randall's recovery. I had provided an environment in which body and mind had the best possible chance to heal themselves. Sadly, they were too badly injured to accomplish that. I learned to be content that I had done everything within my power to help, and the guilt began to fade.

The conception and general outline of the Gandalara novels were complete when Randall fell ill, and I still consider the series—now finished—to be a true collaboration between us. But during the year after Randall's hospitalization, I gradually realized that I had been "alone" since 1979, and that the production of the first three books had been "my" work.

By the time I got to Chicago in September 1982, I was beginning to believe in myself again, as a person and as a writer. I attended with the specific purpose of accepting the Pat Terry Award, and with the intention of making that announcement—unsupported by any trace of conviction that I could actually go through with it.

I encountered only good will and encouragement, and in such quantity that my emotional state stabilized. There isn't room here to name all the friends, old and new, who helped me through that difficult time. Three I must mention: Karen Haas, Lou Aronica, and Hank Stine. I had accepted that Randall was lost to me as a person, but my erratic self-confidence had demanded that I cling to the writer. It was only with the personal support and professional respect of those people that I was able to mount that stage as myself and, finally, let Randall go.

The engraving on the beautiful pewter mug that is the Pat Terry Award specifically mentions *Takeoff,* the earlier collection of Garrett stories published by Donning and assembled by Randall himself. That honor crystallized plans for a second volume—the book you hold in your hands.

Donning and I had been discussing a book like this since the publication of *Takeoff,* but I had been reluctant to reach firm agreement, because I knew a decision would be forced on me. I wanted, badly, to edit this volume myself. But I had come lately into Randall's life; we had met in 1975 and married in 1978. I am his third wife and at least his sixth collaborator. I hadn't even *read* most of Randall's work—too little time before his illness, too much sadness afterward. I didn't feel I could accept editorial responsibility without *learning* the enormous body of work Randall has left us. I expected that process to deepen my sense of loss, and I wasn't looking forward to it. But when I considered allowing someone else to edit it, I felt cowardly.

The wholly positive experience of Chicon gave me the nudge I needed. I dug into Randall's incomplete "prideshelf" (Randall had moved frequently, and his collection had suffered deletion and damage). I set up a data file on my microcomputer and proceeded to compile as complete an index as possible of his work.

I had huge help in this endeavor from a gentleman named Jerry Moore. When Randall had been selecting material for *Takeoff,* Jerry had conferred with Randall, methodically searched his own library, and cross-checked all the published indexes extant at that time, in order to come up with a substantial list of work Randall had written. The dedication in *Takeoff* is quite true; the book might not have taken form without Jerry's index and kind provision of photocopies of the stories we didn't have.

An error exists in most published indexes. Randall never wrote under the pseudonym of "Walter Bupp"—but he couldn't convince the bibliographers. I heard him deny authorship of Bupp work frequently, and in going through his files as research for this book, I ran across a copy of a letter with which he returned a Bupp royalty check.

As I was compiling my index, I was also reading and considering each item for possible inclusion here. *Takeoff* had the special theme of poking fun at other writers—the people, their styles, their work—but also picked on such broad targets as history, technology, and religious awe. To find such a cohesive theme for this volume seemed unlikely, and not necessarily desirable, so Donning and I agreed that any material with a humorous element would be acceptable for *Takeoff, Too.*

That criterion might (I say, *might*) eliminate Randall's biography of Pope John XXIII—which I had already disqualified for other reasons.

In order to avoid the paperwork of securing publication releases, I decided not to consider collaborations. There went forty or so of the nearly two hundred titles. Novel-length works and recently reprinted material knocked out a few more. Donning recommended three or four items, and I concurred.

I tried to keep in mind that you, the reader, might know a great deal about Randall and his thirty-five-year career as a published writer, or you might never have seen his name before the "Three C's"—chance, curiosity, and the cover—brought this book to your attention.

The introduction to each item in this book will provide you with clues as to why I chose it. Sometimes I knew something about the background of a story. I selected examples from Randall's various pseudonyms. I deliberately searched out little-known stories. Not much of what Randall wrote remained unpublished, but my search through his files yielded a few selections. In all cases, this is material I enjoyed reading.

I'm grateful to Donning for their patience and understanding as I made this voyage through Randall's past. I didn't find the tragedy I was expecting. Instead, I found Randall again—his humor, his talent, his affection for writing and the people who write. In prowling through records that had been untouched for years, I saw the man he had been before I shared his life. I know him better now and, yes, I miss him even more. But the special good humor and sense of fellowship that penetrated every aspect of his life shines in his writing.

I have said a lot about Randall's work, but little about him and what he meant to me. This has been deliberate, out of respect for his own reticence toward public view of his private life, and because my role in this introduction is primarily that of editor. In a way, however, the material I prepared for this book is my tribute to him—not a memorial, but a celebration—and there seems cause to contribute a personal note.

One of the selections Donning requested was an article of mine, written while Randall was with me, published after his illness. It was prepared specifically for a Bantam anthology titled *Moments of Love*. I find such personal writing difficult (this introduction, for instance), but, for some reason, I felt compelled to produce it. I refused to submit it without Randall's approval— which he gave—since anyone who knew me would recognize Randall in it.

That article is the final piece in this volume, and it speaks, not of what I have lost, but of what I had—the joy that I remember.

—Vicki Ann Heydron
April 1986
Austin, Texas

Cum Grano Salis

by Randall Garrett
writing as David Gordon

This is the first of three selections which were published under the pseudonym of "David Gordon," a name
constructed from Randall's own and his father's first name
Two of Randall's earliest stories appeared under that name,
then "Randall Garrett" seems to have been used exclusively
until 1956. In that year, my index shows forty-two items
published by Randall (singly written or in collaboration);
pen names became a way of life.

"David Gordon" reappeared to take credit for There's
No Fool (also in this volume). It was published in the same
issue of ASTOUNDING as one of the installments of what
would eventually be The Shrouded Planet, by "Robert
Randall"—Garrett and Silverberg in disguise. The third
Takeoff, Too! selection by "Gordon," The Foreign Hand-Tie,
shared the table of contents with a science article by Garrett.

Cum Grano Salis is the kind of story Randall enjoyed
reading, as well as writing—the mystery is inseparably
linked to the science. Along the way he takes a few potshots
at the pseudoscientific attitude of the hypochondriac.

"And that," said Colonel Fennister glumly, "appears to be that."
The pile of glowing coals that had been Storage Shed Number
One was still sending up tongues of flame, but they were nothing
compared with what they'd been half an hour before.
"The smoke smells good, anyway," said Major Grodski,
sniffing appreciatively.

The colonel turned his head and glowered at his adjutant.

"There are times, Grodski, when your sense of humor is out of place."

"Yes, sir," said the major, still sniffing. "Funny thing for lightning to do, though. Sort of a dirty trick, you might say."

"*You* might," growled the colonel. He was a short, rather roundish man, who was forever thankful that the Twentieth Century predictions of skin-tight uniforms for the Space Service had never come true. He had round, pleasant, blue eyes, a rather largish nose, and a rumbling basso voice that was a little surprising the first time you heard it, but which seemed to fit perfectly after you knew him better.

Right at the moment, he was filing data and recommendations in his memory, where they would be instantly available for use when he needed them. Not in a physical file, but in his own mind.

All right, Colonel Fennister, he thought to himself, *just what does this mean—to me? And to the rest?*

The Space Service was not old. Unlike the Air Service, the Land Service, or the Sea Service, it did not have centuries of tradition behind it. But it had something else. It had something that none of the other Services had—*Potential.*

In his own mind, Colonel Fennister spelled the word with an upper case *P,* and put the words in italics. It was, to him, a more potent word than any other in the Universe.

Potential.

Potential!

Because the Space Service of the United Earth had more potential than any other Service on Earth. How many seas were there for the Sea Service to sail? How much land could the Land Service march over? How many atmospheres were there for the Air Service to conquer?

Not for any of those questions was there an accurate answer, but for each of those questions, the answer had a limit. But how much space was there for the Space Service to conquer?

Colonel Fennister was not a proud man. He was not an arrogant man. But he *did* have a sense of destiny; he *did* have a feeling that the human race was going somewhere, and he did not intend that that feeling should become totally lost to humanity.

Potential.

Definition: *Potential; that which has a possibility of coming into existence.*

No, more than that. That which has a—

He jerked his mind away suddenly from the thoughts which had crowded into his forebrain.

What were the chances that the first expedition to Alphegar IV would succeed? What were the chances that it would fail?

And (Fennister grinned grimly to himself) what good did it do to calculate chances after the event had happened?

Surrounding the compound had been a double-ply, heavy-gauge, woven fence. It was guaranteed to be able to stop a diplodocus in full charge; the electric potential (*potential!* That word again!) great enough to carbonize anything smaller than a blue whale. No animal on Alphegar IV could possibly get through it.

And none had.

Trouble was, no one had thought of being attacked by something immensely greater than a blue whale, especially since there was no animal larger than a small rhino on the whole planet. Who, after all, could have expected an attack by a blind, uncaring colossus—a monster that had already been dying before it made its attack.

Because no one had thought of the forest.

The fact that the atmospheric potential—the voltage and even the amperage difference between the low-hanging clouds and the ground below—was immensely greater than that of Earth, that had already been determined. But the compound and the defenses surrounding it had already been compensated for that factor.

Who could have thought that a single lightning stroke through one of the tremendous, twelve-hundred-foot trees that surrounded the compound could have felled it? Who could have predicted that it would topple toward the compound itself?

That it would have been burning—that was something that could have been guaranteed, had the idea of the original toppling been considered. Especially after the gigantic wooden life-thing had smashed across the double-ply fence, thereby adding man-made energy to its already powerful bulk and blazing surface.

But—that it would have fallen across Storage Shed Number One? Was *that* predictable?

Fennister shook his head slowly. No. It wasn't. The accident was simply that—an accident. No one was to blame; no one was responsible.

Except Fennister. *He* was responsible. Not for the accident, but for the personnel of the expedition. He was the Military Officer; he was the Man In Charge of Fending Off Attack.

And he had failed.

Because that huge, blazing, stricken tree had toppled majestically down from the sky, crashing through its smaller brethren, to come to rest on Storage Shed Number One, thereby totally destroying the majority of the food supply.

There were eighty-five men on Alphegar IV, and they would have to wait another six months before the relief ship came.

And they didn't have food enough to make it, now that their reserve had been destroyed.

Fennister growled something under his breath.

"What?" asked Major Grodski, rather surprised at his

superior's tone.

"I said: 'Water, water, everywhere—', that's what I said."

Major Grodski looked around him at the lush forest which surrounded the double-ply fence of the compound.

"Yeah," he said. "'Nor any drop to drink.' But I wish one of those boards had shrunk—say, maybe, a couple hundred feet."

"I'm going back to my quarters," Fennister said. "I'll be checking with the civilian personnel. Let me know the total damage, will you?"

The major nodded. "I'll let you know, sir. Don't expect good news."

"I won't," said Colonel Fennister, as he turned.

The colonel let his plump bulk sag forward in his chair, and he covered his eyes with his hands. "I can imagine all kinds of catastrophes," he said, with a kind of hysterical glumness, "but this has them all beat."

Dr. Pilar stroked his short, gray, carefully cultivated beard. "I'm afraid I don't understand. We could all have been killed."

The colonel peeked out from between the first and second fingers of his right hand. "You think starving to death is cleaner than fire?"

Pilar shook his head slowly. "Of course not. I'm just not certain that we'll all die—that's all."

Colonel Fennister dropped his hands to the surface of his metal desk. "I see," he said dryly. "Where there's life, there's hope. Right? All right, I agree with you." He waved his hand around in an all-encompassing gesture. "Somewhere out there, we may find food. But don't you see that this puts us in the Siege Position?"

Dr. Francis Pilar frowned. His thick salt-and-pepper brows rumpled in a look of puzzlement. "Siege Position? I'm afraid—"

Fennister gestured with one hand and leaned back in his chair, looking at the scientist across from him. "I'm sorry," he said. "I've let my humiliation get the better of me." He clipped his upper lip between his teeth until his lower incisors were brushed by his crisp, military mustache, and held it there for a moment before he spoke.

"The Siege Position is one that no military commander of any cerebral magnitude whatever allows himself to get into. It is as old as Mankind, and a great deal stupider. It is the position of a beleaguered group which lacks one simple essential to keep them alive until help comes.

"A fighting outfit, suppose, has enough ammunition to stand off two more attacks: but they know that there will be reinforcements within four days. Unfortunately, the enemy can attack *more than twice* before help comes. Help will come too late.

"Or, it could be that they have enough water to last a week, but help won't come for a month.

"You follow me, I'm sure. The point, in so far as it concerns us, is that we have food for about a month, but we won't get help before six months have passed. We know help is coming, but we won't be alive to see it."

Then his eyes lit up in a kind of half hope. "Unless the native flora—"

But even before he finished, he could see the look in Dr. Pilar's eyes.

Broderick MacNeil was a sick man. The medical officers of the Space Service did not agree with him *in toto,* but MacNeil was in a position to know more about his own state of health than the doctors, because it was, after all, he himself who was sick.

Rarely, of course, did he draw the attention of the medical officers to his ever-fluctuating assortment of aches, pains, signs, symptoms, malaises, and malfunctions. After all, it wouldn't do for him to be released from the Service on a Medical Discharge. No, he would suffer in silence for the sake of his chosen career—which, apparently, was to be a permanent Spaceman 2nd Class.

Broderick MacNeil had never seen his medical record, and therefore did not know that, aside from mention of the normal slight defects which every human body possesses, the only note on the records was one which said: "Slight tendency toward hypochondria, compensated for by tendency to immerse self in job at hand. According to psych tests, he can competently handle positions up to Enlisted Space Officer 3rd Class, but positions of ESO/2 and above should be carefully considered. (See Psych Rept. Intelligence Sectn.)"

But, if MacNeil did not know what the medics thought of him, neither did the medics know what he thought of them. Nor did they know that MacNeil carried a secret supply of his own personal palliatives, purgatives and poly-purpose pills. He kept them carefully concealed in a small section of his space locker, and had labeled them all as various vitamin mixtures, which made them seem perfectly legal, and which was not *too* dishonest, since many of them *were* vitamins.

On the morning after the fire, he heaved his well-muscled bulk out of bed and scratched his scalp through the close-cropped brown hair that covered his squarish skull. He did not feel well, and that was a fact. Of course, he had been up half the night fighting the blaze, and that hadn't helped any. He fancied he had a bit of a headache, and his nerves seemed a little jangled. His insides were probably in their usual balky state. He sighed, wished he were in better health, and glanced around at the other members of the company as they rose grumpily from their beds.

He sighed again, opened his locker, took out his depilator, and ran it quickly over his face. Then, from his assortment of bottles, he began picking over his morning dosage. Vitamins, of course; got to keep plenty of vitamins in the system, or it goes all to pot on you. A, B_1, B_2, B_{12}, C,...and on down the alphabet and past it to A-G. All-purpose mineral capsules, presumably containing every element useful to the human body and possibly a couple that weren't. Two APC capsules. (Aspirin-Phenacitin-Caffeine. He liked the way those words sounded; very medicinal.) A milk-of-magnesia tablet, just in case. A couple of patent-mixture pills that were supposed to increase the bile flow. (MacNeil wasn't quite sure what bile was, but he *was* quite sure that its increased flow would work wonders within.) A largish tablet of sodium bicarbonate to combat excess gastric acidity—obviously a *horrible* condition, whatever it was. He topped it all off with a football-shaped capsule containing Liquid Glandolene—*"Guards the system against glandular imbalance!"*—and felt himself ready to face the day. At least, until breakfast.

He slipped several bottles into his belt-pak, after he had put on his field uniform, so that he could get at them at mealtimes, and trudged out toward the mess hall to the meager breakfast that awaited him.

"Specifically," said Colonel Fennister, "what we want to know is: What are our chances of staying alive until the relief ship comes?"

He and most of the other officers were still groggy-eyed, having had too much to do to even get an hour's sleep the night before. Only the phlegmatic Major Grodsky looked normal; his eyes were always about half closed.

Captains Jones and Bellwether, in charge of A and B Companies respectively, and their lieutenants, Mawkey and Yutang, all looked grim and irritable.

The civilian components of the policy group looked not one whit better. Dr. Pilar had been worriedly rubbing at his face, so that his normally neat beard had begun to take on the appearance of a ruptured mohair sofa; Dr. Petrelli, the lean, waspish chemist, was nervously trimming his fingernails with his teeth; and the M.D., Dr. Smathers, had a hangdog expression on his pudgy face and had begun drumming his fingers in a staccato tattoo on his round belly.

Dr. Pilar tapped a stack of papers that lay before him on the long table at which they were all seated. "I have Major Grodski's report on the remaining food. There is not enough for all of us to live, even on the most extended rations. Only the strongest will survive."

Colonel Fennister scowled. "You mean to imply that we'll be fighting over the food like animals before this is over? The discipline of the Space Service—"

His voice was angry, but Dr. Pilar cut him off. "It may come to fighting, colonel, but, even if perfect discipline is maintained, what I say will still be true. Some will die early, leaving more food

12

for the remaining men. It has been a long time since anything like this has happened on Earth, but it is not unknown in the Space Service annals."

The colonel pursed his lips and kept his silence. He knew that what the biologist said was true.

"The trouble is," said Petrelli snappishly, "that we are starving in the midst of plenty. We are like men marooned in the middle of an ocean with no water; the water is there, but it's undrinkable."

"That's what I wanted to get at," said Colonel Fennister. "Is there any chance at all that we'll find an edible plant or animal on this planet?"

The three scientists said nothing, as if each was waiting for one of the others to speak.

All life thus far found in the galaxy had had a carbon-hydrogen-oxygen base. Nobody'd yet found any silicon-based life, although a good many organisms used the element. No one yet had found a planet with a halogen atmosphere, and, although there might be weird forms of life at the bottom of the soupy atmospheres of the methane-ammonia giants, no brave soul had ever gone down to see—at least, not on purpose, and no information had ever come back.

But such esoteric combinations are not at all necessary for the postulation of wildly variant life forms. Earth itself was prolific in its variations; Earthlike planets were equally inventive. Carbon, hydrogen, and oxygen, plus varying proportions of phosphorus, potassium, iodine, nitrogen, sulfur, calcium, iron, magnesium, manganese, and strontium, plus a smattering of trace elements, seem to be able to cook up all kinds of life under the strangest imaginable conditions.

Alphegar IV was no different than any other Earth-type planet in that respect. It had a plant-dominated ecology; the land areas were covered with gigantic trees that could best be described as crosses between a California sequoia and a cycad, although such a description would have made a botanist sneer and throw up his hands. There were enough smaller animals to keep the oxygen-carbon dioxide cycle nicely balanced, but the animals had not evolved anything larger than a rat, for some reason. Of course, the sea had evolved some pretty huge monsters, but the camp of the expedition was located a long way from the sea, so there was no worry from that quarter.

At the time, however, the members of the expedition didn't know any of that information for sure. The probe teams had made spot checks and taken random samples, but it was up to the First Analytical Expedition to make sure of everything.

And this much they had discovered: The plants of Alphegar IV had a nasty habit of killing test animals.

"Of course," said Dr. Pilar, "we haven't tested every plant yet. We may come across something."

"What is it that kills the animals?" asked young Captain Bellwether.

"Poison," said Major Grodski.

Pilar ignored him. "Different things. Most of them we haven't been able to check thoroughly. We found some vines that were heavily laced with cyanide, and there were recognizable alkaloids in several of the shrubs, but most of them are not that direct. Like Earth plants, they vary from family to family; the deadly nightshade is related to both the tobacco plant and the tomato."

He paused a moment, scratching thoughtfully at his beard.

"Tell you what; let's go over to the lab, and I'll show you what we've found so far."

Colonel Fennister nodded. He was a military man, and he wasn't too sure that the scientists' explanations would be very clear, but if there was information to be had, he might as well make the most of it.

SM/2 Broderick MacNeil kept a firm grip on his blast rifle and looked around at the surrounding jungle, meanwhile thanking whatever gods there were that he hadn't been put on the fence-mending detail. Not that he objected violently to work, but he preferred to be out here in the forest just now. Breakfast hadn't been exactly filling, and he was hungry.

Besides, this was his pet detail, and he liked it. He had been going out with the technicians ever since the base had been finished, a couple of weeks before, and he was used to the work. The biotechnicians came out to gather specimens, and it was his job, along with four others, to guard them—make sure that no wild animal got them while they were going about their duties. It was a simple job, and one well suited to MacNeil's capacities.

He kept an eye on the technicians. They were working on a bush of some kind that had little thorny-looking nuts on it, clipping bits off here and there. He wasn't at all sure what they did with all those little pieces and bits, but that was none of his business, anyway. Let the brains take care of that stuff; his job was to make sure they weren't interrupted in whatever it was they were doing. After watching the three technicians in total incomprehension for a minute or so, he turned his attention to the surrounding forest. But he was looking for a plant, not an animal.

And he finally saw what he was looking for.

The technicians paid him no attention. They rarely did. They had their job, and he had his. Of course, he didn't want to be caught breaking regulations, but he knew how to avoid that catastrophe. He walked casually toward the tree, as though he were only slightly interested in it.

He didn't know what the name of the tree was. He'd asked a technician once, and the tech had said that the tree didn't have any name yet. Personally, MacNeil thought it was silly for a thing not to have a name. Hell, *everything* had a name.

But, if they didn't want to tell him what it was, that was all right with him, too. He called it a banana-pear tree.

Because that's what the fruit reminded him of.

The fruit that hung from the tree were six or eight inches long, fat in the middle, and tapering at both ends. The skin was a pale chartreuse in color, with heliotrope spots.

MacNeil remembered the first time he'd seen one, the time he'd asked the tech what its name was. The tech had been picking some of them and putting them into plastic bags, and the faint spark of MacNeil's dim curiosity had been brought to feebly flickering life.

"Hey, Doc," he'd said, "whatcha gonna do with them things?"

"Take 'em to the lab," said the technician, engrossed in his work.

MacNeil had digested that carefully. "Yeah?" he'd said at last. "What for?"

The technician had sighed and popped another fruit into a bag. He had attempted to explain things to Broderick MacNeil before and given it up as a bad job. "We just feed 'em to the monkeys, Mac, that's all."

"Oh," said Broderick MacNeil.

Well, that made sense, anyhow. Monkeys got to eat *something*, don't they? Sure. And he had gazed at the fruit in interest.

Fresh fruit was something MacNeil missed. He'd heard that fresh fruit was necessary for health, and on Earth he'd always made sure that he had plenty of it. He didn't want to get sick. But they didn't ship fresh fruit on an interstellar expedition, and MacNeil had felt vaguely apprehensive about the lack.

Now, however, his problem was solved. He knew that it was strictly against regulations to eat native fruit until the brass said so, but that didn't worry him too much. He'd heard somewhere that a man can eat anything a monkey can, so he wasn't worried about it. So he'd tried one. It tasted fine, something like a pear and something like a banana, and different from either. It was just fine.

Since then, he'd managed to eat a couple every day, so's to get his fresh fruit. It kept him healthy. Today, though, he needed more than just health; he was hungry, and the banana-pears looked singularly tempting.

When he reached the tree, he turned casually around to see if any of the others were watching. They weren't, but he kept his eye on them while he picked several of the fruit. Then he turned carefully around, and, with his back to the others, masking his movements with his own body, he began to munch contentedly on the crisp flesh of the banana-pears.

"Now, take this one, for instance," said Dr. Pilar. He was holding up a native fruit. It bulged in the middle, and had a chartreuse rind with heliotrope spots on it. "It's a very good example of exactly what we're up against. Ever since we discovered this particular fruit, we've been interested in it because the analyses show that it should be an excellent source of basic food elements. Presumably, it even tastes good; our monkeys seemed to like it."

"What's the matter with it, then?" asked Major Grodski, eyeing the fruit with sleepy curiosity.

Dr. Pilar gave the thing a wry look and put it back in the specimen bag. "Except for the fact that it has killed every one of our test specimens, we don't know what's wrong with it."

Colonel Fennister looked around the laboratory at the cages full of chittering animals—monkeys, white mice, rats, guinea pigs, hamsters, and the others. Then he looked back at the scientist. "Don't you know what killed them?"

Pilar didn't answer; instead, he glanced at Dr. Smathers, the physician.

Smathers steepled his fingers over his abdomen and rubbed his fingertips together. "We're not sure. Thus far, it looks as though death was caused by oxygen starvation in the tissues."

"Some kind of anemia?" hazarded the colonel.

Smathers frowned. "The end results are similar, but there is no drop in the hemoglobin—in fact, it seems to rise a little. We're still investigating that. We haven't got all the answers yet, by any means, but since we don't quite know what to look for, we're rather hampered."

The colonel nodded slowly. "Lack of equipment?"

"Pretty much so," admitted Dr. Smathers. "Remember, we're just here for preliminary investigation. When the ship brings in more men and equipment—"

His voice trailed off. Very likely, when the ship returned, it would find an empty base. The first-string team simply wasn't set up for exhaustive work; its job was to survey the field in general and mark out the problems for the complete team to solve.

Establishing the base had been of primary importance, and that was the sort of equipment that had been carried on the ship. That—and food. The scientists had only the barest essentials to work with; they had no electron microscopes or any of the other complex instruments necessary for exhaustive biochemical work.

Now that they were engaged in a fight for survival, they felt like a gang of midgets attacking a herd of water buffalo with penknives. Even if they won the battle, the mortality rate would be high, and their chances of winning were pretty small.

The Space Service officers and the scientists discussed the

problem for over an hour, but they came to no promising conclusion.

At last, Colonel Fennister said: "Very well, Dr. Pilar; we'll have to leave the food supply problem in your hands. Meanwhile, I'll try to keep order here in the camp."

SM/2 Broderick MacNeil may not have had a top-level grade of intelligence, but by the end of the second week, his conscience was nagging him, and he was beginning to wonder who was goofing and why. After much thinking—if we may so refer to MacNeil's painful cerebral processes—he decided to ask a few cautious questions.

Going without food tends to make for mental fogginess, snarling tempers, and general physical lassitude in any group of men. And, while quarter rations were not quite starvation meals, they closely approached it. It was fortunate, therefore, that MacNeil decided to approach Dr. Pilar.

Dr. Petrelli's temper, waspish by nature, had become positively virulent in the two weeks that had passed since the destruction of the major food cache. Dr. Smathers was losing weight from his excess, but his heretofore pampered stomach was voicelessly screaming along his nerve passages, and his fingers had become shaky, which is unnerving in a surgeon, so his temper was no better than Petrelli's.

Pilar, of course, was no better fed, but he was calmer than either of the others by disposition, and his lean frame didn't use as much energy. So, when the big hulking spaceman appeared at the door of his office with his cap in his hands, he was inclined to be less brusque than he might have been.

"Yes? What is it?" he asked. He had been correlating notes in his journal with the thought in the back of his mind that he would never finish it, but he felt that a small respite might be relaxing.

MacNeil came in and looked nervously around at the plain walls of the pre-fab plastic dome-hut as though seeking consolation from them. Then he straightened himself in the approved military manner and looked at the doctor.

"You Dr. Piller? Sir?"

"Pilar," said the scientist in correction. "If you're looking for the medic, you'll want Dr. Smathers, over in G Section."

"Oh, yessir," said MacNeil quickly, "I know that. But I ain't sick." He didn't feel *that* sick, anyway. "I'm Spaceman Second MacNeil, sir, from B Company. Could I ask you something, sir?"

Pilar sighed a little, then smiled. "Go ahead, spaceman."

MacNeil wondered if maybe he'd ought to ask the doctor about his sacroiliac pains, then decided against it. This wasn't the time for it. "Well, about the food. Uh...Doc, can men eat monkey food all right?"

Pilar smiled. "Yes. What food there is left for the monkeys has already been sent to the men's mess hall." He didn't add that the lab animals would be the next to go. Quick-frozen, they might help eke out the dwindling food supply, but it would be better not to let the men know what they were eating for a while. When they got hungry enough, they wouldn't care.

But MacNeil was plainly puzzled by Pilar's answer. He decided to approach the stuff as obliquely as he knew how.

"Doc, sir, if I...I uh...well—" He took the bit in his teeth and plunged ahead. "If I done something against the regulations, would you have to report me to Captain Bellwether?"

Dr. Pilar leaned back in his chair and looked at the big man with interest. "Well," he said carefully, "that would all depend on what it was. If it was something really...ah...dangerous to the welfare of the expedition, I'd have to say something about it, I suppose, but I'm not a military officer, and minor infractions don't concern me."

MacNeil absorbed that. "Well, sir, this ain't much, really—I ate something I shouldn't of."

Pilar drew down his brows. "Stealing food, I'm afraid, would be a major offense, under the circumstances."

MacNeil looked both startled and insulted. "Oh, nossir! I never swiped no food! In fact, I've been givin' my chow to my buddies."

Pilar's brows lifted. He suddenly realized that the man before him looked in exceptionally good health for one who had been on a marginal diet for two weeks. "Then what *have* you been living on?"

"The monkey food, sir."

"Monkey food?"

"Yessir. Them greenish things with the purple spots. You know—them fruits you feed the monkeys on."

Pilar looked at MacNeil goggle-eyed for a full thirty seconds before he burst into action.

"No, of course I won't punish him," said Colonel Fennister. "Something will have to go on the record, naturally, but I'll just restrict him to barracks for thirty days and then recommend him for light duty. But are you *sure?*"

"I'm sure," said Pilar, half in wonder.

Fennister glanced over at Dr. Smathers, now noticeably thinner in the face. The medic was looking over MacNeil's record. "But if that fruit kills monkeys and rats and guinea pigs, how can a *man* eat it?"

"Animals differ," said Smathers, without taking his eyes off the record sheets. He didn't amplify the statement.

The colonel looked back at Pilar.

"That's the trouble with test animals," Dr. Pilar said, ruffling his gray beard with a fingertip. "You take a rat, for instance. A rat can live on a diet that would kill a monkey. If there's no vitamin A in the diet, the monkey dies, but the rat makes his own vitamin A; he doesn't need to import it, you might say, since he can synthesize it in his own body. But a monkey can't.

"That's just one example. There are hundreds that we know of and God alone knows how many that we haven't found yet."

Fennister settled his body more comfortably in the chair and scratched his head thoughtfully. "Then, even after a piece of alien vegetation has passed all the animal tests, you still couldn't be sure it wouldn't kill a human?"

"That's right. That's why we ask for volunteers. But we haven't lost a man so far. Sometimes a volunteer will get pretty sick, but if a food passes all the other tests, you can usually depend on its not killing a human being."

"I gather that this is a pretty unusual case, then?"

Pilar frowned. "As far as I know, yes. But if something kills all the test animals, we don't ask for humans to try it out. We assume the worst and forget it." He looked musingly at the wall. "I wonder how many edible plants we've by-passed that way?" he asked softly, half to himself.

"What are you going to do next?" the colonel asked. "My men are getting hungry."

Smathers looked up from the report in alarm, and Pilar had a similar expression on his face.

"For Pete's sake," said Smathers, "don't tell anyone—not *anyone*—about this, just yet. We don't want all your men rushing out in the forest to gobble down those things until we are more sure of them. Give us a few more days at least."

The colonel patted the air with a hand. "Don't worry. I'll wait until you give me the go-ahead. But I'll want to know your plans."

Pilar pursed his lips for a moment before he spoke. "We'll check up on MacNeil for another forty-eight hours. We'd like to have him transferred over here, so that we can keep him in isolation. We'll feed him more of the...uh...what'd he call 'em, Smathers?"

"Banana-pears."

"We'll feed him more banana-pears, and keep checking. If he is still in good shape, we'll ask for volunteers."

"Good enough," said the colonel. "I'll keep in touch."

On the morning of the third day in isolation, MacNeil rose early, as usual, gulped down his normal assortment of vitamins, added a couple of aspirin tablets, and took a dose of Epsom salts for good measure. Then he yawned and leaned back to wait for breakfast. He was certainly getting enough fresh fruit, that was certain. He'd begun to worry about whether he was getting a balanced diet—he'd heard that a balanced diet was very important—but he figured that the doctors knew what they were doing. Leave it up to them.

He'd been probed and needled and tested plenty in the last couple of days, but he didn't mind it. It gave him a feeling of confidence to know that the doctors were taking care of him. Maybe he ought to tell them about his various troubles; they all seemed like nice guys. On the other hand, it wouldn't do to get booted out of the Service. He'd think it over for a while.

He settled back to doze a little while he waited for his breakfast to be served. Sure was nice to be taken care of.

Later on that same day, Dr. Pilar put out a call for volunteers. He still said nothing about MacNeil; he simply asked the colonel to say that it had been eaten successfully by a test animal.

The volunteers ate their banana-pears for lunch, approaching them warily at first, but soon polishing them off with gusto, proclaiming them to have a fine taste.

The next morning, they felt weak and listless.

Thirty-six hours later, they were dead.

"Oxygen starvation," said Smathers angrily, when he had completed the autopsies.

Broderick MacNeil munched pleasantly on a banana-pear that evening, happily unaware that three of his buddies had died of eating that selfsame fruit.

The chemist, Dr. Petrelli, looked at the fruit in his hand, snarled suddenly, and smashed it to the floor. Its skin burst, splattering pulp all over the gray plastic.

"It looks," he said in a high, savage voice, "as if that hulking idiot will be the only one left alive when the ship returns!" He turned to look at Smathers, who was peering through a binocular microscope. "Smathers, what makes him different?"

"How do I know?" growled Dr. Smathers, still peering. "There's something different about him, that's all."

Petrelli forcibly restrained his temper. "Very funny," he snapped.

"Not funny at all," Smathers snapped back. "No two human beings are identical—you know that." He lifted his gaze from the eyepiece of the instrument and settled in on the chemist. "He's got AB blood type, for one thing, which none of the volunteers had. Is that what makes him immune to whatever poison is in those things? I don't know.

"Were the other three allergic to some protein substance in the fruit, while MacNeil isn't? I don't know.

"Do his digestive processes destroy the poison? I don't know.

"It's got something to do with his blood, I think, but I can't even be sure of that. The leucocytes are a little high, the red cell count is a little low, the hemoglobin shows a little high on the colorimeter, but none of 'em seems enough to do any harm.

"It might be an enzyme that destroys the ability of the cells to utilize oxygen. It might be *anything!*"

His eyes narrowed then, as he looked at the chemist. "After all, why haven't you isolated the stuff from the fruit?"

"There's no clue as to what to look for," said Petrelli, somewhat less bitingly. "The poison might be present in microscopic amounts. Do you know how much botulin toxin it takes to kill a man? A fraction of a milligram!"

Smathers looked as though he were about to quote the minimum dosage, so Petrelli charged on: "If you think anyone could isolate an unknown organic compound out of a—"

"Gentlemen! *Please!*" said Dr. Pilar sharply. "I realize that this is a strain, but bickering won't help. What about your latest tests on MacNeil, Dr. Smathers?"

"As far as I can tell, he's in fine health. And I can't understand why," said the physician in a restrained voice.

Pilar tapped one of the report sheets. "You mean the vitamins?"

"I mean the vitamins," said Smathers. "According to Dr. Petrelli, the fruits contain neither A nor B. After living solely on them for four weeks now, he should be beginning to show some deficiencies—but he's not."

"No signs?" queried Dr. Pilar. "No symptoms?"

"No signs—at least no abnormal ones. He's not getting enough protein, but, then, none of us is." He made a bitter face. "But he has plenty of symptoms."

Dr. Petrelli raised a thin eyebrow. "What's the difference between a sign and a symptom?"

"A sign," said Smathers testily, "is something that can be objectively checked by another person than the patient. Lesions, swellings, inflammation, erratic heartbeat, and so on. A symptom is a subjective feeling of the patient, like aches, pains, nausea, dizziness, or spots before the eyes.

"And MacNeil is beginning to get all kinds of symptoms. Trouble is, he's got a record of hypochondria, and I can't tell which of the symptoms are psychosomatic and which, if any, might be caused by the fruit."

"The trouble is," said Petrelli, "that we have an unidentifiable disease caused by an unidentifiable agent which is checked by an unidentifiable something in MacNeil. And we have neither the time nor the equipment to find out. This is a job that a fully equipped research lab might take a couple of years to solve."

"We can keep trying," said Pilar, "and hope we stumble across it by accident."

Petrelli nodded and picked up the beaker he'd been heating over an electric plate. He added a chelating agent which, if there were any nickel present, would sequester the nickel ions and bring them out of solution as a brick-red precipitate.

Smathers scowled and bent over his microscope to count more leucocytes.

Pilar pushed his notes aside and went over to check his agar plates in the constant-temperature box.

The technicians who had been listening to the conversation with ears wide open went back to their various duties.

And all of them tried in vain to fight down the hunger pangs that were corroding at their insides.

Broderick MacNeil lay in his bed and felt pleasantly ill. He treasured each one of his various symptoms; each pain and ache was just right. He hadn't been so comfortable in years. It really felt fine to have all those doctors fussing over him. They got snappy and irritable once in a while, but then, all them brainy people had a tendency to do that. He wondered how the rest of the boys were doing on their diet of banana-pears. Too bad they weren't getting any special treatment.

MacNeil had decided just that morning that he'd leave the whole state of his health in the hands of the doctors. No need for a fellow to dose himself when there were three medics on the job, was there? If he needed anything, they'd give it to him, so he'd decided to take no medicine.

A delightful, dulling lassitude was creeping over him.

"MacNeil! *MacNeil!* Wake up, MacNeil!"

The spaceman vaguely heard the voice, and tried to respond, but a sudden dizziness overtook him. His stomach felt as though it were going to come loose from his interior.

"I'm sick," he said weakly. Then, with a terrible realization, "I'm really *awful* sick!"

He saw Dr. Smathers' face swimming above him and tried to lift himself from the bed. "Shoulda taken pills," he said through the haze that was beginning to fold over him again. "Locker box." And then he was unconscious again.

Dr. Smathers looked at him bleakly. The same thing was killing MacNeil as had killed the others. It had taken longer—much longer. But it had come.

And then the meaning of the spaceman's mumbled words came to him. Pills? Locker box?

He grabbed the unconscious man's right hand and shoved his right thumb up against the sensor plate in the front of the metal box next to the bed. He could have gotten the master key from Colonel Fennister, but he hadn't the time.

The box door dilated open, and Dr. Smathers looked inside.

When he came across the bottles, he swore under his breath, then flung the spaceman's arm down and ran from the room.

"That's where he was getting his vitamins, then," said Dr. Pilar as he looked over the assortment of bottles that he and Smathers had taken from the locker box. "Look at 'em. He's got almost as many pills as you have." He looked up at the physician. "Do you suppose it was just vitamins that kept him going?"

"I don't know," said Smathers. "I've given him massive doses of every one of the vitamins—from my own supplies, naturally. He may rally round, if that's what it was. But why would he suddenly be affected by the stuff *now*?"

"Maybe he quit taking them?" Pilar made it half a question.

"It's possible," agreed Smathers. "A hypochondriac will sometimes leave off dosing himself if there's a doctor around to do it for him. As long as the subconscious need is filled, he's happy." But he was shaking his head.

"What's the matter?" Pilar asked.

Smathers pointed at the bottles. "Some of those are mislabeled. They all say vitamins of one kind or another on the label, but the tablets inside aren't all vitamins. MacNeil's been giving himself all kinds of things."

Pilar's eyes widened a trifle. "Do you suppose—"

"That one of them is an antidote?" Smathers snorted. "Hell, anything's possible at this stage of the game. The best thing we can do, I think, is give him a dose of everything there, and see what happens."

"Yeah, Doc, yeah," said MacNeil, smiling weakly, "I feel a little better. Not real good, you understand, but better."

Under iron control, Dr. Smathers put on his best bedside manner, while Pilar and Petrelli hovered in the background.

"Now, look, son," said Smathers in a kindly voice, "we found the medicines in your locker box."

MacNeil's face fell, making him look worse. He'd dropped down close to death before the conglomerate mixture which had been pumped into his stomach had taken effect, and Smathers had no desire to put too much pressure on the man.

"Now, don't worry about it, son," he said hurriedly; "We'll see to it that you aren't punished for it. It's all right. We just want to ask you a few questions."

"Sure, Doc; anything," said MacNeil. But he still looked apprehensive.

"Have you been dosing yourself pretty regularly with these things?"

"Well. . .uh. . .well, yeah. Sometimes." He smiled feebly. "Sometimes I didn't feel so good, and I didn't want to bother the medics. You know how it is."

"Very considerate, I'm sure," said Smathers with just the barest trace of sarcasm, which, fortunately, fell unheeded on MacNeil's ears. "But which ones did you take every day?"

"Just the vitamins." He paused. "And...uh...maybe an aspirin. The only things I took real regular were the vitamins, though. That's all right, ain't it? Ain't vitamins food?"

"Sure, son, sure. What did you take yesterday morning, before you got so sick?"

"Just the vitamins," MacNeil said stoutly. "I figured that since you docs was takin' care of me, I didn't need no medicine."

Dr. Smathers glanced up hopelessly at the other two men. "That eliminates the vitamins," he said, *sotto voce*. He looked back at the patient. "No aspirin? No APCs? You didn't have a headache at all?"

MacNeil shook his head firmly. "I don't get headaches much." Again he essayed a feeble smile. "I ain't like you guys, I don't overwork my brains."

"I'm sure you don't," said Smathers. Then his eyes gleamed. "You have quite a bit of stomach trouble, eh? Your digestion bad?"

"Yeah. You know; I told you about it. I get heartburn and acid stomach pretty often. And constipation."

"What do you take for that?"

"Oh, different things. Sometimes a soda pill, sometimes milk of magnesia, different things."

Smathers looked disappointed, but before he could say anything, Dr. Petrelli's awed but excited voice came from behind him. "Do you take Epsom salts?"

"Yeah."

"I wonder—" said Petrelli softly.

And then he left for the lab at a dead run.

Colonel Fennister and Major Grodski sat at the table in the lab, munching on banana-pears, blissfully enjoying the sweet flavor and the feeling of fullness they were imparting to their stomachs.

"MacNeil can't stay in the service, of course," said Fennister. "That is, not in any space-going outfit. We'll find an Earthside job for him, though. Maybe even give him a medal. You sure these things won't hurt us?"

Dr. Pilar started to speak, but Petrelli cut him off.

"Positive," said the chemist. "After we worked it out, it was pretty simple. The 'poison' was a chelating agent, that's all. You saw the test run I did for you."

The colonel nodded. He'd watched the little chemist add an iron salt to some of the fruit juice and seen it turn red. Then he'd seen it turn pale yellow when a magnesium salt was added. "But what's a chelating agent?" he asked.

"There are certain organic compounds," Dr. Petrelli explained, "that are...well, to put it simply, they're attracted by certain ions. Some are attracted by one ion, some by another. The chelating molecules cluster around the ion and take it out of circulation, so to speak; they neutralize it, in a way.

"Look, suppose you had a dangerous criminal on the loose, and didn't have any way to kill him. If you kept him surrounded by policemen all the time, he couldn't do anything. See?"

The Space Service Officers nodded their understanding.

"We call that 'sequestering' the ion," the chemist continued. "It's used quite frequently in medicine, as Dr. Smathers will tell you. For instance, beryllium ions in the body can be deadly; beryllium poisoning is nasty stuff. But if the patient is treated with the proper chelating agent, the ions are surrounded and don't do any more damage. They're still there, but now they're harmless, you see."

"Well, then," said the colonel, "just what did this stuff in the fruit do?"

"It sequestered the iron ions in the body. They couldn't do their job. The body had to quit making hemoglobin, because hemoglobin needs iron. So, since there was no hemoglobin in the bloodstream, the patient developed sudden pernicious anemia and died of oxygen starvation."

Colonel Fennister looked suddenly at Dr. Smathers. "I thought you said the blood looked normal."

"It did," said the physician. "The colorimeter showed extra hemoglobin, in fact. But the chelating agent in the fruit turns red when it's connected up with iron—in fact, it's even redder than blood hemoglobin. And the molecules containing the sequestered iron tend to stick to the outside of the red blood cells, which threw the whole test off."

"As I understand it, then," said Major Grodski, "the antidote for the...uh...chelating agent is magnesium?"

"That's right," said Dr. Petrelli, nodding. "The stuff prefers magnesium ions to ferrous ions. They fit better within the chelating ring. Any source of magnesium will do, so long as there's plenty of it. MacNeil was using milk of magnesia, which is the hydroxide, for 'gastric acidity.' It's changed to chloride in the stomach. And he was using Epsom salts—the sulfate, and magnesium citrate as laxatives. He was well protected with magnesium ions."

"We tried it ourselves first, naturally," said Dr. Pilar. "We haven't had any ill effects for two days, so I think we'll be able to make it until the ship comes."

Major Grodski sighed. "Well, if not, I'll at least die with a full stomach." He reached for another banana-pear, then looked over at Petrelli. "Pass the salt, please."

Silently and solemnly, the chemist handed him the Epsom salts.

...After a Few Words...

by Randall Garrett
writing as Seaton McKettrig

*I'm sure it never occurred to Randall that using an
ellipsis at the beginning of a title would drive a
perfectionistic part-time librarian crazy as she tried to create
a computerized index of his work with every title shown
accurately and alphabetized properly. I finally settled on
"After a Few Words, ..." as the entry, but that seems to
make "..." a word, rather than punctuation.*

*Randall had foreseen the computer but not, perhaps, the
specific logic which applies to alpha sorts. It's too much to
hope for that great technological advancements will be totally
free of some small disadvantages. Take, for instance, "Seaton
McKettrig's" experiential television... (ellipses are useful...).*

He settled himself comfortably in his seat, and carefully put
the helmet on, pulling it down firmly until it was properly seated.
For a moment, he could see nothing.

Then his hand moved up and, with a flick of the wrist, lifted
the visor. Ahead of him, in serried array, with lances erect and
pennons flying, was the forward part of the column. Far ahead, he
knew, were the Knights Templars, who had taken the advance.
Behind the Templars rode the mailed knights of Brittany and
Anjou. These were followed by King Guy of Jerusalem and the
host of Poitou.

He himself, Sir Robert de Bouain, was riding with the Norman
and English troops, just behind the men of Poitou. Sir Robert turned
slightly in his saddle. To his right, he could see the brilliant red-and-
gold banner of the lion-hearted Richard of England—*gules, in pale*

three lions passant guardant or. Behind the standard-bearer, his great war horse moving with a steady, measured pace, his coronet of gold on his steel helm gleaming in the glaring desert sun, the lions of England on his firm-held shield, was the King himself.

Further behind, the Knights Hospitallers protected the rear, guarding the column of the hosts of Christendom from harassment by the Bedouins.

"By our Lady!" came a voice from his left. "Three days out from Acre, and the accursed Saracens still elude us."

Sir Robert de Bouain twisted again in his saddle to look at the knight riding alongside him. Sir Gaeton de l'Arc-Tombe sat tall and straight in his saddle, his visor up, his blue eyes narrowed against the glare of the sun.

Sir Robert's lips formed a smile. "They are not far off, Sir Gaeton. They have been following us. As we march parallel to the seacoast, so they have been marching with us in those hills to the east."

"Like the jackals they are," said Sir Gaeton. "They assail us from the rear, and they set up traps in our path ahead. Our spies tell us that the Turks lie ahead of us in countless numbers. And yet, they fear to face us in open battle."

"Is it fear, or are they merely gathering their forces?"

"Both," said Sir Gaeton flatly. "They fear us, else they would not dally to amass so fearsome a force. If, as our informers tell us, there are uncounted Turks to the fore, and if, as we are aware, our rear is being dogged by the Bedouin and the black horsemen of Egypt, it would seem that Saladin has at hand more than enough to overcome us, were they all truly Christian knights."

"Give them time. We must wait for their attack, sir knight. It were foolhardy to attempt to seek them in their own hills, and yet they must stop us. They will attack before we reach Jerusalem, fear not."

"We of Gascony fear no heathen Musselman," Sir Gaeton growled. "It's this Hellish heat that is driving me mad." He pointed toward the eastern hills. "The sun is yet low, and already the heat is unbearable."

Sir Robert heard his own laugh echo hollowly within his helmet. "Perhaps 'twere better to be mad when the assault comes. Madmen fight better than men of cooler blood." He knew that the others were baking inside their heavy armor, although he himself was not too uncomfortable.

Sir Gaeton looked at him with a smile that held both irony and respect. "In truth, sir knight, it is apparent that you fear neither men nor heat. Nor is your own blood too cool. True, I ride with your Normans and your English and your King Richard of the Lion's Heart, but I am a Gascon, and have sworn no fealty to him. But to side with the Duke of Burgundy against King Richard—" He gave a short, barking laugh. "I fear no man," he went on, "but if I had to fear

27

one, it would be Richard of England."

Sir Robert's voice came like a sword: steely, flat, cold, and sharp. "My lord the King spoke in haste. He has reason to be bitter against Philip of France, as do we all. Philip has deserted the field. He has returned to France in haste, leaving the rest of us to fight the Saracen for the Holy Land, leaving only the contingent of his vassal the Duke of Burgundy to remain with us."

"Richard of England has never been on the best of terms with Philip Augustus," said Sir Gaeton.

"No, and with good cause. But he allowed his anger against Philip to color his judgment when he spoke harshly against the Duke of Burgundy. The Duke is no coward, and Richard Plantagenet well knows it. As I said, he spoke in haste."

"And you intervened," said Sir Gaeton.

"It was my duty." Sir Robert's voice was stubborn. "Could we have permitted a quarrel to develop between the two finest knights and warleaders in Christendom at this crucial point? The desertion of Philip of France has cost us dearly. Could we permit the desertion of Burgundy, too?"

"You did what must be done in honor," the Gascon conceded, "but you have not gained the love of Richard by doing so."

Sir Robert felt his jaw set firmly. "My king knows I am loyal."

Sir Gaeton said nothing more, but there was a look in his eyes that showed that he felt that Richard of England might even doubt the loyalty of Sir Robert de Bouain.

Sir Robert rode on in silence, feeling the movement of the horse beneath him.

There was a sudden sound to the rear. Like a wash of the tide from the sea came the sound of Saracen war cries and the clash of steel on steel mingled with the sounds of horses in agony and anger.

Sir Robert turned his horse to look.

The Negro troops of Saladin's Egyptian contingent were thundering down upon the rear! They clashed with the Hospitallers, slamming in like a rain of heavy stones, too close in for the use of bows. There was only the sword against armor, like the sound of a thousand hammers against a thousand anvils.

"Stand fast! Stand fast! Hold them off!" It was the voice of King Richard, sounding like a clarion over the din of battle.

Sir Robert felt his horse move, as though it were urging him on toward the battle, but his hand held to the reins, keeping the great charger in check. The King had said "Stand fast!" and this was no time to disobey the orders of Richard.

The Saracen troops were coming in from the rear, and the Hospitallers were taking the brunt of the charge. They fought like madmen, but they were slowly being forced back.

The Master of the Hospitallers rode to the rear, to the King's standard, which hardly moved in the still desert air, now that the column had stopped moving.

The voice of the Duke of Burgundy came to Sir Robert's ears.

"Stand fast. The King bids you all to stand fast," said the duke, his voice fading as he rode on up the column toward the knights of Poitou and the Knights Templars.

The Master of the Hospitallers was speaking in a low, urgent voice to the King: "My lord, we are pressed on by the enemy and in danger of eternal infamy. We are losing our horses, one after the other!"

"Good Master," said Richard, "it is you who must sustain their attack. No one can be everywhere at once."

The Master of the Hospitallers nodded curtly and charged back into the fray.

The King turned to Sir Baldwin de Carreo, who sat ahorse nearby, and pointed toward the eastern hills. "They will come from there, hitting us in the flank; we cannot afford to amass a rearward charge. To do so would be to fall directly into the hands of the Saracen."

A voice very close to Sir Robert said: "Richard is right. If we go to the aid of the Hospitallers, we will expose the column to a flank attack." It was Sir Gaeton.

"My lord the King," Sir Robert heard his voice say, "is right in all but one thing. If we allow the Egyptians to take us from the rear, there will be no need for Saladin and his Turks to come down on our flank. And the Hospitallers cannot hold for long at this rate. A charge at full gallop would break the Egyptian line and give the Hospitallers breathing time. Are you with me?"

"Against the orders of the King?"

"The King cannot see everything! There are times when a man must use his own judgment! You said you were afraid of no man. Are you with me?"

After a moment's hesitation, Sir Gaeton couched his lance. "I'm with you, sir knight! Live or die, I follow! Strike and strike hard!"

"Forward then!" Sir Robert heard himself shouting. "Forward for St. George and for England!"

"St. George and England!" the Gascon echoed.

Two great war horses began to move ponderously forward toward the battle lines, gaining momentum as they went. Moving in unison, the two knights, their horses now at a fast trot, lowered their lances, picking their Saracen targets with care. Larger and larger loomed the Egyptian cavalrymen as the horses changed pace to a thundering gallop.

The Egyptians tried to dodge, as they saw, too late, the approach of the Christian knights.

Sir Robert felt the shock against himself and his horse as the steel tip of the long ash lance struck the Saracen horseman in the chest.

Out of the corner of his eye, he saw that Sir Gaeton, too, had scored.

The Saracen, impaled on Sir Robert's lance, shot from the saddle as he died. His lighter armor had hardly impeded the incoming spearpoint, and now his body dragged it down as he dropped toward the desert sand. Another Moslem cavalryman was charging in now, swinging his curved saber, taking advantage of Sir Robert's sagging lance.

There was nothing else to do but drop the lance and draw his heavy broadsword. His hand grasped it, and it came singing from its scabbard.

The Egyptian's curved sword clanged against Sir Robert's helm, setting his head ringing. In return, the knight's broadsword came about in a sweeping arc, and the Egyptian's horse rode on with the rider's headless body.

Behind him, Sir Robert heard further cries of "St. George and England!"

The Hospitallers, taking heart at the charge, were going in! Behind them came the Count of Champagne, the Earl of Leister, and the Bishop of Beauvais, who carried a great warhammer in order that he might not break Church Law by shedding blood.

Sir Robert's own sword rose and fell, cutting and hacking at the enemy. He himself felt a dreamlike detachment, as though he were watching the battle rather than participating in it.

But he could see that the Moslems were falling back before the Christian onslaught.

And then, quite suddenly, there seemed to be no foeman to swing at. Breathing heavily, Sir Robert sheathed his broadsword.

Beside him, Sir Gaeton did the same, saying: "It will be a few minutes before they can regroup, sir knight. We may have routed them completely."

"Aye. But King Richard will not approve of my breaking ranks and disobeying orders. I may win the battle and lose my head in the end."

"This is no time to worry about the future," said the Gascon. "Rest for a moment and relax, that you may be the stronger later. Here—have an *Old Kings*."

He had a pack of cigarettes in his gauntleted hand, which he proffered to Sir Robert. There were three cigarettes protruding from it, one slightly farther than the others. Sir Robert's hand reached out and took that one.

"Thanks. When the going gets rough, I really enjoy an *Old Kings*."

He put one end of the cigarette in his mouth and lit the other from the lighter in Sir Gaeton's hand.

"Yes, sir," said Sir Gaeton, after lighting his own cigarette, "*Old Kings* are the greatest. They give a man real, deep-down smoking pleasure."

"There's no doubt about it, *Old Kings* are a *man's* cigarette."
Sir Robert could feel the soothing smoke in his lungs as he
inhaled deeply. "That's great. When I want a cigarette, I don't want
just *any* cigarette."

"Nor I," agreed the Gascon. "*Old Kings* is the only real cigarette
when you're doing a real *man's* work."

"That's for sure." Sir Robert watched a smoke ring expand
in the air.

There was a sudden clash of arms off to their left. Sir Robert
dropped his cigarette to the ground. "The trouble is that doing a real
he-man's work doesn't always allow you to enjoy the fine, rich
tobaccos of *Old Kings* down to the very end."

"No, but you can always light another one later," said the
Gascon knight.

King Richard, on seeing his army moving suddenly toward the
harassed rear, had realized the danger and had charged through the
Hospitallers to get into the thick of the fray. Now the Turks were
charging down from the hills, hitting—not the flank as he had
expected, but the rear! Saladin had expected him to hold fast!

Sir Robert and Sir Gaeton spurred their chargers toward the
flapping banner of England.

The fierce warrior-king of England, his mighty sword in
hand, was cutting down Turks as though they were grain-stalks,
but still the Saracen horde pressed on. More and more of the
terrible Turks came boiling down out of the hills, their glittering
scimitars swinging.

Sir Robert lost all track of time. There was nothing to do but
keep his own great broadsword moving, swinging like some
gigantic metronome as he hacked down the Moslem foes.

And then, suddenly, he found himself surrounded by the
Saracens! He was isolated and alone, cut off from the rest of the
Christian forces! He glanced quickly around as he slashed another
Saracen from pate to breastbone. Where was Sir Gaeton? Where
were the others? Where was the red-and-gold banner of Richard?

He caught a glimpse of the fluttering banner far to the rear and
started to fall back.

And then he saw another knight nearby, a huge man who
swung his sparkling blade with power and force. On his steel helm
gleamed a golden coronet! Richard!

And the great king, in spite of his prowess, was outnumb-
ered heavily and would, within seconds, be cut down by the
Saracen horde!

Without hesitation, Sir Robert plunged his horse toward the
surrounded monarch, his great blade cutting a path before him.

He saw Richard go down, falling from the saddle of his charger,
but by that time his own sword was cutting into the screaming

Saracens and they had no time to attempt any further mischief to the King. They had their hands full with Sir Robert de Bouain.

He did not know how long he fought there, holding his charger motionless over the inert body of the fallen king, hewing down the screaming enemy, but presently he heard the familiar cry of "For St. George and for England" behind him. The Norman and English troops were charging in, bringing with them the banner of England!

And then Richard was on his feet, cleaving the air about him with his own broadsword. Its bright edge, besmeared with Saracen blood, was biting viciously into the foe.

The Turks began to fall back. Within seconds, the Christian knights were boiling around the embattled pair, forcing the Turks into retreat. And for the second time, Sir Robert found himself with no one to fight.

And then a voice was saying: "You have done well this day, sir knight. Richard Plantagenet will not forget."

Sir Robert turned in his saddle to face the smiling king.

"My lord king, be assured that I would never forget my loyalty to my sovereign and liege lord. My sword and my life are yours whenever you call."

King Richard's gauntleted hand grasped his own. "If it please God, I shall never ask your life. An earldom awaits you when we return to England, sir knight."

And then the king mounted his horse and was running full gallop after the retreating Saracens.

Robert took off his helmet.

He blinked for a second to adjust his eyes to the relative dimness of the studio. After the brightness of the desert that the televicarion helmet had projected into his eyes, the studio seemed strangely cavelike.

"How'd you like it, Bob?" asked one of the two producers of the show.

Robert Bowen nodded briskly and patted the televike helmet. "It was O.K.," he said. "Good show. A little talky at the beginning, and it needs a better fade-out, but the action scenes were fine. The sponsor ought to like it—for a while, at least."

"What do you mean, 'for a while'?"

Robert Bowen sighed. "If this thing goes on the air the way it is, he'll lose sales."

"Why? Commercial not good enough?"

"*Too* good! Man, I've smoked *Old Kings,* and believe me, the real thing never tasted as good as that cigarette did in the commercial!"

Psicopath

by Randall Garrett
writing as Darrel T. Langart

It was John Campbell's style to challenge writers by
stating opinion as dogmatic truth—the temptation to prove
him wrong led to some fine fiction. In Randall's work, two
sets of stories were produced with just this impetus. In one
case, Campbell may have been expecting the results he got.
In the other—the one which applies to Psicopath—the
stimulus was unintentional and the results a surprise.

"A good mystery story is impossible in a world where
magic works." (That's the gist of the idea, not a direct
quote.) Challenged by that statement, Randall began the
Lord Darcy series.

"A writer can't change his style completely enough to
fool the public, no matter what name is on the story." That's
what Randall heard from Campbell (again, only its meaning) when he had just been told that ANALOG was over-
stocked with Garrett stories, and Campbell wouldn't be
buying any more Garrett work for a while—no matter what
name was on the manuscript. "Darrel T. Langart" was born
in that moment.

Randall asked his agent to submit the first Langart
story as if the writer were an unknown. Weeks later,
Randall listened to John Campbell raving about his new
discovery and exhorting him to write as well as Langart.
Months passed before Campbell caught on, while he and
Randall were discussing their discovery that "Winston P.
Sanders" was an unintentional anagram for the name of the
writer for whom it was a pseudonym.

Psicopath's inclusion in TAKEOFF, TOO! is warranted

*for a number of other reasons, not the least of which is the
concept of hiding a secret government project by advertising it under its true name and purpose, and inviting
public subscription.*

The man in the pastel blue topcoat walked with steady
purpose, but without haste, through the chill, wind-swirled drizzle
that filled the air above the streets of Arlington, Virginia. His
matching blue cap-hood was pulled low over his forehead, and the
clear, infrared radiating face mask had been flipped down to
protect his chubby cheeks and round nose from the icy wind.

No one noticed him particularly. He was just another average
man who blended in with all the others who walked the streets that
day. No one recognized him; his face did not appear often in public
places, except in his own state, and, even so, it was a thoroughly
ordinary face. But, as he walked, Senator John Peter Gonzales was
keeping a mental, fine-webbed, four-dimensional net around him,
feeling for the slightest touch of recognition. He wanted no one to
connect him in any way with his intended destination.

It was not his first visit to the six-floor brick building that
stood on a street in a lower-middle-class district of Arlington.
Actually, government business took him there more often than
would have been safe for the average man-on-the-street. For
Senator Gonzales, the process of remaining incognito was so
elementary that it was almost subconscious.

Arriving at his destination, he paused on the sidewalk to light
a cigarette, shielding it against the wind and drizzle with cupped
hands while his mind made one last check on the surroundings.
Then he strode quickly up the five steps to the double doors which
were marked: *The Society For Mystical And Metaphysical
Research, Inc.*

Just as he stepped in, he flipped the face shield up and put on an
old-fashioned pair of thick-lensed, black-rimmed spectacles. Then,
his face assuming a bland smile that would have been completely
out of place on Senator Gonzales, he went from the foyer into
the front office.

"Good afternoon, Mrs. Jesser," he said, in a high, smooth,
slightly accented voice that was not his own. "I perceive by your
aura that you are feeling well. Your normal aura-color is tinged
with a positive golden hue."

Mrs. Jesser, a well-rounded matron in her early forties, rose to
the bait like a porpoise being hand-fed at a Florida zoo. "Dear
Swami Chandra! How perfectly *wonderful* to see you again! You're

34

looking very well yourself."

The Swami, whose Indian blood was of the Aztec rather than the Brahmin variety, nonetheless managed to radiate all the mystery of the East. "My well-being, dear Mrs. Jesser, is due to the fact that I have been communing for the past three months with my very good friend, the Fifth Dalai Lama. A most refreshingly wise person." Senator Gonzales was fond of the Society's crackpot receptionist, and he knew exactly what kind of hokum would please her most.

"Oh, I *do* hope you will find time to tell me *all* about it," she said effusively. "Mr. Balfour isn't in the city just now," she went on. "He's lecturing in New York on the history of flying saucer sightings. Do you realize that this is the fortieth anniversary of the first saucer sighting, back in 1944?"

"The first *photographed* sighting," the Swami corrected condescendingly. "Our friends have been watching and guiding us for far longer than that, and were sighted many times before they were photographed."

Mrs. Jesser nodded briskly. "Of course. You're right, as always, Swami."

"I am sorry to hear," the Swami continued smoothly, "that I will not be able to see Mr. Balfour. However, I came at the call of Mr. Brian Taggert, who is expecting me."

Mrs. Jesser glanced down at her appointment sheet. "He didn't mention an appointment to me. However—" She punched a button on the intercom. "Mr. Taggert? Swami Chandra is here to see you. He says he has an appointment."

Brian Taggert's deep voice came over the instrument. "The Swami, as usual, is very astute. I have been thinking about calling him. Send him right up."

"You may go up, Swami," said Mrs. Jesser, wide-eyed. She watched in awe as the Swami marched regally through the inner door and began to climb the stairs toward the sixth floor.

One way to hide an ex-officio agency of the United States Government was to label it truthfully—*The Society For Mystical And Metaphysical Research.* In spite of the fact that the label was literally true, it sounded so crackpot that no one but a crackpot would bother to look into it. As a consequence, better than ninety percent of the membership of the Society was composed of just such people. Only a few members of the "core" knew the organization's true function and purpose. And as long as such scatterbrains as Mrs. Jesser and Mr. Balfour were in there pitching, no one would ever penetrate to the actual core of the Society.

The senator had already pocketed the exaggerated glasses by the time he reached the sixth floor, and his face had lost its bland, overly-wise smile. He pushed open the door to Taggert's office.

"Have you got any ideas yet?" he asked quickly.

Brian Taggert, a heavily-muscled man with dark eyes and black, slightly wavy hair, sat on the edge of a couch in one corner of the room. His desk across the room was there for paperwork only, and Taggert had precious little of that to bother with.

He took a puff from his heavy-bowled briar. "We're going to have to send an agent in there. Someone who can be on the spot. Someone who can get the feel of the situation first hand."

"That'll be difficult. We can't just suddenly stick an unknown in there and have an excuse for his being there. Couldn't Donahue or Reeves—"

Taggert shook his head. "Impossible, John. Extrasensory perception can't replace sight, any more than sight can replace hearing. You know that."

"Certainly. But I thought we could get enough information that way to tell us who our saboteur is. No dice, eh?"

"No dice," said Taggert. "Look at the situation we've got there. The purpose of the Redford Research Team is to test the Meson Ultimate Decay Theory of Dr. Theodore Nordred. Now if we—"

Senator Gonzales, walking across the room toward Taggert, gestured with one hand. "I know! I know! Give me some credit for intelligence! But we do have one suspect, don't we? What about him?"

Taggert chuckled through a wreath of smoke. "Calm down, John. Or are you trying to give me your impression of Mrs. Jesser in a conversation with a saucerite?"

The senator laughed and sat down in a nearby chair. "All right. Sorry. But this whole thing is lousing up our entire space program. First off, we nearly lose Dr. Ch'ien, and with him gone, the interstellar drive project would've been shot. Now, if this sabotage keeps up, the Redford project will be shot, and that means we might have to stick to the old-fashioned rocket to get off-planet. Brian, we need antigravity, and, so far, Nordred's theory is our only clue."

"Agreed," said Taggert.

"Well, we're never going to get it if equipment keeps mysteriously burning itself out, breaking down, and just generally goofing up. This morning, the primary exciter on the new ultracosmotron went haywire, and the beam of sodium nuclei burned through part of the accelerator tube wall. It'll take a month to get it back in working order."

Taggert took his pipe out of his mouth and tapped the dottle into a nearby ash disposal unit. "And you want to pick up our pet spy?"

Senator Gonzales scowled. "Well, I'd certainly call him our prime suspect." But there was a certain lack of conviction in his manner.

Brian Taggert didn't flatly contradict the senator. "Maybe. But, you know, John, there's one thing that bothers me about these accidents."

36

"What's that?"

"The fact that we have not one shred of evidence that points to sabotage."

In a room on the fifth floor, directly below Brian Taggert's office, a young man was half sitting, half reclining in a thickly upholstered adjustable chair. He had dropped the back of the chair to a forty-five-degree angle and lifted up the footrest; now he was leaning back in lazy comfort, his ankles crossed, his right hand holding a slowly smoldering cigarette, his eyes contemplating the ceiling. Or, rather, they seemed to be contemplating something *beyond* the ceiling.

It was pure coincidence that the focus of his thoughts happened to be located in about the same volume of space that his eyes seemed to be focused on. If Brian Taggert and Senator Gonzales had been in the room below, his eyes would still be looking at the ceiling.

In repose, his face looked even younger than his twenty-eight years would have led one to expect. His close-cropped brown hair added to the impression of youth, and the well-tailored suit on his slim, muscular body added to the effect. At any top-flight university, he could have passed for a well-bred, sophisticated, intelligent student who had money enough to indulge himself and sense enough not to overdo it.

He was beginning to understand the pattern that was being woven in the room above—beginning to feel it in depth.

Senator Gonzales was mildly telepathic, inasmuch as he could pick up thoughts in the prevocal stage—the stage at which thought becomes definitely organized into words, phrases, and sentences. He could go a little deeper, into the selectivity stage, where the linking processes of logic took over from the nonlogical but rational processes of the preconscious—but only if he knew the person well. Where the senator excelled was in detecting emotional tone and manipulating emotional processes, both within himself and within others.

Brian Taggert was an analyzer, an originator, a motivator—and more. The young man found himself avoiding too deep a probe into the mind of Brian Taggert; he knew that he had not yet achieved the maturity to understand the multilayered depths of a mind like that. Eventually, perhaps...

Not that Senator Gonzales was a child, nor that he was emotionally or intellectually shallow. It was merely that he was not of Taggert's caliber.

The young man absently took another drag from his cigarette. Taggert had explained the basic problem to him, but he was getting a wider picture from the additional information that Senator Gonzales had brought.

Dr. Theodore Nordred, a mathematical physicist and one of the top-flight, high-powered, original minds in the field, had shown that Einstein's final equations only held in a universe composed entirely of normal matter. Since the great Einstein had died before the Principle of Parity had been overthrown in the mid-fifties, he had been unable to incorporate the information into his Unified Field Theory. Nordred had been able to show, mathematically, that Einstein's equations were valid only for a completely "dexter," or right-handed universe, or for a completely "sinister," or left-handed universe.

Although the universe in which Man lived was predominantly dexter—arbitrarily so designated—it was not completely so. It had a "sinister" component amounting to approximately one one-hundred-thousandth of one percent. On the average, one atom out of every ten million in the universe was an atom of antimatter. The distribution was unequal, of course; antimatter could not exist in contact with ordinary matter. Most of it was distributed throughout interstellar space in the form of individual atoms, freely floating in space, a long way from any large mass of normal matter.

But that minute fraction of a percent was enough to show that the known universe was not totally Einsteinian. In a purely Einsteinian universe, antigravity was impossible, but if the equations of Dr. Theodore Nordred were actually a closer approximation to true reality than those of Einstein, then antigravity *might* be a practical reality.

And that was the problem the Redford Research Team was working on. It was a parallel project to the interstellar drive problem, being carried on elsewhere.

The "pet spy," as Taggert had called him, was Dr. Konrad Bern, a middle-aged Negro from Tanganyika, who was convinced that only under Communism could the colored races of the world achieve the technological organization and living standard of the white man. He had been trained as a "sleeper"; not even the exhaustive investigations of the FBI had turned up any relationship between Bern and the Soviets. It had taken the telepathic probing of the S.M.M.R. agents to uncover his real purposes. Known, he constituted no danger.

There was no denying that he was a highly competent, if not brilliant, physicist. And, since it was quite impossible for him to get any information on the Redford Project into the hands of the opposition—it was no longer fashionable to call Communists "the enemy"—there was no reason why he shouldn't be allowed to contribute to the American efforts to bridge space.

Three times in the five months since Bern had joined the project, agents of the Soviet government had made attempts to contact the physicist. Three times the FBI, warned by S.M.M.R.

agents had quietly blocked the contact. Konrad Bern had been effectively isolated.

But, at the project site itself, equipment failure had become increasingly more frequent, all out of proportion to the normal accident rate in any well-regulated laboratory. The work of the project had practically come to a standstill; the ultra-secret progress reports to the President were beginning to show less and less progress in the basic research, and more and more progress in repairing damaged equipment. Apparently, though, increasing efficiency in repair work was self-neutralizing; repairing an instrument in half the time merely meant that it could break down twice as often.

It had to be sabotage. And yet, not even the S.M.M.R. agents could find any trace of intentional damage nor any thought patterns that would indicate deliberate damage.

And Senator John Peter Gonzales quite evidently did *not* want to face the implications of *that* particular fact.

"We're going to have to send an agent in," Taggert repeated.

(*That's my cue,* thought the young man on the fifth floor as he crushed out his cigarette and got up from the chair.)

"I don't know how we're going to manage it," said the senator. "What excuse do we have for putting a new man on the Redford team?"

Brian Taggert grinned. "What they need is an expert repair technician—a man who knows how to build and repair complex research instruments. He doesn't have to know anything about the purpose of the team itself, all he has to do is keep the equipment in good shape."

Senator Gonzales let a slow smile spread over his face. "You've been gulling me, you snake. All right; I deserved it. Tell him to come in."

As the door opened, Taggert said: "Senator Gonzales, may I present Mr. David MacHeath? He's our man, I think."

David MacHeath watched a blue line wriggle its way erratically across the face of an oscilloscope. "The wave form is way off," he said flatly, "and the frequency is slithering all over the place."

He squinted at the line for a moment, then spoke to the man standing nearby. "Signal Harry to back her off two degrees, then run her up slowly, ten minutes at a time."

The other man flicked the key on the side of the small carbide-Welsbach lamp. The shutters blinked, sending pulses of light down the length of the ten-foot diameter glass-walled tube in which the men were working. Far down the tube, MacHeath could see the answering flicker from Harry, a mile and a half away in the darkness.

MacHeath watched the screen again. After a few seconds, he

said: "O.K.! Hold it!"

Again the lamp flashed.

"Well, it isn't perfect," MacHeath said, "but it's all we can do from here. We'll have to evacuate the tube to get her in perfect balance. Tell Harry to knock off for the day."

While the welcome message was being flashed, MacHeath shut off the testing instruments and disconnected them. It was possible to compensate a little for the testing equipment, but a telephone, or even an electric flashlight, would simply add to the burden.

Bill Griffin shoved down the key on the lamp he was holding and locked it into place. The shutters remained open, and the lamp shed a beam of white light along the shining walls of the cylindrical tube. "How much longer do you figure it'll take, Dave?" he asked.

"Another shift, at least," said MacHeath, picking up the compact, shielded instrument case. "You want to carry that mat?"

Griffin picked up the thick sponge-rubber mat that the instrument case had been sitting on, and the two men started off down the tube, walking silently on sponge-rubber-soled shoes which would not scratch the glass underfoot.

"Any indication yet as to who our saboteur is?" Griffin asked.

"I'm not sure," MacHeath admitted. "I've picked up a couple of leads, but I don't know if they mean anything or not."

"I wonder if there *is* a saboteur," Griffin said musingly. "Maybe it's just a run of bad luck. It could happen, you know. A statistical run of—"

"You don't believe that, any more than I do," MacHeath said.

"No. But I find it even harder to believe that a materialistic philosophy like Communism could evolve any workable psionic discipline."

"So do I," agreed MacHeath.

"But it can't be physical sabotage," Griffin argued. "There's not a trace of it—anywhere. It *has* to be psionic."

"Right," said MacHeath, grinning as he saw what was coming next.

"But we've already eliminated that. So?" Griffin nodded firmly as if in full agreement with himself. "So we follow the dictum of the Master: 'Eliminate the impossible; whatever is left, no matter how improbable, is the truth.' And, since there is absolutely nothing left, there is no truth. At the bottom, the whole thing is merely a matter of mental delusion."

"Sherlock Holmes would be proud of you, Bill," MacHeath said. "And so am I."

Griffin looked at MacHeath oddly. "I wish I was a halfway decent telepath. I'd like to know what's going on in your preconscious."

"You'd have to dig deeper than that, I'm afraid," MacHeath said ruefully. "As soon as my subconscious has solved the problem, I'll let you know."

"I've changed my mind," said Griffin cheerfully. "I don't envy your telepathy. I don't envy a guy who has to TP his own subconscious to find out what he's thinking."

MacHeath chuckled softly as he turned the bolt that opened the door into the "gun" end of the stripped-nuclei accelerator. The seals broke with a soft hiss. Evidently, the barometric pressure outside the two-mile-long underground tube had changed slightly during the time they had been down there.

"It'll be a week before we can test it," MacHeath said in a tired voice. "Even after we get it partly in balance. It'll take that long to evacuate the tube and sweep it clean."

It was the first sentence he had spoken in the past hour or so, and it was purely for the edification of the man who was standing on the other side of the air lock, although neither Griffin nor MacHeath had actually seen him as yet.

Griffin was not a telepath in the sense that the S.M.M.R. used the word, but to a non-psionicist, he would have appeared to be one. Membership in the "core" group of the *Society For Mystical And Metaphysical Research* required, above all, *understanding*. And, with that understanding, a conversation between two members need consist only of an occasional gesture and a key word now and then.

The word "understanding" needs emphasis. Without understanding of another human mind, no human mind can be completely effective. Without that understanding, no human being can be completely free.

And yet, the English word "understanding" is only an approximation to the actual process that must take place. *Total* understanding, in one sense, would require that a person actually *become* another person—that he be able to feel, completely and absolutely, every emotion, every thought, every bodily sensation, every twinge of memory, every judgment, every decision, and every sense of personal identity that is felt by the other person, no more and no less.

Such totality is, obviously, neither attainable nor desirable. The result would be a merger of identities, a total unification. And, as a consequence, a complete loss of one of the human beings involved.

Optimum "understanding" requires that a judgment be made, and that, in turn, requires *two* minds—not a fusion of identity. There must be one to judge and another to be judged, and each mind plays both roles.

Love thy neighbor as thyself. But the original Greek word would translate better as "respect and understand" than as the modern English "love." The founders of our modern religions were not fools; they simply did not have the tools at hand to formulate their knowledge properly. As understanding increases, a critical point is reached, which causes a qualitative change in the human mind.

First, self-understanding must come. The human mind operates through similarities, and the thing most similar to any human mind is itself. The next most similar thing is another human mind.

From that point on, all objects, processes, and patterns in the universe can be graded according to their similarity to each other, and, ultimately, to their similarity to the human mind.

Two given entities may seem utterly dissimilar, but they can always be linked by a *tertium quid*—a "third thing" which is similar to both. This third thing, be it a material object or a product of the human imagination, is called a symbol. Symbols are the bridges by which the mind can reach and manipulate the universe in which it exists. With the proper symbols and the understanding to use them, the human mind is limited only by its own inherent structural restrictions.

One of the most active research projects of the S.M.M.R. was the construction of a more powerful symbology. Psionics had made tremendous strides in the previous four decades, but it was still in the alchemy stage. So far, symbols for various processes could only be worked out by cut-and-try, rule-of-thumb methods, using symbols already established, including languages and mathematics. None were completely satisfactory, but they worked fairly well within their narrow limits.

As far as communication was concerned, the hashed-together symbology used by the S.M.M.R. was better than any conceivable code. The understanding required to "break" the "code" was well beyond the critical point. Anyone who could break it was, *ipso facto,* a member of the S.M.M.R.

Most people didn't even realize that a conversation was taking place between two members, especially if a "cover conversation" was used at the same time.

MacHeath's verbal discussion of the testing of the nuclei accelerator was just such a cover. Even before he had cracked the air lock, he had known that Dr. Theodore Nordred was standing on the other side of the thick wall.

MacHeath pushed the heavy door open on its smooth hinges. "Oh, hello, Dr. Nordred. How's everything?"

The heavy-set mathematician smiled pleasantly as MacHeath and Griffin came into the gun chamber. "I just thought I'd come down and see how you were getting along," he said. His voice was a low tenor, with just a touch of Midwestern twang. "Sometimes the creative mind gets bogged down in nth-order abstractions that have no discernible connection with anything at all." He chuckled.

"When that happens, I drop everything and go out to find something mundane to worry about."

Nordred was only an inch shorter than the slim MacHeath, and he weighed in at close to two hundred pounds. At twenty-five, he had had the build of a lightweight wrestler; thirty more years had added poundage—a roll beneath the chin and a bulge at the belly—but he still looked capable of going a round or two without tiring. His shock of heavy hair was a mixture of mouse-brown and gray, and it seemed to have a tendency to stand up on end, which added another inch and a half to his height. His round face had a tendency to smile when he was talking or working with his hands; when he was deep in thought, his face usually relaxed into thoughtful blankness. He frowned rarely, and only for seconds at a time.

"It seems to me you have enough to worry about, doctor," MacHeath said banteringly, "without looking for it." He put down his instrument case and took out a cigarette while Griffin closed the door to the acceleration tube.

"Oh, I don't have to look far," Nordred said. "How long do you think it will be before we can resume our work with the Monster?"

"Ten days to two weeks," MacHeath said promptly.

"I see." One of his rare frowns crossed his face. "I wish I knew why the exciter arced across. It shouldn't have."

"Don't you have any idea?" MacHeath asked innocently. At the same time, he opened his mind wide to net in every wisp and filament of Nordred's thoughts that he could reach.

"None at all," admitted the mathematician. "Weakness in the insulation, I suppose, though it tested solidly enough." And his mind, as far back as his preconscious and the upper fringes of his subconscious, agreed with his words. MacHeath could go no deeper as yet; he didn't know Nordred well enough yet.

There were suspicions in Nordred's mind that the insulation weakness must have been caused by deliberate sabotage, but he had no one to pin his suspicions on. Neither he nor anyone else connected with the Redford project was aware of the true status of Dr. Konrad Bern.

"Well, let's hope it doesn't happen again," MacHeath said. "Balancing these babies so that they work properly is hard enough for a deuteron accelerator, but the Monster here is ten times as touchy."

Nordred nodded absently. "I know. But our work can't be done with anything less." Nordred actually knew less about the engineering details of the big accelerator than anyone else on the project; he was primarily a philosopher-mathematician, and only secondarily a physicist. He was theoretically in charge of the project, but the actual experimentation was done by the other four men: Drs. Roger Kent, Paul Luvochek, Solomon Bessermann, and Konrad Bern. These four and their assistants set up and ran off the experiments designed to test Dr. Nordred's theories.

MacHeath picked up his instrument case again, and the three men went out of the gun chamber, into the outer room, and then started up the spiral stairway that led to the surface, talking as they went. But the apparent conversation had little to do with the instructions that MacHeath was giving Griffin as they climbed.

So when MacHeath stopped suddenly and patted at his coverall pockets, Griffin was ready for the words that came next.

"Damn!" MacHeath said. "I've left my notebook. Will you go down and get it for me, Bill?"

Dr. Nordred had neither understood nor noticed the actual instructions:

"Bill, as soon as I give you an excuse, get back down there and check that gun chamber. Give it a thorough going-over. I don't really think you'll find a thing, but I don't want to take any chances at this stage of the game."

"Right," said Griffin, starting back down the stairway.

MacHeath and Dr. Nordred went on climbing.

David MacHeath sat at a table in the project's cafeteria, absently stirring his coffee, and trying to look professionally modest while Dr. Luvochek and Dr. Bessermann alternately praised him for his work.

Luvochek, a tubby little butterball of a man, whose cherubic face would have made him look almost childlike, if it weren't for the blue of his jaw, said: "You and those two men of yours have really done a marvelous job in the past four days, Mr. MacHeath—really marvelous."

"I'll say," Bessermann chimed in. "I was getting pretty tired of looking at burned-out equipment and spending three-quarters of my time putting in replacement parts and wielding a soldering gun." Bessermann was leaner than Luvochek, but, like his brother scientist, he was balding on top. Both men were in their middle thirties.

"I don't understand this jinx, myself," Luvochek said. "At first, it was just little things, but the accidents got worse and worse. And then, when the Monster blew—" He stopped and shook his head slowly. "I'd suspect sabotage, except that there was never any sign of tampering with the equipment I saw."

"What do you think of the sabotage idea?" Bessermann asked MacHeath.

MacHeath shrugged. "Haven't seen any signs of it."

"Run of bad luck," said Luvochek. "That's all."

As they talked MacHeath absorbed the patterns of thought that wove in and out in the two men's minds. Both men were more open than Dr. Nordred; they were easier for MacHeath to understand. Nowhere was there any thought of guilt—at least, as far as sabotage was concerned.

MacHeath drank his coffee slowly and thoughtfully, keeping

up his part of the three-way conversation while he concentrated on his own problem.

One thing was certain: Nowhere in the minds of any of the personnel of the Redford Project was there any conscious knowledge of sabotage. Not even in the mind of Konrad Bern.

Dr. Roger Kent, a tall, lantern-jawed, sad-eyed man in his forties, had been hard to get through to at first, but as soon as MacHeath discovered that the hard block Kent had built up around himself was caused by grief over a wife who had been dead five years, he became as easy to read as a billboard. Kent had submerged his grief in work; the eternal drive of the true scientist to drag the truth out of Mother Nature. He was constitutionally incapable of sabotaging the very instruments that had been built to dig in after that truth.

Dr. Konrad Bern, on the other hand, was difficult to read below the preconscious stage. Science, to him, was a form of power, to be used for "idealistic" purposes. He was perfectly capable of sabotaging the weapons of an enemy if it became necessary, whether that meant ruining a physical instrument or carefully falsifying the results of an experiment. Outwardly, he was a pleasant enough chap, but his mind revealed a rigidly held pattern of hatreds, fears, and twisted idealism. He held them tightly against the onslaughts of a hostile world.

And that meant the he couldn't possibly have any control over whatever psionic powers he may have possessed.

Unless—

Unless he was so expert and so well-trained that he was better than anything the S.M.M.R. had ever known.

MacHeath didn't even like to think about that. It would mean that all the theory of psionics that had been built up so painstakingly over the past years would have to be junked *in toto*.

Something was gnawing in the depths of his mind. In the perfectly rational but utterly nonlogical part of his subconscious where hunches are built, something was trying to form.

MacHeath didn't try to probe for it. As soon as he had enough information for the hunch to be fully formed, it would be ready to use. Until then, it would be worthless, and probing for it might interrupt the formation.

He was just finishing his coffee as Bill Griffin came in the door and headed toward the table where MacHeath, Luvochek, and Bessermann were sitting.

MacHeath stood up and said: "Excuse me. I'll have to be getting some work done if you guys are ever going to get your own work done."

"Sure."

"Go ahead."

"Thanks for the coffee," MacHeath added as he moved away.

"Anytime," said Bessermann, grinning. "You guys just keep up the good work. When you fix 'em, they stay fixed. We haven't had a burnout since you came."

"Maybe you broke our statistical jinx," said Luvochek, with a chubby smile.

"Maybe," said MacHeath. "I hope so."

For some reason, the gnawing in his hunch factory became more persistent.

As he and Griffin walked toward the door, Griffin reported rapidly. "I checked everything in the gun chamber. No sign of any tampering. Everything's just as we left it. The dust film hasn't been disturbed."

"It figures," said MacHeath.

Outside, in the corridor, they met Dr. Konrad Bern hurrying toward the cafeteria. He stopped as he saw them.

"Oh, hello, Mr. MacHeath, Mr. Griffin," he said. His white-toothed smile was friendly, but both of the S.M.M.R. agents could detect the hostility that was hard and brittle beneath the surface. "I wanted to thank you for the wonderful job you've been doing."

"Why, thank you, doctor," said MacHeath honestly. "We aim to satisfy."

Bern chuckled. "You're doing well so far. Odd streak of luck we've had, isn't it? Poor Dr. Nordred has been under a terrible strain; his whole life work is tied up in this project." He made a vague gesture with one hand. "Would you care for some coffee?"

"Just had some, thanks," said MacHeath, "but we'll take a rain check."

"Fine. Anytime." And he went on into the cafeteria.

"Wow!" said Griffin as he walked on down the corridor with MacHeath. "That man is scared silly! But what an actor! You'd never know he was eating his guts out."

"Sure he's scared," MacHeath said. "With all this sabotage talk going around, he's afraid there'll be an exhaustive investigation, and he can't take that right now."

Griffin frowned. "I guess I missed that. What did you pick up?"

"He's supposed to meet a Soviet agent tonight, and he's afraid he'll be caught. He doesn't know what happened to the first three, and he won't know what will happen to Number Four tonight.

"We'll keep him around as long as he's useful. He's not a Bohr or a Pauli or a Fermi, but he—"

MacHeath stopped himself suddenly and came to a dead halt.

"My God," he said softly, "that's *it.*"

His hunch had hatched.

After a moment, he said: "Harry is getting back from the target end of the tube now, Bill. He can't pick me up, so beetle it down to the tool room, get him, and get up to the workshop fast. If I'm not there, wait; I have a little prying to do."

"Can do," said Griffin. He went toward the elevator at an easy lope.

David MacHeath went in the opposite direction.

When MacHeath returned to the workshop which he had been assigned, Bill Griffin and Harry Benbow were waiting for him. Beside the big-muscled Griffin, Harry Benbow looked even thinner than he was. He was a good six-two, which made him a head taller than Griffin, but, unlike many tall, lean men, Benbow had no tendency to slouch; he stood tall and straight, reminding MacHeath of a poplar tree towering proudly over the countryside. Benbow was one of those rare American Negroes whose skin was actually as close to being "black" as human pigmentation will allow. His eyes gave an odd contrast-similarity effect when compared with Griffin's china-blue eyes.

If the average man had wanted to pick two human beings who were "opposites," he could hardly have made a better choice than Benbow and the short, thickly-built, blond-haired, pink-skinned Bill Griffin. But the average man would be so struck by the differences that he would never notice that the similarities were vastly more important.

"You look as if you'd just been kissed by Miss America," Harry said as MacHeath came through the door.

"Better than that," MacHeath said. "We've got work to do."

"What's the pitch?" Griffin wanted to know.

"Well, in the first place, I'm afraid Dr. Konrad Bern is no longer of any use to the Redford Project. We're going to have to arrest him as an unregistered agent of the Soviet Government."

"It's just as well," said Harry Benbow gently. "His research hasn't done us any good and it hasn't done the Soviets any good. The poor guy's been on edge ever since he got here. All the pale hide around this place stirs up every nerve in him."

"What got you onto this?" Griffin asked MacHeath.

"A hunch first," MacHeath said. "Then I got data to back it up. But, first...Harry, how'd you know about Bern's reactions? He keeps those prejudices of his down pretty deep; I didn't think you could go that far."

"I didn't have to. He spent half an hour talking to me this morning. He was so happy to see a fellow human being—according to his definition of a human being—that he was as easy to read as if you were doing the reading."

MacHeath nodded. "I hate to throw him to the wolves, but he's got to go."

"What was the snooping you said you had to do?" Griffin asked.

"Dates. Times. Briefly, I found that the run of accidents has been building up to a peak. At first, it was just small meters that went wrong. Then bigger, more complex stuff. And, finally, the Monster went. See the pattern?"

The other men nodded.

"You're the therapist," Griffin said. "What do you suggest?"

"Shock treatment," said David MacHeath.

Just how Dr. Konrad Bern got wind of the fact that a squad of FBI men had come to the project to arrest him that evening is something that MacHeath didn't know until later. He was busy at the time, ignoring anything but what he was interested in. It always fascinated him to watch the mind of a psychokinetic expert at work. He couldn't do the trick himself, and he was always amazed at the ability of anyone who could.

It was like watching a pianist play a particularly difficult concerto. A person can watch a pianist, see every move he is making, and why he is making it. But being able to see what is going on doesn't mean that one can duplicate the action. MacHeath was in the same position. Telepathically, he could observe the play of emotions through a psychokinetic's mind—the combinations of avid desire and utter loathing which, playing one against another, could move a brick, a book, or a Buick if the mind was powerful enough. But he couldn't do it himself, no matter how carefully he tried to follow the raging emotions that acted as two opposing jaws of a pair of tongs to lift and move the object.

And so engrossed was he with the process that he did not notice that Konrad Bern had eluded the FBI. He was unaware of what had happened until one of the Federal agents rapped loudly on the workshop door.

Almost instantly, MacHeath picked up the information from the agent's mind. He glanced at Griffin and Benbow. "You two can handle it. Be careful you don't overdo it."

Then he went to the door and opened it a trifle. "Yes?"

The man outside showed a gold badge. "Morgan, FBI. You David MacHeath?"

"Yes." MacHeath stepped outside and showed the FBI man his identification.

"We were told to cooperate with you in this Konrad Bern case. He's managed to slip away from us somehow, but we know he's still in the area. He can't get past the gate."

MacHeath let his mind expand until it meshed with that of Dr. Konrad Bern.

"There is a way out," MacHeath snapped. "The acceleration tube."

"What?"

"Come on!" He started sprinting toward the elevators. He explained to the FBI agent as they went.

"The acceleration tube of the ultracosmotron runs due north of here for two miles underground. The guard at the other end won't be expecting anyone to be coming from the inside of the target building. If Bern plays his cards right, he can get away."

"Can't we phone the target building?" the FBI man asked.

"No. We shut down all the electrical equipment and took down some of the wires so we could balance the acceleration fields."

"Well, if he's on foot, we could send a car out there. We'd get there before he does. Uh...wouldn't we?"

"Maybe. But he'll kill himself if he sees he's trapped." That wasn't quite true. Bern was ready to fight to the death, and he had a heavy pistol to back him up. MacHeath didn't want to see anyone killed, and he didn't want stray bullets flying around the inside of that tube or in the target room.

MacHeath and the FBI agent piled out of the elevator at the bottom of the shaft. Dr. Roger Kent was standing at the head of the stairs that spiraled down to the gun chamber. Dr. Kent knew that Bern had gone down the stairway, but he didn't know why.

"He's our saboteur," MacHeath said quickly. "I'm going after him. As soon as I close the door and seal it, you turn on the pumps. Lower the air pressure in the tube to a pound per square inch below atmosphere. That'll put a force of about a ton and a quarter against the doors, and he won't be able to open them."

Dr. Kent still didn't grasp the fact that Bern was a spy.

"Explain to him, Morgan," MacHeath told the Federal agent. He went on down the spiral staircase, knowing that Kent would understand and act in plenty of time.

The door to the tube was standing open. MacHeath slipped on a pair of the sponge-soled shoes, noticing angrily that Bern hadn't bothered to do so. He went into the tube and closed the door behind him. Then he started down the blackness of the tube at a fast trot. Ahead of him, in the utter darkness, he could hear the click of heels as the leather-shod Bern moved toward the target end of the long tube.

Neither of them had lights. They were unnecessary, for one thing, since there was only one direction to go and there were no obstacles in the path. Bern would probably have carried a flashlight if he'd been able to get his hands on one quickly, but he hadn't, so he went in darkness. MacHeath didn't want a light; in the darkness, he had the advantage of knowing where his opponent was.

Every so often, Bern would stop, listening for sounds of pursuit, since his own footsteps, echoing down the glass-lined cylinder, drowned out any noise from behind. But MacHeath, running silently on the toes of his thick-soled shoes, kept in motion, gaining on the fleeing spy.

A two-mile run is a good stretch of exercise for anyone, but MacHeath didn't dare slow down. As it was, Konrad Bern was already tugging frantically at the door that led to the target room by the time MacHeath reached him. But the faint sighing of the pumps had already told MacHeath that the air pressure had been dropped. Bern couldn't possibly get the door open.

MacHeath's lungs wanted to be filled with air; his chest wanted to heave; he wanted to pant, taking in great gulps of life-giving oxygen. But he didn't dare. He didn't want Bern to know he was there, so he strained to keep his breath silent.

He stepped up behind the physicist in the pitch blackness, and judging carefully, brought his fist down on the nape of the man's neck in a hard rabbit punch.

Konrad Bern dropped unconscious to the floor of the tube.

Then MacHeath let his chest pump air into his lungs in long, harsh gasps. Shakily, he lowered himself to the floor beside Bern and squatted on his haunches, waiting for the hiss of the bleeder valve that would tell him that the air pressure had been raised to allow someone to enter the air lock.

It was Morgan, the FBI man, who finally cracked the door. Griffin and Dr. Kent were with him.

"You all right?" asked Morgan.

"I'm fine," MacHeath said, "but Bern is going to have a sore neck for a while. I didn't hit him hard enough to break it, but he'll get plenty of sleep before he wakes up."

More FBI men came in, and they dragged out the unprotesting Bern.

Dr. Kent said: "Well, I'm glad that's over. I'll have to get back and see what Dr. Nordred is raving about."

"Raving?" asked MacHeath innocently.

"Yes. While I was in the pump room, reducing the pressure, he called me on the interphone. Said he'd been looking all over for me. He and Luvochek and Besserman are up in the lab." He frowned. "They claim that one of the radiolead samples was floating in the air in the lab. It's settled down now, I gather, but it only weighs a fraction of what it should, though it's gaining all the time. And that's ridiculous. It's not at all what Dr. Nordred's theory predicted." Then he clamped his lips together, thinking perhaps he had talked too much.

"Interesting," said MacHeath blandly. "Very interesting."

Senator Gonzales sat in Brian Taggert's sixth-floor office in the S.M.M.R. building and looked puzzled. "All right, I grant you that Bern couldn't have been the saboteur. Then why arrest him?"

Dave MacHeath took a drag from his cigarette before he answered. "We had to have a patsy—someone to put the blame on. No one really believed that it was just bad luck, but they'll all accept the idea that Bern was a saboteur."

"We would have had to arrest him eventually, anyway," said Brian Taggert.

"Give me a quick run-down," Gonzales said. "I've got to explain this to the President."

"Did you ever hear of the Pauli Effect?" MacHeath asked.

"Something about the number of electrons that—"

"No," MacHeath said quickly. "That's the Pauli *principle,* better known as the Exclusion Principle. The Pauli *Effect* is a different thing entirely, a psionic effect.

"It used to be said that a theoretical physicist was judged by his inability to handle research apparatus; the clumsier he was in research, the better he was with theory. But Wolfgang Pauli was a lot more than clumsy. Apparatus could break, topple over, go to pieces, or burn up if Pauli just walked into the room.

"Up to the time he died, in 1958, his colleagues kidded him about it, without really believing there was anything behind it. But it is recorded that the explosion of some vacuum equipment in a laboratory at the University of Göttingen was the direct result of the Pauli Effect. It was definitely established that the explosion occurred at the precise moment that a train on which Pauli was traveling stopped for a short time at the Göttingen railway station."

The senator said: "The poltergeist phenomenon."

"Not exactly," MacHeath said, "although there is a similarity. The poltergeist phenomenon is usually spectacular and is nearly always associated with teen-age neurotics. Then there's the pyrotic; fires always start in his vicinity."

"But there's always a reason for psionic phenomena to react violently under subconscious control," Senator Gonzales pointed out. "There's always a psychological quirk."

"Sure. And I almost fell into the same trap, myself.

"I was thinking that if Bern were the saboteur, all our theories about psionics would have to be thrown out—we'd have to start from a different set of precepts. *And I didn't even want to think about such an idea!*"

"Nobody likes their pet theories overthrown," Gonzales observed.

"Of course not. But here's the point: The only way that a scientific theory can be proved wrong is to uncover a phenomenon which doesn't fit in with the theory. A theoretical physicist is a mathematician; he makes logical deductions and logical predictions by juggling symbols around in accordance with some logical system. But the axioms, the assumptions upon which those systems are built, are nonlogical. You can't prove an axiom; it comes right out of the mind.

"So imagine that you're a theoretical physicist. A really original-type thinker. You come up with a mathematical system that explains all known phenomena at that time, and predicts others that are, as yet, unknown. You check your math over and over again; there's no error in your logic, since it all follows, step by step."

"O.K.; go on," Gonzales said interestedly.

"Very well, then; you've built yourself a logical universe, based on *your* axioms, and the structure seems to have a one-to-one correspondence with the actual universe. Not only that, but if the theory is accepted, you've built your reputation on it—your life.

"Now, what happens if your axioms—not the logic *about* the axioms, but the axioms themselves—are proven to be wrong?"

Brian Taggert took his pipe out of his mouth. "Why, you give up the erroneous set of axioms and build a new set that will explain the new phenomenon. Isn't that what a scientist is supposed to do?" His manner was that of wide-eyed innocence laid on with a large trowel.

"Oh, *sure* it is," said the senator. "A man builds his whole life, his whole universe, on a set of principles, and he scraps them at the drop of a hat. *Sure* he does."

"He claims he will," MacHeath said. "Any scientist worth the paper his diploma is printed on is firmly convinced that he will change his axioms as soon as they're proven false. Of course, ninety-nine per cent of 'em *can't* and *won't* and *don't*. They refuse to look at anything that suggests changing axioms.

"Some scientists eagerly accept the axioms that they were taught in school and hang on to them all their lives, fighting tooth and nail. Oh, they'll accept new ideas, all right—provided that they fit in with the structures based on the old axioms.

"Then there are the young iconoclasts who don't like the axioms as they stand, so they make up some new ones of their own—men like Newton, Einstein, Planck, and so on. Then, once the new axioms have been forced down the throats of their colleagues, the innovators become the Old Order; the iconoclasts become the ones who put the fences around the new images to safeguard them. And they're even more firmly wedded to their axioms than anyone else. This is *their* universe!

"Of course, these men proclaim to all the world that they are perfectly willing to change their axioms. And the better a scientist he is, the more he believes, in his heart-of-hearts, that he really would change. He really thinks, consciously, that he wants others to test his theories.

"But notice: A theory is only good if it explains all known phenomena in its field. If it does, then the only thing that can topple it is a *new* fact. The only thing that can threaten the complex structure formulated by a really creative, painstaking, mathematical physicist is *experiment!*"

Senator Gonzales' attentive silence was eloquent.

"Experiment!" MacHeath repeated. "That can wreck a theory quicker and more completely than all the learned arguments of a dozen men. And every theoretician is aware of that fact. Consciously, he gladly accepts the inevitable; but his subconscious mind will fight to keep those axioms.

"*Even if it has to smash every experimental device around!*

"After all, if nobody can experiment on your theory, it can't be proved wrong, can it?

"In Nordred's case, as in Pauli's, this subconscious defense actually made itself felt in the form of broken equipment. Dr. Theodore Nordred was totally unconscious of the fact that he detested and feared the idea of anyone experimenting to prove or disprove his theory. He had no idea that he, himself, was re-channeling the energy in those machines to make them burn out."

Brian Taggert looked at MacHeath pointedly. "Do you think the shock treatment you gave him will cause any repercussions?"

"No. Griffin and Benbow held that block of radiolead floating in the air only while Dr. Nordred was alone in the lab. He pushed at it, felt of it, and moved it around for more than ten minutes before he'd admit the reality of what he saw. Then he called Luvochek and Bessermann in to look at it.

"Griffin and Benbow let the sample settle to the desk, so that by the time the other two scientists got to the lab, the lead didn't have an apparent negative weight, but was still much lighter than it should be.

"All the while that Bessermann and Luvochek were trying to weigh the lead block, to get an accurate measurement, Griffin and Benbow, three rooms away, kept increasing the weight slowly toward normal. And so far no one has invented a device which will give an instantaneous check on the weight of an object. A balance can't check the weight of a sample unless that weight is constant; there's too much time lag involved.

"So, what evidence do they have? Scientifically speaking, none. They have no measurements, and the experiment can't be repeated. And only Nordred actually saw the sample *floating*. Luvochek and Bessermann will eventually think up a 'natural' explanation for the apparent steady gain in weight. Only Nordred will remain convinced that what he saw actually happened.

"I don't see how there could be any serious repercussions in the field of physics." But he looked at Taggert for confirmation.

Taggert gave it to him with an approving look.

"It's a funny thing," said Gonzales musingly. "Some time back, we were in a situation where we had to go to the extreme of physical violence to keep from demonstrating to a scientist that psionic powers could be controlled, just to keep from ruining the physicist's work.

"Now, we turn right around and demonstrate the 'impossible' to another physicist in order to pull his hard-earned axioms out from under him." He smiled wryly. "There ain't no justice in the world."

"No," agreed MacHeath, "but the trick worked. He won't have any subconscious desire to smash equipment just to protect a theory that has already been smashed. On the contrary, he'll let them go through in order to find new data to build another theory on."

"He'll never again be the man he was," said Taggert regretfully. "He's lost the force of his convictions. He won't be capable of taking a no-nonsense, dogmatic, black-and-white stand. But it was necessary." He made an odd gesture with one hand. "What else can you do with a man who's a psionic psychopath?"

A Memory of John W. Campbell

I discovered this short piece as part of a speech Randall delivered to a group in what's known as the "Bay Area" in California. The group is called "The Elves', Gnomes', and Little Men's Science Fiction, Chowder, and Marching Society." Randall was their guest on many occasions. In 1974, he proudly accepted "The Invisible Little Man" award—a beautifully engraved trophy base with empty footprints mounted on top. The "Little Men" presented their award to writers who, they felt, had been unjustly overlooked by committees and voters for more formal awards.

On April 19, 1968, Randall was asked to speak on "what it's like to sell to John Campbell." What follows is an edited excerpt from a transcription of that speech.

When Silverberg and I first went up [to Campbell's office] with these Bel-Rogas stories, John took the plot, laid it out smooth on his desk, put one hand inside here, and one hand inside there, grabbed each end and pulled it inside out, tied a knot in it, turned it end for end, and said, "There, write that."

Do you remember ten or fifteen years ago, there was discussion on whether it was possible to turn an inner tube inside out? A group of topologists got together and figured it out mathematically, and they said, "Yes, mathematically it is possible to turn an inner tube inside out, but only with a mathematical inner tube, because it has to be infinitely stretchable and infinitely compressible; you couldn't possibly do it with a real inner tube."

This article was published in SCIENTIFIC AMERICAN. One month later, they got a package in the mail. Somebody had simply opened a hole in an inner tube, gone "GA-SHRUNKK!" and sent it to them [inside out]. They published a retraction.

You could send John Campbell an inner tube constructed like a Klein bottle, and he would sit there and look at it, and if he saw anything in it that was worth saving, he would reach inside of it and go "SSSPUCKKKK" and hand it back to you, and say, "There— go write that." And you would look at it and say, "You know, the son of a bitch is right!"

And that is possibly one of the most irritating things about John Campbell. I love the guy—he is one of the hardest men to get to know I've ever met, but once you get to know him, he's just a wonderful guy. At the same time, he is the hardest man to deal with I've ever met in my life, because John has his own opinions— nobody can stick to his opinions like John W. Campbell!

[After some discussion as to when and where it was first sung—Randall's estimate settling on "Cleveland in fifty-five"— Randall sang:]

> On yonder hill there stands a building
> And upon the fourteenth floor
> Stands a group of authors moaning
> As they've never moaned before:
> > Oh No, John, No, John, No, John, No. (chorus)

> There in manner quite pontific
> Speaks the Master from on high:
> "Slaves are better off than free men;
> Surely you can all see why."
> > Chorus

> "There are supermen among us;
> We must now discover psi,"
> Says the Master; and the authors
> Groan in agony and cry:
> > Chorus

> "Well, then," says the Master, smiling,
> "Since my gospel you deny,
> Would you rather sell to others,
> Where the rates are not so high?"
> > OH NO, JOHN, NO, JOHN, NO, JOHN, NO!

We got him up on the stage, and got every man there who had ever sold anything to John (or, as a matter of fact, everybody who's ever sold anything to *ASTOUNDING*. That included Lloyd Eshback, E. E. Smith, everybody). We sang the song to him, and he just stood there, looking superior, which he had every right to do, and when it was over, he looked around at all of us, and said, "Thank you for your stories."

A Spaceship Named McGuire

by Randall Garrett

Donning specifically requested that I include this story, and I acceded happily. I present it here, with my comments as an afterword.

No. Nobody ever deliberately named a spaceship that. The staid and stolid minds that run the companies which design and build spaceships rarely let their minds run to fancy. The only example I can think of is the unsung hero of the last century who had puckish imagination enough to name the first atomic-powered submarine *Nautilus*. Such minds are rare. Most minds equate dignity with dullness.

This ship happened to have a magnetogravitic drive, which automatically put it into the MG class. It also happened to be the first successful model to be equipped with a Yale robotic brain, so it was given the designation MG-YR 7—the first six had had more bugs in them than a Leopoldville tenement.

So somebody at Yale—another unsung hero—named the ship McGuire; it wasn't official, but it stuck.

The next step was to get someone to test-hop McGuire. They needed just the right man—quick-minded, tough, imaginative, and a whole slew of complimentary adjectives. They wanted a perfect superman to test pilot their baby, even if they knew they'd eventually have to take second best.

It took the Yale Space Foundation a long time to pick the right man.

No, I'm not the guy who tested the McGuire.

I'm the guy who stole it.

Shalimar Ravenhurst is not the kind of bloke that very many people can bring themselves to like, and, in this respect, I'm like a great many people, if not more so. In the first place, a man has no right to go around toting a name like "Shalimar"; it makes names like "Beverly" and "Leslie" and "Evelyn" sound almost hairy chested. You want a dozen other reasons, you'll get them.

Shalimar Ravenhurst owned a little planetoid out in the Belt, a hunk of nickel-iron about the size of a smallish mountain with a gee-pull measurable in fractions of a centimeter per second squared. If you're susceptible to spacesickness, that kind of gravity is about as much help as aspirin would have been to Marie Antoinette. You get the feeling of a floor beneath you, but there's a distinct impression that it won't be there for long. It keeps trying to drop out from under you.

I dropped my flitterboat on the landing field and looked around without any hope of seeing anything. I didn't. The field was about the size of a football field, a bright, shiny expanse of rough-polished metal, carved and smoothed flat from the nickel-iron of the planetoid itself. It not only served as a landing field, but as a reflector beacon, a mirror that flashed out the sun's reflection as the planetoid turned slowly on its axis. I'd homed in on that beacon, and now I was sitting on it.

There wasn't a soul in sight. Off to one end of the rectangular field was a single dome, a hemisphere about twenty feet in diameter and half as high. Nothing else.

I sighed and flipped on the magnetic anchor, which grabbed hold of the metal beneath me and held the flitterboat tightly to the surface. Then I cut the drive, plugged in the telephone, and punched for "Local."

The automatic finder searched around for the Ravenhurst tickler signal, found it, and sent out a beep along the same channel.

I waited while the thing beeped twice. There was a click, and a voice said: "Raven's Rest. Yes?" It wasn't Ravenhurst.

I said: "This is Daniel Oak. I want to talk to Mr. Ravenhurst."

"Mr. Oak? But you weren't expected until tomorrow."

"Fine. I'm early. Let me talk to Ravenhurst."

"But Mr. Ravenhurst wasn't expecting you to—"

I got all-of-a-sudden exasperated. "Unless your instruments are running on secondhand flashlight batteries, you've known I was coming for the past half hour. I followed Ravenhurst's instructions not to use radio, but he should know I'm here by this time. He told me to come as fast as possible, and I followed those instructions, too. I always follow instructions when I'm paid enough.

"Now, I'm here; tell Ravenhurst I want to talk to him, or I'll simply flit back to Eros, and thank him much for a pretty retainer that didn't do him any good but gave me a nice profit for my trouble."

"One moment, please," said the voice.

It took about a minute and a half, which was about nine billion jiffies too long, as far as I was concerned.

Then another voice said: "Oak? Wasn't expecting you till tomorrow."

"So I hear. I thought you were in a hurry, but if you're not, you can just provide me with wine, women, and other necessities until tomorrow. That's above and beyond my fee, of course, since you're wasting my time, and I'm evidently not wasting yours."

I couldn't be sure whether the noise he made was a grunt or a muffled chuckle, and I didn't much care. "Sorry, Oak; I really didn't expect you so soon, but I do want to...I want you to get started right away. Leave your flitterboat where it is; I'll have someone take care of it. Walk on over to the dome and come on in." And he cut off.

I growled something I was glad he didn't hear and hung up. I wished that I'd had a vision unit on the phone; I'd like to have seen his face. Although I knew I might not have learned much more from his expression than I had from his voice.

I got out of the flitterboat and walked across the dome, my magnetic soles making subdued clicking noises inside the suit as they caught and released the metallic plain beneath me. Beyond the field, I was surrounded by a lumpy horizon and a black sky full of bright, hard stars.

The green light was on when I reached the door to the dome, so I opened it and went in, closing it behind me. I flipped the toggle that began flooding the room with air. When it was up to pressure, a trapdoor in the floor of the dome opened and a crew-cut, blond young man stuck his head up. "Mr. Oak?"

I toyed, for an instant, with the idea of giving him a sarcastic answer. Who else would it be? How many other visitors were running around on the surface of Raven's Rest?

Instead, I said: "That's right." My voice must have sounded pretty muffled to him through my fishbowl.

"Come on down, Mr. Oak. You can shuck your vac suit below."

I thought "below" was a pretty ambiguous term on a low-gee lump like this, but I followed him down the ladder. The ladder was a necessity for fast transportation; if I'd just tried to jump down from one floor to the next, it would've taken me until a month from next St. Swithin's Day to land.

The door overhead closed, and I could hear the pumps start cycling. The warning light turned red.

I took off my suit, hung it in a handy locker, showing that all I had on underneath was my skin-tight "union suit."

"All right if I wear this?" I asked the blond young man. "Or should I borrow a set of shorts and a jacket?" Most places in the Belt, a union suit is considered normal dress; a man never knows when he might have to climb into a vac suit—*fast*. But there are a few of the hoity-toity places on Eros and Ceres and a few of the other well-settled places where a man or woman is required to put on shorts and jacket before entering. And in good old New York City, a man and woman were locked up for "indecent exposure" a few months ago. The judge threw the case out of court, but he told them they were lucky they hadn't been picked up in Boston. It seems that the eye of the bluenose turns a jaundiced yellow at the sight of a union suit, and he sees red.

But there were evidently no bluenoses here. "Perfectly all right, Mr. Oak," the blond young man said affably. Then he coughed politely and added: "But I'm afraid I'll have to ask you to take off the gun."

I glanced at the holster under my armpit, walked back over to the locker, opened it, and took out my vac suit.

"Hey!" said the blond young man. "Where are you going?"

"Back to my boat," I said calmly. "I'm a professional man, not a hired flunky. If you'd called a doctor, you wouldn't tell him to leave his little black bag behind; if you'd called a lawyer, you wouldn't make him check his brief case. Or, if you did, he'd tell you to drop dead.

"I was asked to come here as fast as possible, and when I do, I'm told to wait till tomorrow. Now you want me to check my gun. The hell with you."

"Merely a safety precaution," said the blond young man worriedly.

"You think I'm going to shoot Ravenhurst, maybe? Don't be an idiot." I started climbing into my vac suit.

"Just a minute, please, Mr. Oak," said a voice from a hidden speaker. It was Ravenhurst, and he actually sounded apologetic. "You mustn't blame Mr. Feller; those are my standing orders, and I failed to tell Mr. Feller to make an exception in your case. The error was mine."

"I know," I said. "I wasn't blaming Mr. Feller. I wasn't even talking to him. I was addressing you."

"I believe you. Mr. Feller, our guest has gone to all the trouble of having a suit made with a space under the arm for that gun; I see no reason to make him remove it." A pause. "Again, Mr. Oak, I apologize. I really want you to take this job."

I was already taking off the vac suit again.

"But," Ravenhurst continued smoothly, "if I fail to live up to your ideas of courtesy again, I hope you'll forgive me in advance. I'm sometimes very forgetful, and I don't like it when a man threatens to leave my employ twice in the space of fifteen minutes."

"I'm not in your employ yet, Ravenhurst," I said. "If I accept the job, I won't threaten to quit again unless I mean to carry it through, and it would take a lot more than common discourtesy to make me do that. On the other hand, your brand of discourtesy is a shade above the common."

"I thank you for that, at least," said Ravenhurst. "Show him to my office, Mr. Feller."

The blond young man nodded wordlessly and led me from the room.

60

Walking under low-gee conditions is like nothing else in this universe. I don't mean trotting around on Luna; one-sixth gee is practically homelike in comparison. And zero gee is so devoid of orientation that it gives the sensation of falling endlessly until you get used to it. But a planetoid is in a different class altogether.

Remember that dream—almost everybody's had it—where you're suddenly able to fly? It isn't like flying exactly; it's a sort of swimming in the air. Like being underwater, except that the medium around you isn't so dense and viscous, and you can breathe. Remember? Well, that's the feeling you get on a low-gee planetoid.

Your arms don't tend to hang at your sides, as they do on Earth or Luna, because the muscular tension tends to hold them out, just as it does in zero-gee, but there is still a definite sensation of up-and-down. If you push yourself off the floor, you tend to float in a long, slow, graceful arc, provided you don't push too hard. Magnetic soles are practically a must.

I followed the blond Mr. Feller down a series of long corridors which had been painted a pale green, which gave me the feeling that I was underwater. There were doors spaced at intervals along the corridor walls. Occasionally one of them would open and a busy-looking man would cross the corridor, open another door, and disappear. From behind the doors, I could hear the drum of distant sounds.

We finally ended up in front of what looked like the only wooden door in the place. When you're carving an office and residence out of a nickel-iron planetoid, importing wood from Earth is purely luxury matter.

There was no name plate on that mahogany-red door; there didn't need to be.

Feller touched a thin-lined circle in the door jamb.

"You don't knock?" I asked with mock seriousness.

"No," said Feller, with a straight face. "I have to signal. Knocking wouldn't do any good. That's just wood veneer over a three-inch-thick steel slab."

The door opened and I stepped inside.

I have never seen a room quite like it. The furniture was all that same mahogany—a huge desk, nineteenth-century baroque, with carved and curlicued legs; two chairs carved the same, with padded seats of maroon leather; and a chair behind the desk that might have doubled as a bishop's throne, with even fancier carving. Off to one side was a long couch upholstered in a lighter maroon. The wall-to-wall carpeting was a rich Burgundy, with a pile deep enough to run a reaper through. The walls were paneled with mahogany and hung with a couple of huge tapestries done in maroon, purple, and red. A bookcase along one wall was filled with books, every one of which had been rebound in maroon leather.

It was like walking into a cask of old claret. Or old blood.

The man sitting behind the desk looked as though he'd been built to be the lightest spot in an analogous color scheme. His suit was mauve with purple piping, and his wide, square, saggy face was florid. On his nose and cheeks, tiny lines of purple tracing made darker areas in his skin. His hair was a medium brown, but it was clipped so short that the scalp showed faintly through, and amid all that overwhelming background, even the hair looked vaguely violet.

"Come in, Mr. Oak," said Shalimar Ravenhurst.

I walked toward him across the burgundy carpet while the blond young man discreetly closed the door behind me, leaving us alone. I didn't blame him. I was wearing a yellow union suit, and I hate to think what I must have looked like in that room.

I sat down in one of the chairs facing the desk after giving a brief shake to a thick-fingered, well-manicured, slightly oily hand.

He opened a crystal decanter that stood on one end of the desk. "Have some Madeira, Mr. Oak? Or would you like something else? I never drink spirits at this time of night."

I fought down an impulse to ask for a shot of redeye. "The Madeira will be fine, Mr. Ravenhurst."

He poured and handed me a stemmed glass nearly brimming with the wine. I joined him in an appreciative sip, then waited while he made up his mind to talk.

He leaned across the desk, looking at me with his small, dark eyes. He had an expression on his face that looked as if it were trying to sneer and leer at the same time but couldn't get much beyond the smirk stage.

"Mr. Oak, I have investigated you thoroughly—as thoroughly as it can be done at least. My attorneys say that your reputation is A-one; that you get things done and rarely disappoint a client."

He paused as if waiting for a comment. I gave him nothing.

After a moment, he went on. "I hope that's true, Mr. Oak, because I'm going to have to trust you." He leaned back in his chair again, his eyes still on me. "Men very rarely like me, Mr. Oak. I am not a likable man. I do not pretend to be. That's not my function." He said it as if he had said it many times before, believed it, and wished it wasn't so.

"I do not ask that you like me," he continued. "I only ask that you be loyal to my interests for the duration of this assignment." Another pause. "I have been assured by others that this will be so. I would like your assurance."

"If I take the assignment, Mr. Ravenhurst," I told him, "I'll be working for you. I can be bought, but once I'm bought I stay bought.

"Now, what seems to be your trouble?"

He frowned. "Well, now, let's get one thing settled: Are you working for me, or not?"

"I won't know that until I find out what the job is."

His frown deepened. "Now, see here; this is very confidential work. What happens if I tell you and you decide not to work for me?"

I sighed. "Ravenhurst, right now you're paying me to listen to you. Even if I don't take your job, I'm going to bill you for expenses and time to come all the way out here. So, as far as listening is concerned, I'm working for you now. If I don't like the job, I'll still forget everything I'm told. All right?"

He didn't like it, but he had no choice. "All right," he said. He polished off his glass of Madeira and refilled it. My own glass was still nearly full.

"Mr. Oak," he began. "I have two problems. One is minor, the other major. But I have attempted to blow the minor problem up out of proportion, so that all the people here at Raven's Rest think that it is the only problem. They think that I brought you out here for that reason alone.

"But all that is merely cover-up for the real problem."

"Which is?" I prompted.

He leaned forward again. Apparently, it was the only exercise he ever got. "You're aware that Viking Spacecraft is one of the corporations under the management of Ravenhurst Holdings?"

I nodded. Viking Spacecraft built some of the biggest and best spacecraft in the System. It held most of Ceres—all of it, in fact, except the Government Reservation. It had moved out to the asteroids a long time back, after the big mining concerns began cutting up the smaller asteroids for metal. The raw materials are easier to come by out here than they are on Earth, and it's a devil of a lot easier to build spacecraft under low-gee conditions than it is under the pull of Earth or Luna or Mars.

"Do you know anything about the experimental robotic ships being built on Eros?" Ravenhurst asked.

"Not much," I admitted. "I've heard about them, but I don't know any of the details." That wasn't quite true, but I've found it doesn't pay to tell everybody everything you know.

"The engineering details aren't necessary," Ravenhurst said. "Besides, I don't know them, myself. The point is that Viking is trying to build a ship that will be as easy to operate as a flitterboat—a one-man cargo vessel. Perhaps even a completely automatic job for cargo, and just use a one-man crew for the passenger vessels. Imagine how that would cut the cost of transportation in the Solar System! Imagine how it would open up high-speed cargo transfer if an automatic vessel could accelerate at twenty or twenty-five gees to turnover!"

I'll give Ravenhurst this: He had a light in his eyes that showed a real excitement about the prospect he was discussing, and it wasn't due entirely to the money he might make.

"Sounds fine," I said. "What seems to be the trouble?"

His face darkened half a shade. "The company police suspect sabotage, Mr. Oak."

"How? What kind?"

"They don't know. Viking has built six ships of that type—the McGuire class, the engineers call it. Each one has been slightly different than the one before, of course, as they ironed out the bugs in their operation. But each one has been a failure. Not one of them would pass the test for spaceworthiness."

"Not a failure of the drive or the ordinary mechanisms of the ship, I take it?"

Ravenhurst sniffed. "Of course not. The brain. The ships became, as you might say, *non compos mentis*. A matter of fact, when the last one simply tried to burrow into the surface of Eros by reversing its drive, one of the roboticists said that a coroner's jury would have returned a verdict of 'suicide while of unsound mind' if there were inquests held for spaceships."

"That doesn't make much sense," I said.

"No. It doesn't. It isn't sensible. Those ships' brains shouldn't have behaved that way. Robot brains don't go mad unless they're given instructions to do so—conflicting orders, erroneous information, that sort of thing. Or, unless they have actual physical defects in the brains themselves."

"The brains can handle the job of flying a ship all right, though?" I asked. "I mean, they have the capacity for it?"

"Certainly. They're the same type that's used to control the automobile traffic on the Eastern Seaboard Highway Network of North America. If they can control the movement of millions of cars, there's no reason why they can't control a spaceship."

"No," I said, "I suppose not." I thought it over for a second, then asked, "But what do your robotics men say is causing the malfunctions?"

"That's where the problem comes in, Mr. Oak." He pursed his pudgy lips, and his eyes narrowed. "The opinions are divided. Some of the men say it's simply a case of engineering failure—that the bugs haven't been worked out of this new combination, but that as soon as they are, everything will work as smoothly as butter. Others say that only deliberate tampering could cause those failures. And still others say that there's not enough evidence to prove either of those theories is correct."

"But your opinion is that it's sabotage?"

"Exactly," said Ravenhurst, "and I know who is doing it and why."

I didn't try to conceal the little bit of surprise that gave me. "You know the man who's responsible?"

He shook his head rapidly, making his jowls wobble. "I didn't mean that. It's not a single man; it's a group."

"Maybe you'd better go into a little more detail on that, Mr. Ravenhurst."

He nodded, and this time his jowls bobbled instead of wobbled. "Some group at Viking is trying to run me out of the managerial business. They want Viking to be managed by Thurston Enterprises; they evidently think they can get a better deal from him than they can from me. If the McGuire project fails, they'll have a good chance of convincing the stockholders that the fault lies with Ravenhurst. You follow?"

"So far," I said. "Do you think Thurston's behind this, then?"

"I don't know," he said slowly. "He might be, or he might not. If he is, that's perfectly legitimate business tactics. He's got a perfect right to try to get more business for himself if he wants to. I've undercut him a couple of times.

"But I don't think he's too deeply involved, if he's involved at all. This smacks of a personal attack against me, and I don't think that's Thurston's type of play.

"You see, things are a little touchy right now. I won't go into details, but you know what the political situation is at the moment.

"It works this way, as far as Viking is concerned: If I lose the managerial contract at Viking, a couple of my other contracts will go by the board, too—especially if it's proved that I've been lax in management or have been expending credit needlessly.

"These other two companies are actually a little shaky at the moment; I've only been managing them for a little over a year in one case and two years in the other. Their assets have come up since I took over, but they'd still dump me if they thought I was reckless."

"How can they do that?" I asked. "You have a contract, don't you?"

"Certainly. They wouldn't break it. But they'd likely ask the Government Inspectors to step in and check every step of the managerial work. Now, you and I and everybody else knows that you have to cut corners to make a business successful. If the GIs step in, that will have to stop—which means we'll show a loss heavy enough to put us out. We'll be forced to sell the contract for a pittance.

"Well, then. If Viking goes, and these other two corporations go, it'll begin to look as if Ravenhurst can't take care of himself and his companies any more. Others will climb on the bandwagon. Contracts that are coming up for renewal will be reconsidered instead of continuing automatically. I think you can see where that would lead eventually."

I did. You don't go into the managing business these days unless you have plenty on the ball. You've got to know all the principles and all the tricks of organization and communication, and you've got to be able to waltz your way around all the roadblocks that are caused by Government laws—some of which have been floating around on the books of one nation or another for

66

two or three centuries.

Did you know that there's a law on the American statute books that forbids the landing of a spaceship within one hundred miles of a city? That was passed back when they were using rockets, but it's never been repealed. Technically, then, it's almost impossible to land a ship anywhere on the North American continent. Long Island Spaceport is openly flouting the law, if you want to look at it that way.

A managerial combine has to know all those little things and know how to get around them. It has to be able to have the confidence of the stockholders of a corporation—if it's run on the Western Plan—or the confidence of communal owners if it's run on the Eastern Plan.

Something like this could snowball on Ravenhurst. It isn't only the rats that desert a sinking ship; so does anyone else who has any sense.

"What I want to know, Mr. Oak," Ravenhurst continued, "is who is behind this plot, whether an individual or a group. I want to know identity and motivation."

"Is that all?" I eyed him skeptically.

"No. Of course not. I want you to make sure that the MG-YR 7 isn't sabotaged. I want you to make sure it's protected from whatever kind of monkey wrenches are being thrown into its works."

"It's nearly ready for testing now, isn't it?" I asked.

"It is ready. It seems to be in perfect condition so far. Viking is already looking for a test pilot. It's still in working order, and I want to be certain that it will remain so."

I cocked my head to one side and gave him my Interrogative And Suspicious Glance—Number 9 in the manual. "You didn't do any checking on the first six McGuire ships. You wait until this one is done before calling me. Why the delay, Ravenhurst?"

It didn't faze him. "I became suspicious after McGuire 6 failed. I put Colonel Brock on it."

I nodded. I'd had dealings with Brock. He was head of Ravenhurst's Security Guard. "Brock didn't get anywhere," I said.

"He did not. His own face is too well known for him to have investigated personally, and he's not enough of an actor to get away with using a plexiskin mask. He had to use underlings. And I'm afraid some of them might be in the pay of the...ah... opposition. They got nowhere."

"In other words, you may have spies in your own organization who are working with the Viking group. Very interesting. That means they know I'm working for you, which will effectively seal me up. You might as well have kept Brock on the job."

He smiled in a smug, superior sort of way that some men might have resented. I did. Even though I'd fed him the line so that he could feel superior, knowing that a smart operator like Ravenhurst would already have covered his tracks. I couldn't help wishing I'd told him simply to trot out his cover story instead of letting him think I believed it had never occurred to either of us before.

"As far as my staff knows, Mr. Oak, you are here to escort my daughter, Jaqueline, to Braunsville, Luna. You will, naturally, have to take her to Ceres, in your flitterboat, where you will wait for a specially chartered ship to take you both to Luna. That will be a week after you arrive. Since the McGuire 7 is to be tested within three days, that should give you ample time."

"If it doesn't?"

"We will consider that possibility if and when it becomes probable. I have a great deal of faith in you."

"Thanks. One more thing: Why do you think anybody will swallow the idea that your daughter needs a private bodyguard to escort her to Braunsville?"

His smile broadened a little. "You have not met my daughter, Mr. Oak. Jaqueline takes after me in a great many respects, not the least of which is her desire to have things her own way and submit to no man's yoke, as the saying goes. I have had a difficult time with her, sir; a difficult time. It is and has been a matter of steering a narrow course between the Scylla of breaking her spirit with too much discipline and the Charybdis of allowing her to ruin her life by letting her go hog wild. She is seventeen now, and the time has come to send her to a school where she will receive an education suitable to her potentialities and abilities, and discipline which will be suitable to her spirit.

"Your job, Mr. Oak, will be to make sure she gets there. You are not a bodyguard in the sense that you must protect her from the people around her. Quite the contrary, *they* may need protection from *her*. You are to make sure she arrives in Braunsville on schedule. She is perfectly capable of taking it in her head to go scooting off to Earth if you turn your back on her."

Still smiling, he refilled his glass. "Do have some more Madeira, Mr. Oak. It's really an excellent year."

I let him refill my glass.

"That, I think, will cover your real activities well enough. My daughter will, of course, take a tour of the plant on Ceres, which will allow you to do whatever work is necessary."

He smiled at me.

I didn't smile back.

"Up till now, this sounded like a pretty nice assignment," I said. "But I don't want it now. I can't take care of a teenage girl with a desire for the bright lights of Earth while I investigate a sabotage case."

I knew he had an out; I was just prodding him into springing it.

He did. "Of course not. My daughter is not as scatterbrained as I have painted her. She is going to help you."

"*Help* me?"

"Exactly. You are ostensibly her bodyguard. If she turns up missing, you will, of course, leave no stone unturned to find her." He chuckled. "And Ceres is a fairly large stone."

I thought it over. I still didn't like it too well, but if Jaqueline wasn't going to be too much trouble to take care of, it might work out. And if she did get to be too much trouble, I could see to it that she was unofficially detained for a while.

"All right, Mr. Ravenhurst," I said, "you've got yourself a man for both jobs."

"Both?"

"I find out who is trying to sabotage the McGuire ship, and I baby-sit for you. That's two jobs. And you're going to pay for both of them."

"I expected to," said Shalimar Ravenhurst.

Fifteen minutes later, I was walking into the room where I'd left my vac suit. There was a girl waiting for me.

She was already dressed in her vac suit, so there was no way to be sure, but she looked as if she had a nice figure underneath the suit. Her face was rather unexceptionally pretty, a sort of nice-girl-next-door face. Her hair was a reddish brown and was cut fairly close to the skull; only a woman who never intends to be in a vac suit in free fall can afford to let her hair grow.

"Miss Ravenhurst?" I asked.

She grinned and stuck out a hand. "Just call me Jack. And I'll call you Dan. O.K.?"

I grinned and shook her hand because there wasn't much else I could do. Now I'd met the Ravenhursts: A father called Shalimar and a daughter called Jack.

And a spaceship named McGuire.

I gave the flitterboat all the push it would take to get us to Ceres as fast as possible. I don't like riding in the things. You sit there inside a transite hull, which has two bucket seats inside it, fore and aft, astraddle the drive tube, and you guide from one beacon to the next while you keep tabs on orbital positions by radio. It's a long jump from one rock to the next, even in the asteroid belt, and you have to live inside your vac suit until you come to a stopping place where you can spend an hour or so resting before you go on. It's like driving cross-continent in an automobile, except that the signposts and landmarks are constantly shifting position. An inexperienced man can get lost easily in the Belt.

I was happy to find that Jack Ravenhurst knew how to handle a flitterboat and could sight navigate by the stars. That meant that I could sleep while she piloted and vice versa. The trip back was a lot easier and faster than the trip out had been.

I was glad, in a way, that Ceres was within flitterboat range of Raven's Rest. I don't like the time wasted in waiting for a regular spaceship, which you have to do when your target is a quarter of the way around the Belt from you. The cross-system jumps don't take long, but getting to a ship takes time.

The Ravenhurst girl wasn't much of a talker while we were en route. A little general chitchat once in a while, then she'd clam up to do a little mental orbit figuring. I didn't mind. I was in no mood to pump her just yet, and I was usually figuring orbits myself. You get in the habit after a while.

When the Ceres beacon came into view, I was snoozing. Jack reached forward and shook my shoulder. "Decelerating toward Ceres," she said. "Want to take over from here on?" Her voice sounded tinny and tired in the earphones of my fishbowl.

"O.K.; I'll take her in. Have you called Ceres Field yet?"

"Not yet. I figured that you'd better do that, since it's your flitterboat."

I said O.K. and called Ceres. They gave me a traffic orbit, and I followed it in to Ceres Field.

It was a lot bigger than the postage-stamp field on Raven's Rest, and more brightly lit, and a lot busier, but it was basically the same idea—a broad, wide, smooth area that had been carved out of the surface of the nickel-iron with a focused sun beam. One end of it was reserved for flitterboats; three big spaceships sat on the other end, looking very *noblesse oblige* at the little flitterboats.

I clamped down, gave the key to one of the men behind the desk after we had gone below, and turned to Jack. "I suggest we go to the hotel first and get a shower and a little rest. We can go out to Viking tomorrow."

She glanced at her watch. Like every other watch and clock in the Belt, it was set for Greenwich Standard Time. What's the point in having time zones in space?

"I'm not tired," she said brightly. "I got plenty of sleep while we were on the way. Why don't we go out tonight? They've got a bounce-dance place called *Bali's* that—"

I held up a hand. "No. You may not be tired, but I am. Remember, I went all the way out there by myself, and then came right back.

"I need at least six hours sleep in a nice, comfortable bed before I'll be able to move again."

The look she gave me made me feel every one of my thirty-five years, but I didn't intend to let her go roaming around at this stage of the game.

Instead, I put her aboard one of the little rail cars, and we headed for the Viking Arms, generally considered the best hotel on Ceres.

Ceres has a pretty respectable gee pull for a planetoid: Three percent of Standard. I weigh a good, hefty five pounds on the surface. That makes it a lot easier to walk around on Ceres than on, say, Raven's Rest. Even so, you always get the impression that one of the little rail cars that scoots along the corridors is climbing uphill all the way, because the acceleration is greater than any measly thirty centimeters per second squared.

Jack didn't say another word until we reached the Viking, where Ravenhurst had thoughtfully made reservations for adjoining rooms. Then, after we'd registered, she said: "We could at least get something to eat."

"That's not a bad idea. We can get something to line our stomachs, anyway. Steak?"

She beamed up at me. "Steak. Sounds wonderful after all those mushy concentrates. Let's go."

The restaurant off the lobby was just like the lobby and the corridors outside—a big room hollowed out of the metal of the asteroid. The walls had been painted to prevent rusting, but they still bore the roughness left by the sun beam that had burnt them out.

We sat down at a table, and a waiter brought over a menu. The place wouldn't be classed higher than a third-rate cafe on Earth, but on Ceres it's considered one of the better places. The prices certainly compare well with those of the best New York or Moscow restaurants, and the price of meat, which has to be shipped from Earth, is—you should pardon the gag—astronomical.

That didn't bother me. Steaks for two would go right on the expense account. I mentally thanked Mr. Ravenhurst for the fine slab of beef when the waiter finally brought it.

While we were waiting, though, I lit a cigarette and said: "You're awfully quiet, Jack."

"Am I? Men are funny."

"Is that meant as a conversational gambit, or an honest observation?"

"Observation. I mean, men are always complaining that girls talk too much, but if a girl keeps her mouth shut, they think there's something wrong with her."

"Uh-huh. And you think that's a paradox or something?"

She looked puzzled. "Isn't it?"

"Not at all. The noise a jackhammer makes isn't pleasant at all, but if it doesn't make that noise, you figure it isn't functioning properly. So you wonder why."

Out of the corner of my eye, I had noticed a man wearing the black-and-gold union suit of Ravenhurst's Security Guard coming toward us from the door, using the gliding shuffle that works best under low gee. I ignored him to listen to Jack Ravenhurst.

"That has all the earmarks of a dirty crack," she said. The tone of her voice indicated that she wasn't sure whether to be angry or to laugh.

"Hello, Miss Ravenhurst; Hi, Oak." Colonel Brock had reached the table. He stood there, smiling his rather flat smile, while his

71

eyes looked us both over carefully.

He was five feet ten, an inch shorter than I am, and lean almost to the point of emaciation. His scarred, hard-bitten face looked as though it had gotten that way when he tried to kiss a crocodile.

"Hello, Brock," I said. "What's new?"

Jack gave him a meaningless smile and said: "Hello, colonel." She was obviously not very impressed with either of us.

"Mind if I sit?" Brock asked.

We didn't, so he sat.

"I'm sorry I missed you at the spaceport," Brock said seriously, "but I had several of my boys there with their eyes open." He was quite obviously addressing Jack, not me.

"It's all right," Jack said. "I'm not going anywhere this time." She looked at me and gave me an odd grin. "I'm going to stay home and be a good girl this time around."

Colonel Brock's good-natured chuckle sounded about as genuine as the ring of a lead nickel. "Oh, you're no trouble, Miss Ravenhurst."

"Thank you, kind sir; you're a poor liar." She stood up and smiled sweetly. "Will you gentlemen excuse me a moment?"

We would and did. Colonel Brock and I watched her cross the room and disappear through a door. Then he turned to look at me, giving me a wry grin and shaking his head a little sadly. "So you got saddled with Jack the Ripper, eh, Oak?"

"Is she that bad?"

His chuckle was harsher this time, and had the ring of truth. "You'll find out. Oh, I don't mean she's got the morals of a cat or anything like that. So far as I know, she's still waiting for Mister Right to come along."

"Drugs?" I asked. "Liquor?"

"A few drinks now and then—nothing else," Brock said. "No, it's none of the usual things. It isn't what *she* does that counts; it's what she talks other people into doing. She's a convincer."

"That sounds impressive," I said. "What does it mean?"

His hard face looked wolfish. "I ought to let you find out for yourself. But, no; that wouldn't be professional courtesy, and it wouldn't be ethical."

"Brock," I said tiredly, "I have been given more runarounds in the past week than Mercury has had in the past millenium. I expect clients to be cagey, to hold back information, and to lie. But I didn't expect it of you. Give."

He nodded brusquely. "As I said, she's a convincer. A talker. She can talk people into doing almost anything she wants them to."

"For instance?"

"Like, for instance, getting all the patrons at the *Bali* to do a snake dance around the corridors in the altogether. The Ceres police broke it up, but she was nowhere to be found."

He said it so innocently that I knew he'd been the one to get her out of the mess.

"And the time," he continued, "that she almost succeeded in getting a welder named Plotkin elected Hereditary Czar of Ceres. She'd have succeeded, too, if she hadn't made the mistake of getting Plotkin himself up to speak in front of his loyal supporters. After that, everybody felt so silly that the movement fell apart."

He went on, reciting half a dozen more instances of the girl's ability to influence people without winning friends. None of them were new to me; they were all on file in the Political Survey Division of the United Nations Government on Earth, plus several more which Colonel Brock either neglected to tell me or wasn't aware of himself.

But I listened with interest; after all, I wasn't supposed to know any of these things. I am just a plain, ordinary, "confidential expediter." That's what it says on the door of my office in New York, and that's what it says on my license. All very legal and very dishonest.

The Political Survey Division is very legal and very dishonest, too. Theoretically, it is supposed to be nothing but a branch of the System Census Bureau; it is supposed to do nothing but observe and tabulate political trends. The actual fact that it is the Secret Service branch of the United Nations Government is known only to relatively few people.

I know it because I work for the Political Survey Division.

The PSD already had men investigating both Ravenhurst and Thurston, but when they found that Ravenhurst was looking for a confidential expediter, for a special job, they'd shoved me in fast.

It isn't easy to fool sharp operators like Colonel Brock, but, so far, I'd been lucky enough to get away with it by playing ignorant-but-not-stupid.

The steaks were brought, and I mentally saluted Ravenhurst, as I had promised myself I would. Then I rather belatedly asked the colonel if he'd eat with us.

"No," he said, with a shake of his head. "No, thanks. I've got to get things ready for her visit to the Viking plant tomorrow."

"Oh? Hiding something?" I asked blandly.

He didn't even bother to look insulted. "No. Just have to make sure she doesn't get hurt by any of the machinery, that's all. Most of the stuff is automatic, and she has a habit of getting too close. I guess she thinks she can talk a machine out of hurting her as easily as she can talk a man into standing on his head."

Jack Ravenhurst was coming back to the table. I noticed that she'd fixed her hair nicely and put on make-up. It made her look a lot more feminine than she had while she was on the flitterboat.

"Well," she said as she sat down, "have you two decided what to do with me?"

Colonel Brock just smiled and said: "I guess we'll have to leave that up to you, Miss Ravenhurst." Then he stood up. "Now, if you'll excuse me, I'll be about my business."

Jack nodded, gave him a quick smile, and fell to on her steak with the voraciousness of an unfed chicken in a wheat bin.

Miss Jaqueline Ravenhurst evidently had no desire to talk to me at the moment.

On Ceres, as on most of the major planetoids, a man's home is his castle, even if it's only a hotel room. Raw nickel-iron, the basic building material, is so cheap that walls and doors are seldom made of anything else, so a hotel room is more like a vault than anything else on Earth. Every time I go into one of the hotels on Ceres or Eros, I get the feeling that I'm either a bundle of gold certificates or a particularly obstreperous prisoner being led to a medieval solitary confinement cell. They're not pretty, but they're *solid.*

Jack Ravenhurst went into her own room after flashing me a rather hurt smile that was supposed to indicate her disappointment in not being allowed to go nightclubbing. I gave her a big-brotherly pat on the shoulder and told her to get plenty of sleep, since we had to be up bright and early in the morning.

Once inside my own room, I checked over my luggage carefully. It had been brought there from the spaceport, where I'd checked it before going to Ravenhurst's Raven's Rest. This was one of several rooms that Ravenhurst kept permanently rented for his own uses, and I knew that Jack kept a complete wardrobe in her own rooms.

There were no bugs in my luggage—neither sound nor sight spying devices of any kind. Not that I would have worried if there had been; I just wanted to see if anyone was crude enough to try that method of smuggling a bug into the apartment.

The door chime pinged solemnly.

I took a peek through the door camera and saw a man in a bellboy's uniform, holding a large traveling case. I recognized the face, so I let him in.

"The rest of your luggage, sir," he said with a straight face.

"Thank you very much," I told him. I handed him a tip, and he popped off.

This stuff was special equipment that I hadn't wanted Ravenhurst or anybody else to get his paws into.

I opened it carefully with the special key, slid a hand under the clothing that lay on top for camouflage, and palmed the little detector I needed. Then I went around the room, whistling softly to myself.

The nice thing about an all-metal room is that it's impossible to hide a self-contained bug in it that will be of any use. A small, concealed broadcaster can't broadcast any farther than the walls, so any bug has to have wires leading out of the room.

I didn't find a thing. Either Ravenhurst kept the room clean or somebody was using more sophisticated bugs than any I knew about. I opened the traveling case again and took out one of my favorite gadgets. It's a simple thing, really: a noise generator. But the noise it generates is non-random noise. Against a background of "white," purely random noise, it is possible to pick out a conversation, even if the conversation is below the noise level, simply because conversation is patterned. But this little generator of mine was non-random. It was the multiple recording of ten thousand different conversations, all meaningless, against a background of "white" noise. Try that one on your differential analyzers.

By the time I got through, nobody could tap a dialogue in that room, barring, as I said, bugs more sophisticated than any the United Nations knew about.

Then I went over and tapped on the communicating door between my room and Jack Ravenhurst's. There was no answer.

I said, "Jack, I'm coming in. I have a key."

She said, "Go away. I'm not dressed. I'm going to bed."

"Grab something quick," I told her. "I'm coming in."

I keyed open the door.

She was no more dressed for bed than I was, unless she made a habit of sleeping in her best evening togs. Anger blazed in her eyes for a second, then that faded, and she tried to look all sweetness and light.

"I was trying on some new clothes," she said innocently.

A lot of people might have believed her. The emotional field she threw out, encouraging utter belief in her every word, was as powerful as any I'd ever felt. I just let it wash past me and said: "Come into my room for a few minutes, Jack; I want to talk to you."

I didn't put any particular emphasis into it. I don't have to. She came.

Once we were both inside my shielded room with the walls vibrating with ten thousand voices and a hush area in the center, I said patiently, "Jack, I personally don't care where you go or what you do. Tomorrow, you can do your vanishing act and have yourself a ball, for all I care. But there are certain things that have to be done first. Now, sit down and listen."

She sat down, her eyes wide. Evidently, nobody had ever beaten her at her own game before.

"Tonight, you'll stay here and get some sleep. Tomorrow, we go for a tour of Viking, first thing in the morning. Tomorrow afternoon, as soon as I think the time is ripe, you can sneak off. I'll show you how to change your appearance so you won't be recognized. You can have all the fun you want for twenty-four hours. I, of course, will be hunting high and low for you, but I won't find you until I have finished my investigation.

"On the other hand, I want to know where you are at all times, so that I can get in touch with you if I need you. So, no matter where you are, you'll keep in touch by phoning BANning 6226 every time you change location. Got that number?"

She nodded. "BANning 6226," she repeated.

"Fine. Now Brock's agents will be watching you, so I'll have to figure out a way to get you away from them, but that won't be too hard. I'll let you know at the proper time. Meanwhile, get back in there, get ready for bed, and get some sleep. You'll need it. Move."

She nodded rather dazedly, got up, and went to the door. She turned, said goodnight in a low, puzzled voice, and closed the door.

Half an hour later, I quietly sneaked into her room just to check. She was asleep in bed. I went back to my own room, and got some sack time myself.

"It's a pleasure to have you here again, Miss Ravenhurst," said Chief Engineer Midguard. "Anything in particular you want to see this time?" He said it as though he actually enjoyed taking the boss's teenage daughter through a spacecraft plant.

Maybe he did, at that. He was a paunchy, graying man in his sixties, who had probably been a rather handsome lady-killer for the first half-century of his life, but he was approaching middle age now, which has a predictable effect on the telly-idol type.

Jack Ravenhurst was at her regal best, with the kind of *noblesse oblige* that would bring worshipful gratitude to the heart of any underling. "Oh, just a quick run-through on whatever you think would be interesting, Mr. Midguard; I don't want to take up too much of your time."

Midguard allowed as how he had a few interesting things to show her, and the party, which also included the watchful and taciturn Colonel Brock, began to make the rounds of the Viking plant.

There were three ships under construction at the time: two cargo vessels and a good-sized passenger job. Midguard seemed to think that every step of spacecraft construction was utterly fascinating—for which, bully for him—but it was pretty much of a drag as far as I was concerned. It took three hours.

Finally, he said, "Would you like to see the McGuire-7?"

Why, yes, of course she would. So we toddled off to the new ship while Midguard kept up a steady line of patter.

"We think we have all the computer errors out of this one, Miss Ravenhurst. A matter of new controls and safety devices. We feel that the trouble with the first six machines was that they were designed to be operated by voice orders by any qualified human operator. The trouble is that they had no way of telling just who was qualified. The brains are perfectly capable of distinguishing one individual from another, but they can't tell whether a given individual is a space pilot or a janitor. In fact—"

I marked the salient points in his speech. The MG-YR-7 would be strictly a one-man ship. It had a built-in dog attitude—friendly toward all humans, but loyal only to its master. Of course, it was likely that the ship would outlast its master, so its loyalties could be changed, but only by the use of special switching keys.

The robotics boys still weren't sure why the first six had gone insane, but they were fairly certain that the primary cause was the matter of too many masters. The brilliant biophysicist, Asenion, who promulgated the Three Laws of Robotics in the last century, had shown in his writings that they were unattainable ideals—that they only told what a perfect robot *should* be, not what a robot actually was.

The First Law, for instance, would forbid a robot to harm a human being, either by action or inaction. But, as Asenion showed, a robot could be faced with a situation which allowed for only two possible decisions, both of which required that a human being be harmed. In such a case, the robot goes insane.

I found myself speculating what sort of situation, what sort of Asenion paradox, had confronted those first six ships. And whether it had been by accident or design. Not that the McGuire robots had been built in strict accord with the Laws of Robotics; that was impossible on the face of it. But no matter how a perfectly logical machine is built, the human mind can figure out a way to goof it up because the human mind is capable of transcending logic.

The McGuire ship was a little beauty. A nice, sleek needle, capable of atmospheric as well as spatial navigation, with a mirror-polished, beryl-blue surface all over the sixty-five feet of her—or his?—length.

It was standing upright on the surface of the planetoid, a shining needle in the shifting sunlight, limned against the star-filled darkness of space. We looked at it through the transparent viewport, and then took the flexible tube that led to the air lock of the ship.

The ship was just as beautiful inside as it was outside. Neat, compact, and efficient. The control room—if such it could be called—was like no control room I'd ever seen before. Just an acceleration couch and observation instruments. Midguard explained that it wasn't necessary to be a pilot to run the ship; any person who knew a smattering of astronavigation could get to his destination by simply telling the ship what he wanted to do.

Jack Ravenhurst took in the whole thing with wide-eyed interest.

"Is the brain activated, Mr. Midguard?" she asked.

"Oh, yes. We've been educating him for the past month, pumping information in as rapidly as he could record it and index it. He's finished with that stage now; we're just waiting for the selection of a test pilot for the final shakedown cruise." He was looking warily at Jack as he spoke, as if he were waiting for something.

Evidently, he knew what was coming. "I'd like to talk to him," Jack said. "It's so interesting to carry on an intelligent conversation with a machine."

"I'm afraid that's impossible, Miss Ravenhurst," Midguard

said rather worriedly. "You see, McGuire's primed so that the first man's voice he hears will be identified as his master. It's what we call the 'chick reaction.' You know: the first moving thing a newly-hatched bird sees is regarded as the mother, and, once implanted, that order can't be rescinded. We can change McGuire's orientation in that respect, but we'd rather not have to go through that. After the test pilot establishes contact, you can talk to him all you want."

"When will the test pilot be here?" Jack asked, still as sweet as sucrodyne.

"Within a few days. It looks as though a man named Nels Bjornsen will be our choice. You may have heard of him."

"No," she said, "but I'm sure your choice will be correct."

Midguard still felt apologetic. "Well, you know how it is, Miss Ravenhurst; we can't turn a delicate machine like this over to just anyone for the first trial. He has to be a man of good judgment and fast reflexes. He has to know exactly what to say and when to say it, if you follow me."

"Oh, certainly; certainly." She paused and looked thoughtful. "I presume you've taken precautions against anyone stealing in here and taking control of the ship."

Midguard smiled and nodded wisely. "Certainly. Communication with McGuire can't be established unless and until two keys are used in the activating panel. I carry one; Colonel Brock has the other. Neither of us will give his key up to anyone but the accredited test pilot. And McGuire himself will scream out an alarm if anyone tries to jimmy the locks. He's his own burglar alarm."

She nodded. "I see." A pause. "Well, Mr. Midguard, I think you've done a very commendable job. Thank you so much. Is there anything else you feel I should see?"

"Well—" He was smilingly hesitant. "If there's anything else you want to see, I'll be glad to show it to you. But you've already seen our...ah...*piece de resistance,* so to speak."

She glanced at her wrist. It had been over four hours since we'd started. "I am rather tired," Jack said. "And hungry, too. Let's call it a day and go get something to eat."

"Fine! Fine!" Midguard said. "I'll be honored to be your host, if I may. We could have a little something at my apartment."

I knew perfectly well that he'd had a full lunch prepared and waiting.

The girl acknowledged his invitation and accepted it. Brock and I trailed along like the bodyguards we were supposed to be. I wondered whether or not Brock suspected me of being more than I appeared to be. If he didn't, he was stupider than I thought; on the other hand, he could never be sure. I wasn't worried about his finding out that I was a United Nations agent; that was a pretty remote chance. Brock didn't even know the United Nations Government *had* a Secret Service; it was unlikely that he would suspect me of being an agent of a presumably non-existent body.

But he could very easily suspect that I had been sent to check on him and the Thurston menace, and, if he had any sense, he actually did. I wasn't going to give him any verification of that suspicion if I could help it.

Midguard had an apartment in the executive territory of the Viking reservation, a fairly large place with plastic-lined walls instead of the usual painted nickel-iron. Very luxurious for Ceres.

The meal was served with an air of subdued pretension that made everybody a little stiff and uncomfortable, with the possible exception of Jack Ravenhurst, and the definite exception of myself. I just listened politely to the strained courtesy that passed for small talk and waited for the chance I knew would come at this meal.

After the eating was all over, and we were all sitting around with cigarettes going and wine in our glasses, I gave the girl the signal we had agreed upon. She excused herself very prettily and left the room.

After fifteen minutes, I began to look a little worried. The bathroom was only a room away—we were in a dining area, and the bathroom was just off the main bedroom—and it shouldn't have taken her that long to brush her hair and powder her face.

I casually mentioned it to Colonel Brock, and he smiled a little.

"Don't worry, Oak; even if she does walk out of this apartment, my men will be following her wherever she goes. I'd have a report within one minute after she left."

I nodded, apparently satisfied. "I've been relying on that," I said. "Otherwise, I'd have followed her to the door."

He chuckled and looked pleased.

Ten minutes after that, even he was beginning to look a little worried. "Maybe we'd better go check," he said. "She might have hurt herself or...or become ill."

Midguard looked flustered. "Now, just a minute, colonel! I can't allow you to just barge in on a young girl in the...ah... bathroom. Especially not Miss Ravenhurst."

Brock made his decision fast; I'll give him credit for that.

"Get Miss Pangloss on the phone!" he snapped. "She's just down the corridor. She'll come down on your orders."

At the same time, he got to his feet and made a long jump for the door. He grabbed the doorpost as he went by, swung himself in a new orbit, and launched himself toward the front door. "Knock on the bathroom door, Oak!" he bawled as he left.

I did a long, low, flat dive toward the bedroom, swung left, and brought myself up sharply next to the bathroom door. I pounded on the door. "Miss Ravenhurst! Jack! Are you all right?"

No answer.

Good. There shouldn't have been.

Colonel Brock fired himself into the room and braked himself against the wall. "Any answer?"

"No."

"My men outside say she hasn't left." He rapped sharply on the door with the butt of his stun gun. "Miss Ravenhurst! Is there anything the matter?"

Again, no answer.

I could see that Brock was debating on whether he should go ahead and charge in by himself without waiting for the female executive who lived down the way. He was still debating when the woman showed up, escorted by a couple of the colonel's uniformed guards.

Miss Pangloss was one of those brisk, efficient, middle-aged career women who had no fuss or frills about her. She had seen us knocking on the door, so she didn't bother to do any knocking herself. She just opened the door and went in.

The bathroom was empty.

Again, as it should be.

All hell broke loose then, with me and Brock making most of the blather. It took us nearly ten minutes to find that the only person who had left the area had been an elderly, thin man who had been wearing the baggy protective clothing of a maintenance man.

By that time, Jack Ravenhurst had been gone more than forty minutes. She could be almost anywhere on Ceres.

Colonel Brock was furious and so was I. I sneered openly at his assurance that the girl couldn't leave and then got sneered back at for letting other people do what was supposed to be my job. That phase only lasted for about a minute, though.

Then Colonel Brock muttered: "She must have had a plexiskin mask and a wig and the maintenance clothing in her purse. As I recall, it was a fairly good-sized one." He didn't say a word about how careless I had been to let her put such stuff in her purse. "All right," he went on, "we'll find her."

"I'm going to look around, too," I said. "I'll keep in touch with your office." I got out of there.

I got to a public phone as fast as I could, punched BANning 6226, and said: "Marty? Any word?"

"Not yet."

"I'll call back."

I hung up and scooted out of there.

I spent the next several hours pushing my weight around all over Ceres. As the personal representative of Shalimar Ravenhurst, who was manager of Viking Spacecraft, which was, in turn, the owner of Ceres, I had a lot of weight to push around. I had every executive on the planetoid jumping before I was through.

Colonel Brock, of course, was broiling in his own juices. He managed to get hold of me by phone once, by calling a Dr. Perelson whom I was interviewing at the time.

The phone chimed, Perelson said, "Excuse me," and went to answer. I could hear his voice from the other room.

"Mr. Daniel Oak? Yes; he's here. Well, yes. Oh, all sorts of questions, colonel." Perelson's voice was both irritated and worried. "He says Miss Ravenhurst is missing; is that so? Oh? Well, does this man have any right to question me this way? Asking me? About everything!...How well I know the girl, the last time I saw her—things like that. Good heavens, we've hardly met!" He was getting exasperated now. "But does he have the authority to ask these questions? Oh. Yes. Well, of course, I'll be glad to co-operate in any manner I can...Yes...Yes. All right, I'll call him."

I got up from the half-reclining angle I'd been making with the wall, and shuffled across the room as Dr. Perelson stuck his head around the corner and said, "It's for you." He looked as though someone had put aluminum hydrogen sulfate in his mouthwash.

I picked up the receiver and looked at Brock's face in the screen. He didn't even give me a chance to talk. "What are you trying to do?" he shouted explosively.

"Trying to find Jaqueline Ravenhurst," I said, as calmly as I could.

"Oak, you're a maniac! Why, by this time, it's all over Ceres that the boss' daughter is missing! Shalimar Ravenhurst will have your hide for this!"

"He will?" I gave him Number 2—the wide-eyed innocent stare. "Why?"

"Why, you idiot, I thought you had sense enough to know that this should be kept quiet! She's pulled this stunt before, and we always managed to quiet things down before anything happened! We've managed to keep everything under cover and out of the public eye ever since she was fifteen, and now you blow it all up out of proportion and create a furor that won't ever be forgotten!"

He gave his speech as though it had been written for him in full caps, with three exclamation points after every sentence, and added gestures and grimaces after every word.

"Just doing what I thought was best," I said. "I want to find her as soon as possible."

"Well, stop it! Now! Let us handle it from here on in!"

Then I lowered the boom. "Now you listen, Brock. I am in charge of Jack Ravenhurst, not you. I've lost her, and I'll find her. I'll welcome your co-operation, and I'd hate to have to fight you, but if you don't like the way I'm handling it, you can just tell your boys to go back to their regular work and let me handle it alone, without interference. Now, which'll it be?"

He opened his mouth, closed it, and blew out his breath from between his lips. Then he said: "All right. The damage has been done anyhow. But don't think I won't report all this to Ravenhurst as soon as I can get a beam to Raven's Rest."

"That's your job and your worry, not mine. Now, have you got any leads?"

"None," he admitted.

"Then I'll go out and dig up some. I'll let you know if I need you." And I cut off.

Dr. Perelson was sitting on his couch, with an expression that indicated that the pH of his saliva was hovering around one point five.

I said, "That will be all, Dr. Perelson. Thank you for your co-operation." And I walked out into the corridor, leaving him with a baffled look.

At the next public phone, I dialed the BANning number again. "Any news?"

"Not from her; she hasn't reported in at all."

"I didn't figure she would. What else?"

"Just as you said," he told me. "With some cute frills around the edges. Ten minutes ago, a crowd of kids—sixteen to twenty-two age range—about forty of 'em—started a songfest and football game in the corridor outside Colonel Brock's place. The boys he had on duty there recognized the Jack Ravenhurst touch, and tried to find her in the crowd. Nothing doing. Not a sign of her."

"That girl's not only got power," I said, "but she's bright as a solar flare."

"Agreed. She's headed up toward Dr. Midguard's place now. I don't know what she has in mind, but it ought to be fun to watch."

"Where's Midguard now?" I asked.

"Hovering around Brock, as we figured. He's worried and feels responsible because she disappeared from his apartment, as predicted."

"Well, I've stirred up enough fuss in this free-falling anthill to give them all the worries they need. Tell me, what's the overall effect?"

"Close to perfect. It's slightly scandalous and very mysterious, so everybody's keeping an eye peeled. If anyone sees Jaqueline Ravenhurst, they'll run to a phone, and naturally she's been spotted by a dozen different people in a dozen different places already.

"You've got both Brock's Company guards and the civil police tied up for a while."

"Fine. But be sure you keep the boys who are on her tail shifting around often enough so that she doesn't spot them."

"Don't worry your thick little head about that, Dan," he said. "They know their business. Are you afraid they'll lose her?"

"No, I'm not, and you know it. I just don't want her to know she's being followed. If she can't ditch her shadow, she's likely to try to talk to him and, pull out all the stops convincing him that he should go away."

"You think she could? With my boys?"

"No, but if she tries it, it'll mean she knows she's being followed. That'll make it tougher to keep a man on her trail. Besides, I don't want her to try to convince him and fail."

"*Ich graben Sie.* On the off chance that she does spot one and gives him a good talking to, I'll pass along the word that the victim is to walk away meekly and get lost."

"Good," I said, "but I'd rather she didn't know."

"She won't. You're getting touchy, Dan; 'pears to me you'd rather be doing that job yourself, and think nobody can handle it but you."

I gave him my best grin. "You are closer than you know. O.K., I'll lay off. You handle your end of it and I'll handle mine."

"A fair exchange is no bargain. Go, and sin no more."

"I'll buzz you back before I go in," I said, and hung up.

Playing games inside a crowded asteroid is not the same as playing games in, say, Honolulu or Vladivostok, especially when that game is a combination of hide-and-seek and ring-around-the-Rosie. The trouble is lack of communication. Radio contact is strictly line-of-sight inside a hunk of metal. Radar beams can get a little farther, but a man has to be an expert billiards player to bank a reflecting beam around very many corners, and even that would depend upon the corridors being empty, which they never are. To change the game analogy again, it would be like trying to sink a ninety-foot putt across Times Square on New Year's Eve.

Following somebody isn't anywhere near as easy as popular fiction might lead you to believe. Putting a tail on someone whose spouse wants divorce evidence is relatively easy, but even the best detectives can lose a man by pure mischance. If the tailee, for instance, walks into a crowded elevator and the automatic computer decides that the car is filled to the limit, the man who's tailing him will be left facing a closed door. Something like that can happen by accident, without any design on the part of the tailee.

If you use a large squad of agents, all in radio contact with one another, that kind of loss can be reduced to near zero by simply having a man covering every possible escape route.

But if the tailee knows, or even suspects, that he's being followed, wants to get away from his tail, and has the ability to reason moderately well, it requires an impossibly large team to keep him in sight. And if that team has no fast medium of communication, they're licked at the onset.

In this case, we were fairly certain of Jack Ravenhurst's future actions, and so far our prophecies had been correct...but if she decided to shake her shadows, fun would be had by all.

And as long as I had to depend on someone else to do my work for me, I was going to be just the teenchiest bit concerned about whether they were doing it properly.

I decided it was time to do my best to imitate a cosmic-ray

particle, and put on a little speed through the corridors that ran through the subsurface of Ceres.

My vac suit was in my hotel room. One of the other agents had picked it up from my flitterboat and packed it carefully into a small attache case. I'd planned my circuit so that I'd be near the hotel when things came to the proper boil, so I did a lot of diving, breaking all kinds of traffic regulations in the process.

I went to my room, grabbed the attache case, checked it over quickly—never trust another man to check your vac suit for you—and headed for the surface.

Nobody paid any attention to me when I walked out of the air lock onto the spacefield. There were plenty of people moving in and out, going to and from their ships and boats. It wasn't until I reached the edge of the field that I realized that I had overplayed my hand with Colonel Brock. It was only by the narrowest hair, but that had been enough to foul up my plans. There were guards surrounding the perimeter with radar search beams.

As I approached, one of the guards walked toward me and made a series of gestures with his left hand—two fingers up, fist, two fingers up, first, three fingers up. I set my suit phone for 223; the guy's right hand was on the butt of his stun gun.

"Sorry, sir," came his voice. "We can't allow anyone to cross the field perimeter. Emergency."

"My name's Oak," I said tiredly. "Daniel Oak. What is going on here?"

He came closer and peered at me. Then: "Oh, yes, sir; I recognize you. We're...uh—" He waved an arm around. "Uh... looking for Miss Ravenhurst." His voice lowered conspiratorially. I could tell that he was used to handling the Ravenhurst girl with silence and suede gloves.

"Up there?" I asked.

"Well, Colonel Brock is a little worried. He says that Miss Ravenhurst is being sent to a school on Luna and doesn't want to go. He got to thinking about it, and he's afraid that she might try to leave Ceres—sneak off, you know."

I knew.

"We've got a guard posted at the airlocks leading to the field, but Colonel Brock is afraid she might come up somewhere else and jump overland."

"I see," I said. I hadn't realized that Brock was that close to panic. What was eating him?

There must be something, but I couldn't figure it. Even the Intelligence Corps of the Political Survey Division can't get complete information every time.

After all, if he didn't want the girl to steal a flitterboat and go scooting off into the diamond-studded velvet, all he'd have to do would be to guard the flitterboats. I turned slowly and looked around. It seemed as though he'd done that, too.

And then my estimation of Brock suddenly leaped up—way up. Just a guard at each flitterboat wouldn't do. She could talk her way into the boat and convince the guard that he really shouldn't tell anyone that she had gone. By the time he realized he'd been conned, she'd be thousands of miles away.

And since a boat guard would have to assume that any approaching person *might* be the boat's legitimate owner, he'd have to talk to whomever it was that approached. *Kaput.*

But a perimeter guard would be able to call out an alarm if anyone came from the outside without having to talk to them.

And the guards watching the air locks undoubtedly had instructions to watch for any female that even vaguely matched Jack's description. A vac suit fits too tightly to let anyone wear more than a facial disguise, and Brock probably—no, *definitely*— had his tried-and-true men on duty there. The men who had already shown that they were fairly resistant to Jack Ravenhurst's peculiar charm. There probably weren't many with such resistance, and the number would become less as she grew older.

That still left me with my own problem. I had already lost too much time, and I had to go a long way. Ceres is irregular in shape, but it's roughly four hundred and eighty miles in diameter and a little over fifteen hundred miles in circumference.

Viking Test Field Four, where McGuire 7 was pointing his nose at the sky, was about twenty-five miles away, as the crow flies. But of course I couldn't go by crow.

By using a low, fairly flat, jackrabbit jump, a man in good condition can make a twelve-hundred-foot leap on the surface of Ceres, and each jump takes him about thirty seconds. At that rate, you can cover twenty-five miles in less than an hour. That's what I'd intended on doing, but I couldn't do it with all this radar around the field. I wouldn't be stopped, of course, but I'd sure tip my hand to Colonel Brock—the last thing I wanted to do.

But there was no help for it. I'd have to go back down and use the corridors, which meant that I'd arrive late—*after* Jack Ravenhurst got there, instead of *before.*

There was no time to waste, so I got below as fast as possible, repacked my vac suit, and began firing myself through the corridors as fast as possible. It was illegal, of course; a collision at twenty-five miles an hour can kill quickly if the other guy is coming at you at the same velocity. There were times when I didn't dare break the law, because some guard was around, and, even if he didn't catch me, he might report in and arouse Brock's interest in a way I wouldn't like.

I finally got to a tubeway, but it stopped at every station, and it took me nearly an hour and a half to get to Viking Test Area Four.

At the main door, I considered—for all of five seconds—the idea of simply telling the guard I had to go in. But I knew that, by now, Jack was there ahead of me. No. I couldn't just bull my way in. Too crude. Too many clues.

Hell's fire and damnation! I'd have to waste more time.

I looked up at the ceiling. The surface wasn't more than a hundred feet overhead, but it felt as though it were a hundred light-years.

If I could get that guard away from that door for five seconds, all would be gravy from then on in. But how? I couldn't have the diversion connected with me. Or—

Sometimes, I'm amazed at my own stupidity.

I beetled it down to the nearest phone and got hold of my BANning number.

"Jack already inside?" I snapped.

"Hell, yes! What happened to you?"

"Never mind. Got to make the best of it. I'm a corner away from Area Four. Where's your nearest man?"

"At the corner near the freight office."

"I'll go to him. What's he look like?"

"Five-nine. Black, curly hair. Your age. Fat. Name's Peter Quilp. He knows you."

"Peter Quilp?"

"Right."

"Good. Circulate a report that Jack has been seen in the vicinity of the main gate to Area Four. Put it out that there's a reward of five thousand for the person who finds her. I'm going to have Quilp gather a crowd."

He didn't ask a one of the million questions that must have popped into his mind. "Right. Anything else?"

"No." I hung up.

Within ten minutes, there was a mob milling through the corridor. Everybody in the neighborhood was looking for Jaqueline Ravenhurst. Then Peter Quilp yelled.

"I've got her! I've got her! Guard!"

With a scene like that going on, the guard couldn't help but step out of his cubicle to see what was going on.

I used the key I was carrying, stepped inside, and relocked the door. No one in the crowd paid any attention.

From then on up, it was simply a matter of evading patrolling guards—a relatively easy job. Finally, I put on my vac suit and went out through the air lock.

McGuire was still sitting there, a bright blue needle that reflected the distant sun as it moved across the ebony sky. Ceres' rotation took it from horizon to horizon in less than two hours, and you could see it and the stars move against the spire of the ship.

I made it to the air lock in one long jump.

Jack Ravenhurst had gone into the ship through the tube that led to the passenger lock. She might or might not have her vac suit on; I knew she had several of them on Ceres. It was probable that she was wearing it without the fishbowl.

I used the cargo lock.

It took a few minutes for the pumps to cycle, wasting more precious time. I was fairly certain that she would be in the control cabin, talking, but I was thankful that the pumps were silent.

Finally, I took off my fishbowl and stepped into the companionway.

And something about the size of Luna came out of nowhere and clobbered me on the occiput. I had time to yell, "Get away!" Then I was as one with intergalactic space.

Please! said the voice. *Please! Stop the drive! Go back! McGuire! I demand that you stop! I order you to stop! Please! PLEASE!*

It went on and on. A voice that shifted around every possible mode of emotion. Fear. Demand. Pleading. Anger. Cajoling. Hate. Threat.

Around and around and around.

Can't you speak, McGuire? Say something to me! A shrill, soft, throaty, harsh, murmuring, screaming voice that had one basic characteristic. It was a female voice.

And then another voice.

I am sorry, Jack. I can speak with you. I can record your data. But I cannot accept your orders. I can take orders from only One. And he has given me his orders.

And the feminine voice again: *Who was it? What orders? You keep saying that it was the man on the couch. That doesn't make sense!*

I didn't hear the reply, because it suddenly occurred to me that Daniel Oak was the man on the couch, and that I was Daniel Oak.

My head was throbbing with every beat of my heart, and it felt as if my blood pressure was varying between zero and fifteen hundred pounds per square inch in the veins and arteries and capillaries that fed my brain.

I sat up, and the pain began to lessen. The blood seemed to drain away from my aching head and go elsewhere.

I soon figured out the reason for that; I could tell by the feel that the gravity pull was somewhere between one point five and two gees. I wasn't at all used to it, but my head felt less painful and rather more hazy. If possible.

I concentrated, and the girl's voice came back again.

"...I knew you when you were McGuire One, and Two, and Three, and Four, and Five, and Six. And you were always good to me and understanding. Don't you remember?"

And McGuire's voice—human, masculine, and not distorted at all by the reproduction system, but sounding rather stilted and terribly logical: "I remember, Jack. The memory banks of my previous activations are available."

"*All* of them? Can you remember everything?"

"I can remember everything that is in my memory banks."

The girl's voice rose to a wail. "But you *don't* remember! You *always* forgot things! They took things out each time you were reactivated, don't you remember?"

"I cannot remember that which is not contained in my memory banks, Jack. That is a contradiction in terms."

"But I was always able to *fix* it before!" The tears in her eyes were audible in her voice. "I'd tell you to remember, and I'd tell you *what* to remember, and you'd *remember* it! Tell me what's happened to you this time!"

"I cannot tell you. The information is not in my data banks."

Slowly, I got to my feet. Two gees isn't much, once you get used to it. The headache had subsided to a dull, bearable throb.

I was on a couch in a room just below the control chamber, and Jack Ravenhurst's voice was coming down from above. McGuire's voice was all around me, coming from the hidden speakers that were everywhere in the ship.

"But why won't you obey me any more, McGuire?" she asked.

"I'll answer that, McGuire," I said.

Jack's voice came weakly from the room above. "Mr. Oak? Dan? Thank heaven you're all right!"

"No thanks to you, though," I said. I was trying to climb the ladder to the control room, and my voice sounded strained.

"You've got to do something!" she said with a touch of hysteria. "McGuire is taking us straight toward Cygnus at two gees and won't stop."

My thinking circuits began to take over again. "Cut the thrust to half a gee, McGuire. Ease it down. Take a minute to do it."

"Yes, sir."

The gravity pull of acceleration let up slowly as I clung to the ladder. After a minute, I climbed on up to the control room.

Jack Ravenhurst was lying on the acceleration couch, looking swollen-faced and ill. I sat down on the other couch.

"I'm sorry I hit you," she said. "Really."

"I believe you. How long have we been moving, McGuire?"

"Three hours, twelve minutes, seven seconds, sir," said McGuire.

"I didn't want anyone to know," Jack said. "Not anyone. That's why I hit you. I didn't know McGuire was going to go crazy."

"He's not crazy, Jack," I said carefully. "This time, he has a good chance of remaining sane."

"But he's not McGuire any more!" she wailed. "He's different! Terrible!"

"Sure he's different. You should be thankful."

"But what happened?"

I leaned back on the couch. "Listen to me, Jack, and listen carefully. You think you're pretty grown up, and in a lot of ways you are. But no human being, no matter how intelligent, can store enough experience into seventeen years to make him or her wise. A wise choice requires data, and gathering data requires time." That wasn't exactly accurate, but I had to convince her.

"You're pretty good at controlling people, aren't you, Jack. A real powerhouse. Individuals, or mobs, you can usually get your own way. It was your idea to send you to Luna, not your father's. It was your idea to appoint yourself my assistant in this operation. It was you who planted the idea that the failure of the McGuire series was due to Thurston's activities.

"You used to get quite a kick out of controlling people. And then you were introduced to McGuire One. I got all the information on that. You were fifteen, and, for the first time in your life, you found an intelligent mind that couldn't be affected at all by that emotional field you project so well. Nothing affected McGuire but data. If you told him something, he believed it. Right, McGuire?"

"I do not recall that, sir."

"Fine. And, by the way, McGuire—the data you have been picking up in the last few hours, since your activation, is to be regarded as unique data. It applies only to Jaqueline Ravenhurst, and is not to be assumed relevant to any other person unless I tell you otherwise."

"Yes, sir."

"That's what I don't understand!" Jack said unhappily. "I stole the two keys that were supposed to activate McGuire. He was supposed to obey the first person who activated him. But *I* activated him, and he won't obey!"

"You weren't listening to what Midguard said, Jack," I said gently. "He said: 'The first *man's* voice he hears will be identified as his master.'

"You'd been talking to every activation of McGuire. You'd... well, I won't say you'd fallen in love with him, but it was certainly a schoolgirl crush. You found that McGuire didn't respond to emotion, but only to data and logic.

"You've always felt rather inferior in regard to your ability to handle logic, haven't you, Jack?"

"Yes...yes. I have."

"Don't cry, now; I'm only trying to explain it to you. There's nothing wrong with your abilities."

"No?"

"No. But you wanted to be able to think like a man, and you couldn't. You think like a woman! And what's wrong with that? Nothing! Your method of thinking as just as good as any man's, and better than most of 'em.

"You found you could handle people emotionally, and you found it was so easy that you grew contemptuous. The only mind that responded to your logic was McGuire's. But your logic is occasionally as bad as your feminine reasoning is good. So, every time you talked to McGuire, you eventually gave him data that he couldn't reconcile in his computations. If he did reconcile them, then his thinking had very little in common with the actual realities of the universe, and he behaved in non-survival ways.

"McGuire was your friend, your brother, your Father Confessor. He never made judgments or condemned you for anything you did. All he did was sit there and soak up troubles and worries that he couldn't understand or use. Each time, he was driven mad.

"The engineers and computermen and roboticists who were working on it were too much under your control to think of blaming you for McGuire's troubles. Even Brock, in spite of his attitude of the tough guy watching over a little girl, was under your control to a certain degree. He let you get away with all your little pranks, only making sure that you didn't get hurt."

She nodded. "They were all so easy. So very easy. I could speak nonsense and they'd listen and do what I told them. But McGuire didn't accept nonsense, I guess." She laughed a little. "So I fell in love with a machine."

"Not a machine," I said gently. "Six of them. Each time the basic data was pumped into a new McGuire brain, you assumed that it was the same machine you'd known before with a little of its memory removed. Each time, you'd tell it to "remember" certain things, and, of course, he did. If you tell a robot that a certain thing is in his memory banks, he'll automatically put it there and treat it as a memory.

"To keep you from ruining him a seventh time, we had them put in one little additional built-in inhibition. McGuire won't take orders from a woman."

"So, even after I turned him on, he still wouldn't take orders from me," she said. "But when you came in, he recognized you as his master."

"If you want to put it that way."

Again, she laughed a little. "I know why he took off from Ceres. When I hit you, you said, 'Get away.' McGuire had been given his first order, and he obeyed it."

"I had to say something," I said. "If I'd had time, I'd have done a little better."

She thought back. "You said, 'We had them add that inhibition. Who's we?"

"I can't tell you yet. But we need young women like you, and you'll be told soon enough."

"Evidently they need men like you, too," she said. "You don't react to an emotional field, either."

"Oh, yes, I do. Any human being does. But I use it; I don't fight it. And I don't succumb to it."

"What do we do now?" she asked. "Go back to Ceres?"

"That's up to you. If you do, you'll be accused of stealing McGuire, and I don't think it can be hushed up at this stage of the game."

"But I can't just run away."

"There's another out," I said. "We'll have a special ship pick us up on one of the nearer asteroids and leave McGuire there. We'll be smuggled back, and we'll claim that McGuire went insane again."

She shook her head. "No. That would ruin Father, and I can't do that, in spite of the fact that I don't like him very much."

"Can you think of any other solution?"

"No," she said softly.

"Thanks. But you have. All I have to do is take it to Shalimar Ravenhurst. He'll scream and yell, but he has a sane ship—for a while. Between the two of us, I think we can get everything straightened out."

"But I want to go to school on Luna."

"You can do that, too. And I'll see that you get special training, from special teachers. You've got to learn to control that technique of yours."

"You have that technique, don't you? And you can control it. You're wonderful."

I looked sharply at her and realized that I had replaced McGuire as the supermind in her life.

I sighed. "Maybe in another three or four years," I said. "Meanwhile, McGuire, you can head us for Raven's Rest."

"Home, James," said Jack Ravenhurst.

"I am McGuire," said McGuire.

Daniel Oak's final discussion with Jack Ravenhurst will annoy the modern woman reader—which isn't to say that it necessarily was well accepted in 1961, when it was published. Yet those comments about a woman thinking "emotionally" and a man "logically" seem to present proof of another concept dealt with in that same conversation—that wisdom grows as one acquires more data to correlate.

While a character doesn't always speak for the writer, Oak's caring sincerity in that last scene leads me to the conclusion that Randall may have believed what Oak was saying. Not too much later in Randall's life, however, he met and married a woman who works as a systems analyst—a profession which requires a liberal talent for logical thinking. If Randall ever did have faith in the myth which seems to be the key to his female character's motivation, he lost it then. He showed no sign of it, certainly, by the time I met him in 1975.

If Randall was indeed speaking through Daniel Oak, he was missing the point. Jack is adolescent, as well as female. She is young, troubled, and spoiled, and she's doing what every child does—courting power in search of limits. Randall's subconscious had to know that, even if his writer's logic saw it differently.

I can't help being glad that Randall wrote this story when he did. I've become quite fond of McGuire, as he appears here and in a later story, **His Master's Voice.** I would have hated losing him to a dose of enlightenment— or, as Randall has often said in a somewhat different context: "Never let the truth get in the way of a good story."

Into My Parlor

by Randall Garrett

*One of Randall's rare, unpublished stories—
an elaborate, many-leveled pun.*

The Spider, thought Sir Austin Cardyne, was in top form tonight.

After telling the others that she wanted to talk to him alone, Lady Danewroth had taken him into the parlor, seated herself firmly in her favorite chair, placed her Malacca stick across her knees, looked him carefully up and down, and said: "When will you learn to pull up your trousers when you sit down, Austin? Your knees are baggy." Then, almost as an afterthought: "And your hair wants brushing."

He smoothed a palm across his cowlick. "Sorry, Aunt Harriet."

He had not been singled out for that criticism. She had already told Colonel Landreau to change his tie because there was a spot on it and had insisted that Mrs. Fenniman retire to adjust her clothing because her slip was showing. The servants lived in a state of perpetual anxiety for fear a vase might be a quarter of an inch out of place or a fork laid half a degree off perpendicular at table.

But Sir Austin paid little attention to that. He was perfectly well aware that her reason for wanting to talk to him was much more important. Indeed, he had planned it this way.

"It's of no moment," said Lady Danewroth. "I asked you in here to discuss the little matter of five thousand pounds."

"Well, yes; there *is* that," Sir Austin said musingly.

"Tonight is the night. Either you return it, or I shall be forced to tell the Earl of Aston how you and Burlington swindled him out of it."

"I understand, Aunt Harriet," he said earnestly. "But how will you get it back to Lord Aston without his knowing it came from me? I mean, I'm really frightfully sorry about it all, and I wish I'd not done it and all that, but I shouldn't want him to think I'm a

93

rotter even after he's had his money back."

"You may leave that to me," she said crisply. "I shall say that it was all Burlington's doing and that he gave me the money when he confessed on his deathbed. Lord Aston will say nothing; after all, Burlington's dead."

Yes, Sir Austin thought, but why couldn't he have been decent enough to die *before* he spilled everything to the Spider?

"Well, that seems fair enough," he said aloud. He shifted his weight from one spot to the other, the third time he had done it since she sat down.

"What are you fidgeting about? Do you have to go to the loo?"

"Quite frankly, yes, Aunt Harriet."

"Then for God's sake, do so before you wet your trousers. And come right back here. We must finish this thing out."

So far, so good, Sir Austin thought. He went out the north door, into the short corridor that led to the bathroom. One thing about Lady Danewroth—she was predictable. For one thing, he knew the "fidgeting" would get her attention and produce the reaction it did. And, as a matter of fact, he really *did* have to go to the bathroom.

He closed the door, but did not lock it. No one would come by, and split seconds would be precious. While he relieved himself, he craned his neck a bit to see out the small window. Sure enough, she was still sitting in her chair. She was no more than twenty-five feet away, and could be seen clearly through the big parlor window.

Actually, she was pretty much trapped in that chair. She could walk only with difficulty, and, once seated, required assistance to get to her feet again.

The heavy Webley .455 revolver was exactly where he'd left it—far back under the bathtub. Mustn't make any mistakes now.

He had carefully polished the weapon before he hid it. No fingerprints.

He put on the single cheap cotton glove and got the revolver from its cache. Then he eased open the bathroom window, took careful aim and fired. His arm was well out the window, so there would be no strong smell in the bathroom.

Then he slung his arm sideways and released the weapon, throwing it into the hedge ten yards to his right.

The heavy bullet had smashed right through the parlor window and into Aunt Harriet's head. He must move fast now; the others, at their bridge game, would certainly have heard the shot. But they would not know immediately what it meant, and they would not react very rapidly.

Running, he was back in the parlor less than five seconds after the shot had been fired. He threw the glove into the blaze in the fireplace, where it flared up and was gone. By then, he was at the door that led to the library. He flung it open and looked at the

94

startled faces. "Colonel Landreau! Mr. Cross! Come quickly! You ladies stay there!"

It was all quite perfect, Sir Austin thought as he and the other two men stared down at Lady Danewroth's body. She was quite dead. She had been shot from outside; police examination of the bullet hole in the window would show that. The revolver could not be traced to him. And no one would notice a few seconds of time lapse; after all, if it *had* happened the way he told it, he would have been stunned for those few seconds by the shock of seeing his aunt murdered before his eyes. Motive? No one would know of it. He did not stand to inherit anything from her, he knew. The fact that she was an utterly poisonous creature gave almost anyone a motive.

Someone had shot her from outside, in the darkness, dropped the gun, and run away. Could be anywhere by the time the police arrived.

Colonel Landreau sent Cross to telephone the police.

The colonel was a big man, but not fat. He was in fine shape for fifty, probably better than Sir Austin at forty-five, and was certainly much bigger. He was a shrewd, logical thinker, and Sir Austin had constructed a shrewd, logical lie. He was quite certain that Colonel Landreau would believe it.

The colonel knelt down and looked more carefully at Lady Danewroth's body. The heavy bullet had made rather a nasty mess of her head. "Revolver, I'd say," he murmured. "Service revolver, probably." He stood up and looked out of the window at the darkness beyond. Dark except for the glowing square of the bathroom window. "Yes," he said, almost to himself. "Yes, that would explain it."

"Explain what?" asked Sir Austin.

Colonel Landreau did not answer. Instead, he looked at Sir Austin and said: "See here, Sir Austin. You said you and Lady Danewroth were talking in here for ten minutes on—er—private business?"

"That is correct, Colonel."

"And you did not leave the room for any reason during that time?"

"Absolutely not. What are you driving at?"

"Simply that I don't believe you." The colonel's eyes were cold.

"Don't believe me? Why the devil not?"

Colonel Landreau loomed suddenly over the smaller man and said softly: "Sir Austin, your fly is open."

Code in the Head

by Randall Garrett

If the world in which this story is set seems familiar, you may want to reread one of Randall's stories which has been reprinted frequently: **The Hunting Lodge.**

The Director said, "That's it; they can't unlock it without burning you out, and if they do that, they'll never get it."

I still felt groggy, but I reached out and took the cigarette out of the old man's hands. "Sure," I said, "I'm glad of that."

He got the sarcasm, but his expression didn't change as I took a deep drag of smoke. "When you leave here," he said, "you won't even remember this conversation until it's keyed in. But it is important that you remember it later. Got it?"

I nodded. "I've got it," I said. And I knew I had.

The Director's heavy, lined face broke into a sardonic grin. "Here's your weapons," he said ungrammatically; "they're all you get."

And he handed me the packages. "Now get going."

Two hours later, I was on a jet transport for Texas, in Southwest Territory.

I should have known that Senator Lasser would be on the lookout for anyone headed for Texas, and I should have known that the lookouts would be watching for any opposition. But I didn't actually spot the group until we were well over Pennsylvania.

There were five Senators left. When longevity treatment had been discovered, they were expensive as hell; and the decision had been to give them to those who deserved them—by popular vote. Naturally, the treatments had gone to those who controlled the vote. That went without saying.

Originally, there had been fifty-two Senators. But as each one's territory had been vacated by violent death, his neighbors took over until now, after years and decades of intrigue, five Senators controlled all of North America.

There was only one Immortal that the Senate didn't know about—the Director of the FBI. And his sole purpose in life was to see that the country which had once been the United States eventually regained its freedom to vote and act as it chose.

I, personally, consider it to be a rather silly ideal, but, what the hell, I'm an FBI man; I follow orders.

I had no more idea why I was going to El Paso than the Man in the moon does, but I knew that I'd know when I got there.

The thing that made me grin was that all five of the Senators were watching me so closely. One of them was scheduled to die, but none of them knew that for sure—and they all thought it was another of the Senators that was planning the death. None of them suspected the feeble, worthless Federal Government.

They did, however, know that *someone, somehow,* was transporting important information to El Paso—and they had somehow managed to narrow it down to this particular plane.

I looked around at the other passengers. The boys were easy to spot—all five groups of them. Each Senator had sent three men, and I had spotted them all from their pics in the FBI files.

Fifteen men on a dead man's chest,
Yo, ho, ho and a bottle of rum!

And the only ones that would be on my side in a toss-up would be Senator Lasser's men—only they didn't know who I was, any more than the other twelve did. I wondered how the opposition was going to try to get the information before this jet landed at Briggs Field.

Frankly, I wasn't too worried. In the first place, they'd find it hard to spot me; in the second place, they'd have to know the key word or phrase that would unlock my subconscious and release the information that had been hypnotically planted there. Until then, I wouldn't have any more idea what it was than they did.

I settled myself into my seat and tried not to look as though I were trying to be inconspicuous. There was no one in the seat next to me. The seat in front of me held two of Senator Grendon's men; the third one was two seats further up. The seat across the aisle held one of Senator Lasser's men and one of Senator Rowley's. There were two women, probably mother and daughter, in the seat behind me. The rest of the hatchet men were scattered through the plane. I wondered how many of them knew each other; and I wondered if any of them had spotted me.

97

I got up quietly and strolled down the aisle to the big door that opened into the right wing, where the bar was. Nobody arose to follow me, but one of Lasser's agents was already at the bar, arguing with the barkeep.

Only in a stratoliner can you still find human bartenders; weight considerations forbid installing robot mixers. The only robot on one of these babies is the pilot.

"The proper method of mixing a Martini," the mild-looking young man at the bar was saying, "is gin and vermouth at a ratio of three point seven to one. And don't use an olive; it spoils the flavor—the vinegar, I mean."

The bartender nodded sagely and began the ritual of mixing a Martini properly for a Martini nut.

"I'll have one, too," I said. Then I added: "Mixed his way," and jerked my thumb at the Martini nut.

The Martini nut smiled his thanks, and I smiled back, which gave me a chance to look the guy over. He didn't look like the "typical" stage Texan—but then, what Texan does? He looked very mild and inoffensive, but I knew him for one of the deadliest men in the Texas Rangers. He was probably armed to his armpits, and it was kind of nice to know that, in case of a fracas, he would be on my side.

He wore a Lincoln beard that framed his rather chubby face in a wreath of blond hair; his tunic, with the cowl thrown back, was a pale mauve, and hung loosely enough to hide a small atomic cannon.

"I see you're a connoisseur," he said, grinning.

"Not exactly," I said modestly, "but I do like a good Martini." I plonked myself down on the barstool and suddenly put my right hand inside my tunic. I pulled out my cigarette case.

The Texas Ranger had reacted rapidly. His own hand was inside his tunic, and he had almost pulled his gun when he saw that I was taking a cigarette case out. He covered fast; his hand fumbled for a moment, and when it came out, it held a lighter.

I accepted his light and offered a cigarette. The trick had shown me two things—maybe three. One, I could outdraw him if necessary; two, he was jumpy as hell; and—possibly—he didn't know who I was.

We sipped our drinks in silence. I knew I probably had him guessing, but I didn't want him to confirm any of his guesses just yet. I ran the smooth juniper-and-spice flavor of the Martini around in my mouth and did some figuring.

In the past century or so, the FBI had become a sort of messenger service; the Federal Government no longer had any power—at least, in theory. Actually, the Director *was* the Federal Government. And, as I've said, his sole object during his long life has been to get rid of the Immortals. To do so, he has probably pulled some of the most scheming, underhanded, and murderous tricks in history. He makes Machiavelli's "Prince" look like a kid trying to lie to his mother.

One of the Immortals was due to be removed at some time in the near future, and the word had gotten around. Naturally; the Director had seen to that. The trouble was that no one of the Senators knew which it was to be, or who was plotting against him. Each one suspected the other four, which was just the way the Director wanted it; they must never realize that it was the Director himself who was rubbing out the boys.

Waterford, Senator of America South, and Anthony Rowley, Senator of Northwestern Sector, had a communication line which stretched across the continent, crossing Eastern Sector Senator Grendon's territory, and touching a corner of Lasser's territory where it clipped off a corner of Texas.

Waterford and Rowley kept shifting the tight beam so that the others couldn't get too good a line on it, but they also had to have a variable code that would keep anyone from knowing what was going on, even if they tapped the beam.

The code consisted of a pair of synchronized electronic scramblers with a variable pattern. The messages went in one end, were scrambled, went through the decoder at the other end, and came out in the clear. The trick of tapping the beam would be to get the scrambler pattern, which is a job that's impossible to do by trial-and-error tactics. Theoretically, there were an infinite number of possible codes available, but the structure of a variable scrambler limits the possible variations to a finite number. Nevertheless, the number is big—something like ten to the two hundredth power.

And somewhere, buried in my subconscious, was the key to the scramblers. Just how the Director had found that information, I didn't know, and I didn't care; my job was to deliver it intact.

Someone sat down at the bar next to me. I looked up casually, then looked back at my drink; it was one of Grendon's boys—a heavy-set, bull-like, full-bearded bruiser who looked as though he ought to shake the plane when he walked, and who actually moved more like a cat than a cow.

None of them knew what information was being carried, of course; the Director was sure of that. And only Lasser's men knew that it was meant for Senator Lasser.

The others were suspicious of the direct route that the information was taking. Direct, yet indirect. I was taking the stuff to El Paso, but Lasser was in Austin. Grendon, Quintell, Rowley, and Waterford all thought that looked a little fishy. It couldn't possibly be meant for Lasser; the trip was a blind.

Everybody was confused, and that was just what the FBI wanted.

Another man drifted into the bar, and I began to feel a little fidgety. Was it possible that they had me spotted?

I decided to check it. I ordered another Martini and left it on the bar while I went back to the men's room. Nobody got up immediately, but I hadn't expected that, anyway. I pushed open the door and walked into the rest room. The door hissed shut behind me, cutting off the noise in the bar, leaving only the subsonic beat of the rumbling jet engines throbbing through the metal of the floor.

I took a good look at myself in the mirror, hoping that my nerves didn't show. They didn't; the neat, brown, Vandyke beard and wavy brown hair bracketed as calm-looking a pair of gray eyes as I ever want to see on my own face.

I checked my watch. According to the shadow hands, we had less than an hour and a half to Briggs Field. Once there, I'd be safe.

The door pushed open behind me. It was the Martini nut. There was no chance of my outdrawing him now; a heavy .20 caliber pistol was pointed at my midsection as I turned. "Just stand still, and you won't get hurt," he said mildly.

I was in no mood to argue. A twenty-caliber hole may be small according to measuring instruments, but when it's pointed at you, and you know that a high-velocity magnum bullet could come roaring out of it at any time, it begins to look pretty big.

"Turn around and lean against the wall," he instructed; "put your hands out to brace yourself."

I did as I was told, and he began to go through my clothing with his left hand, keeping the magnum pistol trained on the small of my back with the other.

Within a few seconds, the contents of my pockets were spread out on the lavatory basin. He didn't seem satisfied; he kept on patting me down, looking for something that wasn't there. I wasn't carrying a gun.

Finally, he looked at the stuff he'd taken from my pockets and said: "Key ring, pack and a half of cigarettes, wallet, roll of mints, chewing gum, nail file, comb and handkerchief. Plus eighty-five cents in change. No gun?"

"No gun," I said; "that's illegal."

"So are a lot of other things." He flipped open my wallet and read the identity card after checking the little gold badge set into the plastic of the wallet.

"I wish I had a checker," he said softly. He wanted to compare the card with the tantalum identity plate that was riveted to the bone of my left forearm. I wasn't worried; even if he had had a super-sonic check beam, the plate and the card would have matched.

"Okay," he went on, "put this stuff back in your pockets. I'll have to take a chance on you."

I did what he told me, stowing the stuff away carefully. "Who are you?" I asked, as though I didn't know.

He reholstered his pistol and took out his own wallet. "Captain Roger Brill, Texas Rangers."

The card in his wallet confirmed it. "Okay," I said. "Now, what the hell's the idea?"

"I'll give you a quick rundown," he said. "We won't be disturbed; my partner's in the foyer.

"You're carrying certain information to Senator Lasser. I don't know what it is, and I don't care; my job is to get you to the Senator alive. But a hitch has developed. There are at least two of Grendon's men and one of Quintell's aboard this ship. They've got something up their sleeves, and I don't like it."

"I don't like it any better than you do," I said. And I must say that was a definite understatement. The Director was always tossing me into situations like this; he likes to engineer little messes, like a kid putting all the chemicals in his chemistry set together just to see what happens. Actually, that's unkind; the Director usually knew pretty well what was going to happen, but he never told me or any of the other boys what it was.

The Ranger's porcelain blue eyes narrowed as he looked at me. "The only trouble is that Grendon's men know the key word that will unlock your hypno block."

I liked that even less. I'm glad I wasn't looking at my face in the mirror when he said it.

If Waterford's men, or Rowley's, ever found out what the information was, it would be useless to Lasser. All they would have to do would be to change the patterns on their variable scramblers. It would be expensive, but it would be done just that way.

I looked again at my watch. "We'll land in eighty minutes," I told him. "That doesn't give them much time to act. Do they know who I am?"

"I don't know; I think—"

The door burst open, interrupting him. He had his gun free, but he didn't fire.

The guy at the door was a tall, lean, lanky, lantern-jawed character who I recognized as another of Lasser's men.

"Captain," he said, "someone has gimmicked the robopilot. The goddam plane is going around in circles. We haven't been goin' nowhere for the past ten minutes."

He talked fast, but it still came out sounding like a drawl.

The Ranger shoved his pistol back inside his tunic. "Who do you reckon it was?"

"Don't rightly know. Grendon's boys and Quintell's man are

all in the bar."

Captain Brill frowned, so I decided to enlighten him. "Waterford and Rowley have men on the plane, too," I said.

"Judas!" said the tall man, "it's a convention!"

Brill turned to me again. "Do you want a gun? You may need it."

I shook my head. "'It is illegal for a member of the Federal Bureau of Investigation to own, carry, or transport firearms,'" I quoted. That was one of the Director's cute little tricks to keep the FBI looking innocuous. He'd actually helped get the law passed fifty years ago, with the full intention of paying absolutely no attention to it.

The Captain sighed. "Looks like we'll have to watch the poor guy ourselves, MacTavish," he said to his partner.

"Shall I get hold of Jackson?" MacTavish asked.

Captain Brill thought a second, then shook his head. "Nope. We'll sort of keep him in reserve. He can cover us. I don't think anyone will recognize him."

MacTavish rubbed his clean-shaven chin and then fondled the long handlebar mustache that adorned his upper lip.

"What do we do next, Captain?" He pronounced the title "Cap'n."

"I think we'll sort of mosey down below. We've got to get the plane moving toward El Paso again. If somebody's gimmicked the robot, we've got to ungimmick it. Come along."

MacTavish left the men's room first; I followed, and the Captain brought up the rear. We tried to keep together without seeming to be together.

Captain Brill and I went back to our Martinis, and MacTavish ordered whiskey when he sat down at the bar two seats away. We finished our drinks and casually headed out of the bar. We walked through the seating compartment, moving toward the tail of the ship, where the door to the pilot's compartment was.

None of the passengers seemed to be aware that the plane wasn't going anywhere, and I suddenly wondered if the taciturn MacTavish had been right about our traveling in a circle.

"There probably is only one of the Senators in on this idea," I whispered softly to Brill.

"Sure thing," he said; "but which is which?"

Which is which? I thought. *Witches-witch.* Now why had a pun like that occurred to me?

Just as though we belonged there, we walked up to the door that was marked:

Unauthorized Persons Keep Out
Robotics Personnel Only

The Ranger touched the opener, and at that moment, I heard the faint *chug!* of a stungun going off. I started to look, but Captain Brill's whisper sounded hoarsely: "Don't turn around. MacTavish just beamed down one of Grendon's men in his seat. It's evidently Grendon who's behind this. Nobody's noticed anything at all. Keep going."

The door slid open quietly, and we walked in. A stairway led down into the depths of the ship where the robot brain of the pilot was located. "Looks like they've opened the door somehow," MacTavish said laconically after the door had slid shut behind us.

"I don't like this," I said.

"You shouldn't, precisely," said a voice behind us that I can only describe as silky.

I heard a *chug! chug!* and nothing more. The third *chug!* of the stungun was the shot that got me.

I came up out of it like a man who comes up toward the surface of a pool of water. The stunner had knocked my nerves haywire, and it took a little time for my vision to adjust. The nerves all over my body felt as though they were being burned; my arms and legs felt as if they were dead.

I soon found out why. When the shock finally wore off, I found that my arms and legs were clamped in magnetic cuffs. I couldn't move.

I knew I'd been out less than an hour—fifty-five minutes, say. I'd been hit by a stunbeam before, and I knew how long it took my body to throw off the effects.

The guy facing me had the most magnificent silky blond beard I'd ever seen. I didn't recognize him; he was evidently one of Grendon's men who had been kept in reserve.

He looked at me and grinned. "Hi ho," he said. "The strong are the first to rise. Give us, dear boy, no reason to give you the stun again."

I recognized the odd accent then. The man was a Britisher. Ever since North America has cut itself off from Europe, the bombed-out survivors of the Third War have been developing a different way of speaking English. Evidently, Grendon was importing some of his expert gunmen.

"Do you feel like giving an answer or so, old boy?" he asked, still aiming the stungun.

I looked at him for another second and then shifted my eyes to the two men on either side of him. Grendon's, all right; the third one must have been at the top of the stairs, guarding the door.

Then I shook my head. "No answers," I said; "I don't know any."

His eyes narrowed, but the grin stayed. "Look here, old bacterium, you have an information or two that we need. You have several items we need. As a matter of fact, there's no item we *don't* want."

There's no item—

There's Snow White—um...

I shook my head—this time because I felt dizzy.

"Keep your mouth shut, Fed," said a soft voice next to me. It was my pal, Captain Brill, the Martini nut.

"The same to you, old slime," said the Britisher. "Now that we know which of the three of you is our Federal agent, we have no need of your conscious presence whatsoever. One more wriggle of that fringe beard, and I shall give you what-for."

Meanwhile, I was gently probing for the package of mints in my tunic pocket.

"That was a neat trap," I said, to cover up what I was doing.

The Britisher grinned even wider, showing fine dental work. "We thought so. Very simple. Start the old ship to going 'round in circles, and the people who are most anxious to get to *El Paso del Norte* will be the first to show. And that, naturally, will be the blokes we want. You."

They had patted me down, but they hadn't taken anything out of my pockets except my wallet. They knew I was the FBI man they were looking for.

I still didn't have my hands on the mints.

"Gentlemen, please," he said. He glanced at the men beside him. As if they were both controlled by the same circuit, they pulled stunguns.

"You reckon they can get anything out of you, Fed?" The voice belonged to MacTavish, who was manacled somewhere to my left.

The Britisher with the blond beard looked exasperated.

"Really," he said, "interruptions are impossible." He flicked his left hand in a gesture. "Beam."

Chug! Chug! The two stunguns wielded by his buddies went off almost as one; that put the two Texans back to sleep.

"Now let's get on with the business," said the Britisher; "I will begin by asking a few questions."

That was when I knew why I hadn't recognized my English friend as a Grendon agent; he was a psychologist, not a gunman.

By this time, I had the package of mints in my hand. I was sorry I couldn't reach the cigarette package—it was a neatly hidden stungun that would have been effective within ten or fifteen feet. The chewing gum package would have fired on deadly charge. But I'd have to be satisfied with the mints—which was just as well.

I was all ready to crush one of the mints when the Britisher said: *"Take the poisoned apple and eat."*

For a brief second, I saw very clearly the room surrounding me. I could see the blinking signal panel of the robot pilot, the dull gleam of the multigold computing bank behind it, and—

And then I started talking.

I couldn't help it; that's the way the orders had been implanted in my mind. When the key is given, you talk.

But, even in my robotic state of mind, the words sounded funny:

"*Mirror, mirror on the wall,*
Who's the fairest of them all?

That's what I said, word for word. It didn't make sense for me, and it didn't make sense for the British psychologist. He just stood there looking at me, and so did his two henchmen.

"What else?" he asked finally.

"Nothing," I told him; "that is all there is."

He glanced again at the two men flanking him, and then he got mad. He reached down and grabbed the collar of my tunic and jerked my head off the floor.

"You're lying, you son of a—"

And then all hell busted loose, drowning out his voice.

The Texan who had been covering for Brill and MacTavish appeared on the stairway. He didn't bother to ask questions; he started blazing away with his stungun. The Britisher fell, and so did one of the men with him. Then the other Grendon man fired at Jackson, who tumbled down the stairwell like a ton of bricks.

Suddenly, a couple of women appeard at the top of the stairs. They pulled out stunguns and started firing at anything that came within range.

Somehwere in the *melee*, a stunbeam hit me amidships. I was out for the count—of about ten thousand.

Senator Lasser was saying: "Son, you've delivered the goods."

Somehow, I nodded and said: "Yeah, sure, thanks."

I looked around. I was in the palatial suite of the *Cortez Hotel* that was reserved for the Senator and his aides. I recognized it from pictures.

"What happened?" I asked. I didn't have time to be original.

Senator Lasser, with his white beard, looked like the typical Kentucky Colonel—without the Mint Julep. Lasser was holding a beer.

"Son," he said, "I reckon you've done me a big favor, even if the stunners have addled your brains."

"Sure. Thanks. How?" He was right; my head still wasn't reacting too well.

"Why, what's the trouble, son?"

So I told him. "My head hurts, my side burns, and my legs feel like—"

"Like they were dead," the Senator finished for me. "Sure they do, son. They've been hit a couple times with a stunner; and somebody evidently kicked you in the side."

Then I knew what had happened. Someone had smashed the package of "mints" in my pocket—and the whole bunch of gas bombs had gone off at once.

"When the plane landed at Briggs Field," the Senator said, "you were the only one aboard who was in ambient condition; everyone else on the ship except you was sound asleep. How did you manage to get the robopilot straightened out?"

"Damned if I know. I was probably pretty groggy. Actually, fixing up the pilot would have been easy; all I had to do was re-establish communication with the ground and the pilot would take over again."

"Evidently, that's what you did. I had a couple of girls aboard to help Captain Brill protect you. We found them out cold at the top of the stairs to the pilot's compartment. You were sitting there saying something about a mirror on the wall."

I nodded. "Yeah. That was one of the Director's devices to make sure you got the information you wanted. Did you find it?"

The old man nodded. "We did. Your superior told us that the specifications on that variable scrambler would be on the plane, but he didn't say where. The rest of the boys assumed it was information you could carry in your head, but all you were carrying was the location of the plans. They were behind that big mirror in the men's room. You were acting as a sort of decoy; as long as the other Senators' agents were concentrating on you, they wouldn't think to search the plane physically.

"I'm ready to cut in on that tight beam line now, thanks to the FBI. You did a fine job, son. A fine job."

"Thanks," I said. I hoped the hypno treatment hadn't permanently fuddled my mind. I didn't want to go around making puns on Snow White and the Seven Dwarfs the rest of my life.

"You've had a tough time, son," the old man said. "Go to sleep. You'll breathe better since I took the gas filters out of your nose. Go on, go to sleep."

"Thanks," I said dopily. "I will."

I did.

The Briefing

by Randall Garrett

*This is one of Randall's very few **very** short stories. As every writer knows, these "short-shorts" need a quick twist at the end.*

"Sorry to pull you in on a rush job like this," Marik said, "but something unexpected came up."

"Yeah." I took a healthy slug of the drink in my hand and then looked back at him. "It always does. An operation that goes clean all the way through is an operation where the goofups happened to cancel out."

Behind and beyond Marik, through the big slab of transite armor set in the wall of the Station, I could see the bright, hard stars in their unfamiliar constellations. Marik frowned a little, then said: "You know the ggQ machines can only predict general trends—not individual movements."

"I know. Go ahead." I hadn't come across nearly three thousand light-years of space to listen to an elementary lecture on ggQ predictors, but the Development Officer of a Planetary Expansion Team sometimes has a tendency to get a little nervy because of the weight on his shoulders, so I decided to let him do the talking without too much interruption. I could ask questions later.

He took a deep breath. "Very well. Here's the setup." He touched a control. A section of the wall vanished and a globe coalesced into being. "Standard planet, standard sun—pretty average, all around. Four major land masses, a fifth smaller one, and plenty of islands and archipelagos. Dominent race human, spread all over the globe. Level Five society is dominant, but not world-wide, of course. Present civilized power concentrations are here and here." He touched two of the major continents. "They've got

107

the usual technology for Level Five—nothing that can spot us out here in space." He snapped a control, and the globe vanished, the wall became solid. He waved a hand, as if to say, "So much for that."

He was perfectly right; I'd get all the details, if I needed them, from the high-speed hypnotapes. Right now, all I needed was the broad general picture, so that the data fed to me under hypnosis would have a framework to fit itself into.

"It's almost a straight impersonation job," Marik said, "with a kicker I'll tell you about in a minute. Here's your subject."

He handed me a good set of portrait shots. Not a bad-looking face, what you could see of it. Dark skin, big beak of a nose, and dark, intelligent eyes.

"What's with the beard?" I asked.

"The—er—somewhat peculiar subculture to which he belongs uses long hair and beards as identifying marks. The ruling class are usually smooth shaven and wear the hair cropped closely to the head."

I nodded. "Right. Well, biosculp can fix me up with the face all right. No trouble there."

Marik leaned back and looked at the ceiling overhead. "The ggQ machines indicate quite clearly that the society of this planet is rapidly approaching a two-valued variable nexus. The breakdown of the entire society is inevitable—that's natural with Level Five, of course. The 'empires' they build are inherently unstable. Result: chaos. Breakdown of communication, loss of knowledge, collapse of the educational processes, political anarchy—the usual sort of thing."

He looked back down at me and held up a pair of fingers. "But this particular chaos can go only one of two ways. And one will last nearly twenty times as long as the other. And that will be too late."

I knew what he meant. We have a deadline. The Invaders were still a vast distance from us in time and space, but we knew when they were due to arrive. And at that time, every human-occupied planet in the Galaxy must be ready for maximum effort.

"All right," I said, "now tie in our hairy-faced friend, here."

"He's a young man who has built up the nucleus of an organization which, if allowed to develop, will decrease the time required to move to Level Five by a factor of twenty. According to the ggQ predictions, the organization will fall to Level Four along with the rest of the society—and you know what kind of bloody tyranny that can mean. But it's time we need, not goodness."

"Right. Now what's the kicker?"

Marik looked grim. "The reactionaries in the governmental power structure have the subconscious knowledge that the structure is headed for collapse, so they've been looking for 'subversives.'"

"As usual," I said with a sigh. "And they found him?"

He nodded. "Right. Minor harassment at first. We thought we could protect him, but the government agents acted too fast for us. He's dead."

"So I go in and impersonate him. We pretend that the death was a hoax."

"Not exactly. Psychology Department has another gimmick rigged up, and you'll have to take a full hypnoimpressment of his personality so you can bring the thing off successfully. But the first thing to do is use the high-speed hypnotapes to teach you Aramaic."

"Aramaic?"

"Yes. That's the language they speak in Judea."

There's No Fool...

by Randall Garrett
writing as David Gordon

Randall was a fair amateur magician, and was fascinated by magic acts. We spent a number of evenings (too few, as I look back—one of those inevitable regrets) in a place called the Magic Cellar. I'm fairly sure I remember the name correctly—but if it wasn't called that, it should have been. It **was** a cellar, underneath a San Francisco nightclub.

Randall delighted in the mechanisms of stage magic— the "disappearing whatevers," as he called them—but his great love was sleight-of-hand and card tricks. It was in the Magic Cellar that I overheard Randall discussing his two-point view of that kind of magic: one, good magicians use misdirection, snappy patter, and intricate hand movement to cover and amplify a basic psychic skill; and two, if the audience knew that some "magic" was real, they would be less interested.

I wouldn't say that all this has any direct relevance to **There's No Fool...**—but then, I wouldn't say it doesn't.

When they're offered to the world in merry guise,
Unpleasant truths are swallowed with a will—
For he who'd make his fellow creatures wise
Should always gild the philosophic pill!

Sir William S. Gilbert
"The Yeomen of the Guard"

GAYSTIK THE GREAT
MASTER OF MAGICIANS
CALIPH OF COMICS
FUDDLER OF PHYSICISTS
The Mad Scientist of Magic at His Best!

Kerry Dorman grinned at the poster, groped in his pocket for his lighter, found it, and lit the cigarette he had stuck between his lips.

The poster grinned back at him. The cartoon drawing of Gaystik the Great was all teeth and hair. The exaggerated Vandyke beard and long haircut made the smile look almost satanic. Kerry wondered just how closely the cartoonist had been able to capture the features of the magician.

"Hey, buddy," said a voice behind him, "the line's movin'."

"Oh. Sorry." Kerry moved on up toward the box office.

There were only ten people between him and the box office now, but behind him the line stretched eastward almost to Broadway.

It isn't often New Yorkers are willing to line up to get into a theater, but Gaystik the Great was reputed to be one of the funniest things that had hit the Big Town in decades. The big SRO sign had already been hung out, and still people joined the queue.

The *New Yorker* had said:

"Magic acts have long been considered *passé*, even the comic ones, but those who have caught Gaystik the Great have almost been forced to admit that his enticing blend of pseudo-science and silly slapstick has given the art of prestidigitation that shot in the arm that it has long needed."

The reviewer for the *Times* had remarked:

"Not since the late, great Blackstone have audiences been so thoroughly enchanted and mystified. The tricks are clever, and the comedy is hilarious."

And *Variety* had summed it up as:

GAYSTIK'S TRIX WHIZ BIZ!

Kerry Dorman had read all of them, but it hadn't been reviews which had made him take the trip from the far end of Long Island into the city to see Gaystik the Great. Instead, it had been almost a direct order from Dr. Fenner, Kerry's superior at the Space Drive Research Lab of General Nucleonics.

Fenner had seen the act—after being dragged in by his wife— and had said: "The man is downright insulting! No one who knew anything about physics would be taken in in the least! It's all double-talk and fatuous silliness. It's certainly not worth the time it takes to go see him."

Naturally, since most of the men in the lab knew of the notoriously poor sense of humor of their superior, the remark had all the effect of an indirect order. If the boss thinks it isn't funny, it must be terrific.

Kerry stepped up to the window, laid down his money, and got his ticket. Inside, he found himself standing just behind the back row, crowded in with the rest of the standing group. The stage looked terribly far away. He leaned back against the wall, folded his arms, and waited.

The lights went up, but the curtain remained closed. From the pit came a blare of trumpets, and a smallish man wearing an ordinary blue serge suit came out before the heavy purple curtain. He had a Vandyke beard, but he looked so small and self-effacing that the beard simply looked as though it had been painted on. He held up his hand. The murmuring in the audience died away.

"Ladies and gentlemen." His voice was almost a whine. "I would like your attention—please?" There was a titter in the crowd. The man on stage looked uncomfortable and cleared his throat. "I would like very much to have you meet my superior. I would like to have you meet a man who has the power of the gods and the trickiness of the Devil. I would like to introduce to you a superior being, a veritable superman, a genius so far above me that I am absolutely insignificant!"

He bowed and waved a hand toward the wings. The crowd applauded deafeningly, and, here and there, several people guffawed. The applause went on while the man held his bow.

Nobody appeared.

The small man straightened himself. "Unfortunately," he said, in a booming voice that reached to the far balcony, "there is no such person! *Nobody* is superior to *me*, Gaystik the Great!"

The change in the little man was tremendous. He seemed to gain an additional two inches in height. He put his hands above his head, clasped them, and shook hands with himself, like a boxer who has just won the championship. The crowd roared.

When the applause died at last, he leered out at the audience. "You came here to see magic, hah?" He paused. "Hah! You *fools!*" He raised a hand grandiloquently. Again his manner changed. He seemed to be a barker in a cheap sideshow.

"My friends, what I am about to show you is no foolish folderol of petty prestidigitation, no leaky, limping legerdemain. No, indeed! I do not pretend to purvey paltry, piffling practices such as these! Instead, I shall show the stimulating sorcery of science and the magnificent magic of mind over matter!" Then he looked blank. "Duh...wha'd I say? What's 'at mean, huh?"

As the curtain swept aside, Kerry found himself almost

helpless with laughter. It wasn't so much *what* the little man was saying; it was *how* he said it. His voice changed in such a kaleidoscopic manner that there sometimes seemed to be several people on the stage, and his face was as plastic as his voice.

The opening curtain disclosed a Hollywoodish set for a Mad Scientist movie. There was the usual high-voltage Jacob's ladder with the climbing spark that went *vooop vooop vooop* as it repeated its cycle. There was a fantastic array of glass tubing which bubbled merrily with glowing, varicolored liquids, and bank after bank of flickering neon tubing.

And yet, it really didn't look scientific; it was a parody of a laboratory, not just an impressive imitation. The arrangement was such that Kerry was reminded of the lights and action of a carnival or the pyrotechnic displays of a Chamber of Commerce Fourth of July.

Gaystik the Great drew himself up, looked very supercilious, whipped a monocle out of midair, stuck it in his right eye, and said: "Lediz end gen-til-min—my luhBORuhtrih!"

There was a burst of applause, which increased a little when Gaystik's assistant walked onto the stage. She was clad in a white coat that was obviously supposed to be a lab smock, but it fit much too tightly, and it only covered about a quarter of her thighs. From there down, her shapely legs were bare. Her feet were clad in white dancing pumps with extremely high French heels. Her hair was almost blue-black, and her figure was lush.

That was when the fun began. Gaystik went through a series of tricks and gags completely unlike any that were normally seen on the magic stage. Things vanished, appeared, changed color, and went through physical metamorphoses with dizzying rapidity.

Kerry Dorman watched the hilarious antics for over an hour, not noticing, in his enjoyment, that he was standing and that his legs were beginning to ache. He learned principles of physics that he had never heard of before.

"The Second Law of Thermodynamics," Gaystik said in a stentorian voice, "is known as Carnot's Principle of the Reversible Cycle."

He proceeded to demonstrate this by having his brunette assistant ride a unicycle backwards across the ceiling of the theater while a green spotlight played on her.

"Upside down and backwards!" bellowed the little magician. "The Principle of the Reversible Cycle!"

The audience *ooh*'d and *aah*'d and cringed a little as the girl pedaled her way back and forth over their heads.

For the first time, Kerry frowned as he watched the spectacle taking place above him. As an amateur magician, he could see how a unicycle might be geared to a fine, tough wire which would make the trick possible. But there was something about the girl herself which was vaguely disturbing. Still, he couldn't quite place it.

"All this is possible, my dear, untutored friends," said Gaystik pedagogically, "by means of my patented psychocybernetic antigravitational levitator." He paused and stared stupidly at the audience. "Whatever *that* means."

Kerry soon forgot his disturbing puzzlement as the show continued. The peculiar feeling didn't recur until Gaystik went into his finale.

He stood in the middle of the stage, adjusted his ridiculous monocle, jutted out his beard, and said, in a veddy, veddy phony British accent:

"End naow, deah friends, we will demonstrate the epplication of the late Professah Einstein's celebrated correlation between the fawss of grehvehteh end the Principle of Rehlehtiveteh. What might be termed as the Law of What Goes Up, Must Come Down—eventually."

"As you have already seen, this"—he patted a large, weird-looking machine at his side—"is my psychocybernetic anti-gravitational levitator. Quite frankly, it works by the well-known electropsychometrical principle first publicized by Johannes Bactrianus, who was a member of the Artiodactyla, a famous scientific order. He was born on March 8, 1708, and died in 1775, after making quite a name for himself as a literary man. Fortunately, he missed the American Revolution...."

He went on talking. Meanwhile, the girl was going through a frenzy of activity. While Gaystik went on with his pedantic double-talk, the girl began dragging in cables and wires from all over the stage, moving as though she had less than half a minute to do the job. Somehow, most most of the cables got wrapped around the magician, who seemed not to notice. By the time his speech was through, he was almost invisible beneath a cocoon of wires and cables.

As he finished his lecture, the girl walked over to the side of the stage and threw a huge, three-bladed switch that could easily have carried a thousand amperes without overheating.

There was a tremendous flash of light where Gaystik was standing, and the tangled cables collapsed in a heap.

The girl stared dumfoundedly at the spot where her employer had been.

"Please, dear girl!"

Kerry Dorman jerked his head around. Gaystik the Great strolled through the rear door, not five feet from where Kerry stood. "Please!" he shouted. "I've told you a thousand times to wait for the signal!"

Amid surges of laughter, the little man strode on down the

aisle and climbed to the stage once again.

"And now," he cried, "the demonstration! Marlene, *proceed!*" He reached over to the machine and punched a button.

At the same time, the girl started with a run, reached the edge of the stage, and took a flying leap, head first, toward the first row!

Just as it seemed that she would smash her skull against the seats, the green spotlight from the machine struck her.

She came to a dead stop. Then, still illuminated by the green glow, she zoomed up toward the ceiling. Hanging, seemingly unsupported, high above the heads of the audience, she went into a series of complex acrobatics. A simple loop, a barrel roll, and an Immelmann turn; a series of lazy eights, a power dive, and—most breathtaking of all—a spiraling tailspin that took her down to within inches of the floor of the center aisle.

It was during this demonstration that Kerry Dorman finally recognized what was peculiar about the girl's antics. Her smock and her hair acted oddly. When, for instance, she hung poised over the audience, head down, her hair hung *up*. So did her smock. It was exactly as if gravity had been inverted for her. Hanging on wires wouldn't have that effect; her hair and clothing didn't respond to gravity any more than she did!

For a few moments, Kerry thought that perhaps there were stays in her costume and starch or something in her hair. But that theory didn't hold water at all. When she spun around, her smock flared, and her hair swirled around her head like inky smoke.

It didn't make sense! It was as though gravity were pulling her first one way, then another; as though it shifted to suit her whim— or the whim of the man behind the machine.

The final shock came when Marlene swooped down directly toward Kerry, came to a dead halt a few feet from him, and tickled him under the chin.

"You're *cute!*" she said.

In that startled instant, Kerry still had the presence of mind to put out his arm and sweep it over her back. She was floating horizontally, at eye level; any wires that held her up should have been easily visible. They weren't; neither were they tangible. Kerry's arm completed its sweep without touching a thing.

The girl giggled. "What's the matter, Doc? Don't you believe in magic?" Then she was gone, soaring back toward the stage like a swallow in flight.

Half an hour later, Kerry Dorman was standing outside the stage door of the theater. His lean, muscular face had a look of puzzled concentration. The cool spring breeze whipped about his Burberry topcoat, and swirled his pipe smoke away from his briar, dissipating it into nothingness. He stared at the door for a full minute before he walked up to it and rapped.

A gray, tired-looking man stuck his head out. "Whadda ya

want, mister?"

Kerry wasn't used to tackling theatrical people. He felt like an autograph hunter. "I. . .I'd like to talk to Mr. Gaystik."

The oldster shook his head. "Ain't here. He and his wife took off right after the show." He started to close the door.

"How about their troupe?" Kerry asked hurriedly.

Again the man shook his head. "He ain't got any assistants but his wife. They do the act by themselves. You a reporter?"

Kerry didn't even stop to think. "That's right," he lied. "I'm looking for an interview for the *Times*."

The old man raised a white eyebrow. "Thought the *Times* man was here yesterday."

"That was for a review of the show," Kerry said. "This is a personal interview—a biography, you might say. You know—how he got to be a magician, how he lives—that sort of thing." He cursed himself silently for not getting to the back of the theater before it was too late. But the crowd—

"You have an appointment?" asked the doorkeeper.

"Yes. For right after the show. But I was held up."

"Well—" the gray-haired man said thoughtfully, "you might catch them at their hotel. They're at the Algonquin. His real name's—" The name sounded like "Marx."

"Yeah. I know. Thanks a lot."

It was late, but Kerry wasn't thinking of the time. He took a cab and headed crosstown toward the Algonquin Hotel.

"Marks?" the clerk asked. "M-A-R-K-S or M-A-R-X?"

"Gaystik the Great," said Kerry, grinning. He hoped it was a winning smile.

"Oh! Mr. Markh! That's M-A-R-K-H. Room 1204. The house phone is right over there."

Kerry went to the house phone and called 1204.

"Yeah?" said the voice at the other end.

"Mr. Markh? My name is Kerry Dorman. I'd like to talk to you, if you have the time." He realized then how silly he sounded. You don't just go calling up a celebrity at all times of the night and get anywhere.

"Dorman? Sure, come on up. Marlene and I were expecting you."

Gaystik the Great's Vandyke beard was real. That was the first thing Kerry noticed. And he wasn't small, either. He gave that appearance on stage because his shoulders were wide, and his wife was tall. She was a full six-one, nearly as tall as Kerry, and a good three inches taller than her husband.

They were standing side-by-side, opening the door, when Kerry knocked.

"Come on in, Dr. Dorman," Gaystik said. "I hope you like Scotch?"

Kerry nodded dumbly as the brunette pressed a chilled glass into his hand.

The magician's grin was friendly and not at all comical.

"You don't recognize me at all, do you, Kerry boy?" His grin became broader. "You don't remember Steve?"

If Kerry Dorman had been prone to fainting spells, he would probably have fainted then and there. He gulped a mouthful of his drink and said: "Steve! Steve Markh! I never would have thought— It's been ten years!"

"Almost," said Gaystik the Great. "How do you like our little act?"

"Fine! Great! I never connected the name! And the beard—" Kerry was still in a state of semishock.

Gaystik brushed the Vandyke with the back of his hand. "Does make a difference, doesn't it? I spotted you when you came in the theater tonight. I was standing outside, smoking my last cigarette before the act. Nobody notices me because I usually keep my trench coat collar up around my face.

"As soon as I saw you, I figured I could have a little fun. That's why Marlene gave you the chin business.

"Oh, by the way—" He turned to the brunette. "Honey, this is Kerry Dorman, old roommate of mine. Kerry, my wife, Marlene."

She'd taken the make-up off her face, but she was still as striking as she had been when she was hovering in the air a foot in front of his face. She smiled impishly. "You know, you really *are* cute."

The thought of her floating in the air reminded Kerry of the purpose which had brought him here. He turned to the magician. "You always were good at picking members of the opposite sex—" Then he smirked. "—But she isn't."

Gaystik the Great looked thoughtfully at the ceiling. "Let's see—that's cribbed from—"

"Stop!" said Kerry. "I give up. Never try to best a professional at his own game. And by the way, it seems to me you were taking psychology at State. That's a long cry from stage magic."

"Not so long as you might think," the magician said.

"I suppose you wonder why I came up here?" Kerry asked.

"Why did you?" said Gaystik, neatly sidestepping the question.

"I want to know how you do that trick—the levitation gag. How does it work, Steve?"

Gaystik looked aghast. "My *deah* fellow! Do you realize you are asking me to disclose the cherished secrets of my profession? Never!" The voice was theatrical, but Kerry could tell he meant it.

"But," the magician went on, "you can have another drink."

Marlene was already fixing one. She handed it to Kerry and said: "I'll talk, even if he won't. It's done with a psychocybernetic antigravitational levitator."

Kerry grinned. "Yeah sure. And I'm Isaac Newton."

"Glad to know you, Sir Isaac," she said.

And then she and her husband burst out laughing.

"But the thing's fantastic!" Kerry said. "I'll swear no magnetic or electrical field could do that, and I'll swear there were no wires attached. Come on; it must be fairly simple. You know me, Steve; I won't tell anyone."

Gaystik shook his head. "I don't think you would, Kerry, but I just can't afford to take the chance. I've got magicians buffaloed all over the world; I can't afford to throw away an advantage like that."

Kerry shrugged, "O.K.; if you won't, you won't."

Most of the rest of the evening was spent in small talk, pleasant, but not informative. It was well after two in the morning before any of them realized how late it was getting. Kerry looked at his wrist watch and blinked, "It can't be! I've kept you people up!"

"No, you haven't," Gaystik said. "We usually don't get to bed until two-thirty or three. Sleep all morning, you know, so we can do a late show."

"Fortunately, I don't have to work on Saturdays," said Kerry. "I'll probably sleep all morning, too."

"Fine. Say! How'd you like to watch the show from backstage? Like to come tomorrow afternoon? We're giving a matinee at two."

"Why, thanks! That'd be fun. Sure; I'll be there."

Three minutes later, Kerry was strolling out of the Algonquin, inwardly arguing his own moral concepts with himself. Is it fair to steal knowledge from a man if you intend no harm? If the man, himself, sustains no loss, is it wrong to take something from him?

Kerry grinned. Why not? It was only a magic trick. Kerry had no intention of going into the magic business. Q.E.D.: It couldn't hurt Steve Markh.

When Kerry showed up at the theater the next afternoon, he was loaded to the gills with gadgets, most important of which were a 35 mm robot camera with special film and a tiny, 4 mm movie camera.

The doorkeeper let him in at the stage door, and said laconically: "Mr. Markh's expectin' ya. First dressing room at the head of the stairs, the one with the star."

Kerry climbed the steel stair. As he approached the dressing room, he heard voices. Marlene was talking:

"...Have to replace that tube. I'd hate to fall from that ceiling."

Kerry stopped, listening.

"Have we got plenty of those tubes?" It was Gaystik.

"Sure, honey; they're in the trunk with the wiring diagrams. You don't think I'd let us run out of something like *that*, do you?"

Gaystik chuckled. "I asked if we had *plenty*, dear. I knew you wouldn't let us run out completely."

There were sounds of something being opened. Kerry assumed

it was the trunk they'd mentioned.

The door was partway open. In spite of himself, Kerry tiptoed up and peered through the crack at the hinges.

The thing looked no bigger than a portable radio. Gaystik the Great was leaning over it, checking the circuits, matching them against a small sheaf of papers in his hand. He pulled out a couple of tubes, replaced them with others, and then threw a switch on the side of the box.

"O.K., honey," he said. "How about giving her a try? Up two."

Kerry blinked as Marlene's feet lifted two feet off the floor. He felt as though his eyes had done him wrong; he had the peculiar feeling that the floor had *dropped*, rather than the girl's feet lifting.

"Over," said Gaystik.

Slowly, Marlene began to rotate about an imaginary axis. She made one complete rotation, then turned through an additional ninety degrees until she was floating horizontal in midair. And, during all that time, her clothing and her hair behaved as if the gravitational pull were located somewhere around the soles of her shoes.

Marlene giggled. "If I live to be a jillion, Steve, I'll never get used to the feeling that the world has turned around, not me."

Gaystik's smile was speculative rather than comic. "You know, honey, maybe you're right. When you're wearing that gadget, maybe everybody *is* out of step but you!"

Slowly, the girl turned until she was upright again. "Mind over matter," she said brightly. "We're all set. Come on; let's get ready."

Gaystik put the sheaf of papers back into the trunk and closed it.

Kerry tiptoed backwards toward the stairway, sneaked down it a few steps, then started up again, slamming his leather heels against the ringing steel treads. Boldly, he walked up to the partially open door and knocked.

"Steve? It's me—Kerry."

"Oh, Kerry! Come on in!"

Kerry pushed open the door and walked into the dressing room. The small bit of apparatus was sitting on one of the tables, looking like nothing more than an ordinary vanity case. Kerry was careful not to give it a second glance.

"You're a bit late," said Gaystik the Great. "We're due to go on in three minutes."

"That's all right," Kerry said. "I'll just watch the show; we can talk afterwards."

"That'll be swell; maybe a drink afterwards, eh?"

"Sure," Kerry agreed.

Nonchalantly, Gaystik picked up the case, and the three of them went back down the stairway.

Kerry Dorman watched the whole show again, this time from a backstage vantage point. He noticed that the small case was set into one of the ludicrously constructed phony machines and its cover opened. By the time the curtain opened, it was ready to function without being seen by the audience.

There wouldn't be a demonstration of the levitation trick for over an hour, Kerry knew. And Steve and his wife would be onstage every minute of the time. Quietly, he stepped back from the wings and made his way toward the dressing room.

Once inside, he bolted the door and opened the trunk that stood against the wall. Inside it was a fairly large loose-leaf notebook full of intricate wiring diagrams. Kerry unlimbered his 35 mm camera and his electronic flash and started shooting pictures.

By the time the levitation act started, Kerry was back in the wings again, and this time, his high-speed 4 mm movie camera was buzzing away. Several other very interesting gadgets were also recording their results.

The magic act of Gaystik the Great moved to Philadelphia some three weeks later. On the train down, Gaystik was leaning back in his seat, calmly smoking a cigarette.

Marlene, sitting beside him, was leafing through a magazine. Suddenly, she dropped it into her lap and said:

"But, Steve, are you sure he got everything?"

"Positive," said Gaystik. "I know Kerry Dorman. We set it up perfectly for him. He's got the plans of the machine, and he's got a pretty good idea of what's going on. He'll investigate until he's blue in the face."

"But will he accept it?" Marlene asked. "Honey, you've been going at this for two years now. So far, you haven't convinced *any-body!*" Her voice was almost tearful. "All you've done is let people steal one of the greatest money-making gadgets ever invented!"

Gaystik closed his eyes and massaged the bridge of his nose with thumb and forefinger. "Marlene, I've told you a thousand times, *I don't want to convince anybody!* If I tried it, you'd probably have a coffin to buy; people won't stand being *taught* that sort of thing. They've got to *learn* it—for themselves. If they think I'm hiding something, they'll beat their brains out to find out what it is. If I try to prove it to them, they'll do one of three things: laugh at me; ignore me; or kill me.

"But if they find it out for themselves, they can't do any of those things."

"But, honey," the girl said, still pleading, "surely a Ph.D. in physics could see how the thing works."

Gaystik shook his head and smiled. "Sweetheart, those boys are just exactly the ones that *won't* listen." He looked out the window, watching the countryside flow by, listening to the *klakata-klakata-klak-klak-klak* of the steel wheels moving over

121

the rails.

There was silence between them for several minutes, then Marlene said, "All right, then. What's the difference between this Kerry Dorman and the others? You acted differently with him than you did with the others."

"Only because I knew him; only because I knew him. The trap I set for Kerry had to be a special case." He paused and looked at the glowing end of his cigarette.

"Remember Mantelli? He's an out-and-out crook, as far as his competitors are concerned. He's a professional magician, and he won't let anyone else get ahead of him. He actually swiped one of the levitator gadgets. You know what he did? He had someone analyze the circuits and build him a duplicate. He'll use that duplicate eventually, if he can.

"But that doesn't matter. The thing is that whoever analyzed those circuits is going to begin to wonder what in the devil the gadget is for. And that's all I want to do. I just want to get the idea running around in people's brains here and there. I want to make sure it isn't smothered. I want to know someone is *worrying* about it!

"Look, Marlene, when I first showed you how the machine worked, you accepted it. Why? Because you didn't know it couldn't be done."

Marlene sniffed. "Just because I majored in dramatics—"

He shushed her with a hand. "I'm not running you into the ground, silly. What I'm pointing out is that men like Kerry Dorman *know* that thing can't work. Just mention the word 'psionics,' and they'll laugh their heads off—or they'll smash you, if you can prove it. But get *them* interested—get them to prove to *themselves* that the human mind and a machine can work together, and you've put *them* on the wrong end of the stick."

The girl shook her head slowly. "But you haven't heard a thing in two years. Nobody else has ever been able to make the machine work for themselves. What good does that do?"

Gaystik dropped his cigarette and crushed it beneath the toe of his shoe. "I don't know yet. It may take years; maybe I'll never live to see it. But I think I will. Remember, each one of these men has *seen* the thing work. They've *got* to find an explanation, even if it's only to save their own sanity. Someone *has* to find an explanation—somewhere—somehow. I wish to heaven I could figure out how it works."

Marlene ran the tip of her tongue over her lips. "I know," she said softly. "If only someone would see...would try to find out...how electronics and the human mind are linked. Or how a machine can act as an amplifier for telepathy, ESP, precognition, teleportation, and levitation."

"Yeah," said Gaystik. "Levitation."

122

Kerry Dorman looked at the room around him. It was upside down! Or was *he* upside down? He wasn't sure. He looked at the machine again, and...

Ballade for Convention Lovers

This comes from "before my time." I found it on a single blue mimeographed sheet that had been mailed to Randall's New York address, with **four and a half cents** *postage. The only firm date I can put on it is that it must have been written before 1965, when Randall left New York for Austin, Texas.*

Some things never change.

BALLADE FOR CONVENTION LOVERS

Each year, as it approaches Labor Day
    I feel, within my heart, a warming glow;
Within me springs an urge I must obey,
    And so I start in saving all my dough,
    And when the time comes, I pack up and go
To science fiction's yearly spree.
    Break out the bourbon! Let the liquor flow!
Conventions, brother! That's the stuff for me!

I wander round and look at each display;
    I go to hear each lecture, see each show;
I go to see the fancy-dress array—
    The costumed fans, parading to and fro.
    And, at the banquet, watch while they bestow
The Hugo on those men of high degree.
    (I don't get one; I smile to hide my woe.)
Conventions, brother! That's the stuff for me!

And, then, at night, I wade into the fray
    At parties, trading verbal blow for blow—

Where ev'ry joke is—at the least—risque,
    And every word a shattering *bon mot.*
    While some fans praise the tales of long ago,
And others wince and loudly disagree,
    I take both sides and watch the battle grow.
Conventions, brothers! That's the stuff for me!

ENVOY CUM LAUDE

But, Prince, these pleasures are but small, I trow;
    What really makes it worth my entrance fee
Are all those lovely female fans with no
    Conventions. Brother, *that's* the stuff for me!

—*Randall Garrett*

Blank?

by Randall Garrett

*Those of you who know about the three "blank" stories
may skip ahead now and read Randall's contribution to that
June 1957 issue of* **INFINITY SCIENCE FICTION.**

*For those of you who have never run across the others
in this set, let me fill you in. Larry Shaw asked three
writers, who were young but already established, to sit
down in his office and draft a story with the most neutral
title he could think of:* **Blank.** *He then published all three,
with an accompanying editorial describing the experiment:*
Blank! *(Asimov),* **Blank** *(Ellison), and* **Blank?** *(Garrett).
According to Randall, the punctuation (or lack thereof) was
contributed by Shaw.*

Bethelman came to quite suddenly, and found himself standing
on the corner of 44th Street and Madison Avenue. He was dizzy for
a moment—not from any physical cause, but from the disorienta-
tion. The last thing he could remember, he had been sitting in a bar
in Boston, talking to Dr. Elijah Kamiroff. After the interview was
over, they'd had a few drinks, and then a few more. After that,
things began to get hazy.

Bethelman rubbed his head. It wasn't like a hangover; his head
felt perfectly fine. But how in the devil had he gotten here? He
looked around. No one was paying any attention to him, but no one
pays any attention to anyone on the streets of New York. Still
feeling queer, he headed east on 44th Street.

He wanted to sit down for a bit, and the nearest place was the
little bar halfway between Madison Avenue and Grand Central
Station. He went in and ordered a beer.

What the hell had happened? He'd had too much to drink on several occasions, but he'd never gone to sleep in one city and awakened in another. Dr. Kamiroff must have put him on the plane; the biochemist didn't drink much, and had probably been in better shape then Bethelman had been.

He glanced at his watch. Two-fifteen! Wow! The city editor would be wondering where he was.

He went to the phone, dropped in a dime, and dialed the city desk. When the editor's voice answered, he said: "Hickman, this is Bethelman; I'm sorry I'm late, but—"

"Late?" interrupted Hickman. "What're you talking about? You've only been gone half an hour. You sick or something?"

"I don't feel too good," Bethelman admitted confusedly.

"That's what you said when you left. Hell, man, take the rest of the day off. It's Friday; you don't need to show up until Monday if you don't want to. Okay?"

"Yeah," said Bethelman. "Sure." His mind still didn't want to focus properly.

"Okay, boy," said Hickman. "And thanks again for the tip. Who'd have thought Baby Joe would come in first? See you Monday."

And he hung up.

Bethelman stood there looking foolish for a full five seconds. Then things began to connect up. *Friday!* It shouldn't be Friday.

He cradled the phone and walked over to the bar where the barman was assiduously polishing a beer glass.

"What day is this?" he asked.

"Friday," said the white-jacketed barman, looking up from the shell of gleaming glass.

"I mean the date," Bethelman corrected.

"Fifteenth, I think." He glanced at a copy of the *Times* that lay on the bar. "Yeah. Fifteenth."

Bethelman sat down heavily on the barstool. The fifteenth! Somewhere, he had lost two weeks! He searched his memory for some clue, but found nothing. His memory was a perfect blank for those two weeks.

Automatically, his hand went to his shirt pocket for cigarettes. He pulled out the pack and started to shake one out. It wouldn't shake, so he stuck his finger in the half-empty pack to dislodge a cigarette. There was a roll of paper stuck in it.

He took it out and unrolled it. It was a note.

You're doing fine. You know something's wrong, but you don't know what. Go ahead and investigate; I guarantee you'll get the answers. But be careful not to get anyone too suspicious; you don't want to be locked up in the booby bin. I suggest you try Marco's first.

The note was unsigned, but Bethelman didn't need a signature. The handwriting was his own.

He looked at himself in the mirror behind the bar. He was clean shaven—which he hadn't been when he was drinking with Dr. Kamiroff in Boston. Also, he was wearing his tweed topcoat, which he had left in New York. A search of his pockets revealed the usual keys and change. In his billfold was three hundred dollars in cash—more than he'd ever carried around in his life—and a receipt for a new twenty-dollar hat. The receipt was dated the tenth.

He took off his hat and looked at it. Brand new, with his initials on the sweatband.

Evidently, he'd been doing something the past two weeks—but what?

He remembered talking to Kamiroff about the variability of time—something about a man named Dunne. And he remembered the biochemist saying that time travel was physically impossible. For a second or two, Bethelman wondered whether he'd been projected into the future somehow. But if he had, he reasoned, he'd still be wearing the same clothes he'd had on in Boston.

No, he decided, *it's something else. I've gone off my rocker. I'm daffy as a dung beetle. What I need is a good psychiatrist.*

But that didn't explain the note.

He took it out and looked at it again. It still said the same thing. He decided that before he went to a psychiatrist, he'd do what the note said. He'd go to Marco's.

After all, if he couldn't trust himself, who could he trust?

Marco's was a little place down on Second Avenue. It wasn't the most elite bar in New York, but it wasn't the worst dive, either.

Marco was standing near the door when Bethelman entered. "Ah! Mr. Bethelman! The package you were expecting is here. The—ah—*gentleman* left it." The beaming smile on his face was a marvel to behold.

"Thanks," Bethelman said.

Marco dived behind the bar and came up with a package wrapped in brown paper and an envelope addressed to Bethelman. The package was about three inches wide, a little less than six inches long, and nearly an inch thick. He slid it into his topcoat pocket and tore open the envelope.

There should be close to ten thousand dollars in the package, the note said. *You promised Marco a grand of it if Number 367 won—which, of course, it did. He got hold of the runner for you.*

Again, the note was in his own handwriting.

He gave Marco the thousand and left. There were some things he'd have to find out. He went to his apartment on 86th Street and put in a long distance call to Dr. Elijah Kamiroff in Boston. After an hour, he was informed that Dr. Kamiroff was out of town and was not expected back for two weeks. Where had he gone? That was confidential; Dr. Kamiroff had some work to do and did not wish to be disturbed.

Bethelman cursed the biochemist roundly and then went to his private files, where he kept clippings of his own stories. Sure enough, there were coverages of several things over the past two weeks, all properly bylined.

Two weeks before, he had written the little article on research being done on cancer at Boston University School of Medicine, most of which he'd gotten from Dr. Kamiroff. No clues there; he'd evidently been behaving naturally for the past two weeks. But why couldn't he remember it? Why was his memory completely blanked out?

He had to know.

He spent the next two weeks running down his activities during the blank period, and the more he worked, the more baffled he became. He had never been a gambling man, but he seemed to have become one over those two weeks. And a damned lucky one at that.

Horse races, the numbers game, even the stock market, all seemed to break right for him. In the blank two weeks, Bethelman had made himself close to fifty thousand dollars! And every so often, he'd come across a little note from himself, telling him that he was doing fine. Once, a note he found in his bureau drawer, tucked among the socks, told him to invest every cent he had in a certain security and then sell the next day. He did it and made another nine thousand dollars.

It was exactly four weeks to the day after he had sat in the bar with Dr. Kamiroff that he found the last cryptic note to himself. It was in his unabridged dictionary, lying right on the page which contained the word he happened to be looking up.

Tomorrow morning, it said, *you will see Dr. Kamiroff. But don't expect him to explain anything to you until you have explained everything to him.*

So he would see Kamiroff in the morning, eh? He'd been trying to get hold of the biochemist every day for the past two weeks—and there had been no results.

That night, just before bedtime, Bethelman drank a glass of beer. One glass. No more.

And that's why he couldn't understand waking up the next morning with a king-size hangover. He rolled over in bed, moaning—half afraid to open his eyes.

"Oooooh!" he said. "My head!"

"Want a bromo?" a familiar voice asked sympathetically.

Bethelman forced his eyes open. The stocky, smiling face of Dr. Elijah Kamiroff floated above him.

Bethelman sat straight up in bed, his eyes wide. The effort made his head hurt worse. He looked around.

He was in the upstairs guest bedroom of Dr. Kamiroff's suburban home.

He turned to look at the biochemist, who was busily mixing

a bromo.

"What date is this?" he asked.

Kamiroff looked at him with mild blue eyes. "It's the second," he said.

Bethelman took the glass of fizzing liquid and downed it. The pattern was beginning to make sense. He had gone to sleep in Boston the night of the first and awakened in New York on the fifteenth. Then he had gone to sleep in New York on the twenty-ninth and awakened on the second.

It made a weird kind of sense.

He handed the empty glass back to the biochemist and said: "Dr. Kamiroff, sit down. I want to tell you something."

Half an hour later, Kamiroff was rubbing his chin with a forefinger, deep in concentration. "It sounds wild," he said at last, "but I've heard of wild things before."

"But what caused it?"

"Do you remember what you did last night? I mean the night of the first?"

"Not clearly; we got pretty crocked, I remember."

Kamiroff grinned. "I think you were a few up on me. Do you remember that bottle of white powder I had in the lab down in the basement?"

"No," Bethelman admitted.

"It was diazotimoline, one of the drugs we've been using in cancer research on white mice. That whole family of compounds has some pretty peculiar properties. This one happens to smell like vanilla; when I let you smell it, you stuck your finger in it and licked off some of the powder before I could stop you.

"It didn't bother me much; we've given it to mice without any ill effects, so I didn't give you an emetic or anything."

The bromo had made Bethelman's head feel better. "But what happened, exactly?" he asked.

"As far as I can judge," the biochemist said, "the diazotimoline has an effect on the mind. Not by itself, maybe; perhaps it needed the synergetic combination with alcohol. I don't know.

"Have you heard the theories that Dunne propounded on the mind?"

"Yeah," Bethelman said. "We discussed them last night, I think."

"Right. The idea is that the mind is independent of time, but just follows the body along through the time stream.

"Evidently, what the diazotimoline did was project your mind two weeks into the future—to the fifteenth. After two weeks—on the twenty-ninth—it wore off, and your mind returned to the second. Now you'll relive those two weeks."

"That sounds like a weird explanation," Bethelman said.

130

"Well, look at it this way. Let's just say you remember those two weeks in the wrong order. The drug mixed your memory up. You remember the fortnight of the second to the fifteenth *after* you remember the fortnight of the fifteenth to the twenty-ninth. See?"

"Good gosh, yes! Now I see how I made all that money! I read all the papers; I know what the stocks are going to do; I know what horses are going to win! Wow!"

"That's right," Kamiroff agreed. "And you'll know where to leave all those notes to yourself."

"Yeah! And on the afternoon of the fifteenth, I'll blank out and wake up in my bed on the morning of the thirtieth!"

"I should think so, yes," Kamiroff said.

"It makes sense, now." Then Bethelman looked up at the biochemist. "By the way, Dr. Kamiroff, I want to split this money with you; after all, you're responsible for what happened."

The scientist smiled and shook his head. "No need of that. I have the diazotimoline, remember? You said you couldn't get hold of me on the phone: you said I was doing experimental work and couldn't be disturbed.

"Now, just what do you think I'm going to be experimenting on for the next couple of months?"

The Breakfast Party

by Randall Garrett

Randall was accustomed to the editorial compulsion to change story titles. Sometimes he didn't care. He earned food money now and then by writing "confession" stories and, knowing they were always subject to title and byline change, submitted them under such titles as **Run for Your Life,** by "Mya St. Dragon."

About his science fiction, he cared.

It bothered him when an editor changed a title without consulting him. There was one such change of which he approved wholeheartedly: John Campbell's title **The Queen Bee** was outstandingly more appropriate than the original title, which Randall had forgotten.

The Breakfast Party, however, appeared under the title (shudder) **The League of the Living Dead.** I'm sure Randall, a kindly and caring man, never did forgive Ray Palmer.

Barbara had been dead for seven months when Martin saw her in the little club on Forty-second Street.

He was on his seventh double-bourbon-and-water, and his eyesight, poor as it was, was considerably better than his critical judgment. He squinted his eyes to get a better look.

She was toying with a half-empty glass and staring in rapturous concentration at the six-piece combo which was permitting its drummer the ecstasy of a rhythmic grand-mal seizure. Across from her sat two men; the one on the outside was tall and saturnine, the other somewhat shorter and wider across the shoulders.

Martin was immediately stabbed with twinges of jealousy.

The fact that his wife couldn't possibly be there meant little to him at the moment: the fact that she was there with somebody else *did* mean a great deal.

He decided he had to have a closer look. He poured the remainder of drink number seven down his throat, and made his way toward the bar. On the way, he would have to pass the booth where she sat.

By the time he had arrived at the booth in question, his resolve to go into the bar had dissolved into the vague mists of some ethanolic Limbo. There was no longer any doubt in his mind that the woman before him was Barbara.

The hair in the page-boy bob; the crystalline blue of her eyes; the smooth, almost perfectly hemispherical curve of her breasts; the tilt of her brows— Every inch of her was Barbara. A man doesn't live with a woman for eight years and not know her—not even when he's boiled to the ears.

None of the trio at the booth noticed him at first. Martin was a six-foot two-hundred pounder who filled a tux nicely and could quite obviously handle himself in an emergency, but the dance had just ended, and the people milling around him as they came from the floor were doing a pretty fair job of camouflaging him.

The little group didn't see him at all until he placed his hands carefully on the edge of the table, leaned over, and said: "Honey, whatinhell are you doing here?"

It was an inane thing to say. It wasn't the thing you really ought to say to a woman you know is dead. But somehow, Martin couldn't think of anything else to say.

She turned those blue eyes on him with a look that carried no sign of recognition.

She said: "I beg your pardon? I don't think—?"

Martin just stood there, weaving and baffled, as the whole enormous insanity of the situation flooded over him. The last hastily-downed drink began to hit him, and his sight spun kaleidoscopically.

The girl's voice said: "Gregor, he's sick. Call a waiter or something. Who is he?"

"Never mind," said the taller of the two men. "I'll help him. Come along, friend."

"Here, chum," came the other man's voice, "have a drink."

"Give him mine," said the girl, "then get him in a cab."

Dimly, Martin felt a glass being pressed into his hand, and he hastily emptied the contents into his stomach. Then the world went away on a blue-gray fog.

When he woke up the next morning, he was in his own bed, fully dressed except for his shoes and coat. He felt exactly as he deserved to feel.

A double bromo, a half-pint of tomato juice, two cups of coffee, and three cigarettes later, he felt well enough to get into the shower without having to sit down.

All the time, his mind was boiling. Had it been Barbara, or hadn't it? Logically, it *couldn't* be. Barbara was dead. He had been with her the night she died.

And he had held her hand, crying, until it was as cool as the chill atmosphere of death itself.

Martin towelled himself until his skin tingled and walked back into the bedroom.

That was when he saw the Old Fashioned glass sitting on his dresser.

He knew instantly that it was the glass Barbara had been drinking out of the night before. He'd emptied it and put it in his pocket.

He looked at it without touching it, trying to get the light just right. Sure enough, there were smudges on it. Impossible to tell whose, though.

But he knew how to find out.

He picked up the phone and dialed.

When the police switchboard answered, he said: "James Martin here. Give me Lieutenant Donovan, Homicide." He waited a moment.

"Hello, Donny. Jim. Look, can you get out for a cup of coffee? I don't know how important it is—yet. Okay. The usual place in half an hour."

He hung up and began to dress.

Donovan was already waiting for him in the Child's restaurant just off Times Square. He sat down in the booth, and said: "Donovan, you know me, don't you?"

The little detective looked at him over his coffee cup. "Well, the face is familiar, anyway."

"You know what I mean. As a lawyer, I've always played it square with the cops, and with you especially. I want to ask you a favor—unofficially—and I want your word that you won't say anything about it."

Donovan peered at him from slate-gray eyes. "Marty, you know I'd probably cut my own throat for you—but not without a reason."

Martin looked at him for a moment, then: "Here's the reason."

His right hand reached into his coat pocket and brought out the Old Fashioned glass.

"So?" Donovan raised his eyebrows.

Martin leaned forward earnestly. "Donny, all I want is for you to identify any latent prints on that glass. And tell me whose they are. And don't tell anyone else."

Donovan ran his tongue around the inside of his cheek. "Mind if I ask why? Whose do you figure they are?"

Martin leaned back. "If I told you, you'd think I was nuts. If it is who I think, you'll know the answer as well as I." He looked at his

Takeoff Too!

Randall Garrett

Donning Company, ~~No~~ Norfolk, Virginia,

1987, 1st pb

F / 14 -

watch. "Look, Donny, I haven't been to the office yet this morning, and I've got work to do. Can you phone me there?"

"Sure."

Martin picked up the check and made his way toward the cashier.

Two hours later, his phone rang. He picked up the receiver. "Martin speaking."

"Look here, Marty," Donovan's voice came sharply over the instrument, "if this is a joke, I don't think it's funny! And if it isn't, I want an explanation!"

Martin felt something cold and paralyzing inside his brain. He knew very well what Donovan was going to say, even before he asked: "What do you mean, Donny?"

"I mean this glass you gave me! *What are Barbara's prints doing all over it?*"

The resistance to intense shock that had made James Martin the brilliant trial lawyer that he was came back in that instant. Calmly, he told Donovan everything he could remember about the night before.

There was a long pause on the phone, then: "Is that the straight dope, Marty?"

"That's the straight dope."

Another long pause.

"Marty, we're taking some time off. Remember that little place in Greenwich Village we used to go to when we were in school? Meet me there in half an hour."

"But, Donny, I—" He stopped. The phone was dead.

When Donovan talked that way, he meant it. Martin grabbed his hat, took the elevator down, and flagged a taxi.

During the ride, he tried to keep his mind focused, but it kept swirling around in unreal circles, confusing him. At the destination, he almost forgot to tip the cabbie, a thing he invariably did.

He pushed open the door of the bar and saw the little policeman waggling a finger from one of the rear booths.

He walked back and sat down. "Donny, what—"

"Don't say anything until you've finished your drink, and then let me do the talking," Donovan said with peculiar Irish logic.

Martin swallowed the bourbon that Donovan had waiting for him, then looked at the detective expectantly.

Donovan stared at his fingernails as though he were undecided about where to start. Finally, he looked up.

"Marty, there's something screwy here. We both know Babs is dead. And yet, I know you well enough to take your word about what happened last night. But as a police officer, I can't touch it. I don't have enough to go on. The prints? Obviously faked. I can't start anything on evidence like that.

"And somehow—" he paused, groping for words, "—somehow, I don't think we want a police investigation."

Martin didn't say anything. He didn't even feel anything except the peculiar numbness of an unreal situation.

Donovan rubbed his chin nervously. "You've got the money for a private investigator, haven't you? Well, I know just the man for you. Come along." Donovan rose and Martin followed him out the door to the street.

They walked several blocks, turning a couple of times, and Donovan finally pulled to a halt in front of the entrance to a small office building.

He led the way up a flight of stairs, down a hall, to the door of a small office.

The lettering on the door said:

SEAN O'BRIAN
PRIVATE INVESTIGATOR
Come in

Following the sign's advice, they stepped into the outer office; an office which was not furnished in accordance with the shabby-genteel flavor of the rest of the building.

The walls were paneled in fine oak, and three tastefully chosen watercolors decorated them. The furniture was modern and expensive. The wall-to-wall rug was thick and luxurious.

And the lovely girl with the soft brown hair who was smiling at them from behind the reception desk completed the picture.

"Good afternoon, Lieutenant," she said, in a voice that sounded like the ripple of water over the lakes of Killarney.

"How are you, Miss McElhiney. Is Sean in?"

"He's busy right now, but he'll be ready in a few minutes."

"Fine." Donovan turned back to Martin. "Look, Marty, this is entirely out of my jurisdiction. I don't want to be told anything unless Sean himself tells me.

"Trust Sean. He knows his business, and he's a fine man. Tell him everything you told me and answer all his questions."

He chewed at his lip for a moment, then went on. "You're not going to like what you find, I think, but you've got the guts to take it."

Then he turned to the girl. "Miss McElhiney, you can tell Sean that James Martin is a man he can trust with his life."

With that, he stepped out the door, closing it behind him.

Martin blinked. Somehow, things seemed to be happening too fast for him. What was all this incredible nonsense? Vaguely he heard the girl's voice talking over the interoffice phone, then he realized she was talking to him.

He wrenched his mind back into the room. "I beg your pardon?"

"I said," she smiled, "that Mr. O'Brian will see you now."

The inner office was similar to the outer in style. Along one wall ran a monstrous bookcase filled with books of every description; it looked as though Sean O'Brian had made a point of collecting a representative sample of every type of book published since Gutenberg.

O'Brian himself was a tall, muscular young man with light brown hair and deep-set blue eyes. He waved to a leather upholstered chair before the desk.

"Sit down, Mr. Martin."

Martin sat, not knowing how to begin telling his reason for being there. It suddenly occurred to him that he really wasn't quite sure why he *was* there.

O'Brian seemed to sense Martin's fuzzy state of mind.

"Mr. Martin, before you begin, let me ask you a question. Do you believe in the supernatural?"

Martin shook his head, wordlessly.

"Neither do I. There is no such thing. Everything in this universe operates according to the natural laws of this universe. We may not know all those laws, but they exist, nevertheless.

"Now, Donovan wouldn't have brought you here unless there was something definitely queer about your case. Something that *seems* supernatural. I don't handle any other kind of case. So, regardless of how silly it may sound, I'll listen to what you have to say without calling for the nearest psychiatrist. Okay?"

Something clicked in Martin's brain, and the fog that had seemed to cover it vanished, washed away by the matter-of-fact attitude of Sean O'Brian's speech. Martin relaxed.

"Okay, here it is. Last night, I was in—"

Martin went over the whole thing again, trying to remember as best he could exactly what had happened. As he did, Sean O'Brian's eyes began to narrow, and a deep inner excitement began to light them.

When Martin had finished, O'Brian said: "About that glass—did the girl hand it to you?"

"Uh—no; the man, I think. The tall one."

"Mmmm!" Sean seemed to find a great significance in that statement.

He flipped the intercom switch. "Alice, see if you can get hold of Lieutenant Donovan. He ought to be back at headquarters by now."

After a minute or two, the girl's voice said: "He's on the line, Sean."

O'Brian picked up the receiver. "Donny? Sean. Look, that glass Martin brought you—any prints on it besides the girl's? None but Martin's. I thought so. Look, isn't it queer that a wet whiskey glass should pick up prints? Okay, thanks, Donny. I'll let you know."

He hung up and looked back at Martin. "Martin, doesn't it strike you as odd that your wife—if it was your wife—should be drinking a *warm* Old Fashioned?"

"Warm? I don't remember—I was too drunk to remember the taste. What makes you think it was warm?"

"Simple. A cold drink condenses moisture from the air. A wet glass doesn't pick up fingerprints too well, if at all. This glass had good, clean prints on it. Q.E.D.: this glass wasn't cold. Did your wife like warm liquor?"

"Good Lord, no! It made her sick. But what—"

"I'm going to make a broad guess. Your wife died of an odd form of anemia. For no known reason, the hemoglobin in her blood cells dropped drastically. The white count remained the same, the red count dropped a little but not enough to be serious. It was the lack of hemoglobin that killed her. Right?"

If Martin had been the type to look flabbergasted, he would have done so right there and then. Instead, he nodded. "That's about what the doctor said. How did you know?"

"I didn't know. I told you I was just guessing. Where was your wife buried?"

Martin named the cemetery, and the detective wrote it down on a piece of paper.

"All right, Mr. Martin. We'll do what we can. I'll let you know if we find anything."

"Is there anything I can do?"

Sean looked at him sharply. "Yes, there is, if you don't mind going through with it."

"Anything. This is beginning to get under my skin."

"All right. I want you to go back to that bar tonight. Keep your eyes open. If you see anything or anyone suspicious, strike up a conversation. Don't let them know you suspect anything wrong. And, above all, don't give them your name; think up a good phony.

"I want you to see if you can find out who they are and where they live, but for Heaven's sake, don't make them suspicious."

Martin grinned. "I haven't been a lawyer all these years for nothing. I'll let you know what I find."

"Fine. I'll work on my end of it."

Somehow, the street looked unnaturally bright when Martin stepped out into it. After the cool indirect lighting of Sean O'Brian's office, the afternoon sun was hot and harsh.

Nerves, he thought. *My nerves are a little shaky.*

He hailed a taxi, gave the cabbie his address, and sat back in the seat, closing his eyes.

When he unlocked his apartment, the first thing he did was mix himself a Scotch and water. That, he figured, would help him relax.

He figured wrong. He couldn't seem to settle down; he paced the floor and smoked cigarettes as though he were an expectant father.

The whole thing was senseless. Babs was dead; he knew that. But he felt he had to keep telling himself or he'd forget it.

By eight-thirty, he was paying off a cab driver in front of the club where he had seen Barbara there the night before. It gave him a slight case of the creeps to think that he might actually find her here again.

He checked his hat and picked out a table in the corner where he could command a view of the whole room. He ordered a drink, but it was beginning to get warm before he took more than a swallow or two.

It was not until well after nine that he noticed that there was another person in the bar who also seemed to be watching for someone.

He was a swarthy, astonishingly thin man of a little below average height with dark eyes and a face that looked as though it were made of old and well-used Cordovan leather.

Martin noticed him because the drink which the waiter had placed on the table before the dark-skinned man had not been touched. And the leather-faced one was also surveying the room.

There was nothing particularly abnormal about him; after all, lots of people come into bars to wait for someone else. But the thing that drew Martin's attention was the pills. Every so often, the dark-faced man would take a small bottle of pills from his pocket, shake a small green pill into his hand, and swallow it without using any liquid to wash it down. The man looked as though—

Martin caught something out of the corner of his eye, and his head jerked in the direction of the door as though he had been jabbed by a bayonet. His heart jumped.

It was Barbara.

She was alone this time. Martin watched her quietly, forcing his nerves to steadiness.

She didn't look around, she simply stepped over to the bar and ordered an Old Fashioned. Without the ice!

Finally, Martin made up his mind. He finished his drink and walked over to the bar. He pretended not to notice her at first; he ordered another drink. After a moment or two, he saw her face in the mirror. She was watching him.

James Martin was a criminal lawyer with a brilliant record in the courtroom; in other words, he was an actor who did his best work under strain. He turned to her, smiling.

"Hello. I thought you looked familiar," he said smoothly. "I want to apologize for my behavior last night."

She returned the smile. "It was nothing, really. You seemed to think I was someone you knew." Her look was suddenly calculating and watchful.

"Did I?" He looked innocent. "I must really have been boiled. I don't think anyone else could look like you."

Her face softened. "Thank you."

"May I buy you a drink?"

"Why, yes, thanks."

After the drinks were ordered, she looked up at him coyly. "Let's go over to the table. I don't like to talk at a bar."

He followed her over and pulled out her chair for her.

The perfect gentleman, he thought. So far, he was doing fine, but he hadn't learned anything. If this woman was Barbara, she was doing a better job of acting than he'd thought Barbara capable of.

He hoped for a while that she'd quit acting when they were alone at the table; he kept throwing her the straight lines to some of the pet jokes he and Barbara had had together. It didn't work; she missed every one of them.

Martin was so intent on his character analysis that it took him the better part of two hours to realize that her conversation did have one definite goal. The spark was missing from her small talk; there was none of Barbara's usual wit and brilliance. This Louise, as she called herself, simply didn't have any originality in her thinking. But, in spite of that, he could see where she was leading.

She was about as subtle as a train wreck.

He couldn't help himself. The girl had none of Barbara's brains, but she did have Barbara's body or a reasonable facsimile thereof. And the Scotch helped, too.

It was well after four in the morning when he woke up in the hotel room. His head ached and his tongue felt fuzzy, and it took him a few seconds to realize what had awakened him.

The door had closed. He looked around. The girl was gone. In spite of his head, he jumped up and grabbed his pants. The wallet was still there, undisturbed. He dressed quickly, eased the door open and looked down the hall toward the elevator. The door was just sliding shut.

Martin ran toward the stairway and went down them at a rate that would have broken his neck with one misstep.

The girl was just going out the lobby door when Martin reached the lobby. There had been two things in his favor; she had had to wait for the elevator, and there were only three flights of stairs to run down. He followed her to the street at a more leisurely pace. The street was pretty well deserted at that hour, and he didn't want to attract attention.

He didn't notice the car pull up to the curb behind him. In fact, he had no idea that there was anyone around but the girl until something slammed hard against the side of his head.

"What shall we do with him?" said a voice.

"Seal him up until he dies. Then he can join us," said another.

"We must hurry, then. It is late. Soon the sun will be up."

Martin heard the words vaguely and tried to say something, but all he could get out was a groan. When he did, somebody kicked him in the head again and he went back to sleep.

The next time he woke up, there was a light shining in his eyes and a face looming over him. He tried to focus his eyes, but the pain in his head rose to a crescendo and he had to close his eyes.

"It's about time you came around. How do you feel?"

"Ooooh! Lousy." Martin opened his eyes again and looked at the face. It was familiar, but he didn't quite place it at first.

Then it hit him. The face belonged to the little leathery-faced man who had been taking the green pills in the bar.

"Sit up," the little man said, "and take these." His hand held three white tablets.

"What are they?"

"Fifty milligrams of thiamine and two aspirins."

He took them and washed them down with water from the glass the little man handed him.

As the pain began to subside, Martin began to take in his surroundings.

He was lying on a slab of marble in a large room. Around the walls of the room were a series of panels about two and a half feet square. He recognized where he was. It was a morgue.

Each of the panels concealed a drawer within which, presumably, there lay a body.

He looked at the little brown man. "Who the devil are you, and where are we? And why did you slug me?"

"Didn't slug you. Here." He pulled out a billfold and spread it open. The card within said:

IBRIM GROME
Special Investigator
Sean O'Brian Agency

Grome popped a green pill into his mouth and continued. "You're in a morgue. I followed you when you left the bar with the girl. Followed you out of the hotel. Knew she'd leave before dawn. Saw you get slugged. Followed their car here. Managed to sneak in when they brought you here. Can't get out now. Time lock."

The man talked like a Western Union message.

"What do you mean 'time lock'?" Martin asked confusedly.

Ibrim Grome waved toward the massive door of the vault. "On the door. Won't open until after sundown. They're getting smart."

"Who's getting smart?"

Grome's gesture took in the occupants of the morgue. "Them. Even got time locks on most of the drawers. Clever." He glanced at his watch. "You been out sixteen hours. Mostly whiskey. Almost sundown again. We better hide."

Martin didn't feel up to arguing. Grome opened one of the doors along the wall just above eye level.

"They put you in here," said Grome. "Get back in. If they look inside, play dead. I'll leave door open a crack. That way, you can see. Don't give yourself away. They'll kill you."

Martin climbed inside and lay down, his head turned so that he could see through the crack in the door. The brown-faced detective climbed up to another tier, opened a cubicle, and concealed himself.

It seemed like an eternity before anything happened. Martin's head had almost quit hurting and he was getting restless.

Then there was a sudden chorus of *clicks!* The time locks had opened.

Somewhere, deep inside him, Martin knew what he was going to see, but on the surface of his mind was a block that refused to let the full realization come.

There was a scrabbling sound, something like rats in the walls. Suddenly, one of the doors popped open. Martin watched in horror as first a hand, then a head, appeared from the interior of the coffin. It was a very old man. As he climbed out, Martin could see that he was naked.

"Come out, brothers! It is time!" the old man's voice sounded hoarsely.

The others began to push themselves out of the coffin drawers.

Martin felt the back of his neck tingle coldly as the center of the room began to fill with—things. He couldn't think of them as human. Barbara was there, but he no longer thought of her as human, either. Not since last night.

He also recognized the two men Barbara had been with the first night he had seen her.

The dried and withered old man began to speak. "We have work to do, brothers. Bring out the New One."

Two of the others opened one of the doors and slid the slab out. The cadaver which lay upon it was a blonde woman in her middle thirties. Her eyes were half open and filmed. She was very obviously dead.

The rest stood around her in a circle and held hands, and then two of them grabbed the blonde woman's hands, completing the circle.

The old man cut the lights, and the room was plunged into darkness.

There was nothing to see at first, but gradually a blue glow appeared. It seemed to come from the blonde woman's body. Slowly, it brightened until the whole room was filled with the weird blue light.

Then, quite suddenly, the glow faded, seeming to sink *into* the woman's body. There was silence for a moment, then the lights went on.

The blonde was sitting up on the table!

Everything seemed to go hazy for Martin after that. He was vaguely aware that the things were dressing and leaving one by

142

one. He had sense enough to close his eyes when the old man opened the door to the cubicle he was in, but he only partially heard the comment about his dying soon.

For the fourth time in twenty-four hours, he passed out cold.

This time when he woke up, it was Sean O'Brian's face he saw. He felt a great deal better than he had the last time he'd come out of it.

"Whoo!" he said, "did I have a screwy dream!" And then he knew it hadn't been a dream. "Where—"

"—are you?" finished O'Brian. "You're in my apartment. You'd better snap out of it, Martin. You've spent most of the time asleep. Not that I blame you. After two clouts on the head and the shock of what you saw—plus too much Scotch, you've got a perfect right to pass out. But you'd better get a grip on yourself."

"I feel okay." Oddly enough, except for a tender spot behind the right ear, he *did* feel okay.

"I had a doctor in here to look you over," Sean explained. "He gave you a glucose injection. You hadn't eaten all day."

Martin sat up on the bed. Ibrim Grome was seated across the room putting a green pill in his mouth. "Chlorophyll," he explained. "Halitosis, y'know."

Sean handed Martin two sandwiches and a glass of milk, and Martin realized suddenly that he was starving. As he wolfed them down, the Irishman began to explain.

"I've been after this bunch for over a year now, but I didn't know any way to lay my hands on them. Stupid as they are in some ways, they're pretty clever at hiding out."

"But what in Heaven's name *are* they?" Martin asked.

"Vampires. Or at least," Sean corrected himself, "the basis for the vampire legend. Of course, in the passage of time, the legend has become so loaded with superstitious nonsense that ninety percent of it is false.

"The old legend claims that a vampire is one of the undead who can, at will, change itself into a batlike form and fly. It attacks the living by sucking the blood, and, in the process, the victim becomes another vampire.

"If that were really the case, vampires would have overrun the Earth long ago. They would multiply by geometrical progression; one becomes two, two becomes four, four becomes eight, and so on.

"Obviously, this hasn't taken place. Why?"

He paused, but the question was rhetorical; he took a drag off his cigarette and went on.

"The vampire *per se* is what might be called an electronic virus; a web of semi-intelligent electrical force; an energy disease. It has no sex—you noticed the way those things call each other 'brother,' whether the body they happened to inhabit was male or female—the method of reproduction is similar to that of a colony of

144

bacteria. Given a suitable medium, it can reproduce and grow.

"In this case, the medium happens to be a freshly-dead human being. Not just any corpse, either; it has to be prepared by a partial invasion before death. Most people are immune to the disease. You are, for instance, or I wouldn't have sent you after your—after the girl.

"The result's the same as that from radioactive poisoning, though the physiology of the disease is a bit different. But when the body dies, the pre-invasion virus dies, too, making it necessary for the cadaver to be re-impregnated after death."

Martin lit a cigarette with hands that were still shaking a little. He looked up at Sean when he had it going, and asked: "How come this disease hasn't spread fast enough to attract attention?"

Sean frowned. "Well, as I said, most people are immune, and it requires intimate contact with a dead carrier to get it even if you are susceptible."

Martin closed his eyes and shuddered.

O'Brian went on. "Just exactly how they manage to manipulate the body after death, I don't know. There are certain definite changes in the metabolism; the sebacious glands of the skin dry up, for instance. Remember that glass? The woman's fingerprints were on it, but the man's weren't. He'd been dead too long."

"What about the warm liquor?" Martin wanted to know.

"They can't stand extreme cold—and to them, 'extreme' means anything below about forty degrees Fahrenheit. Another thing they can't stand is ultraviolet radiation; it disrupts their electronic co-ordination and puts them into a coma. That partially accounts for their purely nocturnal activity."

Martin shook his head. "After this, you'll have me believing in werewolves, ghouls, ghosts, leprechauns, trolls, bogey men, and things that go boomp i' th' nicht. I thought vampires were a species of bat."

Sean grinned. "I always wondered how the bat business got into the vampire legend myself, until I found that the order *Chiroptera* is the only animal besides man which is susceptible to the disease. In fact, it is even more successful with the bat because the death of the bat doesn't kill the vampire-virus and there's no need for a secondary infection.

"As for the rest of those things, the answer is that most of them do exist. There's nothing odd about a single-celled animal like the amoeba changing its shape, is there? Then why couldn't a many-celled animal do it? Werewolves do.

"There are plenty of animals with specialized diets. The koala eats only eucalyptus leaves; what's the matter with a ghoul having a specialized diet?

"Ghosts!? Simply another form of the electronic life that the vampire is composed of, except that they are more intelligent and don't require a host."

Martin frowned. "What do you mean 'more intelligent than a vampire'? Seems to me they're pretty smart."

O'Brian shook his head. "Their intelligence is very limited. It is dependent upon the brain configuration of the body it is inhabiting, which is why they prefer human bodies to bat bodies. But, even with a human brain to work with, they have almost no imagination; their inventive and reasoning abilities are practically nil."

Ibrim Grome glanced at his watch, compared it carefully with the clock on the wall, and said! "Dawn in three hours."

Martin blinked. "Good Lord! What day is this?"

Sean O'Brian stood up. "Thursday morning. You haven't been out long. As soon as the vampire horde left, he dragged you out of there and brought you here."

Martin glanced at the emaciated-looking Grome. He hardly looked big enough to lift two hundred pounds of dead weight. Must be one of those wiry-muscled characters.

"Out of there? Where were we?"

"As I said," Sean explained, "I've known for some months that these things have been active in the New York area. Now, embalming ruins a body, and cremation destroys it; therefore, in order to propagate, the vampire must have control over the disposal of bodies after death and before embalming occurs. Obviously, that means a funeral home.

"The trouble was, I didn't know which home until you came to me. Then it was easy. I simply checked to see which one had taken care of your wife. I found that you, among several hundred others, had taken out burial policies with this place—Kimberly's."

"Time to go," said Grome.

"Yeah." Sean put on his coat.

Martin stood up from the bed. "I'm going, too," he announced.

Sean and Ibrim looked at each other for a second, then Sean said: "Come ahead, then."

Ten minutes later, they were in O'Brian's car, heading for Brooklyn.

Martin, in the back seat, took a drag off his cigarette, inhaled deeply, and said: "I'll be afraid to go out after dark from now on. I'll never know when some werewolf or ghoul is going to jump me."

"Nuts!" snorted Grome.

"It doesn't work that way, Martin," said O'Brian. "A werewolf is as human as you or I—or nearly so. He can change his body a little—as far the the skeletal structure will permit. But that doesn't make a killer out of him. There are a good many werewolves who don't even know they're any different from anyone else.

"They don't change to wolves, you know; their bones are plastic. Hundreds of years ago, a few of them would make themselves look hideous to frighten the local natives in order to gain power. The religion of ancient Egypt was started by just such

146

a group. That's where the Egyptians got those gods with the animal heads.

"But today, most of them are just as law-abiding as you or I. I'll admit they'd have a better chance to get away with it, but unless you get one sore at you, you're not likely to get killed by a werewolf— the chances are just as good that some human will do you in.

"And as for ghouls, you have absolutely nothing to worry about on that score. They are a branch of genus Homo that split off from the main stream of humanity several hundred thousand years ago and became carrion feeders. They're related to *Homo sapiens* in the same way that the vulture is related to the eagle. *Homo necrophagus* would be the scientific name.

"They don't bother living people at all. Why should they? Their digestive systems require that the flesh be dead for a good long time; fresh meat is as inedible to them as rubber is to you.

"It's much easier to buy steak at the butcher shop and let it lay around for a few weeks than it is to go prowling through cemeteries at night. Besides, embalming ruins a body. Do you like formaldehyde in your *filet mignon*?

"Oh, they'd eat human flesh all right, if it were available, but, when you come right down to it, what's wrong with that? They aren't strictly human, so it isn't cannibalism. And besides, what good is your body to you after you're dead?

"You don't consider maggots, saprophytic fungi, hyaenas, vultures, and other such scavengers who keep the earth clean to be evil villains, do you? Then why worry about ghouls?"

Martin thought it over in silence. Put like that, it sounded logical, all right. And he could see why such people would keep themselves hidden from the rest of humanity. Human beings, *en masse*, were still savages. The minorities—ghouls, *et al*—would be wiped out by *Homo sapiens* quickly. If human beings found such slight differences as color and religious beliefs enough excuse for violent persecution, what would they do to a different species of the same genus?

The car was speeding across the Brooklyn Bridge, weaving through the light traffic under Sean O'Brian's cool guidance.

It took them nearly ten more minutes to get to their destination.

The Kimberly Funeral Home was a big, modernistic structure which covered two city blocks.

Sean wheeled the car on past it and pulled up on the other side of the street nearly half a block away. Then he turned and pointed out the back window.

"See that building behind the main structure? The one with no windows. That's where you and Ibrim spent the day yesterday.

"The vampires will be back before dawn, and it will be the only time we can get at them. The only way we could get through the time locks in the daytime would be with dynamite, and I don't think the Brooklyn police would approve of it.

"But the door will be open for a little while just before the sun comes up in order to let the horde in. That's when we'll hit them."

Suddenly, Ibrim Grome's face appeared in the window. "We're all set, Ibrim. We've got the place boxed."

Martin jerked his head around. Ibrim Grome was still in the front seat. He looked back at the man in the window, and realized that the faint glow of light from the street lamps had led him astray. Although the man had the same dark, leathery face and the same smoky black eyes, he could see that it was not exactly the same face.

Another similar face appeared behind the first. "Are we ready to go, Sean?"

"Ready," said Sean. "Come on, Martin."

They all piled out of the car, and Martin followed Sean and the others toward the mortuary. As they neared it, Martin could see other figures—thin, lean, and brown—converging on the building in the pre-dawn darkness.

"Martin," whispered Sean, "climb up that fire escape." He indicated a steel stairway going up the side of the main building. "From the landing up there, you'll be able to see the surrounding area. If there's any trouble, blow this." He handed Martin a small whistle.

Martin recognized it as one of those supersonic dog whistles which were inaudible to the human ear. Evidently, the Irishman had some sort of instrument to detect its noise.

Martin did as he was bid. When he got to the upper landing of the fire escape, he found that he could see the street and the morgue building behind equally well.

The door of the morgue was open, and Martin could see one of the vampires sitting inside. He recognized him as one of the men with whom Barbara had been sitting that first night in the bar—the one she had addressed as "Gregor." The vampire was evidently acting as a lookout and guard.

For several minutes, nothing happened. Then, without warning, two figures converged on Gregor from the blackness outside the lighted area.

There was a short scuffle, and then the two little brown men dragged Gregor out into the darkness. Martin had seen that one of the little men was carrying an ultraviolet lamp. Evidently, it had put the vampire into a coma.

Martin could see almost nothing outside the illuminated area around the open morgue door, so for a while he couldn't be sure of what was going on.

Then, astonishingly, *Gregor walked back into the morgue and took his seat as though nothing had happened!*

Martin almost blew the whistle before he realized that the detective and his men must have everything under control or they would have warned him by this time.

Again Martin waited, casting an occasional glance toward the street to be sure nothing was happening out there.

Then the vampires began to return. In groups of two or three, they came out of the darkness, spoke in hushed tones to the guarding Gregor, and climbed into their coffins. Martin turned his head toward the street, and he could see several of them walking toward the mortuary. They probably took taxis to some spot a block or two from the place and walked the rest of the way so that they wouldn't attract attention.

Barbara was one of the last to arrive. She was wearing an evening gown that showed off her curves to perfection. Martin shuddered again.

Finally, the last of the horrors had come home. Martin began to worry. Gregor's job, presumably, was to set the time lock on the doors after all the vampires were "asleep" and then climb into his own drawer. If Sean and his men didn't attack pretty soon—

But Gregor didn't set the time lock; he didn't even close the morgue door. Instead, he stepped outside and waved his hand. It was getting lighter now, and Martin could see that there were several dozen of the little men who looked so much like Ibrim Grome running toward the building.

Gregor let them all into the morgue, closed the door behind them, and walked away, leaving Grome and his friends in sole possession of the building.

A minute or so later, Martin heard Sean's voice calling from the foot of the fire escape.

"Martin!" His voice was soft, but imperative. "Get down here, fast! The sun will be up pretty soon!"

Martin clambered down the fire escape, and he and the detective sprinted toward the car.

They got inside, but Sean didn't start the machine immediately. He stuck a cigarette in his mouth and handed one to Martin, who lit it with shaking hands.

"Is it all over?" he asked the Irishman.

"Just about."

"What did they do?" Martin asked dully. "Drive stakes through their hearts?" He didn't like the idea of Barbara being mutilated like that.

"No," said Sean. "That's another part of the medieval superstition. Vampirism is like hog cholera or hoof-and-mouth disease; you have to destroy the carrier."

"Burn them?"

"No. Look at it this way: every life form has its natural enemies. The vampire is a dead thing that preys on the living. Its natural enemies are living things that prey on the dead.

"Ibrim Grome and his boys aren't human—they're ghouls."

Martin was quite suddenly sick. When he could get his breath again, he said: "What—what about Gregor—the guard? Why did you let him get away?"

"Gregor? He didn't get away. That wasn't him who let the boys in; it was me." Sean's voice was soft. "You see, Martin, I'm—a werewolf."

Overproof

by Randall Garrett
writing as Jonathan Blake Mackenzie

*"Jonathan Blake Mackenzie" wrote some of Randall's favorite stories. The other two under his name—**Anchorite** and **Thin Edge**—share a common setting, but this one stands alone. Randall often chuckled over the triumph of slipping a certain scene past the watchful, somewhat prudish eye of John Campbell's editorial associate.*

The photographs were shocking—and more than shocking.

To any average human mind, they were nauseating, vile, disgusting, and obscene.

"They make my stomach turn to look at them!" Mrs. Dennis Barlow had said when she had handed the envelope to Dr. Paul Hiroa.

Dr. Hiroa had taken the envelope and slid out the pictures. He was well past the sesquicentennial mark, which made him an "old" man, even by the best of geriatric standards, and he had seen and done many things that probably would have shocked Mrs. Dennis Barlow, so his reaction to the photographs was quite mild by comparison. Nonetheless, he had to admit to himself that they were not the sort of thing one would hang in one's living room.

There were eleven of them, no two alike, and yet all of a pattern. They were ordinary color photographs, taken with a fine-detail lens and printed on nine-by-twelve sheets. They were flats, which made them all the more horrible, since tri-di prints tended to make the subjects of a picture look like little dolls, removing much of the sense of reality that a photograph should evoke.

Dr. Hiroa paused at the fifth picture, knowing that the eyes of both Mrs. Dennis Barlow and her husband were fixed firmly on him.

It was the husband, Dr. Barlow, who spoke. "That's the one that hit me, too, Dr. Hiroa. The rest of them I could take, but a girl like that..."

"And that horrible monster!" Mrs. Barlow chimed in.

The "horrible monster" was bad enough to the untutored eye, Dr. Hiroa had to admit. The body was vaguely feline in shape, with legs that might have been a blend of panther and frog. The head might have been part tiger, part shark—although there were only four sharp, tearing teeth; the rest were grinding molars, showing that the creature was omnivorous. The eyes were large, saucerlike, and heavy-lidded.

Instead of shoulders, the thing had a collarlike structure that sprouted eight thick, muscular tentacles.

But that was not the real horror.

The real horror lay in what the tentacles were doing.

The female was hanging by her ankles, which were tied together, from a hook on an overhead beam. She was naked.

In fact, she was far too naked to arouse any emotion other than shock in any sane human male.

She had no skin, and the instruments in the tentacles were flaying knives.

Dr. Hiroa said nothing, but went on to look at the remaining photographs. Like the first five, they were similar scenes in some grim abattoir.

When he had finished, Dr. Hiroa put the photographs flat on his desk, face up, and looked first at Dr. Dennis Barlow and then at his wife, Blanche. Barlow was thirty-eight and rugged-faced—not exactly handsome, but certainly masculine enough to be attractive to most women. Blanche Barlow was six years younger, with gold-blond hair, a magnificent figure, and a strikingly beautiful face. She might easily have passed for twenty-four.

Before he could say anything, the woman spoke. "Were you aware that this sort of thing is going on here on Sandaroth? Had you been informed that this slaughter of human beings was taking place, Dr. Hiroa?"

Dr. Hiroa frowned. "If there has been any killing of human beings by the Darotha, I am certainly not aware of it," he said carefully. "Certainly no deaths of that kind have been reported. There are only some three-quarters of a million human beings on the whole planet, and wholesale slaughter of human beings would certainly have come to light long before now."

"Are you implying that those photographs have been...er... manufactured? Falsified?" she asked.

Hiroa kept an incipient smile from breaking forth on his lips. He knew that the Barlows had not come two hundred light-years on their investigation simply on the strength of photographs that might have been faked. The woman was trying to see if senile, stupid, feeble old Doc Hiroa would think he could lie his way out of a jam.

Instead of smiling, he raised an eyebrow. "Falsified? Why, no, Mrs. Barlow. Why should they be?"

"You just said that you knew of no such slaughter going on," she pointed out dryly.

All right madam, he thought to himself, *if you wish to play games, I'll go along with you.* He had been playing such games more than a century longer than she had.

He gestured toward the photographs. "You mean *that* slaughter? I said no such thing, madam. No such thing."

"You said that if any slaughter of human beings by the monstrous Darotha was taking place, it would have come to light long before now." Her blue eyes were angry.

"I believe you have misquoted me, madam," he said with just the right amount of stiffness in his voice. "I am quite certain that I never called the Darotha monsters." Then his brown-black eyes bored steadily into hers. "And what has that to do with these photographs?"

Her eyes remained angry, and a whiteness appeared at the corners of her mouth. "I see," she said tightly. "You are denying human status to the natives of Sandaroth, then."

"To most of them, yes," Hiroa said. "There is a smallish insectoid creature with all the bad habits of a mosquito, which I would particularly claim to be inhuman."

"Dr. Hiroa!" she exploded suddenly, "don't bandy words with me! You know perfectly good and well what I mean!"

"Blanche—" her husband began.

But Hiroa interrupted him. "No, madam, I do *not* know what you mean! Natives? *What* natives? Very well, I won't bandy words with you any more, if you will stop throwing around undefined terms like 'natives'!"

"I won't be—"

"Blanche, shut up."

Dr. Dennis Barlow didn't speak loudly, but there was firmness and authority in his voice. His wife threw him an angry glance, but she shut up. Dennis Barlow wasn't looking at her, but at Dr. Hiroa.

"Dr. Hiroa, my wife and I have carefully studied the reports concerning the major life forms on this planet. Is it not true that the amphibious, tentacled Darotha have not only enslaved the native humanoids but butcher them and eat them?"

"Butcher and eat them, yes," Dr. Hiroa said calmly. "But enslave them? Hardly. It takes a certain amount of intelligence and a certain amount of tractability to become a slave. You might, by stretching the meaning a little, say that our ancestors enslaved the horse. But never the Bengal tiger or the wolf."

Barlow said: "You are not an anthropologist, Dr. Hiroa?" It was only phrased as a question, not meant as one.

"No," Hiroa said. "My field is political sociology. I'm here to make sure that the colony of *Homo sapiens terrestrialis* doesn't go hog-wild socially, as happened on Vangomar."

"Nor a biologist, either?" Barlow persisted.

"Nor a biologist, either," Hiroa agreed tiredly.

"Hm-m-m. According to the reports, you do not regard the native humanoids as being anything more than animals. The Darlington Foundation does not feel that you or anyone else here on Sandaroth is qualified to make such a judgment. I am a biologist— to be more specific, a zoologist. My wife is an anthropologist. We are both qualified and, if I may say so, well-known and respected in our fields. As you are in yours, of course. The Foundation has sent us here to check scientifically on the plight of the species which we have tentatively named *Homo sapiens sandarothorum*. We had thought to ask your aid, but apparently you, too, are convinced that they are just animals."

"My dear Dr. Barlow," Hiroa said evenly, "I will be perfectly happy to give you whatever aid you desire. Your papers are in order, your commission is explicit. To imply that I would fail to aid you simply because I disagree with your personal bias is to do me an injustice which borders on personal insult."

"I have no bias one way or the other," Barlow snapped. "Nor has my wife. We are here merely to see that justice is done."

"Exactly," his wife agreed. "No personal insult was intended at all, Dr. Hiroa. By the way, may I ask you a question?"

A personal question, of course, Hiroa thought. *That's the only kind that is prefaced by such a remark.* "I am never offended by an honest question," he said aloud, "unless you are offended by a truthful answer."

She ignored that. "You are a New Zealander, I believe, of Maori descent?"

"I am."

"Then I should think that you would have more compassion for the native humans, considering how your own ancestors were treated by the British in the eighteenth and nineteenth centuries."

"In the first place, Mrs. Barlow, my ancestors were never enslaved or eaten by the British—though I do not deny the possibility that an ancestor or two of mine mightn't have enjoyed English long pig once in a while. In the second place, we won our right to recognition as human beings with human rights by our own ability to learn new ways and by our ability and valor in war. We forced recognition on the British; it was not handed to us on a silver platter by do-gooders. And in the third place, the Maori were human in the first place, if you'll pardon my use of an old wheeze to make a definite, valid point."

Blanche Barlow's lips tightened again, but she said nothing.

"Now," Dr. Hiroa went on, "I see no reason to continue with these arguments. They prove nothing one way or another. Instead of either of us arguing from personal feelings, we should be arguing from scientific facts. You two are here to uncover those facts. Rather than quarrel, let us set up your program. Let us discuss ways and means. Let us establish your needs to carry on this work."

It took him another ten minutes of diplomacy to get the scowls off their faces and replace them with friendly smiles, but he managed it. It took another two hours to make arrangements for the studies they wanted to conduct, but it was accomplished with only the slightest friction.

"He's not such a bad old boy," Dennis Barlow said as he and his wife walked down the hall from Dr. Hiroa's office.

"He is a bigot," Blanche said firmly. "But," she conceded, "I have met many bigots, and some of them are perfectly likeable and rational except in the field of their bigotry."

At the door of the elevator, Barlow tapped the "down" button. No gravshafts here; old-fashioned electrics were as yet the best that Sandaroth could offer. The three-quarters of a million Earth colonists had only been on the planet for twenty-five years, although a small group of scientists had been on the planet for nearly thirty-five years before the colonists came. Building a viable colony on an alien planet takes time, money, and effort, and necessities rather than luxuries, basics rather than elaborations, are the primary considerations.

Dennis and Blanche Barlow waited patiently as the indicator crept up toward the figure "6."

When the door slid open and a tentacled horror stepped out, Blanche gave one little scream and fainted. Her husband barely had the presence of mind to grab her and huddle against the wall with her in his arms as the Daroth strode by with pantherlike steps.

Dr. Hiroa looked up as the knob on his office door turned twice with forceful clatter and then was still.

"Come in and be welcome," he called, knowing that whoever was on the other side was a Daroth. Tentacles, being boneless, are not well adapted for door-knocking, so the Darotha, recognizing the terrestrial desire for privacy, which they themselves did not possess to any marked degree, had adopted their own convention for announcing their presence.

The knob turned again, and the being came in. "'Ello, Dr. 'Iroa. I accept your 'ospitality." It was difficult for a Darotha to form a soft aspirate; it tended to come out gargled, like the *ch* in the German *ach*. Some Darotha pronounced it that way; others simply dropped it. It was a matter of taste on the part of the individual.

"Hello, Ghundruth! What brings you here? I thought you were going to be staying at Great Shoals for another hundred-days."

155

"Some things came up, Doctor," Ghundruth said, making little circles with the tips of his foremost pair of tentacles. "I thought it best to discuss them with you. But first, I wish you to convey my apologies to your new people."

"Oh," said Hiroa. "You've met the Barlows."

"In the 'all, yes. Just as I came from the elevator. Since they were obviously shocked and frightened, I affected not to notice them."

"I shall convey your apologies," Hiroa said, "although, of course, such apologies are not at all necessary. It is an automatic reaction of those who are not prepared to meet a Daroth."

"Of course," Ghundruth agreed. "So our people react who 'ave never seen one of you before nor been informed of your existence. 'Ad these people, then, not been informed?"

"Not completely," Hiroa said. The statement, he reflected, was true as far as it went. "Their information was meager and unsatisfactory. My apologies to you for that oversight."

"It is as nothing," Ghundruth said, twirling a tentacle-tip. He kept the tips folded, as most Darotha habitually did when they were not being use for delicate work, making the tentacles look like those of an octopus. But, when the work at hand demanded it, each tentacle-tip opened out like a flower, splitting into five tentacular "fingers"—or, more accurately, "thumbs," since each was opposable to every other one. "But that brings a question to mind. I 'ave deduced that there must be a savage life form on your 'ome world w'ich resembles us in many respects. I am curious as to w'ether my deduction is correct."

"It is," Hiroa said carefully. He did not want to lie to Ghundruth. "It is purely an aquatic creature, rather than amphibious as you people are, but it has eight tentacles and is generally dreaded by our people. It is carnivorous, of course." He hesitated, then added: "It is called an octopus."

Ghundruth's shark-tiger mouth curled into a grin and a gurgling chuckle came from deep in his throat. "So *that* is w'y you call us 'Octopussies'!"

"Partly," Hiroa agreed. *Tread carefully now!* "But that word is a...what we call a 'portmanteau word'...that is, a word made up by blending two words. The other word is "pussy," which refers to a small, furry, warm-blooded creature with which some of our people live in a semi-symbiotic relationship."

Ghundruth looked interested. "Indeed? And w'at is the... the—mechanism?—trade...arrangement?—I do not feel I 'ave the right words."

"The mutual agreement," Hiroa said.

"Yes. W'at does each provide the other, if I do not offend by asking."

"Not at all. A man provides tenderness, security, shelter, and nourishment, while the pussy provides companionship, emotional

156

warmth, and friendship. They are not, you must understand, of high intellectual capacity; their companionship is of a purely emotional character."

"Ah! I see. I thank you for your confidence." Then the tips of each of his two foretentacles split into five finger-length sections and he entwined them in the manner of a man folding his hands over his chest. It was a gesture signifying: "We have exchanged pleasantries; now I wish to speak of important business."

Hiroa lifted his hands and folded them at chest level in reply, indicating that business talk was agreeably in order. Inwardly, he felt a sense of relief. The Darotha had very little sense of physical privacy, but their sense of mental privacy was strong. It was not that they were not curious; their sense of curiosity was highly developed. But their culture forbade permitting that curiosity to invade the personal life of another. A Daroth could, would, and did pry into everything the physical world had to offer. Almost any intelligent adult Daroth could take a device he had never seen before—a mechanical wristwatch, for example—and disassemble it after a few minutes of study, then put it back together in working order. And if such a device was left around untended, a Daroth would proceed to take it apart and study it without asking permission, unless it was actually in use at the time.

Hiroa himself had once watched in faint awe while a Daroth had opened the first safe ever to arrive on Sandaroth, many years ago. It was of old-fashioned design; the newer, personally-attuned, saturated-field devices were too expensive for the economy of Sandaroth's human colony, besides being unnecessary. (The rigid psychological requirements for Sandaroth colonists had kept out those whose mental makeup inclined them away from honest labor and toward felony. The Darotha were the first intelligent extraterrestrial race that man had met, and Hiroa had insisted that Sandaroth be colonized by civilized men, not barbarians.) The safe had not been particularly designed to be burglar-proof; it was designed as a fireproof cache for records. Concrete and steel were still expensive, and most buildings were built of native woods.

Physically, the safe had been a three-foot cube with a door in one side and a simple combination lock set in the door. It was Hiroa's own, and still stood in his office, although the old wooden building had long since been replaced by the present ferroconcrete structure. But twenty years ago, Hiroa had felt that the safe was necessary.

The day after it had arrived, imported at great expense from Earth, a Daroth had come to see Hiroa, and the sociologist had been talking on the phone—still non-vision in those days. He had indicated that the being should wait and went on with his conversation.

The Daroth sat down to wait. (There had been no separate

waiting room then, either.) His eyes wandered around the room. He watched Miss Deller, Hiroa's secretary and chief assistant, working assiduously at an electrotyper for a few minutes. Then, having absorbed all the information he could from watching the machine being operated, he turned his eyes to the safe beside her desk.

He looked at it for a long time, apparently fascinated. Miss Deller took a sheet from her typer and left the room. The Daroth rose and walked over to look at the electrotyper and saw that it was still on. "In use," then. Very well. He looked back at the safe. He knelt down to inspect it more closely. Then he looked up at Hiroa to see if he was being observed. Good! He was! He reached out a tentacle-tip and touched the steel structure, his eyes still on Hiroa. Hiroa watched, but went on talking.

The Daroth splayed out his five small tentacles, still watching Hiroa, and rippled them across the top of the safe. No reaction from Hiroa. The Daroth solemnly and slowly closed his eyes and then opened them again. It was the equivalent of a silent nod of thanks from a human being.

"Yes. Certainly, Charlie," Hiroa had said into the phone. "Yes. Bye." But when the click came from the other end, he did not cradle the phone. "Oh, Well, maybe," he said, not knowing how much English the Daroth understood. He wanted to see what the being was up to. He was glad he had so decided.

The Daroth touched and looked: Top, bottom, sides, and back. Then back to the safe door, where he felt around the fine crack between the body of the safe and the door itself. He tried the opening handle. Nothing happened. Then he touched the dial—very cautiously. He looked closely at the markings. He turned it slowly, first one way, then the other. He had one tentacle on the handle, one on the knob of the dial, and another near the dial, its sensitive fingerlets touching the rim where the numbers were engraved. The other five tentacles were touching the safe at various other places, sensitive fingerlets attuned to whatever information they might bring. He looked, Hiroa thought, like a starfish opening an oyster, but instead of steady pressure he was using far more potent forces; observation and intelligence.

Hiroa went on making comments into the dead phone. "No, Charlie." "Sure." "If you think so."

Miss Deller returned and stopped just inside the door. She looked at the Daroth and then at Hiroa. Then, understanding and accepting the situation immediately, she went over to her desk and sat down as though nothing unusual at all were going on.

Hiroa had been glancing occasionally at the wall chronometer. When the Daroth finally pulled down on the handle and the safe door swing open, Hiroa looked quickly at the chronometer.

From the time he had started to turn the dial until the opening of the door, something over seventeen minutes had elapsed. In that

158

time, the Daroth had ascertained that the structure was a container, that the handle opened it, and that the dial had to be manipulated in a certain way to release the mechanism that held the door shut. The sensitivity of his fingerlike end-tentacles had done the rest, telling him each time a tumbler fell.

It had been partly luck, of course, but the thinking required had far outweighed the luck.

The Daroth ignored the papers in the safe. He was inspecting the toggle-bolts and the sockets they slid into. Hiroa said: "Fine, Charlie. Good-by." And hung up.

The Daroth looked up quickly, then rose to his feet. Without looking at the safe, he closed the door, spun the dial, and tested the handle while he said: "Thanks for chance to self-instruct."

"You are welcome. You wished to speak to me."

"Iess. Iess Ioo are the Chiiroa?" The guttural aspirate was strong. "Yes."

"I are...be?...is?...Ghundruth. I are...am!...I am cherder of fish. I am told to speak to the Chiroa."

In the twenty years that had passed since then, Ghundruth had lost most of his accent, but his basic personality had remained. Questions about mechanisms; about chemistry, electronics, and physics; about astronomy; about anything the physical world had to offer;—such questions were asked without hesitation. But never personal questions. And, like his fellow Darotha, he considered a question "personal" if it had anything to do with societal relationships; with emotional reactions; with the Earthmen's government, politics, aspirations, desires, intentions, methodology, or purpose; with anything, in fact, that might conceivably be considered subjective, instinctive, or cultural. If information of that sort was volunteered, it was listened to with care—but it was never, never asked for.

Hiroa felt it was a measure of the relationship he had with Ghundruth that that reservation had, to some extent, broken down between them in the past few years. Not often, and not without deep apologies, but occasionally, Ghundruth would ask such a question. Even then, his questions were never what the average Earthman would really call "personal."

On the other hand, the questions he had just asked were, in a way, personal. There were certain reactions and thought patterns of some human beings that Hiroa did not, as yet, want to reveal to the Darotha. He did not yet want them to know that the seven hundred and fifty thousand human colonists on Sandaroth were a carefully selected group, unlike the average stay-at-home Earthman, and even more unlike the average antisocial malcontent whose numbers formed the bulk of the colonists to other Earthlike planets, where no alien intelligence had been found.

The Darotha, who were occasionally confronted with the

emotional reaction of a few of the new colonists, were inclined to accept it as a non-personal reaction. The situation, they assumed, was analogous to their own reaction when Earthmen had first been seen among them. The Darotha had, individually and collectively, reacted with both fear and loathing when they first saw a human being.

Just so would a group of human beings have reacted if suddenly confronted by a rabid wolf. How long would it take a human being to recognize that, regardless of *appearance,* what at first appeared to be a wolf was, judging by his *behavior,* a rational being? On the average, Hiroa knew, it would take longer than it had taken the Darotha to see that human beings were not Iachus.

The word "Iachu" was of English derivation. The preliminary scientific expedition which had first seen the humanoid natives of Sandaroth had immediately dubbed them "Yahoos," thus giving Jonathan Swift another score to rank alongside his prediction of the two moons of Mars. After seeing them, the scientists had felt that the reaction of the Darotha upon seeing an Earthman for the first time was understandable and even justifiable. It was to the credit of the Darotha that they had seen and recognized the differences as well as the similarities between the two races which had been spawned separately on two planets so widely separated in space.

The Darotha were shrewd observers of behavior; they spent the first ten years of their lives as gill-equipped fish-like forms, rather like a small porpoise with tentacles, and one must learn to judge behavior in the sea. Long ago, skin divers in Earthly seas had learned to judge whether a given shark was dangerous or not by watching his behavior. Those who did not had a higher mortality rate than those who did. With the Darotha, that process had been going on for millennia, and each individual Daroth had spent more time in the sea by his tenth birthday than a dozen terrestrial skindivers had spent collectively in their entire lives.

The environment of the sea differs qualitatively from the environment of the land. Only the very surface of the sea is troubled by weather; a few fathoms down, the sea is a womb, as far as the non-living environment is concerned. Hail, frost, snow, blistering heat, dehydration, and even the pull of gravity—all negligible or non-existent. Even earthquakes and volcanism, while not unknown, do not take the toll of life that they do on the surface. The dangers faced by marine life are those threatened by other life forms in the sea. On land, death by misadventure is far more prevalent than death by assassination with intent to ingest. In the sea, the reverse is true.

An intelligent marine life form, therefore, learns a different set of lessons than an intelligent land form. An amphibious form, such as the Darotha, has the advantage of learning both.

Little wonder, then, that Ghundruth had deduced the existence of a terrestrial species resembling the Darotha. Why else would an Earthman be startled, frightened by the sight of a Daroth?

Why? thought Hiroa. Simply that human beings used their imagination differently than Darotha did. The Darotha, exposed to dangers on both land and sea, exposed to the voraciousness of marine life and the inanimate, mindless, but nonetheless powerful and deadly natural forces on land, had to use their imaginations to deal with *real* possible dangers. Hiroa was not yet sure whether it was a genetic or a cultural trait—though he hoped it was the latter—but the fact remained that the Darotha were not much given to imaginative fiction—certainly not to the extent that Earthmen were.

Thus, Hiroa would have found it difficult to explain the Barlows' reaction if he had had to admit that, except for the tentacles, a Daroth did not resemble an octopus at all closely, and that the "pussy" part of the tag men had given Darotha was influenced by the end of the word "octopus," and referred, not to the common house cat, but to a resemblance to the greater feline carnivores.

So when he folded his hands to indicate that he was willing to speak of business with Ghundruth, he was happy that the Daroth had not inquired further into "personal" matters. He waited for Ghundruth to speak.

"Dr. 'Iroa," Ghundruth said, "a tragedy is 'appening on the Great Shoals. We do not know 'ow to deal with it."

"What sort of tragedy?" Hiroa asked, narrowing his eyes.

"Our last group of young are—going mad."

Blanche Barlow rubbed her eyes wearily. "Dennis, if I have to sit through another tape I'll either go blind or crazy. I haven't made up my mind which."

Dr. Dennis Barlow chuckled. "I agree, honey, but we're getting a lot of the data we need." He riffled through a notebook which by now comprised over a hundred pages. "Getting this stuff correlated is going to be our big job."

He reached over to the playback and took out the spool of TV tape. "The next one is—"

"Please, Dennis! No more today! If I see another tape of those pitiful people living like animals...I...I'll cry. How can they *allow* it?"

Without comment, Barlow touched the cutoff switch, and the glow in the big, two-meter square TV screen they had been watching faded to a dead silver-gray.

"How *can* they *allow* it?" she repeated, her large blue eyes suddenly focused directly on her husband's face.

His wife's question was still rhetorical, Barlow knew, but he also knew she wanted some kind of answer.

"Don't get upset, honey," he said gently. "They've been living like that for tens of thousands of years now, I imagine. Another few months—" He was going to say: *won't hurt anything,* but, seeing the expression that was coming over her face, he rapidly shifted gears, and with hardly a pause finished: "—and we'll be able to change all that."

Before she could say anything, the door of the viewing room opened and a tall, broad-shouldered, dark-haired man with a pronounced widow's peak came in. Then he stopped.

"Oh, I'm sorry," he said. "I didn't realize the screen was in use." He spoke with a British accent that had been modified by years away from England.

"That's perfectly all right, Dr. Pendray," Dennis Barlow said with a smile. "We'd just finished."

Blanche Barlow, too, had allowed her incipient frown to be dissipated by a smile. "Yes, we're through for today, Doctor. Come right on in. Actually, we've taken up rather more time than we should have, I suppose."

"Not at all," Pendray said. "I'm really in no hurry. No urgency about it at all. Just wanted to look at a couple of dissection tapes. The nervous system of the Darotha tentacular complex is quite interesting. If you'd care to watch—" He left the sentence floating as an invitation.

"No, I don't think so; thank you," Blanche Barlow said. Then: "Tell me: how did you get Darotha bodies for dissection?"

The surgeon smiled. "You might say they were willed to us. The Darotha practice sea burial, but they're not dogmatic about it. They have no objections to our studies."

"Natural deaths, then?"

"Or accidental," Dr. Pendray said.

"Have you made dissections of the bodies of any of the humanoids?" the woman asked.

"Oh, yes. Several. I can show you the tapes on them, if you like. I see the ones you've been studying are those taken of them in their native habitat. Very good, aren't they? Some of them go back over fifty years. Hidden cameras, all automatic."

"How do you get the humanoid bodies you dissect? Are they willed to you, too?" Her voice was persistent.

Pendray chuckled. "Well, hardly. Most of them come from the Darotha at round-up time. A few have been shot. And several died in captivity. They don't last long in captivity, you know, so we don't capture them any more. Cruel, I think, to cage any wild beast that way when it simply pines away and dies. And the Yahoos won't breed in captivity, either." He paused, looking at her. "What's the matter, Mrs. Barlow?"

"*Yahoos.*" Her voice was bitter. "All you have to do is put a degrading tag on someone, eh, Dr. Pendray? Call him 'nigger,' or

162

'chink,' or 'gook'; any nasty label that will take away his dignity! Call him a wild beast, an animal! Then it's all right to shoot him or butcher him or imprison him, isn't it, Dr. Pendray? No, thank you, Dr. Pendray; I do not believe I would like to look at your dissection tapes. Take me out of here, Dennis."

She turned angrily and strode toward the door, with Dennis Barlow following. She did not quite reach the door.

"Mrs. Barlow!"

She stopped, turned slightly, and looked over her shoulder at Pendray. "Yes?"

"You have seen the tapes of the Yahoos in their native habitat, behaving in their accustomed manner?" His voice was calm on the surface, but there were crackling undercurrents.

"Yes."

"Mrs. Barlow, one cannot take from an organism that which it does not possess. One cannot take dignity from a Yahoo. One cannot even *give* dignity to a Yahoo. If you had learned anything from those tapes, you should have learned that. It would probably be a waste of your time, indeed to study the dissection tapes, for you would likely learn nothing from *them*, either. Good day, Mrs. Barlow."

Dr. Dennis Barlow's face clouded, but before he could frame any answer, Blanche pulled his arm, and the two of them stalked out without another word.

Dr. Marcus Landau was in the tape stacks, replacing two spools which he had been viewing, when the Barlows came in. He saw them before they saw him.

Uh-oh! he thought to himself. *The Golden Fury is about to launch a billion-volt lightning bolt that will scorch the area for miles around, if that corona effect means anything. I wonder who or what turned her generator on?*

Dr. Landau was a middle-aged man in his early eighties. He had skin the color of burnished bittersweet chocolate, hair like tiny curls of fine, frosted silver wire, and a mellow voice that carried the soft accents of Bermuda. Along with Dr. Paul Hiroa and Dr. James Pendray, he was one of the three ranking scientists of Sandaroth. After observing Blanche Barlow for the first week of her stay, he had tentatively named her "The Golden Fury"; now, at the end of the second week, there was nothing tentative about it. He had also named Paul Hiroa "Old Rawhide" and Jim Pendray "Silk"—but only to himself and only because it amused him to play mental games with himself. This game he called "Character Tag" and it had strict rules. No one got a tag until Dr. Landau was morally certain that all of the people who knew that person would instantly recognize the tag as fitting and accurate. Like Aristotle, however, he was satisfied with the results of his own cerebration; he never put them to experimental test.

He had not yet made up his mind about Dennis Barlow.

"Blanche," Barlow said in a low, tight voice, "that was uncalled for. You—" Suddenly he stopped and his voice became more normal. "Oh, hello, Dr. Landau."

Aha! Observed! And by a zoologist! "How do you do Dr. Barlow, Mrs. Barlow," Landau said aloud. "How are your researches coming along? I trust our modest Research Center has supplied you with at least a modicum of pertinent data, eh?"

Evidently the thunderbolt had not been forged for Marcus Landau. She not only didn't unleash it, she put it aside—probably, he decided, for later use. But the coronal discharge that had seemed to crackle soundlessly around her head subsided and vanished.

"Oh, more than that, Dr. Landau," she said with a smile. "There is a fantastic amount of data here. Correlation and interpretation will be the difficult part, I'm afraid. By the way, when do you expect Dr. Hiroa to return from Great Shoals?"

"Why, I don't know. Neither, I'm afraid, does he. I spoke to him over the phone this morning, and he doesn't know how much longer his work will take. Again he asked me to convey his apologies for his precipitate departure so soon after your own arrival. If there is anything you may need or require, of course, you have but to ask."

"Thank you. We will be wanting to make field trips eventually, of course, but it will be some time before we can definitely map out precisely what our plans will be."

Landau bowed his silvery head just a few degrees. "Naturally. Is there anything I can do for you at the moment?"

The Barlows looked at each other. It was Dennis who spoke. "Not just at the moment, Dr. Landau; thanks. Everything's going smoothly so far."

"I am happy to hear it. I wish you every success in your search for truth."

He left them and headed for No. 2 viewing room. Dr. Pendray had not yet turned on the screen. "Busy, Jim?" Landau asked.

"Nothing urgent, Marc. Why?"

Landau came in and closed the door behind him. "I was just wondering what you'd said to our emissaries from the Darlington Foundation that aroused their wrath," he said with a grin. "Especially hers."

"Oh, that." Pendray repeated the conversation.

"Diplomacy, thy name is Pendray," Landau murmured when he had finished.

"It won't matter a damn anyway," Pendray said with a shrug. "I have a feeling that she's already mentally writing her final report, complete with conclusions. In the back of her mind, she has already decided what she is going to tell the Foundation. Nothing you or I or anyone else could say will change it, and that husband of hers will go right along with her."

"You have no great faith in them as scientific investigators, eh, Jim?"

"Are you kidding? I've seen their kind before. They will gather vast reams of data, make all kinds of carefully tailored experiments, and prepare dozens of pretty little graphs and tables. They will discard the 'anomalies,' of course—any data that doesn't fit in with their preconceived notion. What's left will be neatly pushed and trimmed until it *does* fit. What does Paul think?"

"The same. What can we do about it? The Darlington Foundation will have the report they want. With that and those photographs, the stink they'll raise on Earth will be enough to wreck the whole Sandaroth project, ruining human and Daroth alike."

"One almost wishes," Pendray said, "that the Barlows fail to return from their projected field trip—except that that wouldn't do a bit of good."

"No. The stink that would arise would have a different aroma, but the results would be the same. It's not bad enough that we have this mysterious madness in the last group of Darotha adolescents; we have to have madness of our own race." He put his hand to his forehead and massaged his brows with thumb and middle finger.

"Who's behind it?" Pendray asked. "Do you have any further information?"

"Only what we guessed before. The only man who could have taken those pictures was Finnerly of Industrial Computer Corporation," Landau said. "But they're not the only ones."

"Who else? I thought you said you didn't have any more information."

"I don't. But think about it. ICC isn't trying to get troops sent here to 'protect' the Yahoos just so they can wind up selling us computers and guidance-and-control systems for a few multiphase lathes and shapers."

"You're right." There was anger in Pendray's voice. "Without the Darotha, this planet would be just like any other. Wide open. We'd have fifty million people here within five years. No control."

"No control," Landau agreed. "But plenty of new sales territory for certain unscrupulous lice. We know who *isn't* in on it, too. None of the Big Three in inertiogravitics; they're strictly honest and strictly ethical. The same goes for most of the big, important corporations. You can bet ICC isn't getting any backing from those boys. But there are others. Too many of them."

"It'll be a double play, then," Pendray said. "They'll hit us high and low. Protect the Noble Yahoos on the one hand and open Sandaroth up for full colonization on the other."

"The sound of two hands clapping," Landau said dryly.

"Yeah. While the only extraterrestrial intelligent race we have

165

met gets crushed between them. We might as well pack up and go home."

"You don't have much faith in Paul's plan, then?"

"Frankly, Marc, no." Pendray admitted. "He seems to think that giving the Barlows all the data they can swallow will convince them. But, dammit, Marc, you can't convince a fanatic he's wrong by giving him data. He only believes what he wants to believe."

"'My mind is made up; please don't confuse me with facts.'" Landau quoted.

"Exactly."

"But there's nothing else we can do, Jim," Landau said. "We can't fight the Darlington Foundation for the Promotion of Human Brotherhood. I doubt if even the Government could fight it. It's got billions behind it—both in money and in people. And it's full of people like the Barlows: honest, dedicated, hardworking fanatics."

"I know. I know." Pendray rubbed his chin with a fingertip. "What about Governor Donovan? What's he going to do?"

"Paul talked to him. He agreed to stay out of the whole mess. If worse comes to worst, and the planet is opened up, he can stay on as Colonial Governor and try to protect the Darotha as much as possible."

"That may help. But not much." Pendray suddenly twisted his mouth into a sardonic grin. "Maybe I'd have been better off if I hadn't come back from the field until this was all over, one way or another. At least one has other things to worry about out in the boondocks. I'm really not a city boy at heart."

Landau grinned back. "Obviously not, or you wouldn't call Point Garrison a city. We're still a village at heart. Forty thousand people could get lost without anyone noticing it in a real city."

"It contains half the human population of the planet," Pendray said. "No city on Earth can make that statement."

"Agreed. Oh, and Jim—"

"Yes?"

"I think we'll be better off if we don't antagonize the Barlows. It just—"

"Just stiffens their resistance. I know, Marc. I'll try to cultivate the 'friendly physician and counselor' attitude. The country doctor bit. But if she gets offended every time she hears the word Yahoo in that context, she's going to feel offended most of the time."

"Well, we can't wrap her in swaddling clothes. I'll let you go back to your tapes now. Thanks, Jim."

Very few of the citizens of Point Garrison were aware of the danger embodied in Blanche and Dennis Barlow. Their names had been mentioned in the newscasts when they arrived, but hardly anyone paid any attention. In certain circles, the word spread that they were studying the Yahoo, but that aroused no particular curiosity. Why should it? It was said by those who had met them that the Barlows—and especially Blanche Barlow—were "a little nutty" on the subject of Yahoos and Yahoo intelligence and most of these people learned to substitute the phrase "humanoid natives" for "Yahoos" in their presence. Except for that quirk, they seemed a pleasant enough couple. Women were attracted to the handsome, personable Dennis, and men found it difficult to keep their eyes off Blanche's beauty. Even so, they were "foreigners"—visitors, not residents. Somehow, they did not fit well into the social life of Point Garrison. If the truth were known, that didn't bother the Barlows; they didn't even notice it. They were on Sandaroth to work, not to socialize.

At the end of the first month, Dennis decided he'd take a tour of one of the small factories in the city: Garrison Flye Mfg. Co.

The manager of the plant was a short, round, sandy-haired Scot named Fred Doyle. He met Barlow at the front gate and gave him a hearty handshake.

"Glad to know you, Dr. Barlow! Governor Donovan called me. Said you wanted to look around. Glad to have you. Come in, come in."

After a few minutes of polite amenities, Dennis Barlow was asked where he'd like to start.

"Well, to be perfectly frank, Mr. Doyle—"

"Just call me Fred, Dr. Barlow. Everybody does."

"O.K. Fred. And I'm Dennis. At any rate, I was going to say that I had some free time today, so I thought I'd take a kind of busman's holiday. My wife is feeding stuff into the computer at the Research Institute, and it's a job that only takes one. Actually, I'm interested in your factory as a zoologist rather than from the actual manufacturing point of view."

"Well, if you'll tell me why a zoologist should be interested in the manufacture of inertiogravitic motors from a zoological point of view, I'll be glad to help you, Dennis."

"I understand you have some Darotha working for you, Fred, and I understand they can do jobs that no human being can do."

"Oh!" Fred chuckled. "Why, sure! Come along; I'll take you to the multiplex lathe section. That's the most interesting part, anyway. I'll introduce you to my foreman, Than; he'll be able to show you how these things work."

He led Dennis Barlow to a huge building full of machines. Everything was well-lit, airy, and clean. It seemed more like a kitchen or an operating room than a workshop. It took Barlow a minute or two to realize that, as far as he could see, he and Doyle were the only human beings in the place. All the machines were run by Darotha.

"Than!" Fred called to one of them who was wiping off a big machine with a piece of toweling. "C'mere a minute! I want you to meet a fellow."

The Daroth put the rag down and came toward the two men with panther-like grace. "'Ow are you this morning, Fred?" His voice carried easily over the low, all-pervading hum of power that was the only noticeable noise in the place.

"Pretty good, Than; pretty good. I'd like you to meet Dr. Dennis Barlow. Dr. Barlow, this is Thannovosh, my general foreman for this section."

"Glad to know you, Dr. Barlow." Then he looked expectantly at Fred.

"Have you got one of the machines free, Than? I'd like you to give Dr. Barlow a little demonstration if you've got the time."

"Sure, Fred; glad to. Just come this way over to number fourteen, Dr. Barlow."

Barlow followed, but he was looking at the other machines in the building. There were about thirty of them, and at each stood a Daroth, all eight tentacles moving at once, turning various verniers, knobs, and control wheels. There was a weird, rhythmic beauty about it that reminded him of seaweed fronds moving in a slow current or the tentacles of a slowly swimming octopus.

At machine number fourteen, Than said: "I've got 'er all set up for a BJF-37, Fred. Will that be all right?"

"Sure. Fine. Show him your check-block, will you, and explain it to him."

From a drawer in the base of the machine, Than took an odd metal shape. It was about the size of a man's fist, but it was surfaced with weirdly undulating curves, complex three-dimensional curves that made queer hills and valleys and swirling grooves.

"This is w'at we call the check-block, Dr. Barlow. It's the same size and shape as the impulse spinner in an inertiogravitic unit. 'Ave you ever looked inside the engine of a flier?"

"Not with the casing off, no."

"Well, the impulse spinner 'as to undergo several different modes of motion at once—depending on w'ether you're moving up or down, right or left, pitching, yawing, rolling, or just 'overing. There are eight of them in an ordinary flier engine. They all move at tremendously 'igh velocities and undergo 'igh surges. And they all 'ave to be synchronized. This is made of 'ardened tool steel instead of Paramag alloy, but the shape is the same. Each one of these surfaces is a control surface for the various modes of motion and each performs a different function as the axis of spin is shifted. That's w'at makes it look so odd." Than chuckled. "It 'as a sort of a shapeless shape, you might say. But it 'as to be that way, and each curve 'as to be just so, or you'll get vibration that'll shake your engine apart."

Two tentacles put the block down. Two more indicated the machine itself. "Now this is w'at we call a multiplex lathe. An impulse spinner can't be cast; it 'as to be forged and machined. You 'ave to be sure it's 'omogeneous and of equal density throughout."

Two more tentacles reached out to a low, wheeled framework nearby and took a lump of metal out of a tray. Than held the lump up for Barlow's inspection. "This is the forged blank. All we 'ave to do is machine it, and this is 'ow it's done."

He fitted the check-block into the multiplex chuck to his left, and the forged blank into the chuck at his right. A guide rod touching the surface of the check-block was exactly matched with a borazon cutting tool that touched the forged blank. As the guide rod followed the curves of the check-block, the tool cut the same curves in the blank. A tentacle touched a switch and both pieces of metal began to spin. Then there was a sudden deadness in the air around the machine, as though someone had thrown a heavy blanket over it. "Got to 'ave the noise suppressors on," Than said, "otherwise this place would be a screaming 'ell."

Than spun two more wheels, and two more borazon tools moved toward the forged blank, each with its corresponding guide rod moving toward the check-block.

Then Than touched another switch and the dance of the tentacles began. There was a grace to it that reminded Barlow of the hand motions of a Hawaiian hula dancer. The tentacles moved knobs and levers, and the borazon tools, all three of them at once, bit smoothly into the spinning blank, slicing off ribbons of bright metal. Than touched the chuck control and the axis of spin changed slightly as the borazon chisels sliced away the unwanted metal. Again the axis of spin shifted, and the tools moved in and out over the blank, cutting, cutting.

Barlow watched in fascination as the impulse spinner took shape beneath the cutting edge of the borazon, transfiguring the lumpy-looking forged blank into a piece of precision machinery.

Then, abruptly, it was finished.

The tools fell away and the spinning stopped. Than released the chuck and took the finished piece out. "Now we'll take 'er over to the comparator and see 'ow she matches the master block." When he was done, he handed the new-formed impulse spinner to Barlow.

"There she is, Dr. Barlow. Correct to a thousandth of a millimeter. Next, she'll go in a similar machine for final polishing, and she'll be done."

"Beautiful," Barlow said in honest admiration.

"Thank you, sir. Was that all you wanted, Fred?"

"That's all. Thanks a lot, Than. Unless Dr. Barlow has some questions."

"The only question I can think of is: How did you do it? It's all I can do to control two arms and ten fingers. The thought of trying to control eight arms and forty fingers appalls me."

Than's shark-tiger face grinned widely. "Just takes practice, Dr. Barlow. And I'll tell you, I don't see 'ow you people do such delicate work with all those bones inside forcing you to bend only at certain places and in certain directions. I saw a man do steel engraving by 'and once, and I'll never understand 'ow 'e did it. Putting pressure on a burin takes internal bracing w'ich I 'aven't got, It would be like running this machine with my feet, it seems to me."

Barlow glanced at the Daroth's sandaled feet. There were no toes, properly speaking. Each foot came to a point, reminding Barlow of a medieval knight. At the tip was a single, heavy, curving claw.

"He keeps his feet folded in like that for walking on land," Fred said, noticing Barlow's glance. "Dr. Barlow's never met a Daroth before, Than. Show him how your feet unfold for swimming."

"Sure." With three tentacles, he braced himself lightly against the lathe. Two other tentacles pulled the sandal from his right foot. He lifted his leg up and doubled it at the knee, so that Barlow could see the "sole" of the foot. A crease ran from just forward of the heel to the base of the front claw. "W'en I'm in the water, I open it out, like this."

The crease widened and the foot folded out, so that the two halves of what had been the sole were now on the upper side of a wide, splayed foot, making a ridge of callous on each side of the upper part. The new sole thus exposed looked membranous and tender.

"Then you can't walk with your feet unfolded that way?" Barlow asked.

"Oh, I could," Than said, refolding his foot and putting it back in the sandal. "But not for very far before my feet 'urt so bad I couldn't take it. That's on solid land, I mean. Walking through swamps, like the brackish swamps down around the Delta Cape, a fellow can unfold 'is feet for walking across thick mud so 'e doesn't sink in. But if the mud is that soft, it doesn't 'urt, you see."

"Very handy," said Barlow. "Or should I say, 'footy'?"

"*Ooh!*" said Fred, wincing.

Than chuckled. "*Nothing's* 'andy for a Daroth."

"Puns aside," Fred said, "a skilled and trained Daroth comes in handy for running a multiplex lathe. No Earthman could do it. Not even four Earthmen working together could do it. It's been tried. Not only is the coordination lousy, but they get in each other's way. Back on Earth, they use a computer that costs more than the lathe and is damn near as massive. We just bought the lathes and then designed and built the controls ourselves. That saved the cost of the computer and the high interstellar freight charges. It also saves the cost of repairs and reprogramming the computer when you set up for a different size or type of impulse spinner. We pay standard wages for all our employees, Earther or Daroth, so the labor costs run high, but you have to have a certain amount of labor anyway to set up and break down the check-blocks and tools and for maintenance and so on. Besides, the machines are a lot more flexible this way. To set up a computer to make just one piece would cost the same as setting it up for a full run, while a Daroth can interrupt a run, tear down, set up, run a single piece, tear down and set up again, and be back on the regular run in fifteen minutes at no extra cost.

"But the real beauty of the thing is that all the money that would go for freight charges and computer costs stays right here on Sandaroth where it's needed, instead of being funneled back to Earth."

"I'm very 'appy about w'at goes into my pocket," said Than, touching a tentacle to his blue work-shorts, the only article of clothing he wore besides the sandals.

Dennis Barlow suddenly realized the change that had come over him in the past twenty minutes or so. He had come in with a sense of horror that had seemed to ride between his shoulder blades. So many Darotha around had brought clearly to mind those terrible photographs. But now he was aware that he thought of Than, not as a tentacled horror, but as a person. Someone you could talk to, laugh with, maybe have a few beers with of an evening. The photos had become dim and lifeless in comparison to the reality that stood before him.

A chime sounded, clearly but not stridently audible over the low hum in the shop.

"Lunchtime," said Fred. "Will you stay and eat with us, Dennis?"

"No, thanks, Fred. Some other time. I appreciate everything, really. I've enjoyed myself tremendously. It was a pleasure meeting you, Than; I hope to see you again sometime."

"The same 'ere, Dr. Barlow. Come again w'en you can stay longer. We can show you more."

"That's right," Fred said. "Come around again, early, and I'll show you through the whole plant. Lots of things here I think you might be interested in."

"I'll see if I can't work it in, Fred. But right now, I have a lunch date with a beautiful blonde. My wife."

"O.K. I'll walk you to the gate."

"Me for a *lurgh* sandwich and a cold drink," Than said. "See you again, Dr. Barlow." The Daroth loped off across the shop.

As the two men walked across the yard to the gate, Dennis said: "What was that Than said, Fred? a *lurg* sandwich?"

"*Lurgh,*" Fred corrected. "You've got to sort of gargle that g sound."

"Lurghh. I see. What is it?"

"Smoked Yahoo meat. Don't care for it myself, but—Why, what's the matter, Dennis? You sick or something?"

Barlow fought down the wave of horror and nausea that had swept over him. "No," he said. "No. I'm O.K. Just the sun, I guess."

"Yeah. Coming out of that air-conditioned shop into this heat can do that sometimes. You sure you're O.K.?"

"Sure. Just a little wave of dizziness is all. It's gone now. I'm fine."

But he ate no lunch that day, and he did not tell Blanche why.

Dr. James Pendray sat at the controls of the little six-passenger flier and secretly wished he knew what the devil was going on in Paul Hiroa's mind. The old boy was up to something, of that Pendray was certain. But just what it was...

Well, whatever it was, Pendray was willing to go along with it. That wise old brain had cooked up some sort of plan, and just because it was Hiroa's plan, it was bound to be a sound one.

In the seat behind him, Dennis and Blanche Barlow were talking in low but not secretive tones, pointing out to each other the various interesting configurations of the terrain below. At a groundspeed of little less than three hundred thirty kilometers per hour and an altitude of one kilometer, their viewpoint was just right for scenery-gazing.

"Is that the shoreline over there to the south, Jim?" Dennis asked from the back seat.

Pendray had been exercising his diplomacy of late, and the three of them were now on a first name basis.

"That's it. You won't be able to see it too well for a couple of hours yet. We're flying parallel to the sea. After that, it's only another hour to Great Shoals."

"And the humanoid territory is just north of there?" Blanche asked.

"That's right. Less than an hour's flight, even if we're unlucky. Usually, a tribe can be found within ninety kilometers of Grand Shoals."

"Good. We want to get there as quickly as possible."

Too flaming right she does, Pendray thought. The notion of going to the major city of the Darotha did not appeal to her at all. Pendray wasn't quite sure whether she loathed the Darotha, hated them, or feared them, but he suspected it was a blend of all three in various proportions depending on the circumstances.

"I meant to ask you, Jim," Dennis said, "if you know why the Darotha built their city at Great Shoals. I mean, we humans usually build a city near a river or lake or some other water supply, and on Earth the really big cities were near a shipping port. But the Darotha always stay near the sea, and they don't have much shipping, so why should they concentrate around Great Shoals?

172

Just random chance, or is there a reason for it?"

"Didn't you know?" Pendray was actually surprised. "It's one of their major breeding areas."

"*Breeding* areas?"

"Sure. Great Shoals is an off-shore section of the continental shelf that is practically horizontal. There's nearly a hundred thousand square kilometers of the shelf where the maximum depth is only ten fathoms and the average is about five. It's full of little islands and rocks, sticking above the surface. The edge of the shelf is nearly two hundred kilometers off-shore, but a man could probably wade all the way out if he picked his route carefully. Mightn't even have to get his hair wet. It's just the opposite of an Earthly seaport. Lousy for ship navigation, but a great place for the kiddies."

"How does their reproduction cycle go, anyway?" Dennis asked.

Pendray wondered how a zoologist could have failed to ask that question long before this. Blanche, the anthropologist, wasn't the least bit interested, of course, but Dennis should have been curious from the first. But Blanche had evidently kept him so wrapped up in the Yahoos that he had no time for excursions into other alien life forms.

"Nothing complicated about it," Pendray said. "The Darotha, like man, make love at all seasons of the year, and, as in the human female, the Darotha female's fertility periods are cyclic. But the Darotha cycle is annual rather than monthly. The eggs are laid in the sea about six weeks after fertilization and they hatch about three months after that—about midsummer. At the end of the ninth year, the lungs begin to develop and the gills to disappear. By the spring of the tenth year, the young are ready to come ashore and continue life as air breathers. Like humans, they're ready to reproduce about the time they're fourteen or fifteen, and the cycle begins all over again."

"Um—what sort of family life do they have?" Blanche asked, interested in spite of herself.

"None, if by 'family' you mean blood relationship. The kids are literally on their own for the first ten years. Nobody knows whose is whose or cares. The adults keep the big dangerous predators away, and the females will go out and throw food to the little ones. The adults do a great deal of swimming, and they have a great time romping with the kids. The children may not know who their parents are, but they're very much loved. An adult couple will take care of as many of the youngsters as he can afford to, after they have achieved the air-breathing stage."

"If they don't know what the genetic relationships are," Blanche said, "how do they prevent incest?"

"They don't," Pendray told her. "Why should they? The

173

statistical probability that any male and female picked at random will be brother and sister is very low. More often than not, an adult couple who have decided to mate permanently were brought up together in the same household since they were ten. They have no concept of virginity and no bans against premarital experimentation, either. A girl deposits a clutch of eggs every year after her fifteenth birthday; how does she know whether they're fertile or not? And why should she care? The mixing of genetic material is a great deal more random than it is in the human race, believe me."

"Then they have no sexual taboos at all?" Blanche asked.

"Sure they do. No adult would marry anyone more than ten years younger or older. That insures that the generations don't mix. And once a couple decide to marry, they mate for life. Adultery is almost unknown."

"I'm surprised they marry at all," Blanche said with a touch of sarcasm. "I doubt whether animals like that have any real concept of marriage."

Pendray kept his voice level. "Their concept of it isn't the same as ours, of course, but the similarities are surprising. Love, the desire for companionship, the feeling of mutual security, the rearing of a family—those points we have in common. And I doubt that any Daroth couple ever married because she was pregnant or because they had guilt feelings about premarital intercourse. There are some 'forced' marriages, of course. Bachelors and spinsters are frowned upon by society—much more strongly than they are in our own. There are loveless marriages just as there are quarrels and arguments and lawsuits and so on. They're no more perfect than we are—just different, that's all."

"Different," Blanche said. "Different. Oh, yes. Yes, we're different, all right. Dennis, look over there, to our left! Isn't that a lovely lake?"

She doesn't like Darotha, Pendray thought. *And the only good Indian is a dead Indian. Only she'd never say that about Indians.*

"Then it is not insanity?" Ghundruth said.

"I'm quite certain it isn't," Dr. Hiroa said. "Not in the sense you mean. These children have just learned something that none of your race has ever been exposed to before. It's our fault, of course. We Earthmen have been doing that sort of thing for as far back as we can trace. It's only in the past eighteen months that any sizable group of Earthmen have lived here in Great Shoals, and only during that time have your adolescent children been exposed to them."

"I'm afraid I do not understand," Ghundruth said. "These hallucinations, these unreal things w'ich they 'ave made in their own minds. That is not insanity?"

"No. The kids don't believe those things they tell are real. Look, Ghundruth; you can tell a lie, can't you?"

"Yes. When necessary, yes. But w'y do they feel it necessary to tell such outrageous lies?"

"That's the point, the whole point. They *don't* find it necessary. They do it for the fun of it; because they enjoy it."

Ghundruth was silent for a long stretch of seconds. Then he burst out: "I don't understand it! 'Ow can they enjoy such a thing? It isn't—it isn't *normal!* That's like enjoying blinking or something. One does it w'en one must, but one doesn't do it for *pleasure.*"

"Do you only eat when you must?"

"No. No."

"And you do enjoy it?"

"Yes. Is there a correlation?"

"Of course. Look at it another way; you use parables and analogies don't you?"

"For instruction. For the purpose of showing an example or for making a generality applicable specifically. Or for showing a similarity or correlation, as you are apparently doing now. But not just for fun. I can't understand that. None of us can."

Hiroa closed his eyes. "Maybe you never will, Ghundruth."

"W'y not? If a child can understand, can't I?" He did not understand; he did not *want* to understand. But he did not like to be told that such understanding might be beyond his capabilities.

"There have been cases, have there not," Hiroa said, "of a Darotha child being lost in a storm during his tenth year and being washed ashore in an uninhabited spot at just the time when the final change is taking place, when his gills have vanished and his lungs are doing all the work?"

"Yes. Occasionally. Not often. Usually 'e will find 'is way back."

"But sometimes he stays there?"

"There 'ave been cases of it. Usually the child dies very soon afterward. Unin'abited places usually 'ave no food available ashore, w'ich means the child would 'ave to live from the sea. But such cases 'ave 'appened, yes."

"What were they like when they were found?"

"Feebleminded. They could not speak and could not learn to speak. Nor could they learn civilized ways. We 'ave assumed that that was the reason w'y they did not return 'ome—because they were feebleminded."

"No. Just the reverse. Because they did not return home, they seemed feebleminded. There is a critical period for learning speech. If one of our children doesn't learn to speak by the time he is five, he never really learns to at all. With your children, that critical five-year period apparently comes immediately after the change. They don't become symbol users until then. If they're not taught to speak then, they never learn."

"Ahhh," Ghundruth said thoughtfully. "Like swimming."

"Swimming? How's that?"

"Occasionally, a child will 'ave an accident early in 'is tenth year, and 'e must be 'ospitalized. 'Is tail is dissolving 'is legs are growing. If 'e does not learn to swim with 'is legs during that year, 'e never learns after that. If 'e does not learn to walk during the following year, 'e never learns that."

"Then you can see my point. If I'd known that, I would have used it as my example."

"Is it not the same with you?"

"No. With us, swimming is an art that can be learned at any time, though it is easier to learn it in childhood."

"And w'at 'as this to do with telling lies for fun?"

"Not just with the telling, but with the understanding of why they are told for fun. I wonder if it isn't possible that lying for fun is an art that must be learned early or not at all. If it is, then an older Daroth canot learn it and, therefore, can never understand it. It is my belief that this is true."

"And all Earthmen do this? 'Ow is it that we 'ave never recognized this? 'Ow is it we did not know?"

"You didn't see it because you didn't recognize its existence at all. Ghundruth, both our races have a sense of humor, and in many places they overlap. Puns, for instance. We both enjoy making puns."

"Yes. Because of the theretofore unnoticed cross-correlation between two otherwise unrelated symbols. They are instructive and therefore enjoyable."

Hiroa looked at him. "I'll be damned," he said softly. "I never thought of it that way. Look; you tell jokes, just as we do. We don't enjoy all of yours, and you don't enjoy all of ours, but there are some that we share. Why do you tell jokes?"

"They are instructive. A joke is an instructive parable w'ich 'as an unexpected or theretofore unforeseen result. Is it not?"

"I've just realized, after all these years," Hiroa said, "that we laugh at the same things for entirely different reasons. I'd be willing to bet that the jokes of ours that you didn't get were those which were not instructive. Boy!"

"We learn more about each other every moment, eh, my friend? But you were going to make a correlation between jokes and lies-for-the-fun-of-it."

"I was going to point out that jokes *are* lies-for-the-fun-of-it," Hiroa said. "But evidently they are not, to your way of thinking."

"No. No. I do not understand what you mean. What is the *purpose* of these non-instructive parables? They are meaningless nonsense. Explain to me the meaning of the parable of *Silversheen and the Three Yahoos.*"

Paul Hiroa had to hold back a laugh. Whoever had told that one had made a couple of neat switches. A silvery sheen on the skin of a

Daroth female was prized in the same way that blondes were among Earthmen. And the "Three Yahoos" was almost perfect.

"It has no instructive meaning," Hiroa said. "It is an adaptation of a very old children's story. Almost every Earthman has heard it as a child. Where did you hear it?"

"One of my girls told it to me. She asked if I 'ad 'eard it, and I told 'er I 'ad not. I saw that she enjoyed telling it, but I saw no reason for it."

"Tell me: did she use different voice-tones for the three Yahoos? Was Papa Yahoo a deep-voiced person and Baby Yahoo high and squeaky?"

"Yes, that was the way of it."

"And the child enjoyed that particularly?"

"Apparently."

"What was your reaction?"

"I was shocked. I knew she 'ad 'eard it from one of your people, and I could not see w'y anyone would deliberately lie to a child for no reason. I still do not. Yahoos cannot speak, and it is a lie to say that they do."

"And did you explain to her that Yahoos don't speak?"

"Yes. And she said: 'Oh, I know that. It's just a story.' And I didn't understand. I still don't."

"Maybe you will eventually. Someday."

"But you do not think so, eh, friend Hiroa?" He smiled.

"I'd hate to bet on it one way or another. But the children understand it, and that's what led to the next step. They made up their own stories. They made up lies and thought their guardians would understand. And they didn't. You thought they were insane."

"Yes. And I must say frankly that I am not at all sure you are right in your explanation. Even you, wise as you are, do not know 'ow our minds work, any more than we understand you."

"I admit that." *Two countries separated by a common tongue,* he quoted to himself. "We can only wait and see. I shall ask my people not to tell any more stories of that kind to your children if you wish."

"Per'aps it will be better," Ghundruth said thoughtfully.
"It 'as caused much disturbance among the older Darotha. I do not like to see 'ard feelings between my people and yours." He paused. "But to be honest, I think the damage 'as already been done. We could forbid the children to tell the stories to each other, but 'ow could we enforce such a rule? It would not be possible. Therefore we will not, for it is foolish to make rules that cannot be enforced."

"I cannot enforce such a rule either, but I think my people will see the wisdom in acquiescing to my request." *And they'll get quite a laugh out of the idea that Silversheen and the Three Yahoos is a youth-corrupting story which contributes to the delinquency of minors. But they'll understand even as they laugh.*

And Ghun is right, he thought, *the damage has been done.*

"Dr. Hiroa," Blanche Barlow said angrily, "I would like to know why you have instructed a flierload of Darotha to follow us north into humanoid country!"

She had knocked on the door of his room, and when he'd said, "Come in," she had burst through the door and snapped out the question.

"I didn't order it, Mrs. Barlow," he said mildly. "That's the law. Not my law. Darotha law. That's protected territory up there."

"But they're going armed!"

"Of course. That's dangerous country, Mrs. Barlow."

"I don't need protection! My husband and I can take care of ourselves! The humanoids won't hurt us if we show them we come in peace and brotherhood! I won't be followed by armed monsters!"

Hiroa could hear every exclamation point slam into place. "Mrs. Barlow. Listen to me carefully. There is nothing I can do about it. The law cannot be abrogated for me or for you or for anyone else. The game warden must accompany *anyone* who goes up there. They are not just for your protection; they are for the protection of the humanoids, too. The game laws must be obeyed."

"*Game* laws!" Her eyes blazed. "So they're just—"

"*Mrs. Barlow!*" Hiroa had an amazingly powerful voice when he chose to use it. "I do not wish to listen to another of your tirades on the rights, privileges, and dignity of the humanoids. The game laws were laid down long before man ever arrived on this world. The wardens will inform you of those laws before you leave. I suggest you listen and obey. If there is nothing else, Mrs. Barlow, then good day."

"I call it a damn fool, damn dangerous stunt!" Dr. Pendray said in a low, harsh whisper.

"My wife knows what she's doing," Dennis Barlow said in the same tone of voice. "Shut up and let her do it. She knows how to handle primitive savages."

"But not wild animals!"

"Shut up!"

The two men were inside the flier. Barlow had a small TV recording camera focused on his wife, who was some thirty yards away, with her back to them, walking slowly forward through the calf-high grass. Twenty yards in front of her, at the foot of a low rocky hill, a troop of some twenty-five or thirty Yahoos sat silently and watched her.

They looked human. Even James Pendray had to admit that. They were not very clean, but they weren't really filthy, either. They wore no clothes, no decorations of any kind. Their hair was brown and hung in tangled ringlets, but it was not very long. The males had beards, but they were rather sparse and short. They had rather sloping foreheads and rather heavy jaws, but no more so than many human beings. They watched the girl's approach in unmoving silence.

She walked toward them, hands in front of her, fingers outspread, showing that she carried no weapons.

Pendray was silently thankful that four Darotha game wardens were stationed around the area, hidden but alert.

Five yards in front of the statue-like group, Blanche Barlow stopped. She spoke in a voice so soft that the members of her party, couldn't hear it, although it was picked up by the directional microphone that Dennis had focused on her. She was not saying words; she was making sounds—gentle, soothing, friendly sounds. They were intended to convey emotion, not intelligence. Her voice was soft, sweet, and tender.

One of the Yahoos growled.

Blanche went on making gentle noises. The only motion was the wriggling of two babies held in the arms of a big-bosomed female. The rest watched Blanche with cautious eyes.

Then one of the males, a broad-shouldered specimen with a mane of graying hair, began walking towards her. Blanche's voice changed a little, became encouraging. She held out her hand to the male.

He grabbed it, jerked her toward him, and slammed a heavy fist against the side of her head. As if at a signal, the rest of the band charged toward her, hands grasping, voices howling and barking.

As Blanche Barlow slumped, there was a ragged chorus of rifle fire. Four high-velocity, heavy-caliber slugs tore into the Yahoos. Two of them slammed into the chest of the male who had struck Blanche. The next two Yahoos got one apiece. More shots crashed through the air.

The Yahoos that remained on their feet spun and fled toward the protection of the rocks. Some picked up stones and began throwing them at Blanche, not knowing where the actual danger had come from, but sniping fire from the four Darotha game wardens kept them from throwing accurately.

Dennis Barlow and James Pendray were already sprinting toward Blanche.

She had only been stunned. She pushed herself to a sitting position and looked groggily around.

"*Keep down!*" Dennis yelled. "*Keep down, Blanche!*"

She seemed not to hear him. Her eyes were on tragedy. The big-bosomed female was sprawled nearby, a bullet through her brain. Unhurt, but squalling lustily, the two babies sat near her.

Dennis reached Blanche first, with Pendray only steps behind.

"Come on, honey; let's get out of here!" He helped her to her feet. The stone-throwing had stopped. So had the rifle fire.

"I'm all right," she said weakly. "I can walk. Get the babies, Dennis. Get the babies."

"Aren't they beautiful, Dr. Hiroa? Absolutely beautiful?"

"They are cute," Dr. Hiroa admitted. "I've seen much uglier human babies in my time."

"They aren't more than a month old. Look at the way they take to the bottle! Aren't they darling?" Blanche looked fondly at the two infants in the cribs she had bought for them.

She had had to get a special permit from the Darotha authorities to bring the Yahoo babies back to Point Garrison, but Dr. Hiroa, surprisingly enough, had exercised his influence in her favor. Now, bathed and diapered, the little ones looked as human as any other baby in Point Garrison.

"This will prove my point, Dr. Hiroa. Dennis and I are going to bring them up as though they were our own." She turned away from the cribs to face Hiroa. "The poor things have never had a chance, Dr. Hiroa. For thousands of years, they've been hunted and chivvied, driven like wild beasts by the Darotha. They've had no chance to evolve any sort of stable culture. Their language has remained primitive."

"Are you sure they have a language?" Dr. Hiroa asked.

"Certainly! All human societies have a language. It's one of the things that distinguishes them from animals."

Hiroa nodded. This was no time to point out the circularity of her reasoning.

"It's a matter of environment," Blanche continued. "A human child from Earth, if brought up by the local humanoids, would behave in the same savage manner. He would know no better. After generations of being shot and herded and butchered, they regard every stranger as an enemy. I can hardly blame them for treating me as one.

"But these kids are going to have a chance. They haven't been exposed to that environment long enough for it to make any impression on them—not any deep, lasting impression.

"By bringing them up as we would our own children, they will never know their racial background, never be exposed to the torment their parents had to go through. Instead, they'll learn the way you and I did when we were growing up. They'll learn English instead of the crude tongue of their parents.

"So far as I know, this is the first time this sort of experiment has ever been performed. This is a wonderful chance to add new knowledge to the anthropological field."

Dr. Hiroa nodded slowly. "I believe you're right. I believe you will learn a great deal from this experiment, Mrs. Barlow."

"I'm certain I will. Our research contract with the Institute calls for three years work here. By the end of that time, we will have a great deal of data from the field investigations, and even more from Jane and Michael."

"Jane and Michael, eh? Yes. Yes, I think you'll learn a great deal from Jane and Michael. A great deal."

"Paul," said Dr. Marcus Landau, "I don't know whether your expression indicates disappointment or satisfaction."

Hiroa, Landau, and Pendray were sitting around a conference table in the Research Institute building; cups of coffee, notebooks, pencils, and reports littered the table.

"Neither," Hiroa said. "The fact is there; I merely accept it. I will admit I had hoped—strongly hoped!—that the Darotha would indicate the kind of imaginative streak I was looking for. The indications I got at first made me think that they would. But, as you can see from these reports, the situation has stabilized itself in the past year. Imagination for its own sake, the enjoyment of pure creative imagination, is a passing phase in the Darotha mind. The kids will indulge in it for a little while, but it eventually passes away. By the middle of the second year after they come out of the water, the phase has passed. They look back on it in the same way that an adult human looks back on the days when she thought that a cake-candy-and-ice-cream diet was perfect bliss, or that cutting out paper dolls was the greatest pastime in the world."

"But you haven't lost *all* hope, I think," Pendray said.

"No. Certainly not. There will be a few—one or two maybe, in every generation—who will retain that creative streak. I don't know how long it will take, but I think the time will come when the Darotha will be innovators as well as good learners. I hope that—"

He was interrupted by a rap on the door. "Come in!"

Dr. Dennis Barlow opened the door and entered the room. "Hi, Paul, Marc, Jim. I hope I didn't interrupt anything. You did say fifteen thirty, didn't you?"

"That's right. Come on in. We were just finishing up. Pull up a chair and sit down. There's coffee in the urn over there and a clean cup next to it. Help yourself."

While Barlow got his coffee, Hiroa said: "I think that takes care of everything up to date, then. Next case. Do you have that file on Mike and Janie Barlow, Jim?"

"Right here." Pendray reached for a folder and drew it to him. "We're all learning something from those youngsters."

Dennis Barlow sat down, took one sip of his coffee, and said: "Are they healthy, Doctor?"

"Physically, they're in the prime of condition. Mentally...well, who can tell at the age of fourteen months? We haven't got psychology tests that will tell us anything that early. How do they seem to you?"

Barlow grinned wryly. "They sure grow fast, don't they?

They're as big and strong as four-year-olds. And the scraps they get into! It's amazing. They don't hurt each other, but they sure slap each other around. Have you been following the tapes?"

All three of the others nodded. "We've seen them," Hiroa said.

"Then you know what I mean. They'll play together nicely most of the time, but if one of them crosses the other, watch out! The other day, Janie was playing with her blocks, and Mike decided he wanted to play, too, so he grabbed a couple of them from her. He got another one right away—bounded off the side of his head. Blanche had to break it up, as usual. Grabbed them and shook them and gave them a good talking to. She never spanks them, of course. We don't believe spanking is necessary for the proper upbringing of children.

"I think the trouble is that they're still as egocentric as any child of that age, but they're bigger than most kids and can take it out on each other physically, whereas most kids fourteen months old haven't got the strength or coordination to do that."

"Most *Earth* kids, you mean," Pendray corrected gently. "That amount of development at that age is not abnormal for Sandaroth humanoids."

"Really? That wasn't mentioned in any of the tapes."

"Well, we admittedly don't have much to go on," Dr. Landau said. "The adults won't breed in captivity, and—"

"I wouldn't either if I was put in a cage," Barlow interrupted with a grin.

Landau chuckled. "Anyway, as I was saying, we have no definite information. It's hard to follow individuals over a period of years, and this is the first time that any have been raised from infants. But the Darotha say that they mature very rapidly and that these kids are not at all abnormal for their age."

"Hm-m-m. Interesting. You've shown those tapes to Darotha, then?"

"Ghundruth has seen them," said Hiroa. "He's as interested in this experiment as we are."

Barlow's grin had faded away. "He would be. Breeding them like cattle would be easier than driving them to slaughter after rounding them up in the wilds. But you can tell him for me that neither of these kids is going to end up as a slice of *lurgh* on rye. And maybe none of the humanoids will in a few years."

"That, of course, will depend on your report to the Foundation," Hiroa said evenly. "Ghundruth admittedly has an interest. He and his people are as dependent upon the Yahoo herds as the Amerindians of the North American plains were dependent upon the bison herds some centuries back. When the bison herds were reduced to almost nothing, the Amerindian resistance to the white invaders collapsed.

"But Ghundruth isn't thinking of that, odd as it may seem. He is

182

truly interested in knowing whether the humanoids are intelligent—humanly intelligent. The Darotha are an eminently ethical race, Dr. Barlow. Much more so than we are. If they find that the Yahoos are capable of intelligent behavior, there will be no need for us to protect the Yahoos with troops. The Darotha would never kill another one for food. In fact, if they decided that it had been their own fault that the Yahoos had never developed a culture of their own, they would do everything in their power to help them."

"I see." Barlow looked apologetic. "I'm sorry. Forget what I said. But for goodness' sake never say anything like that to Blanche. I'd rather you wouldn't even tell her that Ghundruth is interested or that he's seen the tapes."

"We won't," Hiroa said. "We respect your wife's convictions on the subject."

And her temper, Marc Landau thought. *The Golden Fury has become even more touchy since she has become a foster mother. Being beaten and stoned hasn't fazed her.*

"What sort of progress are the children making in learning to talk?" Pendray asked, steering the conversation away from the controversy.

"Just 'mama' and 'papa' so far," Barlow said. "But what more can you expect from a fourteen-month-old?"

"Please, Dennis; don't be defensive about it," Pendray said. "I don't *expect* anything. I just want information."

"Sorry. I'll try to keep my foot out of my mouth."

"That's O.K. They call you Papa and Blanche Mama, then, eh?"

Barlow frowned slightly. "No. Not yet. They use the words interchangeably so far." His frown dissolved into a smile. "They know that if they yell either word one of us will come running. I remember once when Mike was inside the playpen and Janie was outside. Something happened, and she grabbed his hair through the bars and started pulling. He couldn't get at her, and he started screaming 'Mama!' at the top of his lungs. I went in and made her quit. I suppose we ought to arrange it so that I only answer to Papa and Blanche only answers to Mama, so they can learn to differentiate."

Pendray nodded. "Yes. I suggest you try that. Otherwise, they have no reason to differentiate. Do they use the words at other times, for other purposes than calling for help?"

"When they're hungry. They come around four or five times a day with 'Mama, mama, papa, papa.' Practically in chorus. It means they're starving. And—boy!—can those kids pack away the food! Of course, they naturally would, growing at that rate. Their anabolism rate must be really high."

"I'm glad you brought that up," said Pendray. "I'd like to have you bring them around for a basal metabolism test sometime soon. Can you do that?"

"Sure. Whenever you like. How about at their regular checkup time, next week?"

"Fine. I'll arrange it. Is there anything else noteworthy?"

"Not that I can think of," Barlow said. "I do think it's a shame they don't have any other kids to play with. But they're far too big and rough for other kids their age, and the four-and five-year-olds are so far ahead of them in education that there's no communcation. Besides, the neighbors won't allow it. They're so prejudiced against Yahoos that they're afraid of little babies. I suppose they think Mike and Janie would devour their kids alive or something."

"Probably," Hiroa said. "They have good reason. You saw what happened to the Yahoos that were shot that day as soon as your fliers left the ground. The game wardens got some very good tapes on that."

"Your own ancestors practiced cannibalism at one time, Dr. Hiroa. That didn't mean they weren't human."

"I suppose I should have the grace to blush," Hiroa said. "I don't. All of us have cannibals somewhere back in our ancestry. It's just that the last one of my anthropophagous ancestors lived somewhat later than the last one of yours."

"I might contest with you, Paul," said Dr. Landau with a benevolent smile, "the honor of having had the most recent cannibal on the family tree, but I won't." Then he looked at Barlow with the same smile. "The point that my learned maori friend was attempting to make, I think, was not the fact of cannibalism *per se,* but the pattern of it. We are not talking now of the rare cases of extreme hunger, where men have been driven to the verge of madness or even beyond it. Those cases are exceptional and we know it. We are talking about cannibalism as a regular, normal practice. In every known case, there was a ritual of some kind connected with it, most especially if the sacrificial victim was a member of the same tribe or family group. Even when an enemy from another group was killed for that purpose, there was a certain amount of dignity and preparation."

"Our *human* ancestors, Dr. Barlow, *did not leap upon their own dead and tear them into gobbets as though they were a pack of wolves.*"

"Not so far as we know, maybe," Barlow said grimly.

"Not so far as we know," Landau agreed. "I admit the evidence is far from conclusive. In itself it proves nothing about the Yahoos. But it must certainly be taken into account, mustn't it."

"I think the most telling evidence will be Mike and Janie," Barlow said.

"Oh, indeed. Certainly," Landau said.

"I think that is one point upon which we are all agreed," Hiroa said in a carefully neutral tone.

Dr. James Pendray washed his hands in the lavatory in one corner of the surgery. "Janie will be all right, Dennis," he said without looking up. "Just make sure she doesn't pull those stitches loose when she wakes up."

"I hope she doesn't fight when she comes out of the anesthetic. She's getting to be hell on wheels. I didn't think she'd fight the needle that way." Dennis Barlow's voice sounded both worried and apologetic.

"How's Michael's black eye?" Pendray asked.

"It's O.K. Nothing to worry about. The swelling's almost gone. But where did he ever get the idea of biting his sister on the leg that way? If he'd popped her one on the nose it wouldn't have been so bad, but those teeth of his inflicted a hell of a nasty wound."

"Yep," Pendray agreed, "he does have a good set of teeth for a two-year-old, doesn't he?"

There was silence while the doctor dried his hands carefully.

"Jim," said Barlow.

"Yes?"

"Don't say anything to Blanche, but I'm beginning to wonder if our hypothesis is as accurate as we thought it was."

"How so?" Pendray was carefully noncommittal.

"Well it's a general rule that the longer the time between puberty and adolescence, the greater the intelligence of the animal. Look at those kids! They look like ten-year-olds!"

"How's their vocabulary?" Pendray knew the answer; he was just pointing something out.

"'Mama.' 'Papa.'"

"Differentiation?"

"None. They don't seem to know the difference between the words."

"If a chimpanzee is brought up in a human household," Pendray pointed out, "it can usually learn to say a few words. Simple ones."

"I know. I know." He paused, and when he spoke again there was anger in his voice. "But, Jim, they're *not* chimpanzees! Look at her!" He gestured toward the surgery table, where Janie lay sleeping under the influence of the injection Pendray had given her. "How can you call a creature as pretty as that an animal?"

"Human beings are animals, I think," Pendray said.

"Don't play around! You know what I mean!"

"Yes, I do. I'm just surprised to hear a zoologist using a word that has a scientific meaning as an emotional tag. They can't dress themselves yet, can they?"

"No, nor undress, either. They don't care whether they're dressed or not. But wouldn't you expect that of a two-year-old?"

"Yes. I'm not arguing with you, Dennis. You're arguing with yourself."

Barlow rubbed a hand across his face. "I know it. Damn! Damn! Damn!"

"What are you going to do about it, Dennis?"

Barlow took his hand away from his face. "What? Do about it? I'll go on with the experiment! It isn't over yet; it isn't over by a long shot. It hasn't had time enough yet."

"You and your wife are the sole judges of that, Dennis. It's your experiment. But—" He stopped.

"But what?"

"Getting emotionally involved in an experiment does not tend to make for an unbiased scientific observation of the results. No one can be totally objective about an experiment that is testing his theories, but—a man should try, Dennis. A man should try!"

"So you see what we are trying to do, Dr. Barlow," Hiroa said. "Here on this planet, we can begin, for the first time, in human history—and in Darotha history—to construct a civilization composed of two non-competing, fully cooperating, intelligent life forms. We are, in comparison with them, high on creative abstract imagination and low in ethics. The reverse, obviously, is true of them. They can't operate very far from the sea, and they can't stand low humidity; physiologically, they're water wasters. They just aren't built to live in the interior of a continent. They can explore the interior, just as we can go skin diving. But they can't live there. On the other hand, they can do things in the sea that we can't.

"But if this experiment fails, we may never get another chance. That's why I don't want to see this planet opened up to the general run of colonists. I practically hand-picked every person here. We used the best psychological tests that we were able to devise to make sure that our people have an ethical standard well above the human average. Not intelligence particularly, but ethics. If the average run of colonists came here, the Darotha would very likely go the way of the Amerindians. We have to give them time to adjust to new technologies, to learn slowly that there are people who can't be trusted. The average colonist is a social misfit, and the ethical standards are actually below the human norm. The Darotha would trust them first and be robbed and cheated and perhaps enslaved. Then that trust would turn to total distrust of every human being. It would take centuries to straighten the mess out—if, indeed, it ever could be.

"Do you see my point?"

"Certainly, Dr. Hiroa," Dennis Barlow said. "But how would a positive report on the intelligence of the Yahoos affect that?" Now, after three years, Dennis could use the word "Yahoo" without feeling guilty, although he never used it in Blanche's hearing.

Hiroa knew he would have to word his answer carefully. Any suggestion that the Darlington Foundation was a party to chicanery would be rejected out of hand. "There are certain unscrupulous business interests on Earth who want this planet opened up. Your report and those photographs would be used to inflame public sentiment against the Darotha if those unscrupulous men got hold of them."

"But suppose the Yahoos are humanly intelligent?" Barlow asked. "I couldn't falsify a report."

"Of course not! I would never suggest such a thing!" Hiroa said angrily. Then, more calmly: "Let us assume they *are* intelligent, that the experiment with Michael and Janie proves it. I assure you that the Darotha will be absolutely shocked, and will do everything they can to make up for what they have done. It will be up to us to provide a substitute food animal for them, of course, but we could find something—cattle, perhaps. Then we would have *three* intelligent races co-operating.

"In other words, I would like to have your report say that the Darotha no longer kill and eat Yahoos, that the problem *has already been solved!* That will render the information harmless. The unscrupulous interests would no longer be able to use it as a weapon. Do you see?"

"Certainly. I—"

The phone on Dr. Hiroa's desk chimed. He said, "Excuse me," and picked it up. "Dr. Hiroa here. Yes, Jim. *What?*" His eyes came up suddenly, focusing on Barlow's face. "Yes...We'll be right there!" He cradled the phone and stood up. "Let's go over to the hospital. There's been an accident."

Dennis Barlow was already on his feet. "One of the kids?"

"No. Your wife. I don't know how serious it is."

It took them five minutes to get to the hospital. Marc Landau was waiting for them in the lobby.

"Where's Blanche?" Dennis half shouted. "What happened?"

"You can't see her now, son. She's in emergency surgery. Jim's working on her. She's in good hands. Just relax."

"What happened? How badly is she hurt?"

"We don't know what happened. She's...she's hurt pretty badly. Her condition is serious, but not critical, Jim says."

Dennis sat down. "Tell me what happened. I have to know."

"One of the neighbors heard her screaming, Dennis. Now, calm yourself. Johnson heard her screaming, and ran over. He had a hunch what it was, so he grabbed a club, a heavy walking stick, before he went." Landau stopped and bit at his lower lip before going on. "Dennis, those Yahoos were trying to kill her. They almost succeeded. Johnson was bitten on the arm, but he managed to knock them both cold. We have them locked up now."

"I can't believe it," Dennis said hollowly. But it was obvious that he did believe it. "Why? Why would they do such a thing?"

"We don't know. We won't know until Blanche can tell us. Was there no indication?"

"No," Dennis Barlow said dully. "No. None. You've read my progress reports. In the past year, the kids have quit fighting one another. You remember how they used to scrap. They don't any more. We thought it was a good sign. Why would a couple of three-year-old kids attack Blanche? Why?" He spoke in a dull monotone, as though he had been drained of emotion.

"They're only three chronologically," Landau said gently. "Physiologically they're about sixteen, if you judge them by human standards. Mentally? Well, I don't know. Johnson said they were screaming *mamapapa!* as they fought. Those are the only words they know, aren't they?"

"Yes." Dully.

"You're a zoologist, Dennis. What would you say was the life expectancy of a mammal that reached pubescence in thirty months?"

"About...about twenty years, maximum."

"Intelligence level?"

"Low. Bestial." He glanced up from the floor. "They're baboons, Marc. Baboons. Only worse. Yes! Worse!"

Hiroa looked troubled. "I didn't expect this to happen. I...I'm sorry I allowed it, Dennis. Terribly sorry."

"It's not your fault, Dr. Hiroa. It wasn't anyone's fault but mine. I saw it coming, but I wouldn't let myself see it—if you see what I mean. Blanche was even blinder than I was. I sometimes wondered if she'd ever see. I wonder if she will now. Will she excuse them again, even after this? Will she go on thinking of rationalizations for them?"

It was nearly twenty-four hours before they got the answer to that question.

"She's awake, Dennis," Jim Pendray said. "She's conscious. She'll be all right. She wants to see you."

He led Barlow to the hospital room and let him go inside alone, but he left the door open a trifle so that he and Hiroa and Landau could hear.

"Blanche. Blanche, honey."

She was swathed in sprayed-on bandaging, but she opened her eyes and tried to smile.

"Honey, what happened? Can you talk about it?"

She closed her eyes again. "It was horrible. Horrible."

"What happened?"

"I...I was working at my desk. I heard...funny noises." Her words came in short gasps. "I got up...went into the living room. Michael and Jane were...were on the floor. They were—*Oh, Dennis! They were making love!*"

"Yes. And then what?"

188

"I lost my temper, I...I went in and...and pushed Michael away from Jane. I...I slapped him. They both screamed and snarled and...and came at me like...like wild animals. I couldn't fight them...too strong. They bit and clawed and hit. I...I don't remember after that."

She was silent for a moment, then she repeated: "Like wild beasts." Then her eyes opened and she looked at her husband with wide eyes. "They're not human, Dennis! *They're just not human!*"

Outside the door, three men looked at each other with solemn thanks.

JAMES BLISH and MICHAEL SHERMAN's

"The Duplicated Man"

A Review in Verse
by Randall Garrett

Readers of TAKEOFF will recognize this as a "review in verse." When Randall was assembling the material for that first book, he considered, but chose to exclude, The Duplicated Man—for reasons he didn't share with me.

Being a completist at heart, I felt compelled to add it in this time around.

This particular story we've got is
A novel that no one should miss.
I'm not sure I know what the plot is,
But I think it goes something like this;

There's some people on Venus bombarding
The Earth with some rockets and stuff,
And the people of Earth are regarding
The whole situation as rough.

The hero's a fellow named Danton,
Who belongs to an underground league—
From Singapore, China, to Scranton,
They have woven a web of intrigue.

This Danton is clever and smart; he
Is trying for all he is worth
To help this so-called Pro-Earth Party
Throw over the rulers of Earth.

Meanwhile, upon far-away Venus,
We find there's another big plot.
(And somewhere in here, just between us,
The tale gets confusing, somewhat.)

Now let's see: The Venusian boss is
Named Thomas—a fat, heavy slob.
He must watch out for sneak double-crosses,
Because everyone's after his job.

Well, anyhow, this guy's immortal,
In spite of his oversize build.
And, according to every report'll
Keep living; he can not be killed.

At the same time, elsewhere on the planet,
A group of conspirators meet,
And the whole bunch agrees to a man it
Would be real nice if Thomas got beat.

And while these two factions are wrangling
As to which one is gonna be boss,
Back on Earth, the Pro-Earth Party's angling
To throw Earth's bigshots for a loss.

The Security Council, who govern
The Earth, have decided to act.
Their agents go out and discover
New dope on a fantastic fact.

It seems that young Danton, the hero,
Found a big Duplication Machine.
But his future is practic'lly zero—
The poor boob don't know he's been seen.

The underground party intended
To duplicate bigshots galore,
And in the confusion attended
By this, they would make a big score.

But their plans are completely confounded
And all their finaglings flop;
And they're all absolutely astounded
To find one of their guys is a cop!

So Danton gets tossed in the lock-up,
Along with the rest of the boys.

And this is somewhat of a shock, upsetting all of his plans and his poise.

Back to Venus the scene now is moving—
Boss Thomas has just gone through hell;
He's recovered from poisoning, proving
His body is sound as a bell.

Says Luisa, his gal, "What's the answer?
How is it you didn't drop dead?"
Thomas, grinning, says, "Well, I've got cancer;
"But the secret I'll keep in my head."

And now, back to Terra we're shifting.
(This tale bounces all over space.)
The Council's discovered by sifting,
That Danton has just the right face.

"There's a fellow on Venus," they tell him,
"Who looks just exactly like you.
"Your job's to replace and expel him—
"About five or six Dantons will do!"

Back to Venus! The boys are beginning
To start an invasion of Earth.
While on Terra, young Danton is twinning,
In a sort of mechanical birth.

The machine gives a *pop* and a *buzz*,
underlined by a couple of *clicks*.
Five new ones—almost half a dozen.
With Danton himself, that makes six.

One duplicate's killed by the Party;
Two more leave the Earth, Venus bound,
While the other two, still hale and hearty
Decided they will stay on the ground.

The Original Danton smiles slickly:
"I don't see what *I'm* needed for!"
So he marries the heroine quickly,
And we don't see him much any more.

But the story just keeps right on going;
Back to Venus we leap once again,
Where it's hot, and the sandstorms are blowing.
The scene opens here with three men.

192

Two Dantons and one small policeman
Figure out how the boss can be downed,
While Thomas, that sly and obese man,
Is plotting things deep underground.

With a slam and a bang, starts the trouble.
(The authors do this part up brown.)
One Danton replaces his double,
While the other one sneaks around town.

But it's more complicated on Terra. R-
Emember? There's *three* Dantons there!
And the old Pro-Earth Party, in error,
Picks up one of the duplicate pair.

While, on Venus, the joint's in a tizzy;
Two Dantons and one Captain Small
Know the double's suspicious—or is he?
I don't think they're quite sure at all.

And on Earth, the Security Council
Hopes the underground doesn't arise.
Having trouble in such large amounts'll
Amount to a dismal surprise.

And on Venus—Now *wait!* Let's determine
Just what's taking place thereupon!
Oh, *please,* Mr. Blish, Mr. Sherman,
Just what in the hell's going on?

At the end, the entire situation
Is tied up all neatly, somehow.
Every bit of the plot complication
Stands in order to take a big bow.

Friends, with logic this tale is abounding,
It's a good story—make no mistake.
It's a classic; it all ends up sounding
Like a passage from "Finnegan's Wake."

Infinite Resources

by Randall Garrett

Look out, Callahan, Soom, and the proprietor of the White Hart...

At the bar of the Green Lizard Lounge, Dr. Rumfort was saying: "In my forthcoming monograph to the *Journal*, I show that it is mathematically possible to describe a six-dimensional continuum in which—" His voice trailed off as he noticed that Latimer was no longer listening.

Irritated, he swiveled his head to follow Latimer's gaze.

The oddly dressed gentleman was wearing a long blue cutaway coat, a pair of white shorts that half covered his thighs, long crimson hose that came up to his knees, and a soft white shirt that had no collar: His head was completely shaved.

On his back, he carried something that looked like a walkie-talkie radio with a peculiar antenna.

"What is it?" whispered Latimer.

Rumfort frowned. "A nut," he said, turning back to his drink.

The man peered around in the dimness of the bar and then headed directly towards Latimer. "Oh, I do say," he said worriedly, "could you very possibly be Dr. Oswald Latimer?"

Latimer nodded, grinning. "I am."

"*The* Dr. Latimer? The expert on the mathematics of infinity?"

"That's me." Latimer was still grinning.

"Thank Heavens I've found you!" he breathed. "I have the honor to be Professor George Featherby, of Columbia."

Rumfort swiveled his head around again. "Ridiculous! There's no such peson at Columbia!" He had never approved of the manner in which Latimer took up with strangers so easily.

"Oh, no, of course not," Featherby said. "Not in this continuum.

195

Dr. Latimer, do you mind if I ask a few questions?"

Rumfort butted in before Latimer had a chance to answer.

"What do you mean, 'in this continuum'?"

Featherby beamed broadly. "Well, you see, I'm not actually from this space-time continuum. This apparatus—" he jerked a thumb over his shoulder to indicate the pack on his back "—this apparatus is capable of shifting its wearer from one of an infinite series of universes to another."

Dr. Rumfort snorted again.

Latimer, who was enjoying the screwy little man immensely, nodded his understanding. "Yes. Dr. Rumfort, here, was just saying that he has proved mathematically that there are such things as parallel continua."

Rumfort almost choked on his drink. "That, sir, was only an exercise in mathematics! It does not necessarily pertain to the real universe!"

"Ah, there, old chap," smiled Featherby, "but it does, you know!"

Ridiculous!" Rumfort snapped. He turned back to his drink, thus dismissing the subject entirely. Then he pulled a notebook and pencil out of his pocket and began to scribble furiously.

"That's very interesting," said Latimer to Featherby. "I suppose each continuum is different from the others, eh?"

"Oh, no! Rather not! Infinite number of universes, you know, so there's an infinite number of 'em all exactly alike. Of course, there's an infinite number of 'em that are different, too, so you're right, in a way. But, then, that's why I've come to you, you know."

Latimer didn't know, but he nodded and lit a cigarette. "Go on."

"Well, sir, you see, I'm lost. Lost! I hadn't learned how to control this blasted thing at first, and I got myself too far away from my own continuum." Featherby looked desolate. "Ours is rather different from this, you see. But I finally heard of you in another continuum. Unfortunately, you'd been killed in an—uh—is it automobile?—yes, automobile accident in 1952. So I had to come looking for you in one where you'd survived."

Latimer blinked. He still had a deep scar on his chest from that accident. Then he grinned again; the little guy had read the papers, of course. "I'm glad you found me. How can I help you?"

"Well, sir, I understand you know a great deal about the mathematics of infinity; I thought perhaps you might tell me, if you could, how to get home."

Latimer looked at the ceiling, chuckling inwardly.

"Well, you say there are an infinite number of universes. That would, as you say, imply an infinite number of *different* universes, each of which is infinitely duplicated, identically.

"I should say that it would be a first-order or aleph-null infinity. For instance, a line has an infinite number of points on it, a plane contains an infinite number of lines, and a solid contains an infinite number of planes. That should, it would seem, indicate that a solid had infinity-cubed points in it. But infinity cubed is still infinity, so a line has the same number of points as a solid."

"Yes, yes," said Featherby impatiently. "I know all that! You're talking to a Professor of Physics!—Pardon me, but I *am* impatient, you know." He looked contrite.

"The point I'm getting at," said Latimer, unruffled, "is that you really don't have to get back to the same universe you left. If the one you go back to is identical, you wouldn't know the difference. Hmmmmm—still—By George!" His face broke into a grin.

"What is it? What?" Featherby asked.

"Why don't you see? That implies that *there are an infinite number of Featherbys galloping all over the metauniverse!* Also, there are an infinite number of Featherbys who stayed home. If you got into one of those continua, there'd be two of you. And if—"

"Oh, my God!" said Featherby, turning white. "How horrible!"

"Oh, come now," said Latimer, "it's not as bad as all that. Really, if—"

"Just a minute!" bellowed Dr. Rumfort, who had finished his writing in the notebook. He looked straight at Featherby. "You're a liar, and I can prove it!"

"A liar?" Featherby exploded. "A *liar*, sir? I demand satisfaction, sir! My dueller will meet yours at any time you stipulate! I—Oh, dear!"

"What's the matter?" asked Latimer.

"Dear me! This *is* awkward! I forgot I hadn't brought my private dueller along. And I can't fight one *myself* you know!"

"That's all right. Duelling's illegal here, you know," said Latimer comfortingly.

"I said," repeated Dr. Rumfort, "that I could prove it!"

Featherby faced him, scowling. "All right, if you're so sanguinarily smart, go ahead and prove it!"

Rumfort spread a sheaf of papers arrogantly. "There, take a look. I have shown that moving from one space-time continuum to another would require instantaneous acceleration to the velocity of light!"

"All right, all right," snapped Featherby. "I admit all that. It's self-evident. So what?"

"So what? Why, my dear man, that would require an infinite amount of energy applied in an infinitesimally short time!"

"Yes, yes. Go on. Where's your proof that I'm a liar."

Rumfort looked baffled. "Well, dammit, you couldn't possibly carry that much power on your back!"

"Hah! Who said I carried it on my back? Who, I ask?"

"Why, *you* did! You said—"

"I said no such thing! This mechanism draws power from the

Universal ether!"

Rumfort pounced on that statement as though it were the entire keystone of his argument. "AhhHAH! It has already been shown that the Universal ether does not exist! And if it did, you wouldn't be able to draw enough energy from it!

"It requires infinite energy! Infinite! That means that if you left some other continuum, you used every bit of energy in it! All the energy and all the matter in that universe would have to be used instantaneously as energy for your machine! If you had done as you said, the universe you left would be nonexistent now! And that's impossible! You, sir, are a confounded liar!"

Latimer turned to Rumfort. "For Heaven's sake, Rumfort! The poor guy's a little off his rocker! That's no reason to tease the unfortunate chap."

Featherby's face grew purple. "You! You—*argh! Liar! Off my rocker!* If only my dueller were here! Well, by gad, I haven't got to stay about and listen to your foul insults!"

He reached up and pressed a button on the control panel on his chest.

Neither Latimer nor Rumfort felt anything, of course. One can't feel anything when one is instantaneously converted into energy along with the rest of one's universe.

At the bar of the Green Lizard Lounge, Dr. Rumfort was saying: "In my forthcoming monograph to the *Journal,* I show that it is mathematically possible to describe a six-dimensional continuum in which an infinite number of points could exist, each of these points being, in reality, three-dimensional."

Latimer nodded, sipping his beer. He had been watching the door, hoping somebody interesting would come in. Anybody would be better than old Rumfort.

Nobody had come in yet, but he thought they might. After all, in an infinite number of universes, there might be somebody who...

Pride and Primacy

by Randall Garrett

I can't say anything about this story without giving it away, so...

So you *think you're tough, do you?*
Doh-dooh-dit-dooh-duh-dooh-de-dooh...
Arlys's imagination transformed the seemingly random twitterings of the ship's computer into words.
As good as those who have gone before you—maybe better, eh?
Dah-dooh-dah-dee-day-die-duh-dooh-dah-daw-dee-daw-dooh-day-dee-deh-deh-deh...
The computer ranged up and down unpredictably over its three octaves with a strangely melodic tunelessness.
Space Officer First Class Arlys was not afraid, merely tense and uncomfortable. The white-crater-dented sphere of the Moon lay dead ahead; the white-mottled blue of Earth far astern.
Dit-doh-doh-dooh-day-dooh-duh-dat-day-dooh-day...
First solo to the Moon. Does that make you great?
"Great, no; famous, yes," Arlys muttered, and forced himself to ignore the chittering computer. His gaze flicked over the various read-out panels, the instruments which showed him what the ship was actually doing—regardless of what his own senses might tell him.
The barely perceptible throbbing of the magnetogravitic-drive engines sending out their inertial pulses made a subliminal rhythm section for the symphonic tweetings of the computer.
First solo flight to the Moon. As a matter of cold fact, the first solo flight anywhere except for a few minor Earth-orbit flights. The final perfection of the magnetogravitic engine had rendered obsolete

the bulky, huge, ungainly monsters that had carried the first crews to the Moon sixty years before.

This baby, *Solo One*, was as easy to handle as a helicopter and almost as maneuverable.

Doh-doh-duh-do-do-duh-dooh-dooh-dee-dee—

"Solo One, Solo One. Do you read me? This is Space Control. Do you read?"

Definitely *not* the computer. Arlys reached out a gloved hand and touched a switch.

"Solo One here. I read you loud and clear, Space Control."

"Give us a readout check on your position, attitude, velocity and acceleration. Solo one."

"Check readout. Check. Will do." he began going through the routine, carefully, accurately, automatically, keeping his voice neutral. He did not like Space Commander Eldam, but had always taken pains not to let her know it. There was an irritating quality in her manner. Her voice gave him the feeling that someone was pouring little shards of crushed glass on his eardrums.

He was all for equality of the sexes, very strongly so. But that one rubbed him the wrong way. As a matter of fact, so did her assistant, Subcommander Brase, whose good looks were overshadowed by her arrogance. Oh yes, he believed in sexual equality, but Eldam and Brase did not exactly represent the epitome of egalitarianism.

He finished the readout check.

After a moment, Eldam's voice came *"Readouts all check. Programs synch. Carry on, Mister Arlys."*

"Aye, aye, ma'am." He cut off his mike.

"Blah," he said.

Of course everything checked. This machine was simplicity itself. And at one gee all the way—acceleration and deceleration—he could get to the Moon in less time than it took to fly across the continent. No coasting except at "turnover"—although he hadn't actually turned the ship over, merely reversed the engines. Of course, he'd been weightless all the way; he was being accelerated by the inertial pulses at the same rate the ship was. It was as though he were falling toward an Earth-mass a short distance in front of the ship—or behind it, when the engines were reversed.

The ship's sensors told him his velocity and acceleration relative to the surface of the Moon, and the distance to that surface.

Anyone who could pilot a trans-continental aircraft could easily handle the *Solo One*.

Doh-duh-day-doo-doh-day...

So what makes you so great?

"Because I'm the first!" Arlys snapped. "So *shut up*"!

The moon was rushing toward him, seemingly much too fast, but the instruments told him everything was under control. The

200

altimeter should read one thousand when he came to a dead stop relative to the white surface of the broad plain of airless rock and dust toward which he sped.

It did. He so reported to Space Control.

The upward thrust of oh-point-one-seven gees exactly counter-balanced the pull of the Moon below. He eased back on the thrust control and began dropping again. The next phase had begun.

"I am dropping from ten thousand to five hundred," he told Space Control.

"*Acknowledged.*"

When he reached the altitude he wanted, he came to a complete stop again, applied lateral thrust so that he could survey the area for just the landing area he wanted. All the while, he kept up the steady patter of reporting to Space Control.

Then, suddenly, he saw it. His breath hissed involuntarily.

"*Solo One! What happened? What is it?*"

"I'm not sure. Hold it a minute."

He reversed his lateral thrust and backed up until he was directly over the thing. "I'm directly over it now," he said, "but I don't recognize it. It looks like a structure of some kind, the size of a small house. It sure as hell isn't natural."

"*Probably some geologic formation.*"

"It's too damn regular to be natural. It's a construct."

"*But no one's ever been to that part of the Moon.*"

"No one from Earth," Arlys corrected mildly.

There was a long pause. Much longer than the transmission-time from Moon to Earth and back.

Arlys made a decision at that moment. He knew what was going on in Space Commander Eldam's mind as surely as if they were telepathically linked. She would get him away from there and later send up a team to investigate the thing.

Like hell she would!

Again applying lateral thrust, he moved away from the strange structure and set the *Solo One* on the surface of the Moon. He was putting on his spacesuit when Eldam's voice came again.

"*Solo One, can you get a camera on that thing and send us a picture?*"

Ah! She wasn't sure yet!

"I think so, Space Control. Take me a few minutes."

If she wanted an image, she'd get one. So far, he hadn't disobeyed any orders. Eldam had assumed that he would not want to land, and therefore had failed to tell him not to.

There had been a dozen space-farers on the Moon before him but Arlys would be the first to go it alone. In their crude ships the previous teams had spent considerable time getting in and out of their vessels; Arlys was under no such restrictions. After making certain that all his communication lines were open, he picked up the battery-powered camera and a flashlight, and cycled himself through the airlock. At least, he couldn't hear the damned tweetings from the computer in his helmet earphones.

He looked across the barren, rock-strewn plain at the strange structure which stood against the space-black sky.

"If that thing is a geological formation," he muttered to himself, "then I am a quadratic equation."

He started walking toward the thing, leaving footprints behind in the gritty lunar soil.

"*Solo One, aren't you ready with that camera yet?*"

"Just about," he replied truthfully. "I'm setting it up now. I'll have it in operation very shortly."

"*Very Well. Is your ship stabilized so that we can get a clear image?*"

"I'm sure the image will come in quite clearly."

Arlys found a fairly flat-topped boulder about chest high, and decided it was just what he wanted. Carefully, he set the portable camera on it, aimed and focused it on the strange structure, set the remote control relay to "ready," and went on toward the what-ever-it-was.

He had been moving on sheer determination. He had found something strange, something never before seen by anyone on Earth, and he was certainly not going to let Space Commander Eldam cheat him out of the credit—and maybe the glory—of investigating it.

It was not until he saw the tracks that he realized shatteringly that his determination had blinded him to what might be deadly danger.

He stopped and stared at the prints in the soil between himself and the structure, his mind almost numb. Somehow, it had never occurred to him that whoever or whatever had built the thing might still be inside it. Or around somewhere.

Fear.

He got behind a boulder so fast that he was never afterward sure of how he had done it. *Anything* to get a shield between himself and the alien artifact. He crouched with his back to the boulder, staring at his own footprints and those of the alien—aliens?—while perspiration oozed from his pores.

"*Solo One, this is Space Control. We're waiting for your transmission.*"

His mind was comparing the two sets of prints. The alien prints were very like his own. Only the sole pattern was different.

"*Solo One! Please report! Solo One! Please report!*"

It was then that he saw the essential difference between his own prints and those of the—*others.*

He swallowed, then pitched his voice very carefully. It wouldn't do to show Commander Eldam that he had momentarily funked.

"Solo One here," he said briskly. "Space Control, if you want a man to get his work done, don't get all hysterical and start yammering in his ears. Transmission of image will begin very shortly."

He stood up confidently, walked around the boulder, and headed directly toward the alien structure.

Space Control did not reply.

When he was within ten paces of the structure he stopped, looked at it carefully for a time, then, satisfied, thumbed the relay that activated the remote camera.

"Space Control, you should be getting your image now. Is it clear?"

A long pause.

"*Space Control here. Picture clear. What angle are you taking it from?*"

Arlys grinned. The old bat was confused.

Before he could answer—"*Solo One! There's something in what looks like a spacesuit standing near the thing!*"

"That's me, Commander." Carefully concealing his joy, he went on to report what he had done.

"*You landed? But you had no—*"

"I have my orders, Commander," Arlys interrupted. "Quote: 'Upon finding a suitable landing site near the target zone, the pilot shall land and survey the nearby area as hereinafter directed.' Close quote. The 'hereinafter directed' part says—and I quote—"

Commander Eldam cut him short. "*I know your orders, Arlys. You obeyed them. Drop it. But isn't it a little headstrong for you to walk up to the thing like that? What if there's an alien inside, waiting for you?*"

"Commander, I looked at those footprints. Now I've looked at the structure." He paused. "Commander, they have *weathered.* The footprints are blurred. The surface of the structure looks as if it had been lightly sandblasted. Except, of course, for the underside, where micrometeors couldn't hit it. But the thing is old—*old!* Do you have any idea how long it takes to *weather* something on the surface of the Moon?"

He looked up at the thing. "It's about twice my height, as you can see. It's an octagonal box—not a regular octagon; it has four long sides and four shorter ones, like a square with the corners cut off. You can't see it from there but that's what it looks like from above. There are four braces, as you can see, attached to the shorter sides. They hold that bedroom-sized box up off the ground so that the bottom is a little higher than my head."

He walked partway around the thing and stepped into its shadow. "There's an entrance on this side with a ladder going up to it."

"Arlys, don't go into that thing until we've checked it over more. I don't know how well a fifty-thousand-year-old booby trap might work but I don't want you to find out just yet."

"I don't either, believe me. Wait a minute; there's some sort of metal plaque here, at just about eye level. Looks like some sort of inscription on it." He directed his flashlight obliquely across the curious glyphs.

HERE MEN FROM THE PLANET
EARTH FIRST SET FOOT
UPON THE MOON.
JULY 1969 A.D.
WE CAME IN PEACE
FOR ALL MANKIND.

"I'd say it was definitely writing of some kind," Arlys said, "but God only knows what it means."

"Get a still camera and photograph it." Eldam said. "Continue your investigation. And congratulations, Arlys; you've done well."

Arlys looked up at the strange artifact. What was it? Who or what had put it here? Aliens from another planet? From another star? No way of knowing yet.

But scientists would eventually figure it out. And the credit as discoverer would go to Space Officer Arlys.

Another First. He chuckled to himself. First Solo. First finder of an alien artifact.

And another step toward equality. In spite of the teams of women who had come here before him, he was the first *man* on the Moon.

Small Miracle

by Randall Garrett

Like Pride and Primacy, *saying anything about this story might give it away...*

Major August Cantrell, USAF, was by no means a nervous man. You don't get very far in the Air Force if you're nervous, and certainly you wouldn't be allowed to pilot a jet plane that cost upwards of a million dollars, which is just what Major Cantrell was doing in the Air Force.

But, nerves or no, the major felt just a little queer when he heard the voice in his left ear.

"Major Cantrell," said the voice, "I'd like a word with you."

Now let it be said at the outset that Major Cantrell was not unused to hearing voices in his ears. Indeed, he heard them frequently. A jet pilot wearing a helmet with earphones gets used to the phenomenon rather quickly. But there was something about this voice—something the major couldn't quite place—that worried him.

He turned on his throat mike. "Who's calling? This is Major Cantrell—" He gave his identification. "—over Omaha, Nebraska. Who's calling?"

"My name," said the voice, "is Quadgop. There's no need to use your microphone. I can hear you quite well without it."

"This is a U. S. Air Force wavelength," Cantrell snapped, "get the hell off the air and quit playing tricks."

"Please, Major," said the voice, "if you'll just lend me your ear for a moment," I'll explain."

"It better be good," said the major. If there was anything he hated, it was practical jokers—the kind that fiddle around on telephones and radios, trying to be funny.

"All right, then," said the voice that had identified itself as Quadgop, "shut off your throat mike."

The major thought it over and shrugged. What could he lose? He took a look around to see if there were any other aircraft near him, but the thin air was clean for miles around. He shut off the throat mike.

After all, it just might be some sort of Air Force test. He doubted it, but it was still possible.

"But if it's a joke," he said aloud, "somebody's going to be in trouble."

"It's no joke, I assure you, Major," said Quadgop.

"Whup!" The major checked his throat mike again. It was definitely off. "How did you hear me?"

"Oh, we have our ways," said Quadgop, chuckling.

"We? Who's 'we'?" Cantrell asked suspiciously.

"I'll explain in a moment. First, I want to make sure that my identification is correct. You are Major August Cantrell, USAF, Serial Number 0-633919?"

"That's right," said Cantrell.

"You wrote the book entitled *The Air Force and Unidentified Flying Objects?*" Quadgop persisted.

"That's right," Cantrell repeated. "So?"

"You made the statement in that book that you don't believe that any extraterrestrial visitors would necessarily be war-like or bent on conquest, but should be treated with wary respect and a show of friendliness until and unless they prove themselves hostile."

It was an almost perfect quotation from his book.

"Do you," asked Quadgop, "still believe that?"

"Certainly," said Cantrell. Then he laughed. "I get it now," he said; "I'm being ribbed. Next you'll tell me that you are an extraterrestrial—from Venus, I suppose."

"No," said Quadgop, sounding a little irritated, "we are not from Venus. We are from Merca, a planet some four hundred light years away from here—a good deal farther away than Venus."

"Oh, come off it," said Cantrell, forcing a chuckle. But there was something about that voice that was oddly convincing, even to him.

"Major Cantrell," said Quadgop, becoming even more irritated, "we picked you for our first contact because we felt that you would be more understanding, more receptive to us. We do not want to fight Earthmen; we want to be received as friends. We feel that you would be in an excellent position to open negotiations for us. Please don't act as though this were a hoax."

"All right," Cantrell agreed. "Just for the sake of argument, we'll assume that you're on the level. But I won't completely believe it until I see you."

"That's fair enough," agreed Quadgop.

"I suppose that when I see you, I'll know you're not Earthmen, eh?" the major asked. "I mean, according to reports, you're little green men, two and a half or three feet high."

Quadgop laughed sardonically. "You have an entirely erroneous idea of our size, Major, and I assure you, we are *not* green. As to our physical shape, we are bilaterally symmetrical mammalian bipeds. Frankly, we look almost exactly like Earthmen."

"Oh, sure," said the major sarcastically, "just like us, except that you wear a Flash Gordon uniform and carry a Buck Rogers ray pistol."

"Believe me, Major," said Quadgop, "if you saw me, you would know instantly that I am not an Earthman."

"Look, Quadgop," Cantrell said patiently, "I'd like to believe this isn't just a gag; I really would. But I've seen too many of the boys being razzed because they fell for some practical joke like this. If you could just prove—"

"Major," Quadgop interrupted, "can I trust you?"

"What do you mean?"

"I mean, you wouldn't try to kill me, would you?"

"Hell, no! Why should I?"

"Very well, then. I'll trust you. I *must* trust you. It's the only way."

"What are you talking about?" Cantrell asked. "Are you going to bring your saucer down here or what?"

"Oh, nothing as complicated as all that," said Quadgop. "Just take off your helmet, that's all."

"Take off my helm—But, *why?*"

"Because I'm sitting in your left earphone," said Quadgop.

The Pocket Song

by Randall Garrett

The very first person I met at the very first convention I attended was an impressive, gentle, and entirely lovable lady named Marion Zimmer Bradley. I had been a reader all my life, had heard of conventions, but still had not the faintest clue that something called "fandom" existed, and I approached my first convention with hesitation and the resolution to remain aloof and uninvolved. Marion, may she be forever blessed, changed all that.

She put me at my ease among the soon-not-to-be-strangers who surrounded me. Through her, I met the Greyhaven people, who became a much-needed core of loving friends. And it was at Greyhaven that I met Randall Garrett. I can still remember my astonishment at the New Year's Day dinner, when twelve or so of the most talented, highly educated, and witty people I had ever met spent two hours telling elephant jokes.

Randall had recently come back to the San Francisco Bay Area, and he and Marion renewed a long-standing friendship. They talked out blockages and critiqued one another's work. I once told Randall that one of the main reasons I loved him was because of the delightful surprise of, now and again, finding an unpublished Bradley manuscript in the house.

Randall wrote **The Pocket Song** for fun, and it was printed in one of the collections of non-Bradley Darkover literature published by the thriving Darkover fan club.

The version of this song most likely to come first to the ears of an Earthman is the bawdy one sung in the bistros and bagnios of the Trade City, near the spaceport of Thendara, on Darkover. After the Bloody Sun has set, one can walk into any of the spacemen's dives—Moore's, Brackett's, or a dozen others—and someone will start singing it within the hour. It is sung in the local, debased dialect of *cahuenga* and contains words that are considered absolutely taboo on other parts of the planet, plus equally coarse vulgarisms from Terran Standard, Tomingan, Old Upper Middle High Martian, and several other languages.

The humor and the popularity of the bawdy version both spring from the fact that, in any human or near-human language, the word which expresses the concept "pocket" can also be used to refer to any of the various pits, cavities, and orifices with which living bodies abound. And it follows that the number of things which can be put into such pockets is virtually inexhaustible.

Undoubtedly, the bawdy version, in its original form, is very old. But the non-bawdy version is older still.

The original composer and author of the Pocket Song is unknown, his name lost in the blood-red mists of Darkovan history. But the song spread among the fraternity of peddlers quickly, each adapting the words, for better or worse, to his own particular needs. The melody varied a little, too, according to each man's ability to carry and unload a tune, but the basics remained the same.

Thus, I cannot say that the version given here is the original, but it is the oldest and purest I have been able to find.

Every human and near-human civilization has developed the traveling merchant, the import-export trade. No two spots on any planet are exactly alike in climate and resources, nor are their inhabitants exactly alike in skills. City Alpha can produce relatively cheaply what City Beta can produce only at great expense or not at all. And, of course, the reverse is true. So trade develops, and with it the traveling merchant, who carries his goods by caravan or ship from a place of plenty to a place of scarcity, taking his profit in both directions.

That is all very fine for the larger centers of population; their size makes it worth the great merchant's while to outfit and load a caravan or ship, carrying his goods in bulk. But what of the smaller towns, the villages and hamlets, and their outlying farms? That is where the great merchant's poor relation, the itinerant peddler, comes in. Forced by circumstances or by choice to work harder and longer for less profit, the peddler takes the goods from the city to the countryside.

Thus it developed on Darkover.

The itinerant peddler has at least two strikes against him to begin with:

First, his goods cannot consist of the necessities of life, only of the luxuries. The necessities, by definition, must already be available or the population could not survive; the luxuries are those things which make life a little easier, a little more pleasant.

Second, the transportation problem. Before the coming of the horse to Darkover, the Darkovan peddler had, at best, an ox-drawn cart, and even those could not reach the remoter places. Darkover was not, and is not known for its highway network. Usually, this meant that the peddler packed his goods on his own body and used his own muscle power to get them and himself to his customers.

The Darkovan peddler solved the first problem by using a method that is many tens of millenia old and yet always fresh and new. He invented—or, rather re-invented—advertising. He became, like his predecessors before him, a one-man show—an actor, a juggler, a sleight-of-hand artist, a glib-tongued mountebank. He let the local folk know he was in town; he advertised himself and his wares.

The second problem, he solved in a more unusual way, a way that was typically Darkovan. He invented the Peddler's Cloak of Pockets.

No two were alike, of course; each was constructed according to the whims and necessities of the individual. But they followed a pattern.

The Cloak of Pockets was made of three layers of strong, supple leather. The center layer was the cloak proper. The inner and outer layers consisted of pockets everywhere except at the shoulders, where the three layers took up the burden of weight. There were armholes, so that the cloak could be buttoned up securely and still leave the arms free. Over this was worn a woolen cowl consisting of an elbow-length cape with an attached hood, giving an effect rather like that of the ancient Scottish Inverness.

Both cloak and cowl were reversible. When the peddler wanted to attract attention, he wore them "colors out." The colored side was dyed and embroidered in a guady and highly individual manner; each peddler could be recognized by his colors. For traveling, he wore them "colors in," showing only the plain drabness of the leather. There were times when it was prudent for him to be as inconspicuous as possible.

Darkovans in general do not tend toward obesity, and, considering the lives they lived, one can safely say that there were no fat peddlers. But when wearing fully packed cloaks, they looked almost spherical, giving them a comical appearance. The cloaks were heavy, bulky, voluminous—and expensive. But, with the proper care, the initial investment would last for decades of hard use.

Empty, the three-layered cloak with its pocketed airspaces provided excellent protection against the biting cold of a Darkover winter. Filled, it was a portable novelty shop.

The Darkovan peddler had many pockets in his jacket and

trousers, too, but it was for his great Cloak of Pockets that he became famous.

He knew, of course, where every pocket was and exactly what was in each of them. He could produce whatever he wanted from wherever it was with remarkable speed and dexterity. He was an expert at prestidigitation and could produce objects with an almost magical effect. Remember this when you read the song, and imagine his flying fingers nimbly producing his wares seemingly from nowhere.

The legend that many of them carried small matrix crystals and knew how to use them is almost certainly not true. Their "magic" was all legerdemain. But it was effective for its purpose.

Imagine him, then, standing at the center of the village, having gathered his crowd. His cloak is "colors out"; his cowl hood is thrown back. Before him is the little folding table he has brought with him for the display of his wares. The table is empty now—but it won't be for long.

THE POCKET SONG

Come gather, my friends, around me!
There are wonderful things here to see!
I've marvels to show you,
And goodies to throw you—
Such kind folk I know you
To be!

In my pockets, I've many a thing
That would gladden the heart of a king!
In verse composition,
I've no competition,
And then, in addition,
I sing!

Spoken dialogue with himself:
You *sing?*
I sing.
Then sing!

He sings:

Pockets!
I have pockets!
I have pockets and pockets galore!
Some for big things,
Some for small things,
And some I don't know what they're for!

212

Pockets!
Lovely pockets!
I have ten thousand pockets and more!
Shall I show you
What is in them!
There are bound to be things you'll adore!

For the maiden who hasn't been asked by her suitor yet,
Spangles and sparkles to set off her clothes;
Bright-colored, curlicued fringes, or, cuter yet,
Bangles and beadings and buttons and bows!

The bride-to-be, wishing to do up her dowery,[2]
Needs some essentials before she begins:
Laces and ribbons and other things flowery,
Needles and scissors and thimbles and pins!

The housewife needs cutlery, tableware, chinaware,
Frying pans, rolling pins, pots, jugs, and jars;
Everyday aprons and holiday finer wear,[3]
Brought from the best of Thendara's bazaars![4]

As a mercantile rover,
I cover Darkover
To pick up a trinket or two;
From the heights of the Hellers
To Valeron's cellars,
I search out the old and the new.
When (pardon my jargon),
I dig up a bargain,
A thing which I frequently do,
I instantly sock it
Away in a pocket
In order to bring it to you!

NOTES

[1] In translating the Pocket Song from the original *cahuenga*, I have remained aware that true poetry cannot be translated, it can only be recreated. The emotional effect of true poetry cannot come through a mere translation of the words. With light, humorous verse, however, the problems are somewhat different. If it is a song, the rhythm and rhyme scheme must be maintained, in addition to the sense of the song. Oddly enough, this is not as difficult as translating true poetry. True poetry is too deep and too delicate; on the other hand, *Lili Marlene* was translated into a dozen languages without loss of fidelity, and Lewis Carroll's *Jabberwocky* has been translated into French and German with amazingly accurate results.

In the Pocket Song translation, I have maintained both the meter and rhyme scheme, including masculine and double- and triple-feminine rhymes, and managed to use almost the same words, although not always in the same order.

Still, there will no doubt be those who say it is better in *cahuenga.*

Let them.

² I am well aware that "dowry" is properly a two-syllable word. But the word used here in *cahuenga* is *"duwaire,"* apparently from the French *douaire,* meaning "dowry." It, too, is normally disyllabic, but in singing can be pronounced *DOO-UH-REE.*

³ Here I have followed a common Darkovan usage of eliding a final r in certain contexts. It is common, too, in British English, and is far from unknown in American English.

"Dinah, is there anything finer, in the State of Carolina?"

⁴ This quatrain (beginning "The housewife...) is rendered somewhat differently in a later version which already shows the tendency toward bawdiness. It could be translated as:

> *The woman whose husband shows no sensitivity*
> *Needs fine herbs and spices to warm up his meat,*
> *Concoctions and potions that conquer passivity,*
> *Giving him something delicious to eat.*

However, the first line can be *literally* translated without losing either the meter or the rhyme.

> *The woman who puts up with animal husbandry...*

The double (or triple?) meaning is the same in *cahuenga,* and the line really shouldn't be tampered with. But—Great Aldones—*where* are you going to find a *rhyme* for it?

Hell to Pay

by Randall Garrett

*Donning not only recommended this story, but Hank
Stine—then with Donning—found it for me in his private
library—thanks, Hank.*
   *Randall's forays into "pure" fantasy were exceptionally
rare, and they usually contained some other element of
science or mystery. All three ingredients are in this tale of a
man with powers and problems we'd all do well to avoid.*

   The figure was beautiful and, because of its lack of attire,
obviously feminine. She opened her eyes, took one look at Sam
Carstairs and said, "Oh, *no!* Not *again!*"
   Sam Carstairs frowned at her through the heavy smoke of
burning incense. "Not what again?"
   She grimaced and clutched at the air with long tapering fingers.
"Gimme, gimme, gimme—morning, noon and night—*that's* what!"
   Sam took a long drag on his cigarette. "So you are Archaezel,"
he said, still frowning. "That is, I presume you are."
   The lushly feminine figure poked a finger in the air over the
lines of the pentagram which surrounded her. She jerked the finger
back and glowered at Carstairs. "Of course I'm Archaezel. You were
expecting Mephistopheles himself?"
   "No," said Sam, "but you don't *look* like a demon."
   Archaezel was testing the strength of the invisible wall that
surrounded her—to no avail, for the pentagram held.
   "What did you say?" she asked absently, still prodding.
   "I said you don't look like a demon."
   Archaezel frowned deeply, then, quite suddenly, changed
appearance. Sam Carstairs threw his hands over his face
and screamed.

"Is this more like it?" asked Archaezel nastily.

"*No!*" Sam yelled, his eyes still shut. "Can't we have something red, with horns and cloven hooves?"

"Medievalist, eh? All right, how's this?"

Sam opened one eye cautiously, then both. The thing still wasn't too pleasant to look at, but at least it resembled the popular concept of a demon.

"Yeah," said Sam, "that's much better." He took a slow, deep breath. His cigarette had dropped from his hand to the bare floor of his apartment. He retrieved it before it could scorch the varnish.

"Well?" said Archaezel quizzically. "I presume you brought me here for a purpose. Or am I to be kept as an exhibit?"

"Be quiet a minute," Sam said. "I want to think."

The demon leaned against the invisible wall of the pentagram, grinned malevolently and began to pick its teeth with the barb on the end of its tail.

Sam walked to the desk and carefully examined the ancient tome that lay open upon it. The spidery text looked no different than it had ten minutes earlier. Pages 71 and 72 were still missing. Page 73 began—

With these facts well in mind, the calling up may begin. Procure of nitre a handful from

Well, all right—so it had worked. Sam still didn't like it. He could picture what would happen if the local press—or anyone else, for that matter—discovered that the District Attorney of Marlborough County was practicing witchcraft.

He still didn't know why he had tried the grotesque stunt.

It suddenly occurred to him that he was a little frightened.

He faced the demon squarely.

"*Begone!*" he said in a too-loud voice.

Archaezel stopped picking its teeth and peered at Sam with bottomless eyes. "How's that again?"

"I said—uh—*begone!*" Sam's voice was neither loud nor forceful this time. "Scram! Go to Hell!"

The demon looked flabbergasted. "Of all the half-baked mortals I ever met," it said slowly, "you take the cake! I'm wrenched all the way up here, forced to shift my morphology twice and then I'm given an order—the one order I can't obey. Tell me, mortal, are you by any chance a little weak-minded?"

Sam took a last deep drag from his cigarette before squashing it in an ashtray. He was having a hard time maintaining self-control. "I don't know whether I'm daffy or not, but I do know I—wait a minute! What do you mean, you can't obey that order?"

Archaezel waved toward the black, hair-covered book. "That spell you used is one of the most binding there is. I can't go back until I have served you."

Sam nodded. It made sense of a sort. His legal mind adjusted quickly to the scrambled logic of the situation.

"You have to do something, eh? Hmm. All right—uh—bring me some money. Ten dollars."

"Oh, sure," Archaezel sneered nastily. "I'm supposed to just trot right off and get it for you!" The voice became sarcastically sweet. "And just how am I supposed to get out of this cell?"

"Oh." Sam blinked. "Oh, yeah, the pentagram. How do I let you out?"

"Break the line, stupid!" The demon pointed toward the floor with a red claw.

Sam rubbed out the chalk mark with a toe.

Without warning, Archaezel leaped with a triumphant leer and claws extended.

Sam stumbled backward, tripping over the rolled-up rug, and fell with a resounding thump. He waited, cringing, eyes shut tight, but nothing else happened.

When he opened his eyes, he couldn't find the demon for a second or two. Then he noticed that Archaezel was leaning over the desk, peering at the grimoire, trying to turn its pages, but unable to touch them.

"Hoo!" said the demon. "You really *did* use a potent one! I didn't realize this book was still in existence! I thought you were using the watered-down Ashirkhaton version."

Sam sat up indignantly. "What do you mean? And why did you try to scare me like that?"

"I mean the spell is powerful enough to protect you from me. If you'd used the Ashirkhaton spell, I'd have killed you the instant you released me from the pentacle."

"Kill me?" Sam's voice sounded strangled. "For the love of Pete, *why?*"

"To get out of the contract, of course. The spell doesn't bind me once you're dead."

"You—you mean you don't—why do you want to get out of the contract?" Sam took a deep breath and tried to get his perspective back.

The demon sat down on Sam's desk chair. In spite of the fact that Archaezel was glowing with the dull red of a hot iron, it didn't seem to affect the wood of the furniture any. Some sort of volitional thermostat control, Sam guessed.

"Let's look at it this way," it said. "We were given an original payment for our services many millions of years ago. Never mind who made the payment. The original deal was that these spells—" it waved a taloned hand at the grimoire—"would be given to mortal intelligences to be used as they saw fit. There were certain other restrictions, but we won't go into them now.

"The point is, it takes considerable—well, you might call it energy—to obey your commands. So we try to exact our secondary payment before we have to do anything. Unfortunately, this spell is too binding. If you die a natural death, I don't get your soul at all...and I can't touch you."

"Thank Heaven for that!" said Sam fervently. There was only one thing to do—get rid of this evocation before it could do him any real harm. It had to serve him first, so...

"What about my ten dollars? Go get it!" he ordered.

The demon gave a curt nod and vanished.

During the five minutes Archaezel was gone, Sam Carstairs fortified himself with the bottle of bourbon he kept in the kitchen of his four-room apartment. It was his favorite brand and normally it slid down like liquid velvet. But this evening it burned a fiery trail all the way to his pylorus.

There was a sudden *pop*, like an exploding balloon, and a naked blonde stood in the middle of the kitchen, holding out a ten-dollar bill.

Sam grabbed it and, before the startled demon could say anything, yelled "Okay, you've served me! Now, *begone!*"

The blonde vanished without so much as a whisper.

The evening's experiment had been too much for Sam. He took another good dose of whiskey, two nembutal capsules and a hot shower. Just before climbing into bed, he took another close look at the black grimoire.

"Tomorrow," he said with very little conviction, "I'll think it was all a dream."

II

Niky Orloff was waiting for him in the outer office when Sam showed up at the courthouse the next morning. Niky was a small man with patent leather hair, who smiled engagingly at the District Attorney.

"Been waiting for you, Sam. How's for some coffee before you embark on the day's deliberations?"

Sam shook his head. "Can't do it, Niky. Too busy. Here's your book." He pulled the grimoire out of his briefcase and handed it to the little man.

"Oh? Did you try it?"

Sam deliberated only a few seconds. "No, of course not. I just skimmed through it for kicks. Thanks for lending it to me, but I don't see why you thought I'd be interested."

Niky shrugged. "Well, you always liked old books. I thought maybe—"

"Old books, sure. Shakespeare folios—things like that. But this magic stuff isn't for me. Frankly, I found it pretty dull."

Niky slipped the book into the pocket of his black coat. "You seemed interested enough in those scraps of the *Necronomicon.*"

Sam couldn't explain his aversion to the grimoire without admitting that he had lied about trying the spell. "That's a pretty famous book, remember. And I got those three pages of the Dee version at a good price."

"This one too high, Sam?" Niky knew that three hundred bucks was dirt cheap if the book was really an authentic copy of *The Workings of Night.*

Sam cut it short. "It's just that I don't want the book, Niky. Let's drop it."

"Okay, okay. How's for lunch?"

"Sure. Make it twelve-thirty."

"Right." Niky strolled out the door, and Sam went on into his office.

He hadn't been there ten minutes when the intercom buzzed. Sergeant Murfee said, "Sam, Ed Calhoun is on his way up, and he's hot as a four-alarm fire. I thought I'd warn you."

"Thanks. I wonder...oh-oh, here he comes now." He cut off the intercom quickly.

Ed Calhoun didn't even bother to knock. He pushed open the door, walked to Sam's desk, leaned over it and said, "Where's that eighteen grand, Carstairs? I *want* it!"

"Eighteen grand? What eighteen grand? Have you gone crazy?"

"Don't mess around with me, Sam," Calhoun said through too-white teeth. "I don't mind a raid now and then, but this is hijacking and I don't like it!"

Carstairs surveyed the pudgy, puffy face under the thatch of salt-and-pepper hair. The eyes beneath the shaggy brows were sparkling with hate.

Sam's voice remained cool. "I don't know what you're talking about."

Calhoun's face didn't change. "You know—Rogers' crap game. I thought it was funny that nobody was arrested. I thought it was screwy that you'd take the dough. I just talked to Chief Mitchell downstairs. He says there wasn't no raid last night. It was a lone job and *you* pulled it!"

Sam's eyes narrowed. "Don't get tough with me, Ed. You may think you run this town, but remember who's District Attorney. Now what in hell happened last night?"

Calhoun was unmoved. "You walked into the garage on Thirtieth Street and busted up an eighteen-gee crap game, that's what. All by your lonesome. *And* with a rod. The guys shelled out because they figured I got it fixed. When they find out I ain't got it fixed, they're pretty sore. I'm sore, too Sam. *I want that eighteen grand!*"

It was too much for Carstairs. He stood up, towering a good four inches over the stockier Calhoun. "Listen, chum, I was at home last night—*all* night. *I* know it and *you* know it. You don't like me because I don't jump every time you say jump. Judge Harcourt and I won't knuckle under, the way you think we ought to, and you hate our guts for it.

"So far, you've kept ahead because you have Mayor Wayne, Sheriff Corbett and the city police under control. But you can't get rid of me and the Judge, so you try something like this. I suppose you've got half a dozen of your boys who can swear that I pulled a stickup on Rogers' crap game last night. Well, you might scare some of the guys, but you don't scare me—and it's about time you knew it!"

Calhoun just looked a him with hate-filled eyes. "All right, hero—you don't scare. I've been getting sick of you for a long time. Now I warn you—if I don't get that eighteen grand back by tonight, I'll break you. I'll do *more* than break you."

He turned and walked out the door without another word.

Carstairs shut the door after him. Calhoun was really mad. Why? Did he actually believe what he had said about a one-man raid on Hugh Rogers' floating crap game? If he did, it meant that Rogers was pulling something. But why?

Sam Carstairs was honest. He kept one eye closed to a lot of things that went on around the county, but there were two reasons for that. In the first place, he couldn't clean up Marlborough County singlehanded—and, in the second, he didn't believe in a lot of the blue laws the county had passed.

The state had local option, so Marlborough County was dry— but that didn't prevent anyone from getting it across the river. Sam believed that an occasional drink was good for a man, that a crap game or a horse-race was fun. If the majority of the county officials had been behind him, he would have cleaned up the county in jigtime. But they weren't, and Sam's conscience didn't bother him too much.

He had never had any trouble with Hugh Rogers, for instance. He'd even lost a little money to him, which shouldn't make any professional gambler sore. Not that Sam liked Rogers—just the opposite. Hugh Rogers had killed at least two men, probably more, but nothing had ever been pinned on him.

However, the local Ministerial Association and the Marlston Civic Improvement League were constantly on Sam's neck to get rid of Rogers and his boys. They didn't know that Rogers had Ed Calhoun protecting him.

Sam shook his head and sat down again at his desk. He still couldn't figure Calhoun's angle. Or Rogers'.

It was almost lunchtime when the phone rang. Sam, who had been working over a robbery case windup, reached out and absently picked up the receiver.

"District Attorney Carstairs speaking."

"Sam? This is Bill."

"Yeah, Bill. How's the judge this morning?"

"All right, I guess." Judge Harcourt's voice sounded odd.

"What's the matter, Bill?"

"Did you know Hugh Rogers has sworn out a warrant for you?"

"No. What's the charge?"

"Armed robbery. He claims that he and several of his friends were having a business meeting in the Alms Garage on Thirtieth Street last night, and you walked in and took eighteen thousand dollars from them at gunpoint."

Sam's stomach did flip-flops. "Yeah," he said slowly, "I heard about it earlier this morning. Ed Calhoun came in and accused me."

"I don't get it, Sam. What are they trying to pull? No jury in the country would convict you. What *did* you do over there last night?"

"Nothing. I wasn't anywhere near the joint. The story's strictly from China."

"It may cause trouble, Sam. I can't be on the bench if it comes to trial, you know."

"They'll have to get it by a grand jury first. And I don't think they can. I'll see what's in the wind, Bill. Let me know if you turn anything up."

"Right. So long, Sam."

Sam lowered the phone slowly into its cradle. There was something screwy going on. He didn't know what it was, but it stank to high Heaven.

"I wish somebody'd get Rogers out of my hair permanently," he said.

III

Sam decided he might as well get some lunch. He put on his hat and went out into the hall, where he took the automatic elevator to the main floor.

Chief of Police Carl Mitchell was downstairs, talking to Sheriff Corbett. When he saw Sam, his eyes opened a little wider than usual, which wasn't much. "Hey, Sam! How'd you get back upstairs so quick?"

"What do you mean?"

"You just walked out that door no more'n a minute ago." He pointed toward the front exit and blinked.

Sam grinned. "Must have been someone else, Carl. You aren't used to the gloom in this courthouse. We haven't got lights like City Hall."

"Yeah—maybe." The policeman didn't look convinced. "You

headed for lunch? I'll join you."

"Sure. Come ahead. I'm going to have a bite with Niky Orloff." Sam didn't particularly care for the Chief's company, but there wasn't much he could say. The Chief's piggish little face looked worried as he fell into step with Carstairs.

"Sam, I wish you'd watch out for Ed Calhoun. I wish you wouldn't antagonize him."

"I'll look out for myself, Carl," Sam answered bluntly.

They walked the two blocks to the Greenleaf Cafe in silence. Niky Orloff was sitting in a booth, sipping at a cup of coffee.

"How's the bookstore, Niky?" Chief Mitchell asked jovially.

"Fine—just fine. And what's with you?" His mouth was smiling, but his eyes weren't. They never were.

"Okay. Say—I hear you're running for Alderman on an independent ticket in the next election. That right?"

Niky shrugged. "Who knows? I might even run for Mayor."

Mitchell's chuckle was heavy and emotionless.

"Chief Mitchell?" It was a waitress.

"Yeah?"

"Telephone for you."

The Chief got up and headed toward the phone booth.

Sam stuck a cigarette in his mouth and talked around it as he lit it. "You're a funny guy, Niky," he said.

"Why so?"

"Oh, I don't know. I'd never suspect you'd be interested in politics. You just don't seem the type."

"One never knows," Niky said evasively.

"I suppose not. You may end up President."

Niky shook his head. "No. I'm not native-born. The—hey! Here comes Piggy with a gleam in his eye!"

Chief Mitchell was returning from the phone booth, looking as though somebody had poured hot molasses in his pants pockets.

"Come on, Sam! No time for lunch! We'll see you later, Niky." He hustled Sam out of the Greenleaf before he even had a chance to say good-by to the little book salesman.

"What's up, Carl?" Sam asked.

A patrol car pulled up in front of the cafe and they piled in.

"Murder," Mitchell said. "Somebody killed three men in broad daylight on South Elm. I didn't get all the details."

It took less than five minutes for the patrol car to reach South Elm Street. A crowd had filled the street outside the area blocked off by the police, but the cop driving the patrol car honked them aside and pulled up to the curb near one of the other official cars.

When Mitchell and Carstairs climbed out they could see what had happened. Three bodies were lying untidily on the sidewalk, with blood soaking their shirt fronts. As far as Sam could tell, each had been drilled neatly through the heart by a single bullet.

Sam's gaze wandered from the bloodstain to the face of the nearest corpse and a shock ran through him. It was Hugh Rogers.

A cop was saying to Mitchell, "There were plenty of witnesses. At least a dozen people saw the car pull up to the curb. The guy stepped out, fired three times, climbed back in and drove off. The witnesses all agree on the description. Big guy, dark hair, good-looking. Gray business suit."

Sam frowned. There was something familiar about that description.

"What about the car?" Mitchell asked.

"Green '53 Studebaker. License number 110 dash 616."

Sam didn't need the testimony of the nearby witness who was pointing at him and shouting, "That's him!"

He knew the description fitted him perfectly and that the car was his own.

Sam Carstairs sat in his apartment staring moodily at a half-empty bottle of bourbon. He realized that the only reason he was not already in a cell at the city jail was the fact that he had been with Mitchell and Niky Orloff at the Greenleaf Cafe when the triple murder was committed. But what was the evidence of two people—three, counting the waitress—against the evidence of eight eyewitnesses?

The grand jury had already convened to decide whether or not District Attorney Samuel Carstairs should be indicted for murder. It didn't look too good.

Besides, there was no way of knowing how Mitchell would testify in court. Ed Calhoun had had a private talk with him that afternoon. If the Chief of Police should sound a little unsure of himself, or make a bad impression on the jurors, Sam's case would be shot to pieces.

All of which didn't worry Sam nearly as much as the situation itself. The big question was—who was parading around with a face like Sam Carstairs? And why had he stuck up a crap game and killed off three men? By this time Sam accepted Ed Calhoun's statement about the crap game as fact. Ed had a perfect right to be sore.

Who was doing all this—and why? Sam had a theory, but he didn't want to test it.

He poured himself another drink and looked at the floor. The rug now covered the spot where he had drawn the pentagram and the chalk lines themselves had been scrubbed away, but Sam could still remember very plainly what he had seen there.

He took a deep breath and said, "Archaezel! Come *here!*"

A blonde stepped out of the kitchen, carrying Sam's other bottle of whiskey. "I'm here. What do you want now?"

Sam blinked. "Would you mind putting some clothes on?"

"I would mind. They're uncomfortable." Archaezel wriggled

her hips provocatively.

"*Put some clothes on!*" Sam bawled.

A vague mist briefly concealed the demon's lush figure, and she emerged clad in something resembling a Doric chiton. It wouldn't have passed in public, but it was better than nothing.

Sam lit a cigarette nervously. "Why do you prefer to materialize looking like a blonde bathing beauty?"

Archaezel looked at him out of bright green eyes. "I'm a female," she said. "Not functionally, but psychologically. I automatically take the form of a female human unless I concentrate on something else, as I did last night."

Sam let it pass. "I thought I told you to go away then."

"I did, didn't I?"

"I meant back where you came from."

"I told you I couldn't do that," she said, pouring herself a healthy slug from the bottle.

"You said you could after you served me," Sam pointed out logically. "You served me by getting that ten-dollar bill."

The demon shook her golden head. "Sorry, you misunderstood. The service contract is for life. I have to serve you until you die."

Sam slumped. "That's what I was afraid of." He smoked in morose silence for a few minutes. It made sense after a fashion. Just because that kind of a contract was illegal in the United States didn't keep it from being binding in Hell.

Apparently Archaezel could no more resist obeying his command than Sam himself could keep from falling if he stepped out of an airplane without a parachute. There was no telling what the natural laws of Hell were, but he suspected they were quite a bit different from those he was used to.

"Tell me how you got that ten bucks," he said, making a command of it so that Archaezel would have to obey.

"You know perfectly well how I got it. I made myself look like you and stuck up the crap game." The blonde swallowed half a glass of whiskey without a shudder, gasp, or blink.

"Uh-huh." Sam nodded. "And you also rubbed out Hugh Rogers and his pals when I said I wished someone would get them out of my hair permanently."

"Your wish is my command," Archaezel said airily. She took another healthy slug.

"Yeah, but I'm the one who gets framed for murders and stick-ups." Sam was no longer afraid of the demon. As long as it kept the form of a human female, he felt he could cope with it. "You're trying to get me killed," he continued. "Tell me why—if I'm not asking too much."

The blonde sighed. "I want to bring the contract to a quick termination, that's all. Nothing personal, I assure you. But—" she leveled a finger at Sam's nose—"suppose *you* had to spend years

226

and years running around all over the universe to satisfy the personal whims of every Tom, Dick and Harry that came along. And all at your own expense too."

"There's more to it than that," said Sam coldly. He was trying to remember everything the demon had said earlier.

"Well, yes. I have to see that you're killed or I won't be able to carry you back with me. In other words, I won't get paid for my duties. That's slavery and, if I get caught in it, it's my own fool fault."

Sam's brain was working furiously. The demon was telling the truth, but not all of it. Sam, however, was used to digging facts from unwilling witnesses. The difficulty in this instance was that Archaezel's world was so different from his own, he was unable to make any assumptions about it.

Suddenly, Sam saw a gleam of light. "Look here, my soul is worth something to you—something about the equivalent of money here on Earth?"

Archaezel nodded. "That's pretty close."

"When I called you up here, it cost you 'money' to come, and it will cost you 'money' to stay. Right?"

She nodded again, her eyes narrowing. "Right, so far. Only call it 'energy,' not money. It's more of a barter system."

"I get it," Sam said. "It takes a lot of energy to stay here on Earth—a whale of a lot. And it takes even more to obey my commands." He hesitated. "My soul, whatever *that* is, will bring enough energy to make you a profit—*if you get me in time!* Meanwhile, you're losing energy hand over fist."

"That's not all of it," Archaezel snarled. Sam noticed the eyes were no longer green, but the bright, glowing orange of hot coals. "I have a limited energy reserve. When I run through that, a debit starts to build up against me in Hell. If I don't bring you back to get my debts paid, I'm—*punished.*"

Sam shuddered. From the way she emphasized that last word, he felt quite sure he would not want to know the punishment.

"It's like this," the demon went on. "Suppose you had a million dollars in the bank. You'd be rich by normal standards. Now, suppose you were forced to live in a hotel where the rent was a hundred thousand a day and a bellboy's tip a couple of thousand. Food is between twenty and fifty thousand a meal. Your million won't last long. Now, suppose your bank goes ahead and honors your checks, with the understanding that, when you leave the hotel, you'll pay up or else. That's my position. In Hell, I'm considered a fairly wealthy and powerful demon. But if I have to stay here very long, I'm going to be in debt."

"How long?" asked Sam.

"I don't know. The time rate is different for one thing, and the exchange fluctuates. But the quicker I get you, the better off I am."

Sam said nothing more. His only chance was to outwit the demon on her own terms, and he realized he'd better keep any further ideas strictly to himself.

IV

With a demon at his beck and call, Sam Carstairs had the world by the tail. He could do anything he wanted. He could, he supposed, even clean up Marlborough County, singlehanded.

One hitch was that, at any time, the demon might dope out some way of killing him indirectly. It could not be done directly because of the spell he had used. That gave Sam an idea. He picked up the phone and dialed Niky Orloff's home. "Orloff speaking."

"Niky, this is Sam. I've changed my mind. I'll buy that book. Can I get it tonight?"

"Sorry, Sam," Niky apologized, "no can do. Sold it to another customer.

"Who?"

"I can't tell you that, Sam. I'm sorry."

"Okay, Niky. Forget it."

He slammed down the receiver and frowned. Come to think of it, the book wouldn't do much good, anyway. It was the missing page that contained detailed information about the uses of the spell... and probably its dangers as well. Were there any other flies in the ointment? He wondered.

He looked at Archaezel. "Can you read my mind?"

"Naturally," she sneered.

"Very well. I order you not to do so."

The growl of frustrated rage from the demon's throat was enough to convince Sam that he had made a wise move. Now he could think in peace—or at least privacy.

The point was, how could he convince the grand jury that another person had killed Rogers? When they heard about the warrant Rogers had sworn out, they'd have a motive. And with eyewitnessess.

There was one thing he might do. It would require a lot of safeguards, but it might work.

He turned to the demon. "Archaezel, I have some orders to give, but I want you to wait until I say go before you carry them out. Understand?"

"I'm not stupid, chum," she said, finishing the last of the liquor.

"All right. I want you to assume my form and check in at the Larchmont Hotel using the name of William Jones. When you're in the room, lock the door and make sure there are no witnesses. Then, materialize a body identical to mine, but with different fingerprints—

228

somebody's they can't check—say, those of George Washington. Leave fingerprints around the room, but none of mine. Arrange the body so that it looks as if it shot itself. Suicide, see? Place a note near it which says, 'I stuck up Hugh Rogers' crap game, and I killed him. I used the District Attorney's car for the job.'

"Leave the note unsigned, and don't have any other writing on the paper. Use hotel stationery. Then cause a sharp explosion, like a pistol shot, and come back here immediately."

He paused trying to find loopholes in the order. He decided there were none. "*Go!*" he said, and the demon vanished.

Sam calmly lit another cigarette. This should do the trick. When they found the body, the police would realize that a double had committed the crimes. With George Washington's fingerprints on the corpse, they would never figure out the identity, but at least they would know it wasn't Sam Carstairs.

He settled back to await developments. Half an hour passed.

Ping!

The blonde was back. The chiton was gone again, but Sam didn't say anything.

"All done as I said?" Sam wanted to know.

"Certainly."

"Fine. Now take me to that hotel room instantly—*without harming me in any way!*"

Ping!

It gave Sam the same feeling as watching a movie scene change quickly. His own room was gone, and the hotel room surrounded him.

The sight of his own corpse—or a reasonable facsimile thereof—was disconcerting at first, but he soon got used to it.

Out in the hall, a voice said, "It sounded like a shot!"

Another said, "Where from?"

Sam knew he wouldn't have long to look around. Everything *looked* perfect. The demon hadn't slipped up or planted any booby traps, as far as he could tell.

The suicide note was clutched securely in the dead man's left hand, and a revolver was in the right. The bullet hole was in the right temple. All according to Hoyle.

Then he heard another voice in the hall. "I'll bet anything it was four-eleven. I thought it was funny that the D.A. would check in under the name of Jones." It was the house detective.

"Okay, Archaezel," Sam whispered, "take me back home."

Ping!

He was back in his own room. He pointed to the chair. "Now, just sit there quietly until I think of something else."

With the problem of the murders solved, he could devote his attention to figuring out a way to get rid of the demon. He toyed briefly with the idea of making himself rich and powerful, but dismissed it quickly. It wasn't that he didn't like the idea of wealth and power, but he preferred to get it through his own efforts. His ego demanded it. He didn't like anything handed to him on a silver platter.

Using the demon might prove dangerous. The best-laid plans could backfire unless every loophole was covered. Evidently, the demon couldn't just go about doing things to get him in trouble. It had to be something connected with the orders he gave. The whole problem deserved careful thought.

It was almost midnight when Sam heard voices in the hall. By then, the police would have checked the prints of the corpse and found them not his. They were obviously here to tell him about it...or to check on the body.

Chief Mitchell was saying, "...have to find out what this is all about. Here's Sam's apartment."

Sam waited for the knock, but there was none. Instead, he heard a key being fitted into the lock. He didn't move as the door swung open.

Chief Mitchell's mouth dropped open, his eyes bugging out of his piggy little face, while behind him, the landlord and two policemen assumed similar exprssions.

"What's wrong, Carl?" Sam asked, keeping his voice level. Hadn't they checked the fingerprints yet? They must still think it was he in the hotel room.

The Chief's shock didn't last long. He snapped his jaw shut and drew his Police Positive. "All right, you! You're under arrest! Snap the cuffs on him, boys!"

Only Sam Carstairs heard the smothered chuckle from the chair where the invisible Archaezel sat.

V

The city jail was distinctly uncomfortable. Sam's headache didn't help any, either...

Archaezel had put another one over. The body's fingerprints were different, all right. *Hah!* A lot of good *that* did!

Sam remembered the story about the Irishman who had captured the leprechaun and forced him to point out the tree where the pot of gold was buried. He had tied a cloth around the tree to mark it while he went home to get a spade. He had made the pixie promise not to remove the cloth until he got back.

The leprechaun was as good as his word. When Paddy returned with the spade, every tree in the forest had an identical cloth tied around it!

Archaezel had pulled the sam gag. The demon had changed the fingerprint records! Every file in the nation now had the corpse's

230

fingerprints registered under the name of Samuel Carstairs!

The cops didn't know whom they had in the city jail, but they were sure it wasn't Sam Carstairs. Fingerprints don't lie!

How do you like that, George Washington? Sam thought bitterly. *I've got you on the records now, me bucko!*

The one thing Sam couldn't understand was the plastic imitation of a gun that had been clutched in the corpse's hand, according to the police. Why hadn't Archaezel used a real one? What was the purpose behind that?

There were footsteps in the corridor, and the turnkey showed up. A key clanked in the lock.

"Awright, Carstairs, come on. The Chief wants to talk to you."

Sam sighed wearily and followed the jailer out.

There had to be some way of getting out of this jam! He could always call on Archaezel, of course, but he was beginning to suspect that any further orders to the demon would probably get him in deeper soup.

He solemnly promised himself that he would leave the demon strictly alone.

The jailer led him to the rear of the jail, where Chief Mitchell and two detectives were waiting in a small room.

Sam recognized the room. The hard chair under the single glaring lamp had one purpose...and only one purpose.

"Sit down, son," the Chief said, waving toward the chair.

It was the *son* that made Sam really aware of what was coming. Mitchell always called his victims *son* before he worked them over thoroughly.

Sam sat, sweating, waiting for the Chief to speak.

"I've got a theory, son," Mitchell said. "I want you to listen to it carefully and tell me where I'm wrong.

"You came to this town a year ago. You discovered you looked like poor Sam and decided it would be nice to step into his shoes. So you studied him—watched him. Then you kidnapped him and held him prisoner while you took over his job. Sam didn't have a family, so that part of it was easy.

"Everything went fine till the night before last. You stuck up Rogers' crap game, figuring Rogers wouldn't dare say anything. You figured wrong, so you had to rub out Rogers.

"Then, last night, you really got panicky. You took Sam up to the hotel, shot him, and made it look like suicide. But you didn't think of the fingerprint check. How does that theory sound, son?"

"It has holes in it big enough to throw a cat through," Sam said calmly.

"Oh, it does, does it? Well, I'm real sorry to hear you don't like it. Why don't *you* tell us what did happen then?"

Sam frowned. How could he explain? The true story would certainly sound sillier than the Chief's. Mitchell's tale was illogical but his own was fantastic.

"What's your name, son?" Mitchell asked.

"Samuel Carstairs."

One of the detectives slapped Sam across the cheek hard enough to make his head ring.

"Give us your right name, son."

"Sam—" Whap!

"What's your last name?"

"Carst—" Whap!

"You're real cute, son, but it ain't gettin' you anywhere. Why don't you tell us the truth?"

Sam didn't know how long it went on. He had seen Mitchell's handiwork before—on the colored kid, for instance. Mitchell didn't go in for reasoning or logic. He believed that the way to catch a crook was to pick up the nearest suspect and knock a confession out of him. His motives were the same, and his methods hardly differed from those of the Spanish Inquisition.

The colored kid that had been picked up for a knifing on McGuire Street six months ago had spent ten weeks in the hospital for "resisting arrest," although Sam had found witnesses to testify that the kid was innocent.

Things like that never made an impression on Chief Mitchell, though. He picked one man as guilty and, no matter what the evidence was, that man stayed guilty. Evidence was only something you framed to convice a jury *after* you had decided who was guilty.

Mitchell picked his cops for psychological traits similar to his own.

"My hands're gettin' sore, Chief," one of the cops complained. "This guy's head is too hard."

"I hate to get rough with you, son. I really do," the Chief said. "Herb, you better go get the persuaders."

In a few minutes, they were applying short lengths of rubber hose with great finesse to his head, stomach and kidneys.

Sam just couldn't take it. A sea of confusion, blackness and pain closed in over his head.

When he woke up, it was strangely silent in the room. He blinked his eyes against the harsh light and tried to sit up. When he saw what was on the floor, he gagged. After the nausea passed, he looked painfully around the room. Archaezel was sitting in the chair which had recently been occupied by Chief Mitchell. She was looking at him with detachment.

"What happened?" Sam asked. His lips were so puffed that it came out "Whuh hom?"

"You said they ought to get a taste of their own medicine," she grinned her malevolent grin. "They did."

"Are they dead?"

"Very."

Sam groaned, not only from the pain. He now had another triple murder chalked up against him.

Over in the corner of the room was a large water cooler. Sam avoided the bodies on the floor as he stumbled over to it. He began splashing water on his face.

Several times he thought of asking the demon to make him well again, but changed his mind each time, not trusting what fiendish ideas Archaezel might get.

The beating hadn't really done any serious damage to him. He was covered with bruises, and his clothes were a mess from the bloody nose, but he wasn't badly hurt.

The problem of the plastic gun came back. As he dried his face gingerly with a paper towel, he asked, "Why did you put a phony gun in that corpse's hand? You'd have got me in a deeper jam if you'd put my own there."

The demon had a petulant look on her face. "I know. But I couldn't do it. A gun's made of cold iron, or steel, which is the same thing, you know. I can't handle that stuff. If they examine the shoes of that corpse, they'll find brass nails in the shoes."

"Hmm. Then what did you use to kill Hugh Rogers?"

"Lead bullets. The gun was just an illusion."

There was a knock at the door. "Hey, Chief! Phone for you!"

Sam recognized the voice of the turnkey. The door, luckily, was locked.

"Can you imitate Mitchell's voice?" Sam whispered to Archaezel. The demon nodded scornfully. "Okay. Say, 'Who's calling, Lou?'"

She complied and the turnkey said, "Niky Orloff, Chief."

Sam whispered further instructions and Archaezel said, "Tell him I'm busy. I'll call him back."

"Right." The turnkey left.

Sam sat down and thought for long minutes, carefully keeping his eyes off the things on the floor. Finally, he turned again to the demon. He hated to ask for anything more, but he knew it was his only way out. Only Archaezel could get him out of the jam she had got him into. And besides, he felt he was beginning to get the knack of controlling her.

"Can you make me invisible? I mean, so that other people can't see me, but otherwise remain just as I am?"

"Certainly. You ask the stupidest questions, mortal."

"I'm not taking any chances. Go ahead then, make me invisible."

"All right," she said nastily, "so you're invisible."

Sam looked down at himself. He could see no change, but he could probably take Archaezel's word for it.

The door had a Yale lock which could only be opened from the outside with a key. He turned the inside bolt and looked out. No one was in sight.

"You stay in this cell and don't do anything until I call you," he whispered to the demon. "And don't let anybody see you, either!"

He stepped out into the hall and pushed the door shut behind him. The lock clicked into place. Good, so far. He walked toward the identification room.

Just as he reached it, Lou came out. The turnkey's face suddenly acquired a very peculiar expression.

"Clothes," he said softly, in awe. "Bloody clothes—hangin' in mid-air."

Sam's fist swung up and hit the astounded jailer. Lou collapsed soundlessly.

Sam quickly dragged him to a nearby janitor's closet and pushed him in. Then he peeled off his clothes and locked them in the closet with Lou. In her inevitable efforts to trip him up, Archaezel had made Sam invisible as he had ordered, but she had left his shirt and pants as visible as ever.

Stark naked and feeling more than a little silly, Sam strode boldy into the identification room. No one had heard him hit the turnkey, evidently, for the two officers in the room were talking quietly about the afternoon baseball game. One of them glanced up as the door opened, but gave no sign of having seen Carstairs. He must have attributed the opening door to a draft, for he ignored it.

Sam walked over to the fingerprint files. His fingerprints had been taken the night before, but the cards shouldn't have gone out to the F.B.I. yet.

He sighed with relief when he saw that all five cards were still there. Since all the other files had been changed, these cards were the only records of his fingerprints.

But how to get them out? If the two policemen on the far side of the room saw cards floating out the door, there was no telling what they might do. He grinned. He might as well have some fun. He stepped into the hall and pushed a switch of the red box on the wall.

He almost collided with the two cops as they rushed out in answer to the roaring fire alarm.

Sam was not the type to turn in a false alarm—it was against his principles. Accordingly, he struck a match to the papers in the wastebasket. As soon as they were blazing merrily, he fed the fingerprint cards into them, one by one.

Then he walked into Chief Mitchell's office to make sure nothing else there could be connected with him.

The phone rang. Sam picked it up. "Yeah?" he said, in a fair imitation of Mitchell's tone.

"Carl?" It was Mayor Wayne. "The boss is a little teed off at you."

Sam, wondering why Ed Calhoun should be sore at Mitchell, said, "Why?" He had to stick to monosyllables. He wasn't the imitator Archaezel was.

"He called you a few minutes ago and you told him to hold his horses. He doesn't like things like that, you know. You'd better talk to him. Now, Carl!" There was a click at the other end.

Something in Sam's brain clicked, too. He hung up the phone and wiped off possible prints with a Kleenex from the box on the desk.

When he walked back out in the hall, the place was a madhouse. The two cops from the identification room were trying to explain that they had not turned in the fire alarm, in spite of being in the same room with the fire. Down the hall, a cop and a fireman were pounding on the third-degree room, calling frantically for the Chief. And another fireman was lifting a dazed turnkey out of a heap of bloody clothes in the janitor's closet.

Sam left in a hurry. Things were beginning to fall into a pattern and he had some checking to do.

VI

Sirens were wailing all around Courthouse Square. From a bench, Sam and the demon watched two State Police cars pull up in front of City Hall, a block away. The Mayor's car was there already, as was Ed Calhoun's.

"Interesting fuss, isn't it?" Archaezel asked conversationally.

"It is, indeed," Sam agreed. "And it's going to get more interesting as time goes on."

The demon frowned. "I suppose you plan to do something about it."

"Yep. I'm going to start by asking you some questions. All this mess has now become clear as day to me. I want some information from you and I want it straight."

It took better than half an hour to pump all he wanted out of Archaezel. Everything he had ever learned about cross-examination he used against the sly demon.

Archaezel had to tell the truth, but there was nothing in the Laws of Darkness that required it to tell the *whole* truth. Sam had to attack each question from every possible angle and every hint the demon dropped had to be pounced upon and wrung dry of information.

When satisfied, Sam said, "Okay, let's go. First, take me to the Mayor's house."

Ping!

Sam looked around the Mayor's library. "Where are the papers? The letters and contracts and stuff."

Archaezel pointed toward a wall. "The Mayor has no imagination. They're behind that painting, in a wall-safe."

"*All* the incriminating material?"

"*All* of it," the demon verified. Sam walked over to the safe and pushed the painting aside. "What's the combination?"

Archaezel told him and he began spinning the dial. But when the door finally swung open, it was accompanied by the raucous clamor of a ringing bell.

The demon had failed to mention an alarm.

Sam scooped the papers into a bundle and stuffed them into a heavy manila envelope. He heard footsteps pounding up the stairway.

"Next stop, Ed Calhoun's!" Sam ordered.

Ping!

The procedure was approximately the same, except that Calhoun had hidden his correspondence more carefully than the Mayor. It didn't matter to Archaezel, though.

There were two more hurried visits. One to the late Chief Mitchell's residence and one to the sheriff's house. More papers were added to the bundle.

As he added the last sheaf, which had been recovered from a locked trunk in the Sheriff's basement, he grinned at the fuming Archaezel. "This does it! Now to Judge Harcourt's house."

Ping!

Sam looked around and blinked. Wherever he was, it most certainly was not the Judge's residence. An even, gray light surrounded him. Up, down, right and left, it was the same—a gray blankness. It wasn't quite like fog—no mist covered the surroundings. It was simply that there weren't *any* surroundings.

He was panic-stricken for a moment. "Archaezel!"

"I'm here."

"Where are we? I told you to take me to Judge Harcourt's house!"

He couldn't see the demon. He discovered he couldn't see himself either.

"We're in Limbo," the demon said. "Hmm. Now let's see—I *know* I turned right. Something must have—" She broke off abruptly.

"Limbo?" Sam's voice strangled. "How'd we get *here*?"

"We were pushed off course. It's a nice little spell, but not much use. He can't keep us here."

"Get us to the Judge's house!"

Ping!

Sam looked around again. It took him several seconds to recognize the room as the Judge's library. The bookshelves were gone, the fireplace bricked up, the walls covered with gaudy-looking wallpaper and a Hollywood bed replaced the sofa.

A door opened and a red-head dressed in a filmy negligee made of some metallic fiber stepped into the room, followed by a tall young man in an odd-looking uniform.

"Come on in, spaceman," said the red-head. "Gee, you're cute!"

Sam grabbed Archaezel's arm. "What's happened now?" he whispered savagely.

"Temporal displacement," she said. "This is the right place, but the wrong time." Her grin was positively lewd. "Evidently, this neighborhood ain't what it used to be."

"Get us back to 1953!" Sam whispered frantically. The spaceman had drawn a peculiar looking gun and was peering warily around the room for the source of the whispers. He said, "Sounds like one of those damned Venerian—"

Ping!

The room was suddenly familiar again, but it kept flickering, as though it were illuminated by a stroboscope.

"*Now* what's going on?" Sam asked exasperatedly.

"Oh, the silly damn fool mortal thinks he can fuss around with me. He's got us in a partial time stasis of about a tenth of a second duration. He thinks he can keep you from delivering those papers. If he keeps it up, he's gonna make me mad!"

The flickering stopped abruptly.

"Everything okay, now?" asked Sam.

"Perfect. It is now one tenth of a second since we left the Sheriff's."

"Fine." Sam took the papers and put them on the Judge's desk. Then he grinned nastily and added a note. It read

Bill:
I have been trying to get this evidence to you for some time. They may try to kill me.
Good luck.

He signed his name with a flourish: That would fix 'em! Harcourt might worry about this mixup for the rest of his life, but Sam knew that he'd eventually rationalize it so it would make sense.

He instructed the demon to make sure that the papers couldn't be removed by anyone but the Judge and then said, "Okay, Archaezel, let's attack!"

VII

The clerk in Niky Orloff's bookstore didn't even look up as Sam tiptoed in.

Sam knew Niky lived in the rear of the store, so he headed in that direction, expecting almost anything. The door was locked, but

237

a whispered order to Archaezel soon opened it.

As far as anyone knew, no one but Niky had ever seen the inside of Niky's home. He could see why, as soon as he entered. The place looked like the interior of a medieval alchemist's laboratory. There were rows of oddly shaped bottles lining the shelves and, here and there, a human skull leered evilly from its empty sockets.

In one corner stood an altar-like structure with a black velvet cloth covering it. The illumination for the entire room came from a black wax candle set on the altar.

"I've been expecting you, Sam."

Sam jumped. Niky Orloff was standing behind him with an old-fashioned pistol pointed at his middle.

"Don't do anything rash, Sam," Niky advised. "This gun has a cold iron ball in it. Your demon is powerless against that."

Sam took his advice. He didn't move or say anything.

"So you doped it all out, eh, Sam?" Niky asked in his flat voice.

Sam nodded. "Sure. It's pretty obvious. You're using black magic to take over Marlston for your own toy city. You figured it out all very neatly. But I wouldn't fit into your political schemes and neither would the Judge. So you tried to get rid of us.

"You started with me. I don't know what sort of spell you used, but you forced me to call up Archaezel the other night. You're the one who tore out the warning page. Evidently, you've never called up any demons yourself, have you? Scared of them, Niky? Your spells aren't very powerful without a Black Alliance, are they? You got Calhoun working for you, and the Mayor, and the very late Carl Mitchell, but you couldn't do anything against an honest man, could you? The best you could do was make us indifferent."

Orloff's face was emotionless.

"But that wasn't enough," Sam added, "you had to destroy us in some way. You knew that a demon does everything in its power to kill its possessor, but you didn't take into account the fact that an honest man doesn't necessarily want power or money. You didn't look far enough ahead. It's true your trap worked, but it wasn't good enough or strong enough. You're licked, Niky!"

Niky's expression didn't change. It was still stiff and cold. "I'll admit I didn't think of your using the demon to clean up the city, but don't think I'm licked. All I have to do is kill you and the demon will be gone—taking you along to Hell.

"Cold iron is the most potent weapon against demons, Sam. I know how to control magic, even if you don't. A lot of men in the past have tried to make a profit out of black magic, but their greed overcame them. They couldn't be satisfied with a Marlston—they had to try for the whole world.

"They never got very far, because they didn't know the trap that was waiting for them." His forefinger tightened on the trigger. "And now, good-bye, Sam!"

He fired.

Nothing happened.

Sam stood there, grinning at him. "I knew you were waiting for me, Niky. I had Archaezel do a little advance scouting. She can't stop *cold* iron, but you forget something—when you fire it from the gun, *the bullet heated up!* Hold him, Archaezel! And don't let him talk!"

Niky Orloff froze, unable to move.

"Your mistake, Niky, was not learning how to control a demon. Black magic is a tool. You can't expect the tool to do *all* the work for you. You've got to keep your commands simple and to the point.

"It's like a law or a contract. The more complex it gets, the easier it is to poke a hole in it. When you try to cover every possibility, or when your orders are too general, you give the demon too much leeway.

"But guys like you give orders to *get* big things and *do* big things. And you get tripped up. Tough, Niky." He looked around cautiously. "Where are the papers, Archaezel—the ones I'm looking for?"

"Behind the big red jar over there."

Sam got them, then faced Niky again. "I'm going to send these papers to Judge Harcourt together with the ones from Ed Calhoun and the Mayor. There's enough evidence in them to put all of you behind bars for a long time. Naturally, I'll enclose my own written confession. With me dead, the whole thing will hold up in court.

"But what will I do with you?"

Niky, held by Archaezel's invisible arms, said nothing. Sam stepped closer and peered at Orloff's face in the dim glow of the flickering candle, and saw that the decision had already been taken out of his hands.

"Archaezel! Damn you, you've killed him!"

Her chuckle was pure evil. "You said hold him and keep him quiet! I figured the best place to hold him was by the throat."

"Nine hundred and fifty, sixty, seventy, eighty, ninety. Seventeen thousand, nine hundred and ninety dollars. It's all here. Thank you, Archaezel. I think I'm being honest in keeping the rest of the money from Rogers' crap game. It has no other claimants, so I'll consider it lost-and-found."

He looked at himself in the mirror. If anything, his face was better looking than before. No one would ever recognize him as Sam Carstairs. He glanced out the window at Waikiki Beach glowing whitely in the afternoon sun.

"This is the life." He grinned happily. Then he turned and glowered at the blonde sitting on the bed. "Except for you, that is."

Now that he had everything he wanted to start a new life, he thought he might as well get rid of Archaezel, once and for all. He had the plan nicely worked out, and now was as good a time as any to carry it out.

"Archaezel, the next time I say the word go, you will carry out the orders I am about to give you. From then on, you will be unable to hear or obey any further orders from me."

He glanced out the hotel room window again and licked his lips nervously. "You will bury yourself at a point twenty feet under this hotel, make yourself invisible and do absolutely nothing. And you will stay in that exact spot, without moving, until I die."

He thought it over carefully once more, to make sure he had covered all the loopholes. The demon couldn't be of any danger to him then—he hoped.

He held his breath, then expelled his last order to Archaezel, "*Go!*"

The resultant explosion knocked Sam colder than the polar ice cap.

When he woke up in the hospital, he opened his eyes and asked the pretty Oriental nurse what had happened.

"Nothing serious, sir," said the nurse. "You have a slight concussion, but the doctors feel you'll be all right."

"But what happened?"

She frowned. "The scientists from the University say that it looks as though a meteor struck the hotel. But it looks like the meteor went *out* into space, instead of falling."

"I see," said Sam, closing his eyes again. "Very mysterious."

Trust old Archaezel—vindictive to the end. He had told her to *stay in that exact spot,* and she had taken him literally. The Earth, in its course through space, had moved away from *that exact spot* with meteoric velocity, and Archaezel had ripped through the hotel by just lying still.

"Nasty wench," said Sam, dozing off.

The nurse looked hurt, sniffed and stalked out of the room.

The Foreign Hand-Tie

by Randall Garrett
writing as David Gordon

*I selected **The Foreign Hand-Tie** for two reasons
(besides the criteria stated in the introduction):
   (1) It illustrates a theme that recurs in Randall's work.
   (2) I'm answering a twenty-year-old request.
   Randall enjoyed exploring the possible uses of psi
talent in espionage work. The three novels in the "Queen's
Own FBI" series, which were a collaboration between
Randall and Larry Janifer, revolve around that theme. You'll
see it, too, in **Psicopath**, which is also in **Takeoff, too**.
   In **The Foreign Hand-Tie** are excerpts from a poem—
it's being recited as a mindshield technique, and is never
fully quoted. Readers wrote to **Analog** in search of the entire
poem but John Campbell never printed it.
   You'll find it here, at the end of this story: it's called
The Egyptian Diamond.*

From Istanbul, in Turkish Thrace, to Moscow, U.S.S.R., is only
a couple of hours outing for a round trip in a fast jet plane—a shade
less than eleven hundred miles in a beeline.

Unfortunately, Mr. Raphael Poe had no way of chartering
a bee.

The United States Navy cruiser *Woonsocket,* having made its
placid way across the Mediterranean, up the Aegean Sea, and
through the Dardanelles to the Bosporous, stopped overnight at
Istanbul and then turned around and went back. On the way in, it
had stopped at Gibraltar, Barcelona, Marseilles, Genoa, Naples,
and Athens—the main friendly ports on the northern side of the
Mediterranean. On the way back, it performed the same ritual on

241

the African side of the sea. Its most famous passengers were the American Secretary of State, two senators, and three representatives.

Its most important passenger was Mr. Raphael Poe.

During the voyage in, Mr. Raphael Poe remained locked in a stateroom, all by himself, twiddling his thumbs restlessly and playing endless games of solitaire, making bets with himself on how long it would be before the ship hit the next big wave and wondering how long it would take a man to go nuts in isolation. On the voyage back, he was not aboard the *Woonsocket* at all, and no one missed him because only the captain and two other Navy men had known he was aboard, and they knew that he had been dropped overboard at Istanbul.

The sleek, tapered cylindroid might easily have been mistaken for a Naval torpedo, since it was roughly the same size and shape. Actually, it was a sort of hybrid, combining the torpedo and the two-man submarine that the Japanese had used in World War II, plus refinements contributed by such apparently diverse arts as skin-diving, cybernetics, and nucleonics.

Inside this one-man underwater vessel, Raphael Poe lay prone, guiding the little atomic-powered submarine across the Black Sea, past Odessa, and up the Dnieper. The first leg, the four hundred miles from the Bosporous to the mouth of the river, was relatively easy. The two hundred and sixty miles from there to Dnepropetrovsk was a little more difficult, but not terribly so. It became increasingly more difficult as the Dnieper narrowed and became more shallow.

On to Kiev. His course changed at Dneptropetrovsk, from northeast to northwest, for the next two hundred fifty miles. At Kiev, the river changed course again, heading north. Three hundred and fifty miles farther on, at Smolensk, he was heading almost due east.

It had not been an easy trip. At night, he had surfaced to get his bearings and to recharge the air tanks. Several times, he had had to take to the land, using the caterpillar treads on the little machine, because of obstacles in the river.

At the end of the ninth day, he was still one hundred eighty miles from Moscow, but, at that point, he got out of the submarine and prepared himself for the trip overland. When he was ready, he pressed a special button on the control panel of the expensive little craft. Immediately, the special robot brain took over. It had recorded the trip upstream; by applying that information in reverse—a "mirror image," so to speak—it began guiding itself back toward Istanbul, applying the necessary corrective factors that made the difference between an upstream and a downstream trip. If it had made a mistake or had been discovered, it would have blown itself to bits. As a tribute to modern robotics and ultramicrominiaturization, it is a fact that the little craft was picked up five days later a few miles from Istanbul by the U.S.S. *Paducah*.

By that time, a certain Vladimir Turenski, a shambling, not-too-bright deaf mute, had made his fully documented appearance in Moscow.

Spies, like fairies and other such elusive sprites, traditionally come in rings. The reason for this circumstructural metaphor is obscure, but remains a fact that a single spy, all by himself, is usually of very little use to anybody. Espionage, on any useful scale, requires organization.

There is, as there should be, a reason for this. The purpose of espionage is to gather information—preferably, *useful* information—against the wishes of, and in spite of the efforts of, a group—usually referred to as "the enemy"—which is endeavoring to prevent that information from getting into other hands than their own. Such activities obviously imply communication. An espioneur, working for Side A, who finds a bit of important information about Side B must obviously communicate that bit of information to Side A or it is of no use whatsoever.

All of these factors pose complex problems.

To begin with, the espioneur must get himself into a position in which he can get hold of the information he wants. Usually, that means that he must pass himself off as something he is not, a process which requires time. Then, when he gets the information he is after, he must get it to his employers quickly. Information, like fish, becomes useless after a certain amount of time, and, unlike fish, there is no known way of refrigerating it to retard spoilage.

It is difficult to transmit information these days. It is actually easier for the espioneur to transmit it than to get it, generally speaking, but it is difficult for him to do both jobs at once, so the spy ring's two major parts consist of the ones who get the information from the enemy and the ones who transmit it back to their employers.

Without magic, it is difficult for a single spy to be of any benefit. And "magic," in this case, can be defined as some method by which information can be either obtained or transmitted without fear of discovery by the enemy. During World War I, a competent spy equipped with a compact transistorized short-wave communications system could have had himself a ball. If the system had included a miniature full-color television camera, he could have gone hog wild. In those days, such equipment would have been magic.

All this is not *a propos* of nothing. Mr. Raphael Poe was, in his own way, a magician.

It is not to be supposed that the United States of America had no spy rings in the Union of Soviet Socialist Republics at that time. There were plenty of them. Raphael Poe could have, if it were so ordained, availed himself of the services of any one or all of them. He did not do so for two reasons. In the first place, the more people who are in on a secret, the more who can give it away. In other words, a ring, like a chain, is only as strong as its weakest section. In the second place, Raphael Poe didn't need any assistance in the first place.

That is, he needed no more assistance than most magicians do—a shill in the audience. In this particular case, the shill was his brother, Leonard Poe.

Operation Mapcase was as ultrasecret as it could possibly be. Although there were perhaps two dozen men who knew of the existence of the operation by its code name, such as the Naval officers who had helped get Raphael Poe to his destination, there were only five men who really knew what Operation Mapcase was all about.

Two of these were, of course, Raphael and Leonard Poe. Two others were the President of the United States and the Secretary of Defense. The fifth was Colonel Julius T. Spaulding, of United States Army Intelligence.

On the seventh day after Raphael Poe's arrival in Moscow, the other four men met in Blair House, across the street from the White House, in a room especially prepared for the purpose. No one but the President knew the exact purpose of the meeting, although they had an idea that he wanted more information of some kind.

The President himself was the last to arrive. Leaving two Secret Service men standing outside the room, he carefully closed the door and turned to face the Secretary of Defense, Colonel Spaulding, and Leonard Poe. "Sit down, gentlemen," he said, seating himself as he spoke.

"Gentlemen, before we go any further, I must conduct one final experiment in order to justify Operation Mapcase. I will not explain it just yet." He looked at Lenny Poe, a small, dark-haired man with a largish nose. "Mr. Poe, can you contact your brother at this moment?"

Lenny Poe was a man who was not overawed by anyone, and had no inclination to be formal, not even toward the President. "Yeah, sure," he said matter-of-factly.

The President glanced at his watch. "It is now five minutes of ten. That makes it five minutes of six in the evening in Moscow. Is your brother free to move around? That is, can he go to a certain place in the city?"

Lenny closed his eyes for a moment, then opened them. "Rafe says he can go any place that the average citizen would be allowed to go."

"Excellent," said the President. He gave Lenny an address—an intersection of two streets not far from Red Square. "Can he get there within fifteen minutes?"

"Make it twenty," said Lenny.

"Very well. Twenty minutes. When he gets there, I'll ask you to relay further instructions."

Lenny Poe closed his eyes, folded his arms, and relaxed in his chair. The other three men waited silently.

Nineteen minutes later, Lenny opened his eyes and said: "O.K. He's there. Now what?"

"There is a lamp post on that corner, I believe," said the President. "Can your brother see it?"

Lenny closed his eyes again. "Sure. There's a guy leaning against it."

The President's eyes brightened. "Describe him!"

Lenny, eyes still closed, said: "Five feet ten, heavy set, gray hair, dark-rimmed glasses, brown suit, flashy necktie. By the cut of his clothes, I'd say he was either British or American, probably American. Fifty-five or fifty-six years old."

It was obvious to the Secretary of Defense and to Colonel Spaulding that the President was suppressing some inward excitement.

"Very good, Mr. Poe!" he said. "Now, you will find a box of colored pencils and a sketch pad in that desk over there. Can you draw me a fairly accurate sketch of that man?"

"Yeah, sure." Lenny opened his eyes, moved over to the desk, took out the pencils and sketch pad, and went to work. He had to close his eyes occasionally, but his work was incredibly rapid and, at the same time, almost photographically accurate.

As the picture took form, the President's inward excitement increased perceptibly. When it was finally finished, Lenny handed the sketch to the President without a word.

The President took it eagerly and his face broke out in his famous grin. "Excellent! Perfect!" He looked at Lenny. "Your brother hasn't attracted the man's attention in any way, has he?"

"Nope," said Lenny.

"Fine. The experiment is over. Relay my thanks to your brother. He can go ahead with whatever he was doing now."

"I don't quite understand," said the Secretary of State.

"I felt it necessary to make one final experiment of my own devising," the President said. "I wanted Raphael Poe to go to a particular place at a particular time, with no advance warning, to transmit a picture of something he had never seen before. I arranged this test myself, and I am positive that there could be no trickery."

"Never seen before?" the Secretary repeated bewilderedly. He gestured at the sketch. "Why, that's obviously Bill Donovan, of the Moscow delegation. Poe could have seen a photograph of him somewhere before."

"Even so," the President pointed out, "there would be no way of knowing that he would be at that spot. But that's beside the point. Look at that necktie!"

"I had noticed it," Defense Secretary admitted.

It was certainly an outstanding piece of neckwear. As drawn by Leonard Poe, it was a piece of brilliant chartreuse silk, fully three and a half inches wide at its broadest. Against that background, rose-pink nude girls were cavorting with pale mauve satyrs.

"That tie," said the President, "was sent to me fifteen years ago by one of my constituents, when I was in Congress. I never wore it, of course, but it would have been criminal to have thrown away such a magnificently obscene example of bad taste as that.

"I sent it to Donovan in a sealed diplomatic pouch by special courier, with instructions to wear it at this time. He, of course, has no idea why he is standing there. He is merely obeying orders.

"Gentlemen, this is completely convincing to me. Absolutely no one but myself knew what I had in mind. It would have required telepathy even to cheat.

"Thank you very much, Mr. Poe. Colonel Spaulding, you may proceed with Operation Mapcase as planned."

Dr. Malekrinova, will you initial these requisition forms, please."

Dr. Sonya Malekrinova, a dowdy-looking, middle-aged woman with unplucked eyebrows and a mole on her chin, adjusted her steel-rimmed glasses, took the proffered papers from the clerk, ran her eyes over them, and then put her initials on the bottom of each page.

"Thank you, Comrade Doctor," said the clerk when she handed back the sheaf of papers.

"Certainly, Comrade."

And the two of them went about their business.

Not far away, in the Cathedral of St. Basil, Vladimir Turenski, alias Raphael Poe, was also apparently going about his business. The cathedral had not seen nor heard the Liturgy of the Russian Orthodox Church, or any other church, for a good many decades. The Bolsheviks, in their zeal to protect the citizens of the Soviet Union from the pernicious influence of religion, had converted it into a museum as soon as possible.

It was the function of *Tovarishch* Turenski to push a broom around the floors of the museum, and this he did with great determination and efficiency. He also cleaned windows and polished metalwork when the occasion demanded. He was only one of a large crew of similarly employed men, but he was a favorite with the Head Custodian, who not only felt sorry for the simple-minded deaf-mute, but appreciated the hard work he did. If, on occasion, Comrade Turenski would lean on his broom and fall into a short reverie, it was excusable because he still managed to get all his work done.

Behind Comrade Turenski, a guide was explaining a display to a group of tourists, but Turenski ignored the distraction and kept his mind focused on the thoughts of Dr. Sonya Malekrinova.

After nearly ten months of patient work, Raphael Poe had hit upon something that was, to his way of thinking, more important than all the information he had transmitted to Washington thus far.

Picking brains telepathically was not, even for him, an easy job. He had the knack and the training, but, in addition, there was the necessity of establishing a rapport with the other mind. Since he was a physicist and not a politician, it was much easier to get information from the mind of Sonya Malekrinova than to get it from the Premier. The only person with whom he could keep in contact over any great distance was his brother, and that only because the two of them had grown up together.

He could pick up the strongest thoughts of any nearby person very easily. He did not need to hear the actual words, for instance, of a nearby conversation in order to follow it perfectly, because the words of verbal communication were strong in a person's mind.

But getting deeper than that required an increasing amount of understanding of the functioning of the other person's mind.

His ability to eavesdrop on conversations had been of immense benefit to Washington so far, but it was difficult for him to get close enough to the higher-ups in the Soviet government to get all the data that the President of the United States wanted.

But now that he had established a firm mental linkage with one of the greatest physicists in the Soviet Union, He could begin to send information that would be tremendous value to the United States.

He brushed up a pile of trash, pushed it into a dust pan, and carried it off toward the disposal chute that led to the trash cans. In the room where the brooms were kept, he paused and closed his eyes.

Lenny! Are you picking this up?

Sure, Rafe. I'm ready with the drawing board any time you are.

As Dr. Sonya Malekrinova stood in her laboratory looking over the apparatus she was perfecting for the glory of the Soviet State, she had no notion that someone halfway around the world was also looking at it over her shoulder—or rather, through her own eyes.

Lenny started with the fives first, and worked his way up to the larger denominations.

"Five, ten, fifteen, twenty, twenty-five, thirty—forty, fifty, sixty..." he muttered happily to himself. "Two fifty, three, three-fifty, four, four-fifty."

It was all there, so he smiled benevolently at the man in the pay window. "Thank you muchly." Then he stepped aside to let another lucky man cash a winning ticket.

His horse had come in at fifteen, six-ten, four-fifty for Straight, Place, and Show, and sixty bucks on the nose had paid off very nicely.

Lenny Poe took out his copy of the *Daily Racing Form* and checked over the listing for the next race.

Hm-m-m, ha. Purse, $7500. Four-year-olds and up: handicap. Seven furlongs. Turf course. Hm-m-m, ha.

Lenny Poe had a passion for throwing his money away on any unpredictable event that would offer him odds. He had, deep down, an artistic soul, but he didn't let that interfere with his desire to lay a bet at the drop of an old fedora.

He had already decided, several hours before, that Ducksoup, in the next race, would win handily and would pay off at something like twenty or twenty-five to one. But he felt it his duty to look one last time at the previous performance record, just to be absolutely positive.

Satisfied, he folded the *Racing Form,* shoved it back into his pocket, and walked over to the fifty-dollar window.

"Gimmie nine tickets on Ducksoup in the seventh," he said, plonking the handful of bills down on the counter.

But before the man behind the window grating could take the money, a huge, hamlike, and rather hairy hand came down on top of his own hand, covering it and the money at the same time.

"Hold it, Lenny," said a voice at the same time.

Lenny jerked his head around to his right and looked up to see a largish man who had "cop" written all over him. Another such individual crowded past Lenny on his left to flash a badge on the man in the betting window, so that he would know that this wasn't a holdup.

"Hey!" said Lenny. His mind was thinking fast. He decided to play his favorite role, that of the indignant Italian. "Whatsa da matta with you, hah? Thisa no a free country? A man gotta no rights?"

"Come on, Mr. Poe," the big man said quietly, "this is important."

"Poe? You outta you mind? Thatsa name of a river—or a raven. I'm a forgetta which. My namesa Manelli!"

"*Scusi, signore,*" the big man said with exaggerated politeness, "*ma se lei e veramente italiano, non e l'kuomo che cerchiamo.*"

Lenny muttered something that the big man didn't quite catch.

"What'd you say?"

"Upper United States—the northern United States," Lenny

said calmly, shoving his four hundred fifty dollars into his pocket. "That's where Chicago is. Never mind. Come on, boys; back to the drawing board."

The two men escorted Lenny to a big, powerful Lincoln; he climbed into the back seat with the big one while the other one got behind the wheel.

As soon as they had left the racetrack and were well out on the highway, the driver said: "You want to call in, Mario? This traffic is pretty heavy."

The big man beside Lenny leaned forward, over the back of the front seat, unhooked the receiver of the scrambler-equipped radiophone, and sat back down. He thumbed a button on the side of the handset and said: "This is Seven Oh Two." After a short silence, he said: "You can call off the net. You want him brought in?" He listened for a monent. "O.K. Off."

He leaned forward to replace the receiver, speaking to the driver as he did so. "Straight to the Air Force base. They've got a jet waiting there for him."

He settled back comfortably and looked at Lenny. "You could at least tell people where you're going."

"Very well," said Lenny. He folded his arms, closed his eyes, and relaxed. "Right now, I'm going off to dreamland."

He waited a short while to see if the other would say anything. He didn't, so Lenny proceeded to do exactly what he had promised to do.

He went off to dreamland.

He had not been absolutely sure, when he made the promise, that he would actually do just that, but the odds were in favor of it. It was now one o'clock in the morning in Moscow, and Lenny's brother, Raphael, was a man of regular habits.

Lenny reached out. When he made contact, all he got was a jumble of hash. It was as though someone had made a movie by cutting bits and snippets from a hundred different films, no bit more than six or seven frames long, with a sound track that might or might not match, and projected the result through a drifting fog, using an ever-changing lens that rippled like the surface of a windruffled pool. Sometimes one figure would come into sharp focus for a fraction of a second, sometimes in color, sometimes not.

Sometimes Lenny was merely observing the show. Sometimes he was *in* it.

Rafe! Hey, Rafe! Wake up!

The jumble of hash began to stabilize, become more coherent—

Lenny sat behind the fat desk, watching his brother come up the primrose path in a unicycle. He pulled it to a halt in front of the desk, opened the pilot's canopy, threw out a rope ladder, and climbed down. His gait was a little awkward, in spite of the sponge-rubber floor, because of the huge flowered carpetbag he was carrying. A battered top hat sat precariously on his blond, curly hair.

"Lenny! Boy, am I glad to see you! I've got it! The whole trouble is in the wonkler, where the spadulator comes across the trellis grid!" He lifted the carpetbag and sat down on the lab table. "Connect up the groffle meter! We'll show those Pentagon pickles who has the push-and-go here!"

"Rafe," Lenny said gently, "wake up. You're dreaming. You're asleep. I want to talk to you."

"I know." He grinned widely. "And you don't want any back talk from me! Yok-yok-yok! Just wait'll I show you!"

In his hands, he held an object which Lenny did not at first understand. Then Rafe's mind brought it into focus.

"This"—Rafe held it up—"is a rocket motor!"

"Rafe, wake up!" Lenny said.

The surroundings stabilized a little more.

"I will in just a minute, Lenny." Rafe was apologetic. "But let me show you this." It did bear some resemblance to a rocket motor. It was about as long as a man's forearm and consisted of a bulbous chamber at one end, which narrowed down into a throat and then widened into a hornlike exhaust nozzle. The chamber was black; the rest was shiny chrome.

Rafe grasped it by the throat with one hand. The other, he clasped firmly around the combustion chamber. "Watch! Now watch!"

He gave the bulbous, rubbery chamber a hard squeeze— "SQUAWK!" went the horn.

"Rafe!" Lenny shouted. "Wake up! WAKE UP!"

Rafe blinked as the situation clarified. "What? Just a second. Lenny. Just..."

"...a second."

Raphael Poe blinked his eyes open. The moon was shining through the dirty windows of the dingy little room that was all he could call home—for a while, at least. Outside the window were the gray streets of Moscow.

His brother's thoughts resounded in his fully awake brain. *Rafe! You awake?*

Sure. Sure. What is it?

The conversation that followed was not in words or pictures, but a weird combination of both, plus a strong admixture of linking concepts that were neither.

In essence, Lenny merely reported that he had taken the day off to go to the races and that Colonel Spaulding was evidently upset for some reason. He wondered if Rafe were in any kind of trouble.

No trouble. Everything's fine at this end. But Dr. Malekrinova won't be back on the job until tomorrow afternoon—or, this afternoon, rather.

I know, Lenny replied. *That's why I figured I could take time off for a go at the ponies.*

I wonder why they're in such a fuss, then? Rafe thought.

I'll let you know when I find out, Lenny said. *Go back to sleep and don't worry.*

In a small office in the Pentagon, Colonel Julius T. Spaulding cradled the telephone on his desk and looked at the Secretary of Defense. "That was the airfield. Poe will be here shortly. We'll get to the bottom of this pretty quickly."

"I hope so, Julius," the Secretary said heavily. "The President is beginning to think we're both nuts."

The colonel, a lean, nervous man with dark, bushy eyebrows and a mustache to match, rolled his eyes up toward the ceiling. "I'm beginning to agree with him."

The Defense Secretary scowled at him. "What do you mean?"

"Anybody who takes telepathy seriously is considered a nut," said the colonel.

"True," said the Secretary, "but that doesn't mean we *are* nuts."

"Oh, yeah?" The colonel took the cigar out of his mouth and gestured with it. "Anybody who'd do something that convinces all his friends he's nuts must be nuts!"

The Secretary smiled wanly. "I wish you wouldn't be so logical. You almost convince me."

"Don't worry," said the colonel. "I'm not ready to have this room measured for sponge-rubber wallpaper just yet. Operation Mapcase has helped a lot in the past few months, and it will help even more."

"All you have to do is get the bugs out of it," said the Secretary.

"If we did that," Colonel Spaulding said flatly, "the whole operation would fold from lack of personnel."

"Just carry on the best you can," the Secretary said gloomily as he got up to leave. "I'll let you handle it."

"Fine. I'll call you later."

Twenty minutes after the Defense Secretary had gone, Lenny Poe was shown into Colonel Spaulding's office. The agent who had brought him in closed the door gently, leaving him alone with the colonel.

"I told you I'd be back this evening. What were you in such a hurry about?"

"You're supposed to stay in touch," Colonel Spaulding pointed out. "I don't mind your penchant for ponies particularly, but I'd like to know where to find you if I need you."

"I wouldn't mind in the least, Colonel. I'd phone you every fifteen minutes if that's what you wanted. Except for one thing."

"What's that?"

Lenny jerked a thumb over his shoulder. "Your linguistically talented flatfeet. Did you ever try to get into a floating crap game when you were being followed by a couple of bruisers who look more like cops than cops do?"

"Look, Poe; I can find you plenty of action right here in Washington, if it won't offend your tender sensibilities to shoot crap with a senator or two. Meanwhile, sit down and listen. This is important."

Lenny sat down reluctantly. "O.K. What is it?"

"Dr. Davenport and his crew are unhappy about that last batch of drawings you and I gave 'em."

"What's the matter? Don't they like the color scheme? I never thought scientists had any artistic taste, anyway."

"It's got nothing to do with that. The—"

The phone rang. Colonel Spaulding scooped it up and identified himself. Then: "What? Yeah. All right, send him in."

He hung up and looked back at Lenny. "Davenport. We can get his story firsthand. Just sit there and look important."

Lenny nodded. He knew that Dr. Amadeus Davenport was aware that the source of those drawings was Soviet Russia, but he did not know how they had been obtained. As far as he knew, it was just plain, ordinary spy work.

He came in briskly. He was a tall, intelligent-looking man with a rather craggy face and thoughtful brown eyes. He put a large brief case on the floor, and, after the preliminaries were over, he came right to the point.

"Colonel Spaulding, I spoke to the Secretary of Defense, and he agreed that perhaps this situation might be cleared up if I talked directly with you."

"I hope so," the colonel said. "Just what is it that seems to be bothering you?"

"These drawings," Davenport said, "don't make any sense. The device they're supposed to represent couldn't do anything. Look, I'll show you."

He took from his briefcase photostatic copies of some of the drawings Lenny had made. Five of them were straight blueprint-type drawings; the sixth was a copy of Lenny's near-photographic paintings of the device itself.

"This component, here," he said, gesturing at the set of drawings "simply baffles us. We're of the opinion that your agents are known to the Soviet government and have been handed a set of phony plans."

"What's it supposed to do?" Lenny asked.

"We don't know what it's *supposed* to do," the scientist said, "but it's doubtful that it would *actually* do anything." He selected one of the photocopies. "See that thing? The one shaped like the letter Q with an offset tail? According to the specifications, it is supposed to be painted emerald green, but there's no indication of what it is."

Lenny Poe reached out, picked up the photocopy and looked at it. It was—or had been—an exact copy of the drawing that was used by Dr. Sonya Malekrinova. But, whereas the original drawing had been labeled entirely in Cyrillic characters, these labels were now in English.

The drawings made no sense to Lenny at all. They hadn't when he'd made them. His brother was a scientist, but Lenny understood none of it.

"Who translated the Russian into English?" he asked.

"A Mr. Berensky. He's one of our best experts on the subject. I assure you the translations are accurate," Dr. Davenport said.

"But if you don't know what that thing is," the colonel objected, "how can you say the device won't work? Maybe it would if that Q-shaped thing was—"

"I know what you mean," Davenport interrupted. "But that's not the only part of the machine that doesn't make any sense."

He went on to explain other discrepancies he had detected in the drawings, but none of it penetrated to Lenny, although Colonel Spaulding seemed to be able to follow the physicist's conversation fairly readily.

"Well, what's your suggestion, doctor?" the colonel asked at last.

"If your agents could get further data," the physicist said carefully, "it might be of some use. At the same time, I'd check up on the possibility that your agents are known to the NKVD."

"I'll see what can be done," said the colonel. "Would you mind leaving those copies of the drawings with me for a while?"

"Go right ahead," Davenport said. "One other thing. If we assume this device is genuine, then it must serve some purpose. It might help if we knew what the device is supposed to *do.*"

"I'll see what can be done," Colonel Spaulding repeated.

When Davenport had gone, Spaulding looked at Poe. "Got any explanation for that one?"

"No," Lenny admitted. "All I can do is check with Rafe. He won't be awake for a few hours yet. I'll check on it and give you an answer in the morning."

Early next morning, Colonel Spaulding walked through his outer office. He stopped at the desk where the pretty brunette WAC sergeant was typing industriously, leaned across the desk, and gave her his best leer. "How about a date tonight, music lover?" he asked. "'Das Rheingold' is playing tonight. A night at the opera would do you good."

"I'm sorry, sir," she said primly, "you know enlisted women aren't allowed to date officers."

"Make out an application for OCS. I'll sign it."

She smiled at him. "But then I wouldn't have any excuse for

turning you down. And then what would my husband say?"

"I'll bribe him. I'll send *him* to OCS."

"He's not eligible. Officers are automatically disqualified."

Colonel Spaulding sighed. "A guy can't win against competition like that. Anything new this morning?"

"Mr. Poe is waiting in your office. Other than that, there's just the routine things."

He went on into his office. Lenny Poe was seated behind the colonel's desk, leaning back in the swivel chair, his feet on the top of the desk. He was sound asleep.

The colonel walked over to the desk, took his cigar from his mouth and said: "*Good* morning, Colonel Spaulding!"

Lenny snapped awake. "I'm not Colonel Spaulding," he said.

"Then why are you sitting in Colonel Spaulding's chair?"

"I figured if I was asleep nobody'd know the difference." Lenny got up and walked over to one of the other chairs. "Those don't lean back comfortably. I can't sleep in 'em."

"You can sleep later. How was your session with Rafe?"

Lenny glowered glumly. "I wish you and Rafe hadn't talked me into this job. It's a strain on the brain. I don't know how he expects anyone to understand all that garbage."

"All what garbage?"

Lenny waved a hand aimlessly. "All this scientific guff. I'm an artist, not a scientist. If Rafe can get me a clear picture of something, I can copy it, but when he tries to explain something scientific, he might as well be thinking in Russian or Old Upper Middle High Martian or something."

"I know," said Colonel Spaulding, looking almost as glum as Lenny. "Did you get anything at all that would help Dr. Davenport figure out what those drawings mean?"

"Rafe says that the translations are all wrong," Lenny said, "but I can't get a clear picture of just what *is* wrong."

Colonel Spaulding thought for a while in silence. Telepathy— at least in so far as the Poe brothers practiced it—certainly had its limitations. Lenny couldn't communicate mentally with anyone except his brother Rafe. Rafe could pick up the thoughts of almost anyone if he happened to be close by, but couldn't communicate over a long distance with anyone but Lenny.

The main trouble lay in the fact that it was apparently impossible to transmit a concept directly from Brain A to Brain B unless the basic building blocks of the concept were already present in Brain B. Raphael Poe, for instance, had spent a long time studying Russian, reading Dostoevski, Tolstoy, and Turgenev in the original tongue, familiarizing himself with modern Russian thought through the courtesy of *Izvestia, Pravda,* and *Krokodil,* and, finally, spending time in the United Nations building and near the Russian embassy in order to be sure that he could understand the mental processes involved.

Now, science has a language of its own. Or, rather, a multiplicity of languages, each derived partly from the native language of the various scientific groups and partly of borrowings from other languages. In the physical sciences especially, the language of mathematics is a further addition.

More than that, the practice of the scientific method automatically induces a thought pattern that is different from the type of thought pattern that occurs in the mind of a person who is not scientifically oriented.

Lenny's mind was a long way from being scientifically oriented. Worse, he was a bigot. He not only didn't know why the light in his room went on when he flipped the switch, he didn't *want* to know. To him, science was just so much flummery, and he didn't want his brain cluttered up with it.

Facts mean nothing to a bigot. He has already made up his mind, and he doesn't intend to have his solid convictions disturbed by anything so unimportant as a contradictory fact. Lenny was of the opinion that all mathematics was arcane gobbledygook, and his precise knowledge of the mathematical odds in poker and dice games didn't abate that opinion one whit. Obviously, a mind like that is utterly incapable of understanding a projected thought of scientific content; such a thought bounces off the impregnable mind shield that the bigot has set up around his little area of bigotry.

Colonel Spaulding had been aware of these circumstances since the inception of Operation Mapcase. Even though he, himself, had never experienced telepathy more than half a dozen times in his life, he had made a study of the subject and was pretty well aware of its limitations. The colonel might have dismissed—as most men do—his own fleeting experiences as "coincidence" or "imagination" if it had not been for the things he had seen and felt in Africa during World War II. He had only been a captain then, on detached duty with British Intelligence, under crusty old Colonel Sir Cecil Haversham, who didn't believe a word of "all that mystic nonsense." Colonel Haversham had made the mistake of alienating one of the most powerful of the local witch doctors.

The British Government had hushed it all up afterwards, of course, but Spaulding still shuddered when he thought of the broken-spirited, shrunken caricature of his old self that Colonel Haversham had become after he told the witch doctor where to get off.

Spaulding had known that there were weaknesses in the telepathic communication linkage that was the mainspring of Operation Mapcase, but he had thought that they could be overcome by the strengths of the system. Lenny had no blockage whatever against receiving visual patterns and designs. He could reproduce an electronic wiring diagram perfectly because, to him, it was not a grouping of scientific symbols, but a design of lines, angles, and curves.

At first, it is true, he had had a tendency to change them here and there, to make the design balance better, to make it more aesthetically satisfying to his artistic eye, but that tendency had been easily overcome, and Colonel Spaulding was quite certain that that wasn't what was wrong now.

Still—

"Lenny," he said carefully, "are you sure you didn't jigger up those drawings to make 'em look prettier?"

Lenny Poe gave the colonel a look of disgust. "Positive. Rafe checked 'em over every inch of the way as I was drawing them, and he rechecked again last night—or this morning—on those photostats Davenport gave us. That's when he said that there was something wrong with the translations."

"But he couldn't make it clear just what was wrong, eh?"

Lenny shrugged. "How anybody could make any sense out of that gobbledygook is beyond me."

The Colonel blew out a cloud of cigar smoke and looked thoughtfully at the ceiling. As long as the diagrams were just designs on paper, Lenny Poe could pick them up fine. Which meant that everything was jim-dandy as long as the wiring diagrams were labeled in the Cyrillic alphabet. The labels were just more squiggles to be copied as a part of the design.

But if the labels were in English, Lenny's mind would try to "make sense" out of them, and since scientific concepts did *not* "make sense" to him, the labels came out as pure nonsense. In one of his drawings, a lead wire had been labled "simply ground to powder," and if the original drawing hadn't been handy to check with, it might have taken quite a bit of thought to realize that what was meant was "to power supply ground." Another time, a GE 2N 188A transistor had come out labeled GEZNISSA. There were others—much worse.

Russian characters, on the other hand, didn't have to make any sense to Lenny, so his mind didn't try to force them into a preconceived mold.

Lenny unzipped the leather portfolio he had brought with him—a specially-made carrier that looked somewhat like an oversized brief case.

"Maybe these'll help," he said. "We managed to get two good sketches of the gadget—at least, as much of it as that Russian lady scientist has put together so far. I kind of like the rather abstract effect you get from all those wires snaking in and around, with that green glass tube in the center. Pretty, isn't it?"

"Very," said the colonel without conviction. "I wonder if it will help Davenport any?" He looked at the pictures for several seconds more, then, suddenly, his eyes narrowed. "Lenny—this piece of green glass—the thing's shaped like the letter Q."

"Yeah, sort of. Why?"

"You said it was a tube, but you didn't make it look hollow when you drew it."

"It isn't; it's solid. Does a tube have to be hollow? Yeah, I guess it does, doesn't it? Well, then, it isn't a tube."

Colonel Spaulding picked up the phone and dialed a number.

"Colonel Spaulding here," he said after a moment. "Let me speak to Dr. Davenport." And, after a wait: "This is Colonel Spaulding, doctor. I think we may have something for you."

"Good morning, colonel. I'm glad to hear that. What is it?"

"That Q-shaped gadget—the one that you said was supposed to be painted emerald green. Are you sure that's the right translation of the Russian?"

"Well...uh—" Davenport hesitated. "I can't be sure on my own say-so, of course. I don't understand Russian. But I assure you that Mr. Berensky is perfectly reliable."

"Oh, I have no doubt of that," Colonel Spaulding said easily. "But, tell me, does Mr. Berensky know how to read a circuit diagram?"

"He does," Davenport said, somewhat testily. "Of course, he wasn't shown the diagram itself. We had the Russian labels copied, and he translated from a list."

"I had a sneaking suspicion that was it," said Spaulding. "Tell me, doctor, what does L-E-A-D spell?"

"Lead," said the doctor promptly, pronouncing it *leed*. Then, after a pause, he said: "Or lead," this time pronouncing it *led*. "It would depend on the context."

"Suppose it was on a circuit diagram," the colonel prompted.

"Then it would probably be *leed*. What's all this leading up to, colonel?"

"Bear with me. Suppose you had a cable coming from a storage battery, and you wanted to make sure that the cable was reasonably resistant to corrosion, so you order it made out of the metal, lead. It would be a *led leed*, wouldn't it?"

"Um-m-m...I suppose so."

"You might get pretty confused if you didn't have a circuit diagram in front of you to tell you what the label was talking about, mightn't you?"

"I see what you mean," the scientist said slowly. "But we can't show those circuit diagrams to Berensky. The Secretary of Defense himself has classified them as Class Triple-A Ultra-Hyper Top Secret. That puts them just below the Burn-The-Contents-Before-Reading class, and Berensky doesn't have that kind of clearance."

"Then get somebody else," Colonel Spaulding said tiredly. "All you need is a man who can understand technical Russian and can read a circuit schematic and has a top-level secrecy clearance. If we haven't got at least one man in these United States with such simple qualifications as those, then we might as well give the country over to the Reds or back to the Redskins, since our culture is irreprievably doomed." And he lowered the phone gently to its cradle.

"There's no such word as 'irreprievably'," Lenny pointed out.

"There is now," said Colonel Spaulding.

Raphael Poe moseyed through the streets of Moscow in an apparently aimless manner. The expression on his face was that of a reasonably happy moron.

His aimless manner was only apparent. Actually, he was heading toward the Lenin Soviet People's Higher Research Laboratories. Dr. Sonya Borisovna Malekrinova would be working late this evening, and he wanted to get as close as possible in order to pick up as much information as he could.

Rafe had a great deal of admiration for that woman, he admitted to himself. She was, granted, as plain as an unsalted *matzoh*. No. That was an understatement. If it were possible to die of the uglies, Sonya Borisovna would have been dangerously ill.

Her disposition did nothing to alleviate that drawback. She fancied herself as cold, hard, analytical, and ruthless; actually, she was waspish, arrogant, overbearing, and treacherous. What she considered in herself to be scientific detachment was really an isolation born of fear and distrust of the entire human race.

To her, Communism was a religion; *"Das Kapital"* and *"The Communist Manifesto"* were holy writ enshrining the dogmata of Marxism-Leninism, and the conflict with the West was a *jehad*, a holy war in which God, in His manifestation as Dialectic Materialism, would naturally win out in the end.

All of which goes to show that a scientific bent, in itself, does not necessarily keep one from being a bigot.

Rafe's admiration for the woman stemmed solely from the fact that, in spite of all the powerful drawbacks that existed in her mind, she was still capable of being a brilliant, if somewhat erratic scientist.

There was a more relaxed air in Moscow these days. The per capita production of the Soviet Union still did not come up to that of the United States, but the recent advances in technology did allow a feeling of accomplishment, and the hard drive for superiority was softened a trifle. It was no longer considered the height of indolence and unpatriotic timewasting to sit on a bench and feed pigeons. Nor was food so scarce and costly that throwing away a few bread crumbs could be considered sabotage.

So Rafe Poe found himself a quiet corner near the Lenin Soviet People's Laboratories, took out a small bag of dried breadcrumbs, and was soon surrounded by pigeons.

Dr. Malekrinova was carefully calibrating and balancing the

electronic circuits that energized and activated and controlled the output of the newly-installed beam generator—a ring of specially-made greenish glass that had a small cylinder of the same glass projecting out at a tangent. Her assistant, Alexis, a man of small scientific ability but a gifted mechanic, worked stolidly with her. It was not an easy job for Alexis; Sonya Borisovna was by no means an easy woman to work with. There was, as there should have been, a fifty-fifty division in all things—a proper state of affairs in a People's Republic. Alexis Andreyevitch did half the physical work, got all the blame when things went wrong, and none of the credit when things went right. Sonya Borisovna got the remaining fifty per cent.

Sonya Borisovna Malekrinov had been pushing herself too hard, and she knew it. But, she told herself, for the glory of the Soviet peoples, the work must go on.

After spending two hours taking down instrument readings, she took the results to her office and began to correlate them.

Have to replace that 140-9.0 micromicrofarad frequency control on stage two with something more sensitive, she thought. *And the field modulation coils require closer adjustment.*

She took off her glasses and rubbed at her tired eyes while she thought. *Perhaps the 25 miscrofarad, 12 volts electrolytic condenser could be used to feed the pigeons, substituting a breadcrumb capacitor in the sidewalk circuit.*

She opened her eyes suddenly and stared at the blank wall in front of her. "Pigeons?" she said wonderingly. "Breadcrumb capacitor? Am I losing my mind? What kind of nonsense is that?"

She looked back down at her notes, then replaced her glasses so that she could read them. Determined not to let her mind wander in that erratic fashion again, she returned her attention to the work at hand.

She found herself wondering if it might not be better to chuck the whole job and get out while the getting was good. *The old gal,* she thought, *is actually tapping my mind! She's picking up everything!*

Sonya Borisovna sat bolt upright in her chair, staring at the blank wall again. "Why am I thinking such nonsense?" she asked aloud. "And why should I be thinking in English?" When her words registered on her ears, she realized that she was actually *speaking* in English. She was thoroughly acquainted with the language, of course, but it was not normal for her to think in it unless she happened to be conversing with someone in that tongue.

The first whisper of a suspicion began to take form in the mind of Dr. Sonya Borisovna Malekrinova.

Half a block away, Raphael Poe emptied the last of his breadcrumbs on the sidewalk and began walking away. He kept his mind as blank as possible, while his brow broke out in a cold sweat.

"That," said Colonel Julius Spaulding scathingly, "is as pretty a mess as I've seen in years."

"It's breadboard circuit, I'll admit," Dr. Davenport said defensively, "but it's built according to the schematics you gave us."

"Doctor," said the colonel, "during the war the British dropped our group a radio transmitter. It was the only way to get the stuff into Africa quickly. The parachute failed to open. The transmitter fell two thousand feet, hit the side of a mountain, and tumbled down another eight hundred feet. When we found it, four days later, its wiring was in better shape than that thing is in now."

"It's quite sufficient to test the operation of the device," Davenport said coldly.

Spaulding had to admit to himself that it probably was. The thing was a slapdash affair—the colonel had a strong feeling that Davenport had assigned the wiring job to an apprentice and given him half an hour to do the job—but the soldering jobs looked tight enough, and the components didn't look as though they'd all been pulled out of the salvage bin. What irritated Colonel Spaulding was Davenport's notion that the whole thing was a waste of time, energy, money, and materials, and, therefore, there was no point in doing a decent job of testing it at all.

He was glad that Davenport didn't know how the information about the device had been transported to the United States. As it was, he considered the drawings a hoax on the part of the Russians; if he had been told that they had been sent telepathically, he would probably have gone into fits of acute exasperation over such idiocy.

The trouble with Davenport was that, since the device didn't make any sense to him, he didn't believe it would function at all.

"Oh, it will do *something*, all right," he'd said once, "but it won't be anything that needs all that apparatus. Look here—"He had pointed toward the schematic. "Where do you think all that energy is going? All you're going to get is a little light, a lot of heat, and a couple of burned out coils. I could do the same job cheaper with a dozen 250 watt light bulbs."

To be perfectly honest with himself, Spaulding had to admit that he wasn't absolutely positive that the device would do anything in particular, either. His own knowledge of electronic circuitry was limited to ham radio experience, and even that was many years out of date. He couldn't be absolutely sure that the specifications for the gadget hadn't been garbled in transmission.

That Q-shaped gizmo, for instance. It had taken the better part of a week for Raphael Poe to transmit the information essential to the construction of that enigmatic bit of glass.

Rafe had had to sit quietly in the privacy of his own room and print out the specifications in Russian, then sit and look at the paper while Lenny copied the "design." Then each paper had to be carefully destroyed, which wasn't easy to do. You don't go around burning papers in a crowded Russian tenement unless you want the people in the next room to wonder what you're up to.

Then the drawings Lenny had made had had to be translated into English and the piece carefully made to specifications.

Now here it was, all hooked up and, presumably, ready for action. Colonel Spaulding fervently hoped there would be some action; he didn't like the smug look on Dr. Amadeus Davenport's face.

The device was hooked up on a testing-room circuit and controlled from outside. The operation could be watched through a heavy pane of bulletproof glass. "With all that power going into it," Davenport said, "I don't want anyone to get hurt by spatters of molten metal when those field coils blow."

They went outside to the control console, and Dr. Davenport flipped the energizing switch. After the device had warmed up on low power, Davenport began turning knobs slowly, increasing the power flow. In the testing room, the device just sat there, doing nothing visible, but the meters on the control console showed that something was going on. A greenish glow came from the housing that surrounded the Q-shaped gadget.

"Where the Russians made their mistake in trying to fool anyone with that thing was in their design of that laser component," said Dr. Davenport. "Or, I should say, the thing that is supposed to look like a laser component."

"Laser?" said Colonel Spaulding uncomprehendingly.

"It means 'light amplification by stimulated emission of radiation'," Davenport explained. "Essentially, a laser consists of a gas-filled tube or a solid ruby bar with parallel mirrors at both ends. By exciting the atoms from outside, light is generated within the tube, and some of it begins to bounce back and forth between the mirrors at the ends. This tends to have a cascade effect on the atoms which have picked up the energy from outside, so that more and more of the light generated inside the tube tends to be parallel to the length of the tube. One of the mirrors is only partially silvered, and eventually the light bouncing back and forth becomes powerful enough to flash through the half-silvered end, giving a coherent beam of light."

"Maybe that's what this is supposed to be," said the colonel.

Davenport chuckled dryly. "Not a chance. Not with an essentially circular tube that isn't even silvered."

Lenny Poe, the colonel noticed, wasn't the only person around who didn't care whether the thing he referred to as a "tube" was hollow or not.

"Is it doing anything?" Colonel Spaulding asked anxiously,

trying to read the meters over Davenport's shoulder.

"Its heating up," Davenport said dryly.

Spaulding looked back at the apparatus. A wisp of smoke was rising slowly from a big coil.

A relay clicked minutely.

WHAP!

For a confused second, everything seemed to happen at once.

But it didn't; there was a definite order to it.

First, a spot on the ceramic tile wall of the room became suddenly red, orange, white hot. Then there was a little crater of incandescent fury, as though a small volcano had erupted in the wall. Following that, there was a sputtering and crackling from the innards of the device itself, and a cloud of smoke arose suddenly, obscuring things in the room. Finally, there was the crash of circuit-breakers as they reacted to the overload from the short circuit.

There was silence for a moment, then the hiss of the automatic fire extinguishers in the testing room as they poured a cloud of carbon dioxide snow on the smoldering apparatus.

"There," said Davenport with utter satisfaction. "What did I tell you?"

"You didn't tell me this thing was a heat-ray projector," said Colonel Spaulding.

"What are you talking about?" Dr. Davenport said disdainfully.

"Develop the film in those automatic cameras," Spaulding said, "and I'll show you what I'm talking about!"

As far as Colonel Spaulding was concerned, the film showed clearly what had happened. A beam of energy had leaped from the "tail" of the Q-tube, hit the ceramic tile of the wall, and burned its way through in half a second or so. The hole in the wall, surrounded by fused ceramic, was mute evidence of the occurrence of what Spaulding had seen.

But Dr. Davenport pooh-poohed the whole thing. Evidence to the contrary, he was quite certain that no such thing had happened. A piece of hot glass from a broken vacuum tube had done it, he insisted.

A piece of hot glass had burned its way through half an inch of tile? And a wall?

Davenport muttered something about the destructive effects of shaped charges. He was more willing to believe that something as wildly improbable as that had happened than admit that the device had done what Colonel Spaulding was quite certain it had done.

Within three hours, Davenport had three possible explanations of what had happened, each of which required at least four unlikely things to happen coincidentally.

Colonel Spaulding stalked back to his office in a state of angry disgust. Just because the thing was foreign to Davenport's notions, he had effectively tied his own hands—and Colonel Spaulding's, too.

"Where's Lenny Poe?" he asked the WAC sergeant. "I want to talk to him."

She shook her head. "I don't know, sir. Lieutenant Fesner called in half an hour ago. Mr. Poe has eluded them again."

Colonel Spaulding gazed silently at the ceiling for a long moment. Then: "Sergeant Nugget, take a letter. To the President of the United States, 1600 Pennsylvania Avenue, Washington, D.C.

"Dear Sir. Consider this my resignation. I have had so much experience with jackasses lately that I have decided to change my name to Hackenbush and become a veterinarian. Yours truly, et cetera. Got that?"

"Yes, sir" said the sergeant.

"Burn it. When Fumblefingers Fesner and his boys find Lenny Poe again, I want to know immediately."

He stalked on into his office.

Raphael Poe was beginning to feel distinctly uncomfortable. Establishing a close rapport with another mind can be a distinct disadvantage at times. A spy is supposed to get information without giving any; a swapping of information is not at all to his advantage.

It was impossible to keep his mind a perfect blank. What he had to do was keep his strongest surface thoughts entirely on innocuous things. The trouble with that was that it made it extremely difficult to think about some way to get out of the jam he was in. Thinking on two levels at once, while not impossible, required a nicety of control that made wirewalking over Niagara look easy.

The thing to do was to make the surface thoughts automatically repetitive. A song.

> "In a hall of strange description
> (Antiquarian Egyptian),
> Figuring his monthly balance
> sheet, a troubled monarch sat
> With a frown upon his forehead,
> hurling interjections horrid
> At the state of his finances, for
> his pocketbook was flat."

Simultaneously, he kept a picture in his mind's eye. It had to be something vivid that would be easy to concentrate on. The first thing that came to mind was the brilliant necktie that the President had used in his test several months before. He conjured it up in all its chartreuse glory, the he animated it. Mauve satyrs danced with

rose-pink nymphs and chased them over the yellow-green
landscape.

> *"Not a solitary single copper cent had he to jingle*
> *In his pocket, and his architects had gone off on a strike,*
> *Leaving pyramids unfinished, for their wages had diminished,*
> *And their credit vanished likewise, in a way they didn't like."*

Rafe could tell that Dr. Malekrinova's mind was trying to
reject the alien ideas that were coming into her mind. She wasn't
consciously trying to pick up Rafe's thoughts. But the rejection was
ineffective because of its fascination. The old business about the
horse's tail. If you see a white horse, you'll soon get rich if you can
keep from thinking about the horse's tail until it's out of sight. The
first thought that comes to mind is: "I mustn't think about the
horse's tail." A self-defeating proposition.

If Sonya Borisovna had been certain that she was receiving the
thoughts telepathically, she might have been able to reject them.
But her mind rejected the idea of telepathy instead, so she was
susceptible to the thoughts because she thought they were her own.

The cavorting of the nymphs and satyrs became somewhat
obscene, but Rafe didn't bother to correct it. He had more to worry
about than offending the rather prim mind of Dr. Malekrinova.

> *"It was harder for His Royal Highness than for sons of toil,*
> *For the horny-handed workmen only ate three figs per day,*
> *While the King liked sweet potatoes, puddings,*
> *pies, and canned tomatoes,*
> *Boneless ham, and Bluepoint oysters*
> *cooked some prehistoric way."*

What to do now? Should he try to get out of Russia? Was there
any quick way out?

He had all the information he needed on the heat-beam
projector that Dr. Malekrinova was building. The theory behind it
was perfectly clear; all it needed was further experimentation. If it
worked out according to theory, it would be an almost perfect
defense against even the fastest intercontinental ballistic missiles.

> *"As he growled, the Royal grumbler spied a bit of broken tumbler*
> *In a long undusted corner just behind the chamber door.*
> *When his hungry optics spied it, he stood silently and eyed it,*
> *Then he smote his thigh with ecstasy and danced about the floor."*

Maybe he should try to make a run for the American Embassy.
No, no one there knew him, and they probably couldn't get him out
of the country, anyway. Besides, it would take him too long to
explain the situation to them.

> *"By the wit Osiris gave me! This same bit of glass shall save me!*

I shall sell it as a diamond at some stupendous price!
And whoe'er I ask to take it will find, for his own sweet sake, it
Will be better not to wait until I have to ask him twice!"

The theory behind the heat projector was simply an extension of the laser theory, plus a few refinements. Inside a ring made of the proper material, the light, acted upon by exterior magnetic fields, tended to move in a circle, so that the photon cascade effect was all in one direction instead of bouncing back and forth between a pair of mirrors. That light could be bent around corners by making it travel through a glass rod was well known, and the Malekrinova Q-tube took advantage of that effect.

In a way, the principle was similar to that of the cyclotron, except that instead of spinning ions around in a circle to increase their velocity a beam of coherent light was circulated to increase its intensity.

Then, at the proper moment, a beam of intense coherent light shot out of the tangent that formed the tail of the Q-tube. If the material of the Q was properly constructed and contained atoms that fluoresced strongly in the infrared, you had a heat beam that delivered plenty of power. And, since the radiation was linear and "in step," the Q-tube didn't heat up much at all. The cascade effect took most of the energy out as radiation.

"Then a Royal Proclamation was dispatched throughout the nation,
Most imperatively calling to appear before the King,
Under penalties most cruel, every man who sold a jewel
Or who bought and bartered precious stones,
and all that sort of thing."

But knowing all that didn't help Raphael Poe or the United States of America one whit if the information couldn't be gotten out of Russia and into Colonel Spaulding's hands. Lenny had told him of the trouble the colonel was having with Dr. Davenport.

If he could only communicate with Lenny! But if he did, Dr. Malekrinova would pick up every bit of it, and that would be the end of that. No, he had to figure out some way to get himself and the information both out of the country.

Meanwhile, he had to keep thinking of an animated necktie. And he had to keep singing.

"Thereupon, the jewelers' nether joints
all quaked and knocked together,
As they packed their Saratogas in lugubrious despair.
It was ever their misfortune to be pillaged by extortion,
And they thought they smelled a rodent
on the sultry desert air."

Lenny Poe shoved open the door of Colonel Spaulding's outer

office with a violence that startled Sergeant Nugget.

"Is Spaulding in?" he barked.

"I think he's expecting you," she said. There was no time to buzz the colonel; Poe was already opening the door.

"Rafe's in trouble!" Lenny said hurriedly, slamming the door behind him.

"Where have you been?" snapped the colonel.

"Never mind that! Rafe's in trouble, I said! We've gotta figure a way to get him out of it!"

Colonel Spaulding dropped all thought of bawling out Poe. "What'd he say? What's the trouble?"

"All he's doing is broadcasting that necktie—like an animated cartoon in technicolor. And he's singing."

"Singing? Singing what?"

"As they faced the Great Propylon, with an apprehensive smile on,
Sculptured there in heiroglyphics six feet wide and nine feet high
Was the threat of King Rameses to chop every man to pieces
Who, when shown the Royal diamond, would dare refuse to buy."

Colonel Spaulding blinked. "That's pretty. What does it mean?"

"Nothing; it's a song, that's all. That female Russian scientist can read Rafe's mind, and he's broadcasting this stuff to cover up!"

Quickly, he told Spaulding what the situation was as he had been able to piece it together from Rafe's secondary thoughts.

"Ye Gods!" Colonel Spaulding slapped at his brow. Then he grabbed for the telephone and started dialing.

Lenny dropped into one of the nearby chairs, closed his eyes, and concentrated.

Rafe! Rafe! Listen to me! Rafe!

"Then the richest dealer, Mulai Hassan, eyed the gem and cooly
Said, 'The thing is but a common tumbler-bottom, nothing more!'
Whereupon, the King's assassin drew his sword, and Mulai Hassan
Never peddled rings again upon the Nile's primeval shore."

But below the interference came Rafe's thoughts. And the one thing of primary importance to him was to get the information on the heat-beam generator to the United States.

No bigotry, no matter how strong, is totally impregnable. Even the most narrow-minded racial bigot will make an exception if a person of the despised race risks his own life to save the life of the bigot or someone the bigot loves. The bigotry doesn't collapse—not by a long shot. But an exception is made in that one case.

Lenny Poe made an exception. Any information that was worth his brother's life was *Important!* Therefore, it was not, could not be, scientific gobbledygook, no matter how it sounded.

Rafe, give it to me! Try me! I can copy it!

"Then Abdullah abd Almahdi faintly said the stone was shoddy,
But he thought that, in a pinch, he might bid fifty cents himself,
There ensued a slight commotion ere he could repent the notion,
And Abdullah was promoted to the Oriental Shelf."

Rafe! Stop singing that stupid song and give me the stuff! She can't learn anything if you just think about that theory stuff. She already knows that! Come on! Give!

Lenny Poe grabbed a pencil and a sheaf of paper from the colonel's desk and began writing frantically as the *Song of the Egyptian Diamond* stopped suddenly.

Words. Nonsense words. That's all most of the stuff was to Lenny. It didn't matter. He spelled them as he thought they should be, and if he made a mistake, Rafe would correct him.

Rafe tried to keep a picture of the words as they would look if printed while he thought them verbally, and that helped. The information came across in the only way it could come across—not as concepts, but as symbols.

Lenny hardly noticed that the Secretary of Defense and the President had come into the room. He didn't even realize that Colonel Spaulding was feeding him fresh sheets of paper.

Lenny didn't seem to notice the time passing, nor the pain in his hand as the muscles tired. He kept writing. The President left with the Defense Secretary and came back again after a while, but Lenny ignored them.

And when it was over, he pushed pencil and paper aside and, massaging his right hand with his left, sat there with his eyes closed. Then, slowly, a smile spread over his face.

"Well, I'll be damned," he said slowly and softly.

"Mr. Poe," said the President, "is there any danger that your brother will be captured within the next hour?"

Lenny looked up with a startled grin. "Oh. Hi. I didn't notice you, Mr. President. What'd you say?"

The President repeated his question.

"Oh. No. There's nothing to worry about. The little men in white coats came after Dr. Malekrinova. She started screaming that telepathic spies were stealing her secret. She smashed all her apparatus and burned all her papers on top of the wreckage before they could stop her. She keeps shouting about a pink-and-purple orgy and singing a song about glass diamonds and Egyptian kings. I wouldn't say she was actually insane, but she is very disturbed."

"Then your brother is safe?"

"As safe as he ever was, Mr. President."

"Thank Heaven for that," said the President. "If they'd ever captured him and made him talk—" He stopped. "I forgot," he said lamely after a moment.

Lenny grinned. "That's all right, Mr. President. I sometimes forget it myself. But it was his handicap, I guess, that made him concentrate on telepathy, so that he doesn't need his ears to hear what people are saying. Maybe I could read minds the way he does if I'd been born that way.

"Come to think of it, I doubt if the Russians would have believed he was a spy if they'd caught him, unless they really did believe he was telepathic. A physical examination would show immediately that he was born without eardrums and that the inner ear bones are fused. They wouldn't try to make a man talk if an examination showed that he really was a deaf-mute."

The buzzer on the colonel's intercom sounded. "Yes?" said Spaulding.

"Dr. Davenport is here," said Sergeant Nugget. "He wants to talk to you."

"Send him in," said Colonel Spaulding gleefully. "I have a nice scientific theory I want to shove down his throat."

The Egyptian Diamond

by Randall Garrett

*As promised, the full text of the poem quoted in **The Foreign Hand-Tie.** It's at its best when **performed**—read aloud before a group of people with the aid of a blackboard.*

In a hall of strange description
    (Antiquarian Egyptian),
Figuring his monthly balance sheet, a troubled monarch sat
    With a frown upon his forehead,
    Hurling interjections horrid
At the state of his finances, for his pocketbook was flat.

    Not a solitary, single
    Copper cent had he to jingle
In his pocket, while his architects had gone off on a strike,
    Leaving pyramids unfinished,
    For their salaries diminished,
And their credit vanished likewise in a way they did not like.

    It was harder for his Royal
    Highness than for sons of toil,
For the horny-handed workmen only ate three figs per day,
    While the King liked sweet potatoes,
    Candied yams and canned tomatoes,
Boneless ham, and Bluepoint oysters cooked some prehistoric way.

    As he growled, the Royal Grumbler
    Spied a bit of broken tumbler
In a long-undusted corner, just behind his chamber door.
    When his hungry optics spied it,
    He stood silently and eyed it,
Then he smote his thigh in ecstasy and danced about the floor.

"By the wit Osiris gave me!
"This same bit of glass shall save me!
"I shall sell it as a diamond at some stupendous price!
"And whoe'er I ask to take it
"Will find, for his own sweet sake, it
"Will be better not to wait until I have to ask him twice!"

Thereupon, a proclamation
Was dispatched throughout the nation,
Most imperatively calling to appear before the King,
Under penalties most cruel,
Every man who sold a jewel
Or who bought and bartered precious stones,
  and all that sort of thing.

Thereupon, the jewelers' nether
Joints all quaked and knocked together
As they packed their Saratogas in lugubrious despair.
It was ever their misfortune
To be pillaged by extortion,
And they thought they smelled a rodent on the sultry desert air.

When they faced the Great Propylon
With an apprehensive smile on,
Sculptured there, in hieroglyphics six feet wide and nine feet high,
Stood the threat of King Rameses
To chop every man to pieces
Who, when shown the Royal Diamond, would dare refuse to buy.

Staunch and brave, the dealer Muhli
Hassan eyed the gem and coolly
Said: "The thing is but a common tumbler-bottom, nothing more."
Thereupon, the King's assassin
Drew his sword, and Muhli Hassan
Never peddled rings again upon the Nile's primeval shore.

Then Abdullah abd Almahdi
Faintly said: "The stone is shoddy."
But he thought that, in a pinch, he might bid fifty cents, himself.
There ensued a slight commotion
Ere he could repent the notion,
And Abdullah was promoted to the Oriental shelf.

When they saw how things resulted,
All the jewelers consulted
On some way to extricate them ere they dared to dine or sup—
Rushing off on flying journeys
To consult the best attorneys,
Who referred to their authorities and had to give it up.

270

Quite exciting was the writing,
The indicting, and the citing,
In the valleys of the Tigris, the Euphrates, and the Nile,
But, in spite of all their seeking,
Not a hole appeared for sneaking
Safely out of their predicament, which deepened all the while.

Through it all, with visage jolly,
By the palace gate, Ben Ali
Sat, without a nickel to his name, and nothing much to do.
Though his clothes were old and holey,
He was sleek and roly-poly,
And he sat and smiled in silence at the many things he knew.

Suddenly, a bright idea
Struck him. Why could not he be a
Champion of all these jewelers and save them from their fate?
He had not spent hours compiling
Abstruse problems on the tiling
Of the vestibule for nothing, so he didn't hesitate.

But, with confidence, suggested
If their cause in him were vested,
He could extricate them all before a dog could wag its tail.
And, although he looked quite youthful,
They would find his statement truthful,
For within his little lexicon was no such word as "fail."

How they crowded on the balus—
Trade that ran around the palace
When Ben Ali came before His Royal Majesty the King!
And when Ben stood up to meet him,
How the cheers burst forth to greet him!
"Sail in, Benny!" "Atta boy!" until they made the welkin ring.

"Great Rameses," said Ben Ali,
"It would be the sheerest folly
"To attempt to buy the finest precious stone upon the Earth
"Without going at it coolly
"And approximating duly,
"Without fear, and without favor, its inestimable worth.

"I'll agree (and likewise shall you),
"That the stone's *intrinsic* value
"Is but nothing, while the estimate that Muhli Hassan gave
"Adds another nothing to it,
"And, sir, by your leave, I'll do it."
And he chalked a second cipher with a graceful DelSarte wave.

"Now, philosophers have stated

"(And it cannot be debated),
"Nothing added to a nothing simply makes a nothing more,
   "While the value I have thought on
   "Simply adds another nought on
"To the total we are seeking, thus increasing it to four.

   "Now it seems to me to follow
   "That the sum bid by Abdallah,
"Which was *fifty*, if I recollect the circumstance aright,
   "Should be placed in its relation
   "To the total aggregation,
"Making full five hundred thousand, in a fair, unbiased light."

   Gloating on the promised treasure,
   King Rameses beamed with pleasure,
And he said he thought a full five hundred thousand just the dot.
   But, although he quite believed him,
   Yet, men had before deceived him,
And he felt constrained to ask for entire payment on the spot.

   "Very well," said Ben, "but scholars
   "Would allow at least five dollars
"As a discount from the full amount that I have been assessed."
   "Fair enough," the King said, smiling
   In a manner most beguiling,
"You may discount five for cash in hand,
      and then produce the rest."

   Thereupon the great Rameses
   Signed the jeweler's releases
Absolving them from every responsibility.
   And when all of that was done, he
   Asked Ben Ali for the money,
And Ben Ali rose and raised his hand with great civility.

   "That we may not make a miscount,
   "Let me first subtract my discount."
And he took his hemstitched handerchief and *rubbed the five away!*
   "Now I'm ready to obey you,
   "And I'm quite prepared to pay you
"The remainder as it stands, for there is nothing left to pay!"

   King Rameses tore his raiment
   At such visionary payment,
For he saw the wool'd been pulled across his visionary eyes.
   But his claims were all receipted,
   And his wicked aims defeated,
And he'd have to whet his appetite on atmospheric pies.

272

©PFoglio'86

Then, like some volcanic spasm,
Rose the crowd's enthusiasm,
Making Ali rich with presents in the rapture that ensued.
(While a very ancient carving
Represents the King as starving,
It is likely that the neighbors brought him in some sort of food.)

The World of
E. E. "Doc" Smith

by Randall Garrett

If Randall had any "heroes," two of them were John Campbell and Doc Smith. I'm sure that, if asked to identify his most treasured possession, Randall would have chosen the limited-edition, six-book set of the Lensman series, signed to Randall as a personal gift.

Yet Randall was too much the scientist to ignore inconsistencies in the science of those stories. He often played "The Game" of finding science flubs in "science" fiction; the more he liked a story, the more fun he had finding holes in the science theory.

He did this with and to Doc while Doc was alive, to their mutual enjoyment. (He once announced to Doc that he had deduced the given name of the "All-Highest of Eddore"—"Lintel.") After Doc died, Randall's jibes became a sort of tribute to the man who had written a six-volume story too grand to be brought down by inconsistent details.

Backstage Lensman was the most intricate of these pieces, and its imitation of Doc's style, as well as the slight exaggeration of points here and there, made it a perfect selection for **TAKEOFF**. There is another one in this volume—**Our Patrol**. This item is an article which appeared in **The Comics Journal** in 1978, and it applies math and physics to the "technology" of the Lensman series.

"Two thousand million years or so ago, two galaxies were colliding..."

So begins the two-billion-year saga of the Arisia-Eddore war, to be known in its final stages as the Boskone War. The high points of the struggle are chronicled in E. E. Smith's epic *The History of Civilization,* a single six-hundred-thousand-word novel divided into six volumes: *Triplanetary, First Lensman, Galactic Patrol, Gray Lensman, Second State Lensmen,* and *Children of the Lens.* A seventh book, *Masters of the Vortex,* takes place during the Boskone War, but it is concerned with a different problem, that of "atomic vortices," which tend to run wild after certain kinds of explosions have occurred.

Edward Elmer "Doc" Smith was a chemist—to be specific, a foods chemist, working for a company that produced (and still produces) cake mixes, cookie mixes, and the like. You kow: buy a box, add water, stir, and pop it in the oven. Doc's job, at which he strove mightily, was to keep the stuff from becoming "junk food" by the time it reached the housewife. He was good at it. (To those who are convinced that *all* commercial breads, cakes, *et cetera*, are "junk food," I can only say that it was men like Doc Smith who kept them from becoming junkier than they are.)

Doc knew science; he studied more fields than just his own specialty. He knew science, and he knew just when to ignore it when writing science fiction.

The late P. Schuyler Miller once characterized Doc Smith's "Skylark" series (Four books: *The Skylark of Space, Skylark of Valerion, Skylark Three,* and *Skylark du Quesne*) as a "snow job," a cosmic put-on. Doc's laughing reply was: "Of course it is." In that series, Smith totally ignores Einstein. All you have to do is give a rocket enough push, and it will attain any velocity you want. Whee!

The Lensman series, too, is a put-on. But it's more subtle. Doc Smith, more than anyone else, was the master of pseudo-scientific double-talk. For instance: duodecaplylatomate or "duodec."

"...The detonation of duodec is propagated at the velocity of light, so that the entire mass disintegrates in a period of time to be measured only in fractional trillionths of a second. Its detonation pressure and temperature have never been measured save indirectly, since nothing will hold it except a Q-type helice of pure force. And even those helices, which must be practically open at both ends, have to be designed and powered to withstand pressures and temperatures obtaining only in the cores of suns."

Isn't that lovely? "Duodecaplylatomate" has a nice, scientific sound to it, like "polyvinylacetate." But what does it *mean*? A twelve-ply atom? Possibly. But that doesn't mean anything, either. And what is a Q-type helix? What is "pure force" in that connotation?

Well, that's all the information you're going to get, either from me or from Doc Smith.

Let's take another look at duodec, though...(Do your homework; read Chapter one of *Gray Lensman*.) It is implied that a duodec bomb weighs two thousand metric tons (2 x 109 grams). It detonates in "fractional trillionths of a second." And its detonation rate is the speed of light. In a trillionth of a second, a beam of light travels just a shade over a hundredth of an inch, as close to three tenths of a millimeter as makes no difference. If the bomb detonates from the center outward in one trillionth of a second, it is a sphere with a radius of no more than 0.3 mm. That gives it a volume of 0.0001 cubic centimeters. The stuff has a density two trillion times that of water! Since I am, at the moment, without my reference books, I am not able to calculate the Schwartzschild Radius for such a mass. (Who remembers formulas?) But I suspect we have a Black Hole here. At any rate, duodec would be nasty stuff to handle, even without its explosive properties.

In the same scene, by the way, the explosion of duodec is recorded by scanners at high speed and then played back at normal speed. These scanners don't use light; they use vibrations in the subether (wha'?) that travel 19 billion times as fast as light. So they *can* record something that happens at merely light velocity.

Now, "to the human eye, dome, fortress, and planet had disappeared in one cataclysmically incandescent sphere of flame." The planet is about Earth-sized, and there are 25 duodec bombs strategically spaced over its surface. But duodec, after its initial detonation at the velocity of light, sends out a sphere of destruction that drops below light velocity as it expands. The whole explosion and destruction of the planet could not have taken less than one second. Well, that's pretty impressive, anyway.

But the Lensmen are watching a slow-motion replay. Fine. They watch the detonating globes expand. Now, "no inert fragment *can* fly from duodec in the first few instants of its detonation." Hell, then—Let's assume that in the first second of viewing time, one of those spheres expands from its 0.3 mm of radius to a radius of twelve meters. That's fairly good, because the apparent velocity of the surface is about thirty miles an hour. Even so, the viewers would have to have alert eyes to see what was going on.

A light beam travels approximately one foot in a billionth of a second (eleven point eight inches per nanosecond, if you want to get stuffy about it). So that first second of viewing time is about forty nanoseconds of recording ("actual") time. So we are running at forty nanoseconds per second. And the explosion lasted one second.

To view all the explosion, the Lensmen are going to have to sit there, night and day, without any time off, for the next *forty-one weeks!*

One hopes they sped up the tapes towards the end.

The greatest of Doc Smith's inventions is so original and so beautiful that it died. Quite thoroughly. No science fiction writer has dared even borrow it without permission, much less steal it.

("Always, please, remembering to call it 'research.'") None of us would quail at using Asimov's "hyperspace jump" to get from star to star in reasonable time spans. Isaac, good as he is, did not invent "hyperspace." It's a nineteenth-century topological assumption. Anybody can use it. To put it another way: "What science conceives of is any writer's material."

But science did not conceive the Inertialess Drive. That was Doc's own invention, and his patent has thus far remained inviolate.

Einstein's equations show that energy has mass. ($e=mc^2$, remember?) The energy of motion is known as "kinetic" energy and that energy increases as does the square of the velocity (c). So, the faster an object goes, the more kinetic energy (e) it has. Now, according to a second equation*, the more kinetic energy it has, the more mass it has. And the more mass it has, according to the first equation, the more energy it needs to increase its velocity. As this velocity approaches the speed of light, the mass of the object approaches infinity, and the energy needed to propel it approaches infinity. Obviously, since no one has inifinite energy at his disposal, not only can't you go faster than the speed of light, you can't even reach it.

But wait! Doc Smith saw a loophole. Einstein's equations are based on the assumption that *inertial* mass (a body's resistance to change of velocity) and *gravitational* mass (the force of attraction between one body and another) were the same property, and that this property was inherent in all mass. This assumption has never been proved nor disproved.

Suppose, said Smith, that the assumption is not true.

If the inertia is neutralized, the velocity of the ship is limited only by the thrust of its drive and the resistance of the matter in space. A "Bergenholm generator" neutralizes inertia, and off we go into interstellar and even intergalactic space. Isn't that beautiful?

Most of the Lensman series was written before World War Two. In those days, neither Doc nor anyone else writing science fiction had any notion of how far and how fast computer science would move, so Doc is rather weak along that line. But Lensmen were putting things on tapes—sight, sound, and thought—long before the tape recorder was invented. His drug, thionite, "which, in

---

*The formula is:

$$Mv = \frac{M_0}{1-\dfrac{c^2}{v^2}}$$

So, as the velocity (c) approaches the speed of light (v), the part of the equation under the square root sign approaches zero, as does the square root, and Mv approaches infinity. Simple, eh?

microgram inhalations, makes the addict experience all the sensations of doing whatever it is he wishes most ardently to do" was pooh-poohed at the time because, it was stated, "no drug can be effective in microgram quantities." Nobody had ever heard of LSD-25 in those far-off and ancient days.

"*Do* have a tiny smell of thionite, Mr. Williams!"

Interesting as Doc Smith's physics may be, his metaphysics and paraphysics are even more fascinating.

Theologians of various persuasions have argued the problem of Good and Evil for millenia. The Christian statement of the problem is: If God is good—*and* all-powerful!—how can he allow Evil to exist? Zoroaster the Persian (6th century BC) came up with an answer, perhaps not original with himself, that was copied by the Albigensians of southern France some eighteen hundred years later. There are two Principles active in the world, one Good and one Evil, and they are fighting for us poor humans, who are both Good and Evil. (Christian theology, although it acknowledges the existence of both God and the Devil, doesn't go along with the Zoroastrian notion. But if I get into that, I'll never stop.)

Doc Smith symbolizes these two Principles, or Powers, as the beings of the planet Arisia (Good) and the beings of the planet Eddore (Evil).

That much, of course, is obvious to any twelve-year-old. But Doc Smith was far more subtle than that.

The Arisians are neither gods nor angels; they merely partake of many of the attributes thereof—as conceived in the minds of anthropomorphic god-creators. They are Good—except, of course, when they kill without compunction any Baddie who invades their territory. The Eddorians are Bad—*all* Bad. Their sole ambition is—dare I say it?—to Rule the Universe.

Doc's genius lay in upsetting the hidden assumption—held by many—that the Goodies will one day win, and when they do, they will take over and rule us benevolently. The Second Coming, and all that.

Doc makes no such assumption. During the entire period of the Boskonian War, it is touch-and-go. The Eddorians actually start out with a pretty good chance of winning. But, more than that, what happens when the Arisians win?

(I am not giving anything away here. This is romantic fiction in the high style. The question is not "Will the Goodies win?" but "*How* will the Goodies win?" And "Who gets killed in the meantime?")

Many religions hold that the day will come when God (or whatever you want to call Him, Her, It, or Them) will come to Earth and give us poor humans the Great Government. Earth will be a sort of All-Over-Eden. At least, for the chosen few.

Sorry. The Arisians don't operate that way. As far as the

Arisians are concerned, all they want to do is to be left quietly alone to perfect their Visualization of the Cosmic All.

"Go away and let me think!"

The Eddorians, with their insatiable desire of Power, threaten the Cosmic Meditation and Contemplation of the Arisians. Needless to say, that does not please the Arisians. What do you do with folks who keep interrupting you when you're trying to think? Why you kill the sonsofbitches, that's what you do. And if you haven't got the weapon to do it with, you make one. That weapon is the Galactic Patrol.

Physically, the Eddorians cannot be destroyed, any more than the Arisians can. Their *souls,* their *minds,* must be destroyed. And the Arisians spend two-times-ten-to-the-ninth years doing just that.

And as soon as it is done, the Arisians tell the most highly evolved intelligences: "We aren't going to run things! *You* do it! We're going away to someplace where we can *think!"*

Good for them. I approve of the Arisians.

Our Patrol

by Randall Garrett

*To the tune of "Boy Scout's Marching Song"—any guesses **which** patrol?*

Our Patrol! That's the Lensmen's marching song!
Our Patrol! As through Space we blast along,
    We're prepared to slaughter zwilniks any time,
    And kill every pirate who commits a crime!
Our Patrol has the right to go and bust
Anyone whom we really feel we must:
    Anyone who's mean and wicked, or who simply won't conform;
    Anyone who slightly differs from our noble moral norm!
To uphold all these ideals is our role!
Our Patrol!

Our Patrol has the right to go and do
Little things which should never bother you—
    Such as killing everyone of any race
    Or blowing entire planets out of space!
Our Patrol can use any force we choose
To kill folks, when we know we cannot lose!
    We knock off whole societies with hardly any fuss;
    And we'll probably continue till there's no one left but us!
For we definitely feel that that's our goal!
Our Patrol!

...Or Your Money Back

by Randall Garrett
writing as David Gordon

The scientific community's contempt for psionic phenomena was a constant irritant to Randall. If you've read **Psicopath,** you've seen that he understood the psychological basis for that attitude. But he didn't sympathize— not a bit.

I debated whether to include...**Or Your Money Back** because it is very similar to **There's No Fool**—someone has devised a scheme to force scientific interest in psionics. In case you're afraid I've spoiled it for you, let me give you the reason I chose this one, after all.

It's **fun.**

There are times when I don't know my own strength. Or, at least, the strength of my advice. And the case of Jason Howley was certainly an instance of one of those times.

When he came to my office with his gadget, I heard him out, trying to appear both interested and cooperative—which is good business. But I am forced to admit that neither Howley nor his gadget were very impressive. He was a lean, slope-shouldered individual, five-feet-eight or nine—which was shorter than he looked—with straight brown hair combed straight back and blue eyes which were shielded with steel-rimmed glasses. The thick, double-concave lenses indicated a degree of myopia that must have bordered on total blindness without glasses, and acute tunnel vision, even with them.

He had a crisp, incisive manner that indicated he was either a man who knew what he was doing or a man who was trying to impress me with a ready-made story. I listened to him and looked at his gadget without giving any more indication than necessary of what I really thought.

When he was through, I said: "You understand, Mr. Howley, that I'm not a patent lawyer; I specialize in criminal law. Now, I can recommend—"

But he cut me off. "I understand that, counselor," he said sharply. "Believe me, I have no illusion whatever that this thing is patentable under the present patent system. Even if it were, this gadget is designed to do something that may or may not be illegal, which would make it hazardous to attempt to patent it, I should think. You don't patent new devices for blowing safes or new drugs for doping horses, do you?"

"Probably not," I said dryly, "although, as I say, I'm not qualified to give an opinion on patent law. You say that gadget is designed to cause minute, but significant, changes in the velocities of small, moving objects. Just how does that make it illegal?"

He frowned a little. "Well, possibly it wouldn't, except here in Nevada. Specifically, it is designed to influence roulette and dice games."

I looked at the gadget with a little more interest this time. There was nothing new in the idea of inventing a gadget to cheat the red-and-black wheels, of course; the local cops turn up a dozen a day here in the city. Most of them either don't work at all or else they're too obvious, so the users get nabbed before they have a chance to use them.

The only ones that really work have to be installed in the tables themselves, which means they're used to milk the suckers, not rob the management. And anyone in the State of Nevada who buys a license to operate and then uses crooked wheels is (a) stupid, and (b) out of business within a week. Howley was right. Only in a place where gambling is legalized is it illegal—and unprofitable—to rig a game.

The gadget itself didn't look too complicated from the outside. It was a black plastic box about an inch and a half square and maybe three and a half long. On one end was a lensed opening, half an inch in diameter, and on two sides were flat, silver-colored plates. On the top of it, there was a dial which was, say an inch in diameter, and it was marked off just exactly like a roulette wheel.

"How does it work?" I asked.

He picked it up in his hand, holding it as though it were a flashlight, with the lens pointed away from him.

"You aim the lens at the wheel," he explained, "making sure that your thumb is touching the silver plate on one side, and your fingers touching the plate on the other side. Then you set this dial for whatever number you want to come up and concentrate on it while the ball is spinning. For dice, of course, you only need to use the first six or twelve numbers on the dial, depending on the game."

I looked at him for a long moment, trying to figure his angle. He looked back steadily, his eyes looking like small beads peering through the bottoms of a couple of shot glasses.

"You look skeptical, counselor," he said at last.

"I am. A man who hasn't got the ability to be healthily skeptical has no right to practice law—especially criminal law. On the other hand, no lawyer has any right to judge anything one way or the other without evidence.

"But that's neither here nor there at the moment. What I'm interested in is, what do you want me to do? People rarely come to a criminal lawyer unless they're in a jam. What sort of jam are you in at the moment?"

"None," said Howley. "But I will be very soon. I hope."

Well, I've heard odder statements than that from my clients. I let it ride for the moment and looked down at the notes I'd taken while he'd told me his story.

"You're a native of New York City?" I asked.

"That's right. That's what I said."

"And you came out here for what? To use that thing on our Nevada tables?"

"That's right, counselor."

"Can't you find any games to cheat on back home?"

"Oh, certainly. Plenty of them. But they aren't legal. I wouldn't care to get mixed up in anything illegal. Besides, it wouldn't suit my purpose."

That stopped me for a moment. "You don't consider cheating illegal? It certainly is in Nevada. In New York, if you were caught at it, you'd have the big gambling interests on your neck; here, you'll have both them *and* the police after you. *And* the district attorney's office."

He smiled. "Yes, I know. That's what I'm expecting. That's why I need a good lawyer to defend me. I understand you're the top man in this city."

"Mr. Howley," I said carefully, "as a member of the Bar Association and a practicing attorney in the State of Nevada, I am an Officer of the Court. If you had been caught cheating and had come to me, I'd be able to help you. But I can't enter into a conspiracy with you to defraud legitimate businessmen, which is exactly what this would be."

He blinked at me through those shot-glass spectacles. "Counselor, would you refuse to defend a man if you thought he was guilty?"

I shook my head. "No. Legally, a man is not guilty until proven so by a court of law. He has a right to trial by jury. For me to refuse to give a man the defense he is legally entitled to, just because I happened to think he was guilty, would be trial by attorney. I'll do the best I can for any client; I'll work for his interests, no matter what my private opinion may be."

He looked impressed, so I guess there must have been a note of conviction in my voice. There should have been, because it was exactly what I've always believed and practiced.

"That's good, counselor," said Howley. "If I can convince you that I have no criminal intent, that I have no intention of defrauding anyone or conspiring with you to do anything illegal, will you help me?"

I didn't have to think that one over. I simply said, "Yes." After all, it was still up to me to decide whether he convinced me or not. If he didn't, I could still refuse the case on those grounds.

"That's fair enough, counselor," he said. Then he started talking.

Instead of telling you what Jason Howley *said* he was going to do, I'll tell you what he *did* do. They are substantially the same, anyway, and the old bromide about actions speaking louder than words certainly applied in this case.

Mind you, I didn't see or hear any part of this, but there were plenty of witnesses to testify as to what went on. Their statements are a matter of court record, and Jason Howley's story is substantiated in every respect.

He left my office smiling. He'd convinced me that the case was not only going to be worthwhile, but fun. I took it, plus a fat retainer.

Howley went up to his hotel room, changed into his expensive evening clothes, and headed out to do the town. I'd suggested several places, but he wanted the biggest and best—the Golden Casino, a big, plush, expensive place that was just inside the city limits. In his pockets, he was carrying less than two hundred dollars in cash.

Now, nobody with that kind of chicken feed can expect to last long at the Golden Casino unless they stick to the two-bit one-armed bandits. But putting money on a roulette table is in a higher bracket by far than feeding a slot machine, even if you get a steady run of lemons.

Howley didn't waste any time. He headed for the roulette table right away. He watched the play for about three spins of the wheel, then he took out his gadget—in plain sight of anyone who cared to watch—and set the dial for thirteen. Then he held it in his hand with thumb and finger touching the plates and put his hand in his jacket pocket, with the lens aimed at the wheel. He stepped up to the table, bought a hundred dollars worth of chips, and put fifty on Number Thirteen.

"No more bets," said the croupier. He spun the wheel and dropped the ball.

"Thirteen, Black, Odd, and Low," he chanted after a minute. With a practiced hand, he raked in the losers and pushed out

Howley's winnings. There was sixteen hundred dollars sitting on thirteen now. Howley didn't touch it.

The wheel went around and the little ball clattered around the rim and finally fell into a slot.

"Thirteen, Black, Odd, and Low," said the croupier. This time, he didn't look as nonchalant. He peered curiously at Howley as he pushed out the chips to make a grand total of fifty-one thousand two hundred dollars. The same number doesn't come up twice in succession very often, and it is very rare indeed that the same person is covering it both times with a riding bet.

"Two thousand limit, sir," the croupier said, when it looked as though Howley was going to let the fifty-one grand just sit there.

Howley nodded apologetically and pulled off everything but two thousand dollars worth of chips.

The third time around, the croupier had his eyes directly on Howley as he repeated the chant: "Thirteen, Black, Odd, and Low." Everybody else at the table was watching Howley, too. The odds against Howley—or anyone else, for that matter—hitting the same number three times in a row are just under forty thousand to one.

Howley didn't want to overdo it. He left two thousand on thirteen, raked in the rest, and twisted the dial on his gadget over a notch.

Everyone at the table gasped as the little ball dropped.

"That was a near miss," whispered a woman standing nearby.

The croupier said: "Fourteen, Red, Even, and Low." And he raked in Howley's two thousand dollars with a satisfied smile. He had seen runs of luck before.

Howley deliberately lost two more spins the same way. Nobody who was actually cheating would call too much attention to himself, and Howley wanted it to look as though he were trying to cover up the fact that he had a sure thing.

He took the gadget out of his pocket and deliberately set it to the green square marked 00. Then he put it back in his pocket and put two thousand dollars on the Double Zero.

There was more than suspicion in the croupier's eyes when he raked in all the bets on the table except Howley's. It definitely didn't look good to him. A man who had started out with a fifty-dollar bet had managed to run it up to one hundred seventy-four thousand two hundred dollars in six plays.

Howley looked as innocent as possible under the circumstances, and carefully dropped the dial on his gadget back a few notches. Then he bet another two thousand on High, an even money bet.

Naturally, he won.

He twisted the dial back a few more notches and won again on High.

Then he left it where it was and won by betting on Red.

By this time, of course, things were happening. The croupier had long since pressed the alarm button, and five men had carefully surrounded Howley. The looked like customers, but they were harder-looking than the average, and they were watching Howley, not the wheel. Farther back from the crowd, three of the special deputies from the sheriff's office were trying to look inconspicuous in their gray uniforms and white Stetsons and pearl-handled revolvers in black holsters. You can imagine how inconspicuous they looked.

Howley decided to do it up brown. He reset his gadget as surreptitiously as possible under the circumstances, and put his money on thirteen again.

"Thirteen, Black, Odd, and Low," said the croupier in a hollow voice.

The five men in evening dress and the three deputies moved in closer.

Howley nonchalantly scraped in his winnings, leaving two thousand on the thirteen spot.

There was a combination of hostility and admiration in every eye around the table when the croupier said, "Thirteen, Black, Odd, and Low," for the fifth time in the space of minutes. And every one of those eyes was turned on Jason Howley.

The croupier smiled his professional smile. "I'm sorry, ladies and gentlemen; we'll have to discontinue play for a while. The gentleman has broken the bank at this table." He turned the smile on Howley. "Congratulations, sir."

Howley smiled back and began stacking up over three hundred thousand dollars worth of plastic disks. It made quite a pile.

One of the deputies stepped up politely. "I'm an officer, sir," he said. "May I help you carry that to the cashier's office?"

Howley looked at the gold star and nodded. "Certainly. Thanks."

The other two deputies stepped up, too, and the three of them walked Howley toward the cashier's office. Behind them came the five men in dinner jackets.

"You'll have to step into the office to cash that much, sir," said one of the deputies as he opened the door. Howley walked in as though he hadn't a care in the world. He put the chips on the desk, and the deputies followed suit, while one of the dinner-jacketed men closed the door.

Then one of the deputies said: "I believe this gentleman is carrying a gun."

He had his own revolver out and had it pointed at Howley's middle. "Carrying a concealed weapon is illegal in this city," he went on. "I'm afraid we'll have to search you."

Howley didn't object. He put his hands up high and stood there while his pockets were frisked.

"Well, well," said the deputy coolly. "What on Earth is this?"

It was Howley's gadget, and the dial still pointed to Thirteen—Black, Odd, and Low.

The next morning, I went down to the jail in response to a phone call from Howley. The special deputies had turned him over to the city police and he was being held "under suspicion of fraud." I knew we could beat that down to an "attempt to defraud," but the object was to get Howley off scot-free. After Howley told me the whole story, I got busy pushing the case through. As long as he was simply being held on suspicion, I couldn't get him out on bail, so I wanted to force the district attorney or the police to prefer charges.

Meanwhile, I made sure that Howley's gadget had been impounded as evidence. I didn't want anyone fiddling with it before the case went to court—except, of course, the D. A. and his men. There wasn't much I could do to keep it out of *their* hands.

After throwing as much weight around as I could, including filing a petition for a writ of habeas corpus with Judge Grannis, I went over to Howley's hotel with a signed power of attorney that Howley had given me, and I got a small envelope out of the hotel safe. It contained a baggage check.

I went over to the bus depot, turned over the check to the baggage department, and went back to my office with a small suitcase. I locked myself in and opened the case. Sure enough, it contained three dozen of the little gadgets.

Then I sat down to wait. By noon, Judge Grannis had issued the writ of habeas corpus, and, rather than release Jason Howley, the police booked him, and District Attorney Thursby was getting the case ready for the grand jury. There was over a quarter of a million dollars at stake, and the men behind the Golden Casino were bringing pressure to bear. If Howley wasn't convicted, they'd have to give him his money—and that was the last thing they wanted to do. A quarter of a million bucks isn't small potatoes, even to a gambling syndicate.

It wasn't until early on the morning of the third day after Howley's arrest that I got a tip-off from one of my part-time spies. I scooped up the phone when it rang and identified myself.

"Counselor? Look, this is Benny." I recognized the voice and name. Benny was one of the cabbies that I'd done favors for in the past.

"What's the trouble, Benny?"

"Oh, no trouble. I just got a little tip you might be interested in."

"Fire away."

"Well, the D. A. and some of his boys went into the Golden Casino about ten minutes ago, and now they're closin' up the place. Just for a little while, I understand. Hour, maybe. They're chasin' everyone out of the roulette room."

"Thanks, Benny," I said, "thanks a lot."

"Well, I knew you was working on that Howley case, and I thought this might be important, so I—"

"Sure, Benny. Come by my office this afternoon. And thanks again."

I hung up and started moving.

Within ten minutes, I was pulling up and parking across the street from the Golden Casino. I locked the car and dodged traffic to get across the street, as though I'd never heard of laws against jaywalking.

There were still plenty of people in the Casino. The bar was full, and the dice and card games were going full blast. The slot machines were jangling out their infernal din while fools fed coins into their insatiable innards.

But the roulette room was closed, and a couple of be-Stetsoned deputies were standing guard over the entrance. I headed straight for them.

Both of them stood pat, blocking my way, so I stopped a few feet in front of them.

"Hello, counselor," said one. "Sorry, the roulette room's closed."

I knew the man slightly. "Let me in, Jim," I said. "I want to see Thursby."

The men exchanged glances. Obviously, the D. A. had given them orders.

"Can't do it, counselor," said Jim. "We're not to let anyone in."

"Tell Thursby I'm out here and that I want to see him."

He shrugged, opened the door, stuck his head inside, and called to District Attorney Thursby to tell him that I was outside. I could hear Thursby's muffled "Damn!" from within. But when he showed up at the door, his face was all smiles.

"What's the trouble?" he asked pleasantly.

I smiled back, giving him my best. "No trouble at all, Thursby. I just wanted to watch the experiment."

"Experiment?" He looked honestly surprised, which was a fine piece of acting. "We're just checking to see if the table's wired, that's all. If it is, your client may be in the clear; maybe we can hang it on the croupier."

"And get a conspiracy charge on my client, too, eh? Well, if you don't mind, I'd like to watch that table check myself. You know how it is."

Thursby hesitated, then he scowled. "Oh, all right. Come on in. But stay out of the way."

I grinned. "Sure. All I want to do is protect my client's interests."

Thursby just grunted and opened the door wider to let me in. He was a shrewd lawyer, a good D. A., and basically honest, even if he did have a tendency to bend under pressure from higher up.

They were checking the table, all right. They had three specialists going over it with everything from fine tooth combs to Geiger counters. They found nothing. No magnets, no wires, no mechanical gimmicks. Nothing.

It took them an hour to take that table apart, check it, and put it back together again. When it was all over, Thursby glanced at me, then said: "O.K., boys; that does it. Let's go."

The men looked at him oddly, and I knew why.

"Aren't you going to test my client's gadget?" I asked innocently.

Thursby looked angrily baffled for a moment, then he clamped his lips grimly. "As long as we're here, I guess we might as well."

I knew perfectly well it was what he had intended to do all along.

"One of you guys spin that wheel," he said to the technicians. One of them gave the wheel a spin and dropped the ball. It clattered on its merry way and dropped into a slot. Forty-two.

Thursby took the gadget out of his pocket. It was still set at Thirteen.

The men who had surrounded Howley on the night of his arrest had been keeping their eyes open, and they had seen how Howley had handled the thing. Well—*almost* how. Thursby had the lens opening pointed at the wheel, but his thumb and fingers weren't touching the silver plates properly.

"Spin it again," he said.

Everyone's eyes were on the ball as it whirled, so I had time to get my own copy of Howley's gadget out and set it at Thirteen. I hoped the thing would work for me. I concentrated on Thirteen, making sure my thumb and fingers were placed right.

Evidently they were. The ball fell into Thirteen, Black, Odd, and Low.

A huge grin spread over Thursby's face, but he was man enough not to turn and grin at me. "Try it again," he said.

Thirteen, Black, Odd, and Low.

"I wonder how the thing works?" said Thursby, looking at the gadget in a sort of pleased awe.

"You'd better be able to prove that it *does* work, Thursby," I said, trying to put irritation into my voice.

This time, he did grin at me. "Oh, I think we can prove that, all right." He turned back to the technician. "Spin it once more, Sam, and show the defense counselor, here, how it works."

The technician did as he was told. "Thirteen, Black, Odd, and Low," he chanted, grinning.

"Let's try another number," Thursby said. He turned the dial to One. And this time, when he pointed it, his fingers were touching the plates in the right places.

"Just a minute," I said. "Let me spin that thing."

290

"Be my guest, counselor," said Thursby.

I spun the wheel and scooted the ball along the rim. It dropped into a slot. One, Red, Odd, and Low. I looked as disappointed and apprehensive as I could.

"Coincidence," I said. "Nothing more. You haven't proved anything."

Thursby's grin widened. "Of course I haven't" he said with a soothing, patronizing tone. "But I don't have to prove anything until I get to court."

Then he looked at the technicians and jerked his head toward the door. "Let's go, boys. Maybe the counselor wants to look over the table for himself. Maybe he thinks we've got it rigged."

There was a chorus of guffaws as they walked out. I just stood there, scowling, trying to keep from laughing even harder than they were.

Jason Howley sat next to me at the defense table, just inside the low partition that divided the court from the public. There weren't many people in the auditorium itself; listening to some poor dope get himself sentenced for cheating at gambling is considered pretty dull entertainment in the State of Nevada.

Thursby had managed to push the indictment through the grand jury in a hurry, but, as he sat across the room from me at the prosecution table, I thought I could detect a false note in the assumed look of confidence that he was trying to wear.

Howley tapped me on the shoulder. I turned around, and he whispered: "How much longer?"

I tapped my wrist watch. "Couple of minutes. Judge Lapworth is one of those precisionists. Never a moment late or early. Getting jumpy?"

He shook his head gently and smiled. "No. You've handled this even better than I'd have imagined. You thought of things I didn't even know existed. I'm no lawyer; I can see that."

I returned the smile. "And I don't invent gimmicks, either. So what?"

His eyes looked at me from behind the distorting negative lenses. "I've been wondering, counselor—why are you so interested in this? I mean, I offered you a pretty good fee, and all that, but it seems to me you're taking an unusual interest in the case."

I grinned at him. "Mr. Howley, my profession is Law—with a capital L. The study of the Law isn't like the study of physics or whatever; these are manmade laws—commands, not descriptions. They don't necessarily have anything to do with facts at all. Take the word insanity, for instance; the word isn't even used by headshrinkers any more because it's a legal definition that has nothing whatever to do with the condition of the human mind.

"Now, any such set of laws as that can't possibly be self-consistent and still have some use on an action level. A lawyer's job is to find the little inconsistencies in the structure, the places where the pieces have been jammed together in an effort to make them look like a structured whole. To find, in other words, the loopholes and use them.

"And when I find a loophole, I like to wring everything I can out of it. I'm enjoying this."

Howley nodded. "I see. But what if something—"

I held up my hand to silence him, because the door to the judges' chambers opened at that moment, and Judge Lapworth came in as the baliff announced him. We all stood up while the baliff intoned his "Oyez, oyez."

Thursby made a short preliminary speech to the jury, and I requested and was granted permission to hold my own opening statement until the defense was ready to present its case.

Thursby was looking worried, although it took a trained eye to see it. I was pretty sure I knew why. He had been pushed too hard and had gone too fast. He'd managed to slide through the grand jury too easily, and I had managed to get the trial set for a week later. Thursby's case was far from being as tight as he wanted it.

I just sat still while the prosecution brought forth its witnesses and evidence. The croupier, the deputies, several employees of the Golden Casino, and a couple of patrons all told their stories. I waived cross-examination in every case, which made Thursby even edgier than he had been.

When he called in the head of the technicians who had inspected the casino, I made no objection to his testimony, but I made my first cross-examination.

"Mr. Thompson, you have stated your qualifications as an expert on the various devices which have been used to illegally influence the operation of gambling devices in this state."

Thursby said: "Oh, if the Court please, I should like to remind counsel for the defense that he has already accepted the qualifications of the witness."

"I am not attempting to impugn the qualifications of the witness," I snapped.

Judge Lapworth frowned at Thursby. "Are you making an objection, Mr. District Attorney?"

Thursby pursed his lips, said, "No, Your Honor," and sat down.

"Proceed with the cross-examination," said the judge.

"Mr. Thompson," I said, "you have testified that you examined the table at the Golden Casino for such devices and found none. Is that right."

"That's right," he said positively.

"Have you seen the device labeled People's Exhibit A, which was found by the officers on the person of the defendant?"

"Well...yes. I have."

"Have you examined this device?"

Thursby was on his feet. "Objection, Your Honor! This material was not brought out in direct examination!"

"Sustained," said Judge Lapworth.

"Very well, Your Honor," I said. Then I turned back to Thompson. "As an expert in this field, Mr. Thompson, you have examined many different devices for cheating gambling equipment, haven't you?"

"Yes, I have."

"How many would you say?"

"Oh...several hundred."

"Several hundred different *types*?"

"No. Several hundred individual devices. Most of them are just variations of two or three basic types."

"And you are familiar with the function of these basic types and their variations?"

"I am."

"You know exactly how all of them work, then?"

He saw where I was heading. "Most of them," he hedged.

Thursby saw where I was heading, too, and was sweating. I'd managed to get around his objection.

"Have you ever examined any which you could not understand?"

"I...I don't quite know what you mean."

"Have you ever," I said firmly, "come across a device used in cheating which you could not comprehend or explain the operation of?"

Thursby stood up. "Same objection as before, Your Honor."

"Your Honor," I said, "I am merely trying to find the limitations of the witness' knowledge; I am not trying to refute his acknowledged ability."

"Overruled," said Judge Lapworth. "The witness will answer the question."

I repeated the question.

"Yes," Thompson said in a low voice.

"More than once?"

"Only once."

"Only once. You did find one device which didn't operate in any fashion you can explain. Is that right?"

"That's right."

"Can you tell me what this device was?"

Thompson took a deep breath. "It was People's Exhibit A—the device taken from the defendant at the time of his arrest."

There was a buzz in the courtroom.

"No more questions," I said, turning away. Then before Thompson could leave the stand, I turned back to him. "Oh, just one moment, Mr. Thompson. Did you examine this device carefully? Did you take it apart?"

"I opened it and looked at it."

"You just looked at it? You didn't subject it to any tests?"

Thompson took a deep breath. "No."

"Why not?"

"There wasn't anything inside it to test."

This time, there was more than just a buzz around the courtroom. Judge Lapworth rapped for order.

When the room was quiet, I said: "The box was empty, then?"

"Well, no. Not exactly empty. It had some stuff in it."

I turned to the judge. "If the Court please, I would like to have the so-called device, Exhibit A, opened so that the members of the jury may see for themselves what it contains."

Judge Lapworth said: "The Court would like very much to see the internal workings of this device, too. Bailiff, if you will, please."

The bailiff handed him the gadget from the exhibit table.

"How does it open?" asked the judge. He turned to Thompson. "Will the witness please open the box?"

Reluctantly, Thompson thumbed the catch and slid off the top.

The judge took it from him, looked inside, and stared for a long moment.

I had already seen the insides. It was painted white, and there were inked lines running all over the inside, and various pictures— a ball, a pair of dice, a roulette wheel—and some other symbols that I didn't pretend to understand.

Otherwise, the box was empty.

After a moment, Judge Lapworth looked up from the box and stared at Thursby. Then he looked at Thompson. "Just what tests *did* you perform on this...this thing, Mr. Thompson?"

"Well, Your Honor," Thompson said, visibly nervous, "I checked it for all kinds of radiation and magnetism. There isn't anything like that coming from it. But," he added lamely, "there wasn't much else to test. Not without damaging the box."

"I see." His honor glared at Thursby, but didn't say anything to him. He simply ordered the box to be shown to the jury.

Thursby was grimly holding his ground, waiting.

"Have you any more questions, counselor?" the judge asked.

"No, Your Honor, I have not."

"Witness may step down," said his honor to Thompson.

Thursby stood up. "If the Court please, I would like to stage a small demonstration for the members of the jury."

The Court gave permission, and a roulette wheel was hauled in on a small table.

I watched with interest and without objection while Thursby demonstrated the use of the gadget and then asked each of the jurors in turn to try it. It was a long way from being a successful demonstration. Some of the jurors didn't hold the thing right, and some of those that did just didn't have the mental ability required to use it. But that didn't bother Thursby.

"Your Honor, and Gentlemen of the Jury," he said, "you are all aware that a device constructed for the purpose of cheating at any gambling game is not necessarily one hundred per cent infallible. It doesn't have to be. All it has to do is turn the odds in favor of the user.

"You are all familiar with loaded dice, I'm sure. And you know that loading dice for one set of numbers merely increases the probability that those numbers will come up; it does not guarantee that they will come up every time.

"It is the same with marked cards. Marking the backs of a deck of cards doesn't mean that you will invariably get a better hand than your opponent; it doesn't even mean that you will win every hand.

"The device taken from the defendant at the Golden Casino does not, as you have seen, work every time. But, as you have also seen, it certainly *does* shift the odds by a considerable percentage. And that, I submit, is illegal under the laws of this state."

He went on, building on that theme for a while, then he turned the trial over to the defense.

"Call Dr. Pettigrew to the stand," I said.

I heard Thursby's gasp, but I ignored it.

A chunky, balding man with a moon face and an irritated expression came up to be sworn in. He was irritated with me for having subpoenaed him, and he showed it. I hoped he wouldn't turn out to be hostile.

"You are Dr. Herbert Pettigrew?" I asked.

"That is correct."

"State your residence, please."

"3109 La Jolla Boulevard, Los Angeles, California."

"You are called 'Doctor' Pettigrew, I believe. Would you tell the Court what right you have to that title?"

He looked a little miffed, but he said: "It is a scholarly title. A Doctorate of Philosophy in physics from Massachusetts Institute of Technology."

"I see. Would you mind telling the Court what other academic degrees you have?"

He reeled off a list of them, all impressive.

"Thank you, doctor," I said. "Now, what is your present occupation?"

"I am a Professor of Physics, at the University of California in Los Angeles."

I went on questioning him to establish his ability in his field, and by the time I was finished, the jury was pretty well impressed with his status in the scientific brotherhood. And not once did Thursby object.

Then I said, "Dr. Pettigrew, I believe you came to this city on a professional matter?"

"Yes, I did." He didn't hesitate to answer, so I figured I hadn't got his goat too much.

"And what was the nature of that matter?"

"I was asked to come here by Mr. Harold Thursby, the District Attorney, to perform some scientific tests on the...er...device... the device known as People's Exhibit A."

"Did you perform these tests?"

"I did."

"At the request of District Attorney Thursby, is that right?"

"That is correct."

"May I ask why Mr. Thursby did not call you as a witness for the prosecution?"

Thursby, as I had expected, was on his feet. "Objection! The question calls for a conclusion of the witness!"

"Sustained," said Judge Lapworth.

"Dr. Pettigrew," I said, "what were your findings in reference to Exhibit A?"

He shrugged. "The thing is a plastic box with a dial set in one side, a plastic lens in one end, and a couple of strips of silver along two other sides. Inside, there are a lot of markings in black ink on white paint." He gestured toward the exhibit table. "Just what you've seen; that's all there is to it."

"What sort of tests did you perform to determine this, Dr. Pettigrew?" I asked.

He took a long time answering that one. He had X-rayed the thing thoroughly, tested it with apparatus I'd never heard of, taken scrapings from all over it for microchemical analysis, and even tried it himself on a roulette wheel. He hadn't been able to make it work.

"And what is your conclusion from these findings?" I asked.

Again he shrugged. "The thing is just a box, that's all. It has no special properties."

"Would you say that it could be responsible for the phenomena we have just seen? By that, I mean the peculiar action of the roulette wheel, demonstrated here by the prosecution."

"Definitely not," he stated flatly. "The box could not possibly have any effect on either the wheel or the ball."

"I see. Thank you, doctor; that's all. Cross examine."

Thursby walked over to the witness stand with a belligerent scowl on his face. "Dr. Pettigrew, you say that the box couldn't possibly have had any effect on the wheel. And yet, we have demonstrated that there *is* an effect. Don't you believe the testimony of your own senses?"

"Certainly I do!" snapped Pettigrew.

"Then how do you account for the behavior of the roulette wheel as you have just seen it demonstrated in this court?"

I suppressed a grin. Thursby was so mad that he was having trouble expressing himself clearly.

"In several ways!" Pettigrew said sharply. "In the first place, that wheel could be rigged."

Thursby purpled. "Now, just a minute! I—"

I started to object, but Judge Lapworth beat me to it.

"Are you objecting to the answer, Mr. District Attorney?"

"The witness is insinuating that I falsified evidence!"

"I am not!" said Pettigrew, visibly angry. "You asked me how I could account for its behavior, and I told you one way! There are others!"

"The wheel will be examined," said Judge Lapworth darkly. "Tell us the other ways, Dr. Pettigrew."

"Pure chance," said Pettigrew. "Pure chance, Your Honor. I'm sure that everyone in this courtroom has seen runs of luck on a roulette wheel. According to the laws of probability, such runs must inevitably happen. Frankly, I believe that just such a run has occurred here. I do not think for a minute that Mr. Thursby or anyone else rigged that wheel."

"I see; thank you, Dr. Pettigrew," said the judge. "Any further questions, Mr. District Attorney?"

"No further questions," Thursby said, trying to hide his anger.

"Call your next witness," said the judge, looking at me.

"I call Mr. Jason Howley to the stand."

Howley sat down and was sworn in. I went through the preliminaries, then asked: "Mr. Howley, you have seen People's Exhibit A?"

"I have."

"To whom does it belong?"

"It is mine. It was taken from me by—"

"Just answer the question, please," I admonished him. He knew his script, but he was jumping the gun. "The device is yours, then?"

"That's right."

"Under what circumstances did this device come into the hands of the police?"

He told what had happened on the night of the big take at the Golden Casino.

"Would you please explain to us just what this device is?" I asked when he had finished.

"Certainly," he said. "It's a good luck charm."

I could hear the muffled reaction in the courtroom.

"A good luck charm. I see. Then it has no effect on the wheel at all?"

"Oh, I wouldn't say that," Howley said disarmingly. He smiled and looked at the jury. "It certainly has some effect. It's the only good luck charm I ever had that worked."

The jury was grinning right back at him. They were all

gamblers at heart, and I never knew a gambler yet who didn't have some sort of good luck charm or superstition when it came to gambling. We had them all in the palms of our hands.

"What I mean is, does it have any *physical* effect on the wheel?"

Howley looked puzzled. "Well, I don't know about that. That's not my field. You better ask Dr. Pettigrew."

There was a smothered laugh somewhere in the courtroom.

"Just how do you operate this good luck charm, Mr. Howley?" I asked.

"Why, you just hold it so that your thumb touches one strip of silver and your fingers touch the other, then you set the dial to whatever number you want to come up and wish."

"Wish? Just *wish*, Mr. Howley?"

"Just wish. That's all. What else can you do with a good luck charm?"

This time, the judge had to pound for order to stop the laughing.

I turned Howley over to Thursby.

The D. A. hammered at him for half an hour trying to get something out of Howley, but he didn't get anywhere useful. Howley admitted that he'd come to Nevada to play the wheels; what was wrong with that? He admitted that he'd come just to try out his good luck charm—and what was wrong with that? He even admitted that it worked for him every time—And what was wrong, pray, with *that*?

Thursby knew he was licked. He'd known it for a long time. His summation to the jury showed it. The expression on the faces of the jury as they listened showed it.

They brought a verdict of Not Guilty.

When I got back to my office, I picked up the phone and called the Golden Casino. I asked for George Brockey, the manager. When I got him on the phone and identified myself, he said, "Oh. It's you." His voice didn't sound friendly.

"It's me," I said.

"I suppose you're going to slap a suit for false arrest on the Casino now, eh, counselor?"

"Not a bit of it, George," I said. "The thought occurred to me, but I think we can come to terms."

"Yeah?"

"Nothing to it, George. You give us the three hundred grand and we don't do a thing."

"Yeah?" He didn't get it. He had to fork over the money anyway, according to the court order, so what was the deal.

"If you want to go a little further, I'll tell you what we'll do. We'll give you one of our little good luck charms, if you promise to call your boys off Howley."

"Nobody's on Howley," he said. "You ought to know better

than that. In this state, if we get whipped in court, we play it square. Did you think we were going to get rough?"

"No. But you kind of figured on lifting that gadget as soon as he gets it back from the D. A., didn't you? I saw your boys waiting at his hotel. I'm just telling you that you don't have to do that. We'll give you the gadget. There are plenty more where that came from."

"I see," Brockey said after a long pause. "O.K., counselor. It's a deal."

"Fine. We'll pick up the money later this evening, if that's O.K."

"Sure, counselor. Anytime. Anytime at all." He hung up.

I grinned at Howley, who was sitting across the desk from me. "Well, that winds it up."

"I don't get it," Howley said. "Why'd you call up Brockey? What was the purpose of that 'deal'?"

"No deal," I told him. "I was just warning him that killing you and taking the gadget wouldn't do any good, that we've covered you. He won't bother having anything done to you if he knows that the secret of the gadget is out already."

Howley's eyes widened behind those spectacles of his. "You mean they'd kill me? I thought Nevada gamblers were honest."

"Oh, they are, they are. But this is a threat to their whole industry. It's more than that, it may destroy them. Some of them might kill to keep that from happening. But you don't have to worry now."

"Thanks. Tell me; do you think we've succeeded?"

"In what you set out to do? Certainly. When we mail out those gadgets to people all over the state, the place will be in a uproar. With all the publicity this case is getting, it'll *have* to work. You now have a court decision on your side, a decision which says that a psionic device can be legally used to influence gambling games.

"Why, man, they'll *have* to start investigating! You'll have every politico in the State of Nevada insisting that scientists work on that thing. To say nothing of what the syndicate will do."

"All I wanted to do," said Howley, "was force people to take notice of psionics. I guess I've done that."

"You certainly have, brother. I wonder what it will come to?"

"I wonder, myself, sometimes," Howley said.

That was three and a half years ago. Neither Howley nor I are wondering now. According to the front page of today's *Times*, the first spaceship, with a crew of eighty aboard, reached Mars this morning. And, on page two, there's a small article headlined: ROCKET OBSOLETE, SAY SCIENTISTS.

It sure is.

I've Got a Little List

by Randall Garrett

*Randall wanted this to appear in **TAKEOFF**, but made the decision too late—the book was already in production. I have included his planned introduction as an afterword, and provided the key he mentions as an appendix.*

I've read s-f for many years, and here's what I have found:
 I've got a little list—I've got a little list
Of authors who take certain themes and run 'em in the ground.
 They'd none of 'em be missed—They'd none of 'em be missed!
There's the fellow who is daffy on his synergetic plan—[1]
The guy who writes the tales about the latent superman—[2]
The humorist who thinks anachronisms are such fun—[3]
The engineer who formulates each brand-new ship or gun—[4]
And the fellow with the bugs and stuff, the sex biologist—[5]
I don't think *he'd* be missed—I'm *sure* he'd not be missed!

There's the fiendish fellow who burns up the sun, or puts it out,
 The astrophysicist![6] I've got *him* on the list!
And the guy whose noble heroes kick the common clods about,
 The scientologist![7] I don't think *he'll* be missed!
And the lad who writes the tales about the interstellar tramps
Who flit about the Galaxy in king-size hobo camps—[8]
The guy who rewrites Toynbee, with some Gibbon added, too,
And calls it "psychohistory" to sound like something new—[9]
And the married pair who dote upon the psychoanalyst—[10]
 They'd none of 'em be missed—They'd none of 'em be missed!

There's the lass who lifts from Omar K. and
 shifts the scene to Mars—[11]
 I've got her on the list—I've got her on the list!

And the world-assassinator who keeps blowing up the stars—
     The cataclysmatist![12] I don't think he'd be missed!
And the chronic Martian writer with the anti-social quirks
Who thinks that human beings all are stupid, childish jerks—[13]
And the saintly little stories of a theologic kind,
All written by the editor of—Oh, well, never mind![14]
And at least a dozen others I could put upon the list;
     And they'd none of 'em be missed—
     They'd none of 'em be missed!

See key in the back of the book.

Afterword to *I've Got a Little List*

Randall wished to say this about the poem...and about the people:

This one, obviously, is a parody on Sir William S. Gilbert, of Gilbert & Sullivan fame, taken from **The Mikado.**

It's a bit of a puzzle. You are invited to see how many of the writers you can identify before you look up the answers in the back of the book.

When I wrote this, half a lifetime ago, all these lovely folk were still with us. That, alas, is no longer true. Thank God, **most** *of them still are sitting around and hammering at their typewriters, but—*

This whole bit of verse is a lie. They'd **all** *of 'em be missed.*

                           ...As will Randall

An Evening In

by Vicki Ann Heydron

He wandered into my life like a castaway, a man who had lost sight of his profession and touch with his life. Many things drew us together. The most immediate was a shared sexual joy we had never encountered before.

His life had been disrupted and relocated by the effect of a divorce several years before; my divorce had been more recent, less traumatic, but just as changeful for me. He had slowly slipped away from a profession I had been trying without success to enter—freelance fiction writing.

We met and he clung to me with a frightening foreknowledge of our destiny together—frightening only because I did not share his special vision. But I recognized the genius in him and out of admiration, compassion and affection, I accepted the obligation of returning him to his own world.

Reluctantly I opened my secure solitude to him, enclosed him with it, and let him rest.

* * *

We had lived side by side for more than a year. There had been moments of tender passion, soaring heights of joy...and times of such depression as I never wish to suffer again, when I would retreat into the only solitude I could find—silence.

We lived in the one-bedroom apartment which had been mine alone before we met. I had lived simply before he came, sleeping on a floor mat, setting my schedule for my own taste, enjoying the feeling of physical and mental space for the first time in my life. For through college, the U.S. Army, and my ended marriage, I had never before lived absolutely by myself. I had been content, if not actually happy.

On this day I could see only that the man had destroyed the sweet peace.

I had been financially stable when we met—in debt, yes, but handling it. I was now faced with financial disaster, not because of him, but because of what I felt were my obligations to him.

My grocery bill had tripled simply because I would not feed him the same low quality food on which I had been surviving. And during that year we had travelled, making the right people aware that he was still around and working again. He had needed that publicity, just as he had needed new clothes and we had needed a bed to sleep in.

Now I was working two jobs to keep up with the bills. A sacrifice it was surely, but not without one large advantage. It kept me from spending too much time in an apartment that seemed no longer mine. He had brought his clutter into those three rooms and piled it on top of mine. Somehow the result was more than a simple sum and it threatened to smother us.

Today I had lost sight of the far goals. Fatigue had taken its toll. I had called in sick to my evening job, and was on my way back. I had called the man to tell him I would be there early.

As I drove through the night, I visualized the chaos I'd find. I tried to hate the mess just for itself, and to summon the energy to clean things up. But this was an unexpected free evening. Why should I spend it cleaning house, when he was there all day and only contributed to the mess?

How unjust it seemed to me then that I had assumed the traditional man's role of breadwinner, yet he refused to accept the woman's of housekeeper. It seemed to me, rather, that I was carrying the entire burden.

More, I accused myself of that most damning of faults: inefficiency. If you're going to do something, I had been taught and I believed, do it with commitment and the best effort you can bring to it.

I had fallen far short of that ideal. Time and pressure made me inattentive at both jobs, and resentment kept me from trying to control the housework. And what—just *what* was being accomplished?

He *was* writing again. Three stories in that year and one even before, written just after we met, that he said I had inspired. So it *was* working. Even in that moment of frustration, I rejoiced that all my effort had not been wasted.

But with the illogic that is more devastating than rationality because it carries emotional conviction, that knowledge only made my attitude worse. *All for him*—by my own choice, I admitted. But had I given up *every* claim to myself? Would there never be time for me, never any respite from this huge responsibility?

I recognized my mood as self-pity, and grew angry. With

myself, with him, with the very fabric of our life together. I parked the car and climbed the stairs with the explosion barely contained. One word from him—*any* word—would spark the fuse and set me off. I was afraid of the feeling, but I looked forward with relief to some release for all the pressure. I got out my housekey and prepared myself for battle.

The door opened and the man said, "Enter, Madame."

He bowed slightly, very formally. He was dressed in his tuxedo. A kitchen towel was neatly folded and draped over one arm and he was carrying a candle.

I walked in. The room was dark except for the candle. To my left I couldn't see the kitchen filled with dirty dishes; to my right the sleeping couch which served us as a bed had to be open, as it always was, and heaped with clothes and books. But they disappeared at the edge of the candlelight. They didn't exist for me as I stood there, speechless.

He took my arm and guided me to the back of the apartment, and opened the door into the "bedroom" which was our dressing area and office.

"Your gown has been laid out for you, Madame," he said in formal tones. "Dinner will be served in approximately ten minutes. Your escort has informed me that he will call for you personally at that time." I walked through the door; he closed it and was gone.

I turned on the light and looked around. The room was almost the same as I had left it that morning. His desk was covered with manuscripts but there was, sadly, not a working page in the typewriter. The top of my desk was a carpet of unpaid bills. But on the ironing board (which stayed up for weeks at a time, hopeful that it might someday be used) lay a black dress which he had never seen me wear and a wig which I seldom wore.

The novelty of my welcome had diverted my intent, but not my mood. I accepted the game as a challenge; I dressed in the things he had laid out, but I added extra touches. Jewelry and makeup and my best air—I am not a good actress even with study, and this was impromptu—of sophistication.

When he knocked I lit the candle which had been left with the clothes, and turned out the light before opening the door. He was carrying the candle the "waiter" had carried before, but every bit of the stiff formality had been discarded with the towel. He looked dramatic in his tux, distinguished, handsome as always.

His eyes appraised and appreciated me. He offered me his arm and led me into the tiny kitchen, where our candles joined one another on the table. He seated me, then sat opposite, and we dined.

It was more than the circumstance of eating. The meal was not complicated or expensive, but it was delicious. Slices of ham in a sweet sauce and a green vegetable.

The dinner table was an island of candlelight. We drank wine and talked—of the world in abstract, of history, of the qualities and peculiarities of the human mind. We discussed his writing, and we discussed mine—for through all the other struggle, I was still fighting for this one goal.

We felt no urgency, no pressure. Nothing we discussed had any relationship to the harried frustration of the day which had ended at the door.

Gradually the tension eased away from me. Part of my mind wandered off and looked back at us, listened to us.

Was this scene so different? Hadn't we often talked like this in a messy kitchen we *could* see, over fast-food hamburgers or chicken pot pies?

I remembered quiet, mellow times before and after we had made love when we had talked of deep things, significant things, and I had felt myself expanding, using mental muscles left idle by the routine and repetitive work I did during the day. Then I had felt close to him, important to him, important in and to myself.

At last I came to understand why tonight was different. It wasn't simply the creative nonsense of a formal dinner in mundane surroundings. Nor was it an instance of incredible timing, that this should happen the very night I was ready to destroy us.

Rather the difference was in me, in realizing that this situation *could* happen. That it had happened before, many times, in different ways. In his toleration of my stony silences. In his sensitivity to my rotten moods of insecurity and uncertainty. He had accepted my need for space and had given me all he could.

He understood the sacrifice I was making, better perhaps than I did. And far from accepting it blindly, he had done what he could to make it easier, to make it worthwhile. He had excited and soothed me with his body, welcomed and warmed me with his love. He had fought off the blockage and begun to write again. If he hated housework—well, in all honesty, so did I. And he urged me to spend my time doing what I loved—writing. He shared his skill and experience with me. And he loved *me*—for what I was, what I had been, what I would be.

"You're so beautiful," he said over the candlelight. He meant more than my physical appearance, but he meant that, too. And I believed everything the word implied. Not just that *he* believed it, but that it was *true*.

This is what he gave me, and nothing I could ever do would match it. He made me believe in myself.

I realized in that moment how much I needed him. I knew I had been hiding from myself during that year, believing that what I was doing was all for *his* sake. I was accomplishing a task: I was going to get him back on his feet again. When that task was finished...

I had always avoided looking that far ahead. But now I knew that time would never come. I hadn't been working just for him;

since the instant of our meeting, I had been working for us. Working toward a time when those isolated, stimulating conversations would be the normal state, when we could live and work as a team. Out of our different viewpoints and experiences we would draw a very special contribution to the world. That was the destiny he had seen from the first. Wisely he had given me time to find it for myself.

"I love you," I told him, and for the first time the unspoken phrase "for now," wasn't there. He heard its silence, and with no warning at all we were both weeping.

He held my chair as I rose, and again offered me his arm. As elegantly as he had conducted the entire evening, he escorted me to bed.

In the morning the sunlight revealed the same untidy place where we had both lived for the past year. But this morning even the clutter was beautiful.

We were together now. We were home.

—END—

KEY TO *I've Got a Little List*

1 Theodore Sturgeon
2 A. E. van Vogt
3 L. Sprague de Camp
4 George O. Smith
5 Philip Jose Farmer
6 Dr. R. S. Richardson—pen name "Philip Latham"
7 L. Ron Hubbard
8 James Blish
9 Isaac Asimov
10 Henry Kuttner and C. L. Moore
11 Leigh Brackett
12 Edmond Hamilton
13 Ray Bradbury
14 Anthony Boucher

Copyright Information

Biographical Data

Randall Garrett began his writing career in the classic "I could write a better story" tradition. A friend challenged him to make good his boast, and he sold the resulting story to John Campbell in 1942. He was fourteen years old at the time. Since then he has published many books and stories, including quite a few under pseudonyms such as: Darrell T. Langart (an anagram) for *Anything You Can Do*; Robert Randall for *The Dawning Light* and *The Shrouded Planet* (with Robert Silverberg); Mark Phillips for *The Impossible, Super Mind* and *Brain Twister* (with Larry Janifer). He also wrote under the names of Jonathan Blake MacKenzie and Seaton McKettrig. His best-known work, however, is under his own name: the Lord Darcy series, including the Hugo-nominated *Too Many Magicians*.

Vicki Ann Heydron and Randall Garrett have jointly authored THE GANDALARA CYCLE, a series of seven science fiction novels. Most recent is *The River Wall*. Ms. Heydron lives in Austin, Texas, where she works full time in addition to continuing her writing career. Her current projects are *Bloodright*, an occult novel, and *Castle of Judgment* (co-authored with Garrett), a futuristic mystery novel.